JaKobe's Assignment

Book 1:
Angel Trilogy

Elizabeth Baker

JaKobe's Assignment

**EBB Publications
Pittsburg, Texas
2012**

ISBN 978-0-9839919-9-1 Copyright: Elizabeth Baker, 2012. Classification: Fiction / Christian/ Suspense / Supernatural. Cover art from Phatpuppy.com. & BookishBrunette.com. For permissions, questions, bulk stock, or interviews contact staff@elizabethbakerbooks.com

Elizabeth Baker

JaKobe's Assignment is a work of fiction. All characters, plots, and circumstances are fiction and not intended to represent any person living or dead. Churches and customs are also fiction. While reflective of author's experience they do not necessary reflect any denomination as a whole, specific assembly, or individual religious practices.

JaKobe's Assignment

Dedication:

To my dear friend, Kathy Marie Lundquist, a woman of God whose heart lives up to the meaning of her name.

JaKobe's Assignment

Elizabeth Baker

Time: Eternity

Place: Heaven

It was the pause that got him in trouble. That brief moment when he hung suspended between simply processing Rachael's request and considering its implications. If only he had not paused things might have been different. But he did pause, and in that brief instant everything changed.

JaKobe[1] had been quietly sitting at his workstation with fingers spread wide over the processing screen. An endless stream of requests, reports, and comments flowed through his hands and he managed each with ease. Then Rachael sent her strange request and the entire well-organized process came to a stop. His first instinct was to pass it on through normal channels, but the moment he paused a mystery piqued his curiosity and he was trapped.

Rachael was involved in such a simple assignment. Why was she backing out at the last moment? She even suggested the one to take her place should be an angel of Superior rank.

Superior for such a simple task? That was *his* rank!

Then an unexpected thought crossed his mind. A thought he instinctively knew had long been weaving itself together in some deep corner, waiting for an opportune moment to spring on him. A moment like this. If Superior rank was needed, why not go himself?

Removing his hand from the screen, the angel allowed the flow of information to be channeled to others while he sat at his station and toyed with the possibility.

It couldn't be time to go back. Not yet. He liked this secluded place of healing. The work might not be glamorous, but it had its perks. And, best of all, it was as far removed from humans as heaven allowed. Why mess up a good thing?

Closing his eyes the angel tilted back his head and calculated according to earth years. Could they really total seven hundred? Impossible! Memory of the wounds inflicted in that place still seemed too fresh. He had never considered returning. Until now.

The idea was preposterous. While it was true he had not been created for the work which now occupied him why did that matter? He served where he was assigned and the Final Authority never expressed any displeasure with the arrangement.

He straightened and looked around the processing station. This was a friendly, efficient, valuable place. He wasn't even bored with the repetitive tasks. Why should he be? For angels everything held a curious fascination and investigation was second nature.

A short distance away, Mallobi caught his eye and smiled. There was nothing wrong with being assigned here.

Yet, the smell of battle became strangely enticing and something stirred in the ancient warrior. What would it be like to experience earth again? He went over Rachael's message a second time. Exactly where was this place called, Thyme?

JaKobe's Assignment

8:05 AM

Sidewalks of Thyme

It was an ordinary Sunday in Thyme. School started two months ago. Thanksgiving was still weeks away. Even the weather was boring. It was not one of those spectacular Indian summers that often visit East Texas in the fall. There were no storms threatening and certainly no snow. The sunrise had come and gone unnoticed by most of the still sleeping residents.

Jonathan was the only man in town dressed in a suit and smelling of aftershave as he stepped from the shelter of his large front porch and blinked his way into the strong morning light.

The cool air was invigorating as he looked up and down the street taking in familiar surroundings. Each house was at least seventy-five years old and most of the trees a hundred or more. If one ignored an occasional satellite dish clamped to the edge of a roof or modern car by the curb the date could have been 1950—or even 1890.

It was a tranquil view that should have brought feelings of comfort and stability but Jonathan only pushed out a tired breath and hurried on untouched by the peaceful scene.

Halfway down the front walk a particularly tall pile of leaves gathered in a brown lump. Frowning, he pushed them aside with the toe of a polished shoe.

Yesterday, Melody suggested a good raking was past due, but why should he bother? Raking was like his life: an endless round of effort that never yielded permanent results.

He laced his fingers and stretched his arms above his head then inhaled deeply and let them fall. Perhaps fresh air would clear his head and improve his mood.

No change. Resigned, he began his three block walk from the parsonage to Grace Community Church where he had served as pastor for the past five years.

"Five years," he mused. "How many Sunday walks would that be?" He worked the math while chewing the inside of one cheek, a habit acquired in the third grade.

Of course the total number would need to be reduced by those Sundays when vacations made the trip unnecessary or bad weather forced him to drive. The figures began to blur and he gave up. What did it matter?

*****

JaKobe's Assignment

Half a block away an unseen figure watched the pastor's reluctant stroll with intense, ageless eyes. If the light had not been passing through her, the appearance would have been that of a slender woman dressed in delicate sea-blue.

A loose fitting tunic hung just below her hips and gathered about the thin waist with a wide, turquoise sash. Her trousers were of the same lightweight fabric and auburn hair hung just below her shoulders. Everything about her moved as though stirred by a gentle breeze while not a leaf moved on nearby trees.

The only article of jewelry was a three inch wide silver cuff circling one wrist. It looked heavy and was nearly an inch thick but the scrolls and vine carvings covering it were delicate and inlayed with gold. She twisted the band slowly as though its reassuring presence helped her think.

Ruch-El was the official name. But long ago JaKobe had dubbed her Rachael. The fact that the womanly form was something chosen, not birthed, didn't seem to matter to anyone and after a few years of protest, the angel gave up resisting. His teasing had outlasted her objections and the feminine earth-name stuck.

She watched as Jonathan finished crossing his yard and turned north. The man moved with slow steps and slumped posture. He was either coming down with some illness or discouraged.

She would guess the latter.

Humans were such strange creatures. They had so much potential and such a fantastic future!

Yet, they were often morose, slow to see reality, easily confused, and surprisingly quick to give in to discouragement.

The angel cocked her head and studied the man more deeply. What amazing creatures these descendants of Adam had turned out to be.

JaKobe's Assignment

Time: Eternity

Place: Heaven

Stepping back from the busy activity around him JaKobe moved quietly from his work station and left without saying goodbye. One or two of the workers looked up, curious, but paid him little mind. No big deal. His work now flowed to others and in a place where time had little meaning they knew they would see him again.

Their lack of attention didn't surprise him. Freedom was one of the things he enjoyed most about heaven. That, and the ever changing environment surrounding him. Even the architecture held infinite variety.

Gardens were interspaced with workstations and homes snuggled against expansive gathering spaces. The active bustle of city streets was never far from fields of solitude and the light corridors made moving from one to another quick and pleasant. One could even travel by thought, if they possessed the power and had developed the skill.

JaKobe had that power and as his methodical walk continued he closed his eyes visualizing a meadow he often visited. The pleasant scene, sounds and smells took shape in his mind: Trees in a thousand shades of green. Flowers. The small stream leading to the river.

His feet never broke their constant stride as the hard surface softened and the atmosphere around him changed. The scent of fresh grass filled his senses and the low hum of insects was distinct. He opened his eyes and smiled. It was all just as he left it.

Ambling toward the river with an easy grace, the angel considered the new feelings stirring inside him. Why should he return to earth? Why now?

A small animal covered with light blue fur tipped in black, peeked at him from her burrow at the base of a tree. She gave a chirping sound then turned back down the hole only to appear a moment later pushing three young offspring into the open for his inspection.

He bent to pet the tiny creatures. Life. It was such a wondrous adventure and heaven was so full of it!

Of course, earth had life, too. But it was only a distorted reflection of what he enjoyed. Life there was adulterated with struggle, shame and pain. And battle.

He stood as he watched the little mother return to the comfort of her den. Seven hundred years was a long time to be gone but he knew about the changes taking place in his absence. Everyone watched that sad, significant planet. But observation was far different than participation. What would it be like to experience earth again?

The angel grew pensive. Why did any of his kind ever leave this world for that one? Adventure? Compassion for the creatures of the planet? To satisfy curiosity? The opportunity to learn? It was all of that and more.

Yet, there was no denying the one true reason they left home behind: Obedience.

Slowly the internal stirring that brought him to the meadow birthed into desire. He twisted the silver band on his wrist feeling its heft and pent up energy while doubts faded. It was time to go back. He knew it.

The Final Authority had commissioned his race to serve the children of Adam. Earth was where the most intense service to Adam took place. It was that simple.

Yet, like any faithful soldier, JaKobe would not initiate a move on his own until permission was granted and specific duties assigned.

Fortunately, obtaining those things was neither hard nor complex. The Final Authority was very accessible; even welcoming. God dwelt in the midst of heaven. His throne was never far away and all citizens of the Kingdom were allowed access.

*****

Reverently, quietly, JaKobe joined the ranks of several million others surrounding the throne and waited. Access did not mean familiarity between subjects and King.

The brightness of the throne was scorching and heavily armed seraphim constantly circled the core of Light with cries of "Holy, Holy, Holy."

Even though an angel of superior rank, JaKobe was grateful for the seraphim's protective blur as they whirled around the throne creating a permeably shield between creatures and Creator.

The sounds and colors emanating from the core of Light wrapped around him and blended into a throbbing, musical whole. Although not loud, it gathered the emotions of listeners and moved them along on a wave of unity with the source. It would have been easy to stand for a century doing nothing but being enraptured by the sight and sound.

Some described the sound as many voices speaking at once. Or, ocean surf. Or, heavy rain. But, in truth, the sound was One voice speaking thousands of soft words simultaneously and as he listened, JaKobe began to hear certain sounds above others. Slowly, individual words became distinct. Words meant for him alone.

"How much will change cost? Assist Ruch-El. Make a way for the answer."

He wasn't sure he fully understood all the meaning, but one thing was very clear. He had a new assignment. Earth had another warrior on the way.

JaKobe's Assignment

*****

JaKobe returned to his private space to prepare for the journey. He needed to decide on a method of travel, besides, there were tools to collect and test.

Several avenues existed between heaven and earth. He seriously considered each. The light corridors took less energy, but if he avoided them and move directly between the dimensions of spirit and matter, he was less likely to be detected by dark spirits. Considering his last trip, that might have definite advantages.

He had not used an Evaluator since his last trip but when the glossy black box was lifted from its place, it nestled comfortably in his hand as though made for him. Indeed, it had been.

About one inch thick, three inches wide and five long, the top was covered with row upon row of colored stones. He smiled and ran his finger down one row rehearsing the name and purpose of each stone. Then, he smiled. He might have been gone seven hundred years but he could still recite them all with ease.

Satisfied, he settled cross legged on the floor and reverently slipped the silver band from his wrist. It dropped to the floor with a solid, metallic sound.

JaKobe reached forward placing the fingers of each hand on the inside of the ring. Holding the outside with his thumbs, he pulled gently. The ring opened, and then flattened to a three by one inch bar several inches long.

The angel set up straight admiring the object before him then leaned forwards a second time and drew his finger down the length of the bar.

As though some organic instinct had taken over the object releasing long confined energy it began to grow and unfold. Pummel, grip, ornately carved guard and finally the blade lay before him. His sword.

JaKobe picked up the light weight object and held it with a practice reverence. Although pointed, the instrument was not sharp. It didn't have to be. Only humans needed sharp objects to slice and pierce each other. Angelic warfare was decided by the smallest of touches.

While on earth, everything about him—his clothes, hair, skin—would be equal extensions of his essence rather than objects to be put on and taken off. Any part of his being touched by a messenger of darkness would create an arc like that between positive and negative poles of electricity or matter touching antimatter.

At the slightest touch, an explosion of spiritual power would take place. He would be sapped of life-force like air rushing from its source to fill a vacuum. Only this weapon would guard him in a fight by absorbing blows from the enemy while keeping direct contact at bay. Its tip was also a contact point that disabled an enemy.

He stood. Then, he lifted the sword before his face in a salute to the King.

The blade began to glow as Shekinah[2] glory shot streams of light in every direction. It was a blessing; a benediction; a parting gift from the Final Authority reminding him of the true nature of the battle.

Warfare was not, and would never be, a question of his power against the power of evil. Victory hinged on the angel's ability to tap and channel a Power beyond himself. That was one thing angels and humans had in common.

Gradually the light faded and JaKobe lowered the sword. He paused a moment then grabbed the guards on each side of the blade and gently urged them toward the middle. The motion set off a chain reaction and soon only a single strip of silver lay on the floor.

He picked it up, wrapped it to his wrist and the ends melded seamlessly together.

Visualizing the meadow once more, JaKobe walked across the room and directly onto the grass. Reminding himself to relax, he squared his shoulders and concentrated on the task at hand.

Deliberately, the angel pulled the surrounding energy of spirit closer to him. Closer and closer he gathered it around his body like layer after layer of a large, hooded cape while pulling back from all that was familiar; all that was home. His world tightened as the life within him grew less, colder, slower.

The process was not painful, only unpleasant and lonely. His world turned red then faded to lavender followed by a deep shade of purple-

Elizabeth Baker

black. Numbness surrounded him as one reality faded and the next was not yet fully born

JaKobe's Assignment

Time: 8:10 AM

Place: Pecan Street

The jolt of deceleration was sudden as the angel's speed slowed to that of light. A blinding yellow aura engulfed him. Shapes and colors took form and sensations of a new world touched the edges of awareness. He felt sunlight passing through him. Smelled the morning. Tasted the air. Sensations that were warm and vaguely familiar. Then, his feet settled against a rough, cement sidewalk and he stood momentarily, back bent forward and head hanging down.

Becoming fully conscious within his new surroundings, the angel pulled himself upright, threw his arms wide and stretched backward turning his face to the sky. Earth was beneath his feet again.

JaKobe had settled on the form of a human male and he took a moment to check out the results of his labors. The angular jaw was covered by short, brown beard and his full hair was cut in a modern, business style. He had salted both the beard and his hair with grey which resulted in a look that was dignified as well as ageless.

Dressed according to styles worn by humans of this century, his tan khakis held a sharp crease and a light blue dress shirt with open collar and long sleeves covered his top half while starched cuffs hid the silver bracelet. Loafers completed the ensemble and if human eyes had observed the angel, he might have been mistaken for a successful businessman on holiday.

Looking down at his body, the angel ran his hand over his bearded chin, pleased with the results. Dressing to fit the role was one of the perks involved in working earth. The process was fun, but it also had a serious purpose. Looking something like a human helped one identify with the race and should it become necessary to step inside the range of visible light, others were less likely to notice he was not a native of the planet.

Taking a final, long look at the sky, he felt like a traveler rounding the last corner from which one can see home. He sighed then turned his full attention to this new world.

JaKobe walked the last few steps to Grace Community Church, settled himself on one of the wide, concrete banisters and casually began swinging his new feet. He had time. He would wait.

*****

As he neared the church, Jonathan stepped from the sidewalk intending to cross to the other side, but stopped. Instead, he backed up a few steps and leaned against a tree.

Across the street the white steeple of Grace Community glistened against the bright blue sky and the wide banisters curving down each side of the front steps looked like open arms inviting all to come inside. Was life in Thyme really so bad? He wondered.

Nineteen years serving God was a good thing. Wasn't it? There had even been scattered moments when the daily effort seemed to produce something of worth. But, those moments had grown fewer and farther between. At the present he felt completely alone in a vast universe that stubbornly refused to make sense.

When he placed those empty feelings alongside the faith he professed and the sermons he preached each Sunday, nothing added up. The only way he could explain the conflict was to assume somewhere in the past he must have missed God's direction. Maybe he was in the wrong place or attempting something God couldn't bless. Maybe it was time to move on.

He paused.

Melody would throw a fit if he suggested moving again. She had put down roots and learned to appreciate the piney woods. At times he thought he could even hear subtle Texas accents replacing her Midwestern brogue.

Why move now? The kids were settled in school. Benjamin would start his junior year next fall. Stephanie, at thirteen, was all hormones and braces. He could see the drama on her face as she moaned that a move would ruin her life. But then, these days he ruined her life at least once a week over far more minor things. Traci wouldn't mind moving. At ten, life was still an adventure to his red-haired tomboy.

What did he expect to find by moving on? He liked this place. Indeed, he liked the people of Thyme and his role as their pastor. Even though the hours were long and people slow to respond, he knew he wouldn't trade being a pastor for any other job in the world.

How could a man, fully employed at a job he enjoyed, who had a perfect wife, healthy kids and enough money to buy an almost-new car last year, be so alone and discontent? He had never known the answer. And so far, Thyme had only made the questions less clear.

While Jonathan studied the church, Rachael looked past him and studied the angel relaxing on the banister. A smile softened her features. So, the long absent warrior had returned at last.

JaKobe caught her glance, hopped from his perch and moved toward her with the slow familiar strides she had seen so often before. He was very near before he spoke.

"I assume that's the human in question," he said with a slight tilt of his head toward Jonathan.

She nodded but said no more.

JaKobe's Assignment

"And the problem is . . .," he prompted.

Rachael changed her position, folding and refolding her arms as she studied the man. "No problem," she said. Then modified, "Not really."

Neither spoke for a long moment until JaKobe prompted again. "He looks rather ordinary."

"He is."

They stood together some twenty feet behind the subject and waited until JaKobe became restless. If he had not known better, he would have suspected Rachael was playing some odd kind of human game. But, he did know better, so he bridled his impatience and waited until she finally chose to speak.

"Jonathan has processed forty-three earth years," she said at last. "Each has been—as you said—'ordinary'." She glanced at him with eyes that matched the sash she wore. "You absorbed the basic facts before leaving?"

"Of course. Married, three children, nineteen years as pastor of four different churches ranging from very small to a mega-church in Colorado before coming here. Grace Community would be termed an old-fashion church by current earth tastes but its scores on love and service are acceptable."

She acknowledged the facts with a nod. "I am not sure I can explain why, but humans seem to need more."

The incomplete statement left him puzzled. "More, what?"

"Just more." She unfolded her arms and waved them. "More than statistics. More than facts. More than they should logically be given considering their physical limitations and dull wits."

She grew silent again. This was not like the Rachael he remembered. He was about to say as much when she decided to continue.

"I'm not sure where it started. Probably Bible College. They made a lot of noise in those years about doing big things for God. You know, *'Jesus has a wonderful plan for your life!'* that sort of thing."

"Is that bad?" JaKobe's eyebrows drew slightly higher and the tilt of his head followed.

"Don't be absurd," she defended. "But how often have you seen a human who could accurately describe what a *'big thing'* or a *'wonderful plan'* might look like in ordinary life?"

She had a point. He shrugged one shoulder.

Jonathan kicked a stray nut sending it into the street. He liked this view of Grace. It was postcard perfect. A glimpse of bygone days. A slice of yesterday. Although most American churches had abandoned the tradition, Grace still held services both Sunday morning and Sunday evening. There was even a Wednesday night "prayer" service though no one but the preacher did any actual praying. The schedule had been the same for eighty-five years.

He remembered those first enthusiastic messages and the plan he developed for church growth. Looking back, the only significant changes he could identify were his secretarial help had increased from 15 to 25 hours per week and a part-time janitor had been hired. A small army of volunteers accomplished the rest of the work. While attendance of three hundred hadn't fallen, neither had it increased.

Worse, it hadn't taken long to discover the same petty egos, dull routines, and problems without answers that plagued every church he had ever known were also part of Grace Community. He exhaled slowly. If this was the Kingdom of God, it certainly wasn't much to brag about.

Behind him, JaKobe was becoming exasperated. "I'm here because I received your message. Exactly what is the problem as you see it?"

"The problem is heaven," she stated bluntly. A look of shock flashed across her companion's face and she quickly apologized.

"I didn't mean that like it sounded."

She made an effort to relax then continued. "It seems Jonathan has petitioned the throne for over twenty years—always the same request. He longs to understand the significance of his life. Now, the Final Authority desires to grant that petition."

"It's an admirable request."

"Yes, but the human has no idea about the cost! Jonathan can never see spiritual realities as long as he is chained to the pleasures and securities of earth! Breaking those chains will not be easy."

Silence fell between them and the words from heaven echoed in his mind. *How much will change cost? Assist Rach-El. Make a way for the answer.*

"Will you be recommending a different opposition level?"

"Not unless I have to."

Those five words and the downward tilt of her head communicated all he needed to know. JaKobe's mood shifted from irritation to sympathy for his long time friend.

"I see." He spoke softly and averted his gaze while shuffling his feet.

A short distance away, Jonathan pulled himself upright from the support of the tree and shook his head as if the motion might clear the cloud of discouragement clinging to him.

Walking quickly across the street, he fished keys from his pants pocket, bounded up the steps two at a time and unlocked one of the large double doors. It shut behind him with a thud.

JaKobe watched as the pastor disappeared then with calm efficiency followed the human up the steps, melted through the wooden panels, and slipped inside. He had every intention of completing this assignment before midnight.

JaKobe's Assignment

8:15 AM

Inside Grace Community Church

The heavy double doors showed no trace of movement as he faded through the wood and entered the small narthex. Soft morning light filtered through a stained glass transom and the aroma of polished wood permeated the air. JaKobe turned around taking in every detail. The years of service clearly showed, but there was something warm and well cared for about the space. Walls, paneled half way up. Cream colored stucco above the wainscoting. Large, wooden table with printed literature.

That last item caught his attention. He studied the illustrations and lettering. Nice. The print was sharper than what Gutenberg produced but the color and style of those illustrations could use some work.

He craned his neck first one direction than another: There was so much to fascinate him. So much to study. Seeing earth's changes first hand was exciting.

Directly across from the outside doors, a second set of lighter ones led into the auditorium. Jonathan had left one of them open and JaKobe walked through moving quickly up the aisle shoving his hands in his pockets as he had seen Jonathan do while walking the last half block to the church.

The angel enjoyed the texture of fabric rolling over his finger tips. *Pockets. What a marvelous invention! Much more convenient than the leather bag strapped to my waist during the last visit.*

He looked around noting that the arrangement of the room was exactly as he expected. The space was divided by three aisles—one central, two against the walls—splitting the benches into two sections. At the front of the room, three steps led to a low stage anchored by a large pulpit in the center. Behind it, a low wall modestly hid the knees and laps of the choir. An organ was to the right and small grand piano to the left. Red and white decor. Soft light. Nice place.

Jonathan was nowhere to be seen, but JaKobe had no trouble following his steps. A dog would have traced the pastor by scent. A friend might have reasoned and guessed the way. But the angel simply knew and after taking a last look at the

JaKobe's Assignment

auditorium he followed Jonathan's exact path out a side door.

Of course, he could have walked through the wall or dropped through the ceiling but adapting to human manners and conventions was one way of demonstrating respect for the race. It was one of the primary differences between servants of Righteousness and those who served Destruction.

Beyond the door, the hall was wide but dark. Walls of paneled wood and a floor of brown-glazed concrete gave a dreary feel. He passed the women's restroom, drinking fountain, men's restroom, janitor's closet, and then paused at the next door which stood slightly open and looked in.

The nameplate on the desk identified LeeAnn Gentry as the owner of the neatly organized space. He recalled the name from heaven's files. Church secretary.

A few steps farther another sign read, *Pastor's Office*. JaKobe positioned himself directly in front of the closed door then passed through it.

The Reverend Jonathan A. Phelps sat at a worn desk in the middle of the room. His head was bent over an open Bible but a smaller book lay open on top of the pages. The angel bent until he could watch the pastor's eyes. They moved in quick jumps. Jonathan was reading.

He straightened and looked at the small book. *"Thank God for the sight of all you have never yet been. You have had the vision, but you are not there yet by any means. It is when we are in the valley, where we prove whether we will be the choice ones, that most of us turn back. We are not quite prepared for the blows which must come if we are going to be turned into the shape of the vision. We have seen what we are not, and what God wants us to be, but are we willing to have the vision "Batter'd to shape and use" by God? The batterings always come in commonplace ways and through commonplace people."*[3]

It was a quote from *My Utmost For His Highest* and JaKobe had memorized the text long ago. If Jonathan took its message seriously, perhaps his task would not be as odious as he had feared.

The angel turned studied all four walls taking in every detail just as he had done in the narthex and auditorium.

It was possible to learn much about a human by observing his environment and it would be necessary to know the man in detail before he could be confident his recommendation was the right one.

Books covered three walls and a sofa took up most of the forth. There were family pictures on one shelf and a section of trophies on another. Baseball trophies. Looking closer he saw they were dated early 70s. *Must be childhood keepsakes,* he thought. He read the titles on all the books noting that biographies of famous preachers were the most worn. Jonathan evidently preferred the *New King James Bible* and had saved old Bibles since his teens. An antique copy of *Pilgrim's Progress* was on a small stand. It needed dusting.

JaKobe's Assignment

Satisfied, he spread his feet and squared his shoulders then reached to his pocket intending to draw out the Evaluator. Precise indentions on the back were designed to fit each finger. The instrument would spring to action when nestled against his palm, drawing energy directly from his being.

Three hundred colored stones marched across the face of the device arranged in twenty rows of fifteen each. Each stone served as a measurement of a specific human character trait and brightened or dulled according to the level of information received. Data from the three hundred fed into three larger stones resting near the angel's wrist. These served as summations of the whole.

A narrow gage ran along the side and measured the same quality from two viewpoints. The first, the amount of opposition allowed for a particular human and the second, the amount of opposition currently being received. Keeping Hell within these boundaries consumed a large portion of Heavenly energy.

It's hard to surprise an angel, but JaKobe's eyes grew wide as his fingers touched the Evaluator and drew it into the light. Three small, blue boxes grew from the left side like organic appendages.

The boxes bore the stamp of Ruch-El and they undoubtedly contained information about Jonathan she deemed critical. He smiled. If nothing else, Rachael always had been efficient.

JaKobe broke off the first box, closed his eyes and crushed it in his right hand. The box shattered into dust then vanished while the information it contained played across the screen of his closed eyes. Events unfolded before him exactly as Rachael had viewed them through her eyes years before.

*****

The school lunchroom was a cacophony of young voices. Plastic trays scraped against tables and metallic sounds came from a nearby kitchen. Jonathan was carrying a paper sack to his seat and settling down with his classmates. He unrolled the top of the bag and cautiously peered inside. With a sigh, he pulled out a bologna sandwich, corn chips and half an apple. He looked up and down the table keeping the food hidden closely behind the brown paper bag then spoke to a boy with black hair seated directly across from him.

"I'll trade for your Twinkies."

"I don't know," said the boy reluctantly. "What ya got?"

Jonathan rested his fingers on the bag of chips then passed them and picked up a different item. "How 'bout this juicy apple? It's nice and red."

"Are you kid'n? Ain't no apple worth a Twinkie!"

The boys were silent for a moment then the black haired child stretched his neck trying to see

JaKobe's Assignment

the other side of Jonathan's paper sack. "Is that a bag o' Frito's you got there?"

"Maybe," replied Jonathan. "You wanna swap the Twinkies for a bologna sandwich?"

"If you want my Twinkies, I get y'er Frito's."

The boys were silent again. Jonathan tore open his bag and tasted a salty chip. The boy with black hair pushed his package of Twinkie's out into open view. Jonathan obviously wanted both the Twinkies and his Fritos and was reluctant to let either slip away. He frowned, studying the situation then suddenly brightened.

"I got somethin' special to trade for y'er ol' Twinkies," he said confidently. "I'm Line Leader this week. I even get to go first on the bus. You can be Line Leader instead o' me if you'll let me have the Twinkies."

The black haired boy considered this, but didn't move.

"You can even have my turn for the rest of the year!" he sweetened the deal.

"Okay." The Twinkies slid across the table and Jonathan placed them firmly beside the Frito's. "But, it's fer the whole year and ya gotta promise!"

"I promise," he said.

The vision paused to freeze frame then after a moment continued. The children had evidently been dismissed to the playground. Swings drifted back and forth. Running feet. Kids in pants and T-shirts were milling around in all directions. Surely, there was some significance in all this but JaKobe couldn't imagine what.

As the playground scene continued, Jonathan mixed among the other children. He swung across an open space holding onto a series of bars, then chunked a rock at a stick and hit it, but gradually drifted off alone. He hung around the steps leading into the building and seemed apprehensive as he draped himself across the handrail.

There was a shrill whistle and an overweight teacher in a blue flowered dress waved her hand. "Second Grade!" she yelled. "Line up!"

The boy with black hair raced from a distant tree and headed toward the steps. He arrived with a dozen other little humans all of whom seemed to be pushing as they adjusted into what could loosely be called a line.

"I'm Line Leader!" the black-haired boy demanded and pushed at Jonathan trying to remove him from the handrail so he could have the coveted position on the first step.

"We can't trade!" whined Jonathan. "I asked Mrs. Mallory and she said we couldn't switch."

"Y'er lyin! You never ask no such thing!"

"Yes, I did. Y'er gonna get in trouble if ya push."

"What is the matter up there?" The formidable presence of what must have been Mrs. Mallory strode with authority to the front of the line as yards of flowered fabric swished around her.

JaKobe's Assignment

"Freddy! Jonathan! You boys stop pushing this instant!"

"But he's cheatin'," protested Freddy and his eyes flashed with anger.

"Freddy, go to the back of the line. Jonathan, that's no way for a Line Leader to act. The rest of you straighten up. And, don't forget to use the restroom before going back to class."

Mrs. Mallory turned her head and Freddy shook his fist at Jonathan who shrugged his shoulders and held both hands palm upward signaling that none of this was his fault.

JaKobe thought the scene would end at that point, but Rachael's notes did not appear and after a moment's pause the vision continued with what must have been later the same day.

The math class of Mrs. Mallory was well in progress and the room of twenty tired children sat relatively silent as they struggled over papers on their desk. Jonathan was on the front row, his paper half finished. With one eye on Mrs. Mallory, he cast furtive glances at Freddy on the back row. Twice Freddy caught his glance and—with an equally cautious eye on the teacher—silently pounded his small fist into his hand giving clear intention of a fight.

Jonathan squirmed. He fingered a small car in his desk and pretended to work on his math. The snap was barely audible as he pushed his pencil point against the paper at an angle breaking the tip.

"Mrs. Mallory?" he asked raising his hand. "Can I sharpen my pencil? It broke. See?"

"All right," she sighed. "Just be quick about it."

In one smooth motion he slipped his rear from the seat and his hand swiped the cubbyhole beneath the desk's writing surface. His treasured, red Mustang Match Box with doors that really opened hid in his palm.

Walking to the back of the room with his eyes straight ahead, he slipped the car on top of Freddy's math page and kept moving. He didn't turn to see what reaction the offer might solicit until the grinding of the pencil sharpener made such a move less noticeable.

Freddy wasn't smiling. He glared briefly at Jonathan, risking the wrath of Mrs. Mallory. But, the car had vanished from the math page and was peeking ever so slightly over the top edge of Freddy's back pocket. Jonathan breathed a sigh. The deal had been made.

*****

The vision ended and at last Rachael's voice was heard. She had also pasted a picture of her Evaluator in the lower right hand corner of the last frame.

"This scene demonstrates one of the first and most significant things I have observed about my human. He is amiable, but seeks his own comfort and appetite satisfaction above all else. He is also conflict avoidant as demonstrated by his offering to Freddy. He really liked that car but he liked his skin more."

JaKobe memorized the exact brightness of each light on Rachel's Evaluator and their overall pattern but was surprised to note the allowable opposition scale only reached to 3.7. He had certainly seen more significant readings.

Breaking the second pod from his instrument, he again closed his eyes as he crushed the box to dust. This time, Jonathan looked to be about eleven.

*****

The little boy with blond hair raced his bicycle up the street at a fast pace. Panting, he peddled across the lawn and threw the bike down by the wooden steps. Looking determined and anxious, he raced up the steps and pushed open a door with a creaking sound.

The building was large and old. The ornately lettered sign by the curb declared it to be the King's Hotel of Preston, Kansas but the words seemed absurd. If there had ever been anything royal about that pile of dilapidated shutters and graying boards, it had vanished years before.

Once inside, the dim light made it difficult to see and he stumbled on a wrinkle of carpet then regained his balance and walked to an old man who stood behind the counter shuffling papers with absent-minded boredom.

"Mr. Peterson," he asked breathlessly, "Where's my dad?"

"Whoa, Johnny! Hang on just a minute." A frown flickered across Jonathan's face. He evidently didn't like being called, "Johnny."

"Where's my dad?" he repeated. "What room?"

"Does your mama know you're here?"

"It's all right. I got a letter. He wrote and told me he'd come today."

"Your dad has been here since Tuesday, Johnny, but I ain't so sure you ought to go tearing up to his room. What's your mama say 'bout this?"

"We got new uniforms. See?" he backed away from the counter and proudly displayed a baseball uniform. White pants, red jersey shirt and red striped socks with a cap announcing he was part of the *Mighty Tigers*.

"I got to show my dad. He sent me a letter."

The scene jerked with an abrupt motion. Interference had caught Rachael's attention and the video swirled to the right. JaKobe saw a shadow of something evil attacking from that direction then, another shadow came through the ceiling, above and to the left. Jonathan's voice could be heard in the background as he continued to argue with the clerk.

"I got to see him. He sent me a letter."

"Your dad's in room 203, but I don't think . . ." Mr. Peterson's words were cut short by the sound of running feet and a quickly shouted, "Thanks!"

Rachael jerked away from the enemy and turned to follow Jonathan as he bounded up the stairs but a huge, dark adversary stepped between her and the boy. JaKobe could have sworn it was Doltar however the video suddenly stopped. Rachael had evidently edited the presentation eliminating the battle scene so JaKobe's attention would remain on Jonathan, not her.

He wasn't surprised. Rachael was good in battle but everyone knew she had a strong distaste for the process. If the enemy was Doltar, he could imagine what must have taken place. He didn't need video to remember.

There was static then the recording continued. The picture was somewhat blurred and he wondered if Rachael was crying.

The furious little boy pushed his bicycle to its maximum speed. Down Lilac Lane and across McKenzie he raced standing on the pedals to give each stroke all the pressure his small body could exert. Past houses, parked cars, and friends who called but received no answer.

He threw the bicycle in the middle of a front yard, tearing up small chunks of damp grass, and ran inside slamming the door behind him.

"You lied to me!" he screamed throwing himself on the living room floor.

Lee Ida was drying dishes and still had the towel in her hand as she rushed to his side, alarmed by the outburst of terror and sobbing. "Are you all right? Where have you been?"

"You lied to me!" he screamed over and over again. "You told me my daddy was sick. He ain't sick. He's drunk!"

"Oh, Jonathan! No!" Her tears began to flow. "Oh, my little boy!"

"You lied!" he accused again. He thrashed and kicked away as she tried to hold him.

"Kenny told me. Even dumb ol' Susie knew. They said he was in jail 'cause he was drunk. But you said he was sick and I told 'em they didn't know what they was talking 'bout." He screamed again. "You lied to me!"

"No, Johnny, no!" The frantic mother sobbed and reached for her son. "Your daddy got out of jail after the first day. He's been in a hospital. It's just a different kind of hospital, that's all."

"No he ain't!" Jonathan sobbed. "I'm no baby. I know what drunk is. I saw him! I saw the bottles! I couldn't wake him up! He ain't sick. You lied!"

She grabbed hold of him with the force of a broken heart and sat on the floor with both arms and legs wrapped around his small, heaving body. Slowly the thrashing stopped, replaced by wracked sobs and intermittent struggle. She turned her face toward heaven. It was contorted with tears and anguish. "Oh, God!" she prayed. "My poor, little boy!"

They rocked together as Jonathan repeated over and over, "You lied to me. My daddy is a drunk. All the kids knew. My daddy's a drunk. You lied."

JaKobe's Assignment

*****

The scene faded mercifully to a muted shade of gray then cleared. For a second time, Rachael had pasted a copy of her Evaluator reading in the right corner and added a voice overlay.

"I knew I couldn't get an accurate character read until the emotions subsided. This reading was taken three days later. Notice the change in the trust level—violet light in the upper left quadrant."

JaKobe was almost offended that she should think it necessary to inform him of the position of the trust indicator. Knowing the significance of every light, the degree of accepted intensity and the character quality each represented was basic to any angel's job. Reliability: royal blue, third row, fifth position. Aggression: orange, first row, fifteenth position. Generosity: clear green, tenth row, seventh position. Blaming: maze brown, seventh row, fourth position. Compassion: Teal, second row, twelfth position. But he pushed aside the temptation to defend his knowledge and listened as her voice continued.

"I suppose I will never grow accustomed to the way pain leaves scars that last for generations. Like the rest of creation, I struggle and wait and long for the time when all of this is over and God's children come into their inheritance.

"There have been many scars for Jonathan that added to his caution and reinforced his reluctance to risk. While this is not an excuse for current lack of faith, I thought showing you these events might aid better understanding of your responsibility and explain more fully why I called for help."

The angel felt sadness as he reached for the last pod, disconnected it and closed his eyes as the pod disintegrated in his hand. This time, the Jonathan who entered the kitchen door appeared to be about the same age as the man he had just observed reading at the desk, however, the date in the lower, left indicated the event took place three years previous.

*****

"I'm home, Honey!" he called passing through the kitchen and into the dining area. A woman with honey-blond hair sat at a table sorting through sheet music. He crossed the room and nuzzled the back of her neck. "My, you smell good."

"Jonathan! What a surprise! Are you home for lunch, again? This makes the third day in a row! I am afraid we don't have much."

"That's okay. I just thought I would drop by since I was in the neighborhood." He peered over her shoulder at the stacks of paper. "What ya doin'?" he asked.

His wife laughed. "I believe your diction is getting worse the longer we live in this area. If we stay in Thyme another five years, you won't be able to speak English at all!"

He visibly cooled and she realized her mistake.

"I'm sorry," she apologized. "I was only teasing."

They were silent for a moment then he asked, "Mailman come yet?" Still smarting from her remark about his English he continued, "Or, should I say, 'Has the mailperson arrived?'"

She wrinkled her nose at him and at last he grinned.

"No, not yet. You've really been interested in the mail lately. Are you expecting something important?

"No, just wondering."

She straightened one pile of music and began thumbing through another. "Well, for myself, I have spent all morning finishing out this semester of piano assignments for my students. When I add teaching on top of what I do at the church, ten is almost too many. I had not even considered what to have for lunch."

Melody talked on about her students and various music needs but Jonathan didn't seem to be listening. He kept glancing past her and out the living room windows.

There was a clatter on the front porch as the mailman lifted the metal lid and dropped several items into the small box attached beside the front door. "I'll get it," he said and crossed the room in large strides.

"For someone who isn't expecting anything important, you sure move fast."

Jonathan dug into the box retrieving several pieces of mail then checked to make sure nothing was left behind. He shuffled through the letters and found a tan envelope which he folded and slipped into his back pocket. He opened the screen door with a squeak letting it slam shut behind him. "Just the usual," he reported, tossing the mail on top of the sheet music. He hugged his wife. "Hey, why don't we go out for lunch?"

"Again?" she quizzed. She pushed back the chair and stood. Looking at him with a glint in her eye, she cocked her head to one side. "I'm all for it. I must say things are a lot easier in the money department since you took over the checkbook. I'm impressed!"

The video stopped, then after a moment's pause, continued.

Jonathan entered his office and took off his jacket, settled into his chair, and picked up a phone message LeeAnn had written on a Post-It Note and attached to his computer screen.

Suddenly, he stood and slapped at his back pocket digging out the tan envelope. He tore it in pieces and dropped it in the trash receptacle under his desk, then returned to the Post-It Note with his chin in his hand.

The action paused to a still frame.

"For a while this action confused me," Rachael's voice said. "The first day Jonathan came to the house, he appeared to find nothing in the mail that interested him. The next day, a tan envelope was taken from the stack and, as you could see, the same thing happened on this day. I knew the letters were from his bank, but I only realized their significance when I talked with Phennia. She said the letters were likely generated automatically when he wrote several checks and did not have enough money to pay them. He is evidently hiding the error from his wife. This is consistent with character problems noted in this report.

"I sympathize with Jonathan's request to know his significance and see the dynamics of God in action, but the flaws that blind him are deep and removing them will not be simple. Unlike us, humans must live by faith rather than directly seeing into the spirit world. This human has no idea of all that will be required to move him to a new level of spiritual sight. But as a child of the Most High he has a right to ask difficult things. Ours is to obey the Master and serve them as a new world order dawns.

"Welcome back to the battle noble warrior!"

*****

The notes ended at that point and JaKobe stood for a moment, thinking. Of course, he would only be recommending a new level of opposition. The Final Authority would make the official judgment. Still, the responsibility was heavy and he sighed as he settled the Evaluator against the palm of his left hand.

He appreciated Rachael's work, but if he were going to be responsible for this decision, he would take several of his own readings and study them his own way.

He aimed the instrument directly at the pastor's head and desired a reading. It instantly sprang to life measuring the character of the man before its beam. Three hundred lights blinked and settled into a consistent pattern, and then, slowly, the larger summation lights at the base began to glow. Faith gleamed with mellow amber light. Next in line, the robin-egg blue of Hope shown clear. The last light—a deep, garnet red—pulsated like something alive as it measured Jonathan's ability to Love.

For Jonathan, the glow of all three stones was softer than expected for a child of the King, but Faith flickered with the faintest light of all.

JaKobe's Assignment

9:18 AM

The Pastor's Office

He was intently studying the lights on his Evaluator when a glow from a different source made him look up. Although JaKobe instinctively knew where it came from the phenomenon still created mild surprise. Nothing like this ever happened in heaven.

It had started with that strange promise Jesus made. He told his followers they would not be left orphans but he would send another Comforter — One like Himself — who would actually live inside their individual bodies and never leave them.

JaKobe had been on earth at the time and was one of the few who realized the huge implication of those strange words. It was so fantastic — so outside the realm of possibility — that he kept his thoughts to himself but slightly more than fifty days later it all came true. The sky split open, the earth shook and the Holy Spirit — a second member of the Trinity — appeared as a ball of fire.

Splitting himself into individual flames, he rested on each of the hundred and twenty human present igniting the faces and the hearts.

But, it didn't stop there.

For the next fifteen hundred years JaKobe watched as one by one the fallen offspring of Adam—creatures of dust—caught the flame.

For some, the experience was so gentle that the recipient felt little more than a whisper. For others, it was almost violent as the old life shattered and ripped away while the new took possession.

Yet, whatever the experience was like for the one receiving it, the view from the spirit world was always the same. The birth of the Spirit of God inside a human body showed through the skin—especially the face—and glowed in the eyes. It was a light that brightened when the mind of the human connected with the Spirit of God.

Jonathan was still bent over his Bible but now the light which moments before had been a steady, gentle glow, danced and glistened with many colors. The man was praying

Moses[4] had seen it when the glory of God filled the tabernacle. Isaiah[5] saw it when he caught a glimpse of the Almighty, high and lifted up. The disciples[6] were overwhelmed when they looked up and Jesus was covered with it. The Hebrews called it *Shekina*.[1]

There was a feeling of holiness in the room but it abruptly vanished as quickly as it had come

JaKobe's Assignment

when a soft knock drew Jonathan's attention to the door and Melody peeked inside.

"Got time to say good morning?" she asked with a grin.

A large purse was slung over her shoulder and her arms loaded with several music books. A huge plate of cookies topped the stack and the loads made her slim figure look even more petite.

She wore a dress of light wool cream set off by a pumpkin colored scarf. The combination drew warm tones from her peach-soft skin and large brown eyes.

Jonathan smiled back. Every aspect of the woman—from her two inch, closed toe pumps to her carefully styled hair and perfect smile—fit the role of a conservative pastor's wife. She was always supportive, unfailingly kind, given to gracious hospitality and after twenty years of marriage he could count the times she had given way to outbursts of anger on the fingers of one hand.

There was no doubt he loved Melody but—if he had been honest with himself—he would have admitted that through the years she had become both intimidating and boring.

However, Jonathan had a lifelong habit of avoiding unpleasant facts, so these feelings were pushed to the back of his mind and hidden behind a smile.

"Of course," he said. "A man would be a fool not to have time for a wife like you. Your morning going okay? What are the cookies for?"

Elizabeth Baker

He gave neither the statement nor the questions emphasis and ran them together as though not really expecting answers. Melody grimaced. It was an irritating habit.

She sat primly in a straight backed chair balancing the music and cookies on her lap while swinging her purse by its strap. "The cookies are for the shower this afternoon," she began in a soft, slightly breathless voice.

"Shower? What shower?" he interrupted.

"You remember. The baby shower for Miranda." He looked puzzled. "Tina's niece?" she prompted. "Her *unmarried* niece?"

Jonathan groaned inwardly and winced. The complications of giving a baby shower for some unmarried girl the church members hardly knew came back to haunt him.

"But before we get into that, we really need to discuss your first question about how the morning went." She paused and looked directly at him. "When I left home your son was still in bed."

"My son?" he raised his eyebrows in mock surprise. "I thought he was our son. But, of course, I haven't read that birth certificate in a while."

Melody knew her husband often avoided unpleasant situations with a joke but she found no humor in the current situation.

What she did find was anger rising up inside. For seventeen years this man had loaded her with 100% of the care of Ben while he played everybody's favorite preacher. She was the one who nursed him, diapered him, sat up with him at night and still managed a part time job during the day. She was the one who went to his Little League practices and baked cupcakes for the class party and attended the school meetings even while giving birth to his two sisters, managing their multiple moves and juggling her duties in the church. She was the one who . . .

Abruptly, she stopped the thoughts midstream and forced her resentment into the background.

"I'm worried, Jonathan. Ben's sixteen—almost seventeen. A boy that age needs a stronger hand than his mother can give."

"I know," he conceded. "I'll have a talk with him."

She had heard that before. Why couldn't this man just be more like her own dear father? If only Gerald Stonemeyer were still alive, he would be able to fix Ben. He knew how to be a godly man. Faithful. Strong. Wise.

A backlash of guilt engulfed her. It wasn't right to compare her husband with her father. If she were a better wife Jonathan would grow strong. Eventually.

"Could you talk with him this afternoon?" she asked.

He thought of his crowded schedule and his much treasured Sunday afternoon nap. "Isn't Luke coming over this afternoon?"

"Oh, yes. I forgot about Luke."

They were silent for a moment. The faint smell of chocolate-chips drifted from under the plastic wrap.

"Got any extra on that plate?" he asked, reaching behind him for a coffee pot. It would be his first pot of five. LeeAnn's last assignment each evening was to set up the coffee maker and he personally kept it going through the day. "There's an empty cup in the kitchen if you'd like to join me."

Melody pulled the plastic wrap away from the edge of the plate and reached in with two polished fingernails. Like everything else she did, the cookies were perfect. Brown and crisp on the outside, soft and chewy inside with a generous serving of toasted pecans and melted chocolate chips evenly divided throughout each.

"No thanks," she said. "Eating would mess up my lipstick." She hardly paused before adding, "And don't forget, you can only have one. You know what the doctor said about your cholesterol."

He frowned but said nothing. Watching his cholesterol was one more job his wife had taken on her already overloaded shoulders. This conversation was not going well. First she reminded him of his duties as a father, now she was harping on his diet. It was time to change the subject. He opted for a topic where he felt more authority.

"I am still not comfortable with that shower this afternoon."

JaKobe's Assignment

The resentment Melody had so recently pushed down flooded back with a vengeance. If he were not *comfortable* with the situation, why hadn't he done something about it?

When the call first came from Tina, she had been like a bulldozer pushing plans and dates before Melody could even understand the request but the moment she sensed reluctance, the woman switched from demanding to morally superiority arguing that the church had no right to judge her niece just because Miranda and Brad were not married. They had a committed relationship and had been living together for three years. That was longer than some marriages lasted.

Melody couldn't keep up with the onslaught. Until that moment, she hadn't even realized Miranda was not married. Her only concern had been asking the women of the church to buy gifts and produce a shower for someone they had never seen or even heard of until two months ago. The moral issue that Tina was fighting to defend had never occurred to her.

As soon as Jonathan returned she laid the problem in his lap but the man had been no help at all. He said giving Miranda the same honor as married mothers would set a bad example for teenage girls. He griped about the decline of morals in the United States. He argued the homosexual issue, the abortion issue, the balanced budget issue and the Supreme Court issue. Yet, he would not make a clear decision either for or against the shower.

To his credit, Jonathan tried to set up a meeting with Miranda and Brad so he could encourage them to follow a more traditional path, but the meeting never happened. Melody suspected Tina never passed on his request.

Instead, Tina waited until she knew Jonathan was out of town then called the church secretary insisting the shower be put on the church calendar.

LeeAnn, in turn, called Melody and tearfully asked what she should do. With no other authority around, Melody made the best decision she could and authorized the shower then suddenly found herself persuading church members to cook and buy gifts for someone they did not know in order to have a party that no one was sure should be taking place.

Remembering all this pushed unguarded words from her mouth. Sarcasm dripped from her words like acid and she felt her lips curl as she spit them out. "Well, if the church leadership had been a little more actively involved, we might not be in this mess!"

Jonathan's eyes widened as two different emotions hit him simultaneously. One emotion was anger. How could his wife be so insensitive? She was dragging him into an argument when she knew he had to preach in a couple of hours!

But the second emotion held a surprising taste of pleasure. There was something satisfying about watching this always perfect woman lose it. Somehow it made her more real. He stared at her with mouth slightly agape. Then, guilt crept in, winning the emotional toss-up.

"Perhaps you are right," he said. "I should have made a decision rather than letting the issue slide."

His humble admission did nothing to help the situation. Melody was mortified by her cutting remark. No matter how hard she tried to be a good Christian wife, her mouth was always getting in the way.

Tears, which had been just below the surface for months, threatened to spill over. She was such a failure. Her family was slipping through her fingers and she was helpless to stop the decline. Ben was swinging wildly between being ultra religious and subtly rebelling. Stephanie had lost her head to boys, Christian rock, and sexy clothes. Traci was like a lost lamb, oblivious to danger yet intuitively knowing her mother was sad and trying in her childish way to comfort her drifting parents.

An unutterable weariness swept over her. She tried so hard. Year after year the battle went on. Demands of the children. Demands of the community. Demands at church. Demands of God. The list never shortened. She was tired. So very tired.

It hadn't always been this way. As a little girl, she dreamed of one day growing up to be a smiling, confident mommy. In high school, while other girls looked forward to careers, she gave them only lip service for she knew in her heart she wanted nothing more than to be a good wife to a good man and raise a good family. She prayed about it, planned for it and built her identity around it.

Her first year in college, she kept her virginity even when Shawn changed from commending her purity to complaining about his unfulfilled needs.

She thought she'd die when he left her. But, she still had her purity and surely God would reward her for that. All the books said He would.

When Jonathan came into her life, she believed God had sent him. The Almighty was rewarding her for good deeds.

Their wedding was sweet and simple, and the honeymoon physically exciting. The first two years she worked as a bank teller and worried that she might never become pregnant but she stayed faithful in prayer and again God rewarded her. This time with a healthy baby boy.

It had been so simple in those early years. Do good, be nice, work hard, and things go like they should. Nothing worked that way anymore.

On the outside, she was still good; she worked hard at being nice and always went above and beyond the expected. Yet, on the inside—in her mind and heart—a continual war raged. She thought things and felt things that shocked and shamed her. She pushed and battled with herself. It was like being caged inside her body with a lion.

JaKobe's Assignment

Melody blinked back the tears but her smile barely faded. "I'm sorry. I should not have said that."

"It's all right," he mumbled.

Silence settled in the room like a suffocating, palatable, fog. Melody adjusted her position in the chair. Jonathan broke his cookie into bite size pieces and swirled the coffee in his cup.

At last he cleared his throat and tried to approach a safe subject.

"You all ready for the recital? How will you fit both that event and the shower into one afternoon?"

Melody wanted to throw her hands over her ears and scream! How many times had she reminded him not to ask more than one question at a time! She took a deep breath and tried to answer each in the order it was received.

"Yes, I'm ready. Most of the students are doing great. Luke is a genius at the keyboard. He intimidates me with his power and precision. He should be teaching me.

"As for your second question, it will be tight but I feel sure it will work. Didn't you see this week's bulletin?"

Jonathan fished through several piles on his desk. "Here it is," he said locating the neatly folded copy of announcements, events, and church schedule.

Every week LeeAnn placed a stack of bulletins in the narthex and one copy on the pastor's chaotic desk. He usually unearthed it before church started but seldom actually read it until the end of the morning service when he made the announcements.

"Shower at two, recital and reception at four-thirty, and church at seven. That's do-able?"

"I think so. The shower should take about two hours; the recital and reception another two. That leaves thirty minutes between each event to clear the parking lot and set up for the next thing on the schedule."

"Melody, . . ." he began but couldn't find words to finish the sentence. How could he correct someone for serving to the maximum, scheduling to the minute and being perfect in every way?

"Go ahead, say it."

"Nothing. I am sure it will all come together. You always manage to make everything fit."

Voices from the hall let them know others were beginning to arrive for Sunday school. She nodded in the direction of the door.

"It sounds like it's about time to get started." She shuffled her arm into the purse strap swinging it free from the back of the chair and stood balancing the cookies and music. "I'll try not to schedule so closely again." She was almost to the door when Jonathan called to her.

"Melody. . ."

She turned toward him and forced another smile. The face was so perfect and so foreign. He longed to share his confusion and feelings of failure with the gentle, vulnerable girl he once married. But, this perfect creature before him bore

JaKobe's Assignment

little resemblance to his bride. The only words he could manage were the same, safe, words that he uttered every day, "I love you."

Her eyes were bright with unshed tears. "I love you, too, Jonathan."

JaKobe watched the scene without embarrassment. His deep respect for all things human and the fact that they were an altogether different strain of being prevented any sense of privacy infringement.

However, he did have an angel-size capacity for compassion and Melody touched him deeply. Dark shadows clung all around her. There was no glow. No Life.

8:37 AM

Old Enemies

JaKobe left the office shortly after Melody and for a brief while roamed about the halls. Humans had been arriving for the past several minutes and most rooms contained at least a few of them. There were also spirit beings whose assorted task, various ranks and numerous relationships added to the busy, excited feeling permeating the air.

JaKobe drifted back to the auditorium.

Thoughtful, dark, eyes looked over the empty room then he slowly walked up the center aisle and took a position behind the pulpit. What must it be like for Jonathan to stand in this spot week after week? He tried hard to imagine.

It was strange how humans and spirits could be so much alike while remaining fundamentally different. They both shared the same Creator. Both communicated, felt emotion, used logic, made choices, and possessed the ability to suffer.

JaKobe's Assignment

Yet, in other ways, angels and mortals were different and totally unique within their own spheres.

Humans experienced many capacities angels did not. Things like hunger, thirst, sex, sleep and a dozen other attributes of which JaKobe had only academic knowledge.

On the other hand, as long as humans occupied the current time and space, angels were superior in ways people could only imagine. JaKobe could absorb and process information at a phenomenal rate. He became curious about microbiology before Socrates walked the earth and could easily have discussed time/space warps with Einstein.

But the factor that divided someone like him from the pastor in the other room was a spiritual element. A simple, obvious, difference that more than anything else formed a watershed between angels and mortals: Faith.

Angels neither had need for faith nor possessed the ability to experience it. They could see the Throne. They could walk between the worlds of spirit and flesh. Long ago, the apostle Paul described faith as *evidence of things not seen*. JaKobe could see and touch things of the spirit so how could he experience depending on what he could not see?

It must be difficult to be human. He considered the mystery. *They gather knowledge of God from what they can see then jump into the unknown believing Someone out there will catch them as they fall.*

The process seemed an awesome thing to a being like him.

How could he accurately and compassionately serve humans when something so fundamental as faith was outside his experience? Was he familiar with any personal event that might be similar?

His memory slipped back to the earth year of 879 AD.

He had just come from one of the few fights he ever lost. Weary beyond endurance, stripped of power and discouraged, JaKobe spent day after day on a windswept bluff in Asia Minor where he had been left to heal and slowly regain strength. It was a long, painful process and as the seasons changed, so did the colors of the sea.

It was also a place to think.

Separate from the excitement of battle, relieved from the responsibility of assignment, he not only exercised his body but his mind. He entertained many thoughts, but the one mystery that tantalized him most was the sad shape of earth and the nature of the Kingdom he had sworn to protect.

Almost four centuries earlier he had been encouraged and wondered if the final victory might be near. Persecution of the saints had ceased. Rome had fallen and although much of Europe was drifting into darkness, there were hopeful signs elsewhere.

Across the continent small pockets of true believers were willing to die for the truth. Antioch and Constantinople and Alexandria and Rome

JaKobe's Assignment

were salted with a few good men of faith. Hundreds of monks along the rocky shores of Ireland had sequestered themselves in beehive-looking houses where they took tireless delight in copying page after page of scripture and the classics. They filled parchment scrolls and cortex with art and graceful script. Humans in East Asia were being set spiritually free by the thousands.

But four hundred years later, progress on scripture production came to a halt when Vikings attacked the monasteries stopping the work and stealing or destroying treasures they could not understand. Darkness deepened as dependence on magic replaced faith and corruption permeated even the highest levels of ecclesiastical leadership.

Only one year before his fateful battle the Tang dynasty had been ripped apart. One hundred thousand foreign merchants were killed in Canton and the fledgling Christian community there was destroyed. The gospel of Jesus, which had been brought to India and lower China by the Apostle Thomas, was making only slow progress. There were Bibles—both whole and in portions— but only the very rich had access to anything significant. Paper would not be used for books for another twenty years and the printing press would have to wait almost six hundred.

Making matters worse, the organized church had drifted into the same excesses and power manipulations as the rest of earth. The pope of Constantinople had just excommunicated the patriarch of the same, who in turn decided the pope could not drive him out and issued an order excommunicating the pope instead.

As he watched the sea change colors, Jakobe had wondered how the Kingdom of God could possibly survive on earth.

He was grateful when orders came at last for a new assignment. But the directions were not at all what he expected.

It was not a call to battle in some hot spot of the planet. He was not given a human to evaluate or protect. There was no territory or nation or project he was to supervise. He was simply told to count the lights. So, he did.

Beginning where he was, he moved around the earth following the path of the sun. Village after village, city after city, country after country, and continent after continent he counted on. Some lights were so intense that holiness burned around them. Others were just a glimmer of hope in a dark land.

He remembered a peasant child in upper France. She was only seven and consumed by a wracking cough that would take her life. A guardian angel stood by keeping the way clear of evil influence as a grieving mother shared the story of Jesus while the Holy Spirit worked drawing, comforting and enlightening the tiny human. An inner light began to burn only hours before the child's outer shell fell away.

JaKobe remained on the earth another 520 years before taking an assignment heavenward,

JaKobe's Assignment

but he never forgot the experience of counting the lights.

He had seen the Kingdom begin at Pentecost with drama and open flame, but after counting the lights he realized that in the future it would be less like open power and more like a mighty, underground river flowing just below the surface and giving life to the land.

The Kingdom of God on earth was neither insipid nor in decline but growing step by step just as the Master planned. The words of the psalmist echoed in his mind: *"Indeed, of Zion it will be said, 'This one and that one were born in her, and the Most High Himself will establish her.'"*[7]

A teenage boy raced in a side door, bringing the angel's full attention back to the present. Crossing the auditorium, he slammed against the set of swinging double doors, stomped across the narthex and tore through the outside doors. He didn't seem angry or fearful just filled with the physical energy and exuberance of youth. Before the automatic closure had time to pull the heavy outside doors fully closed the boy was back again holding a CD in his hand and striding purposefully across the room as though on an urgent mission.

JaKobe knew of CDs and was mildly curious about the one the boy held, but the object was too far away to read the title and it was turned backwards as well. He could have used his energy to look through the boy's hand, through the CD case and read the English as a mirror image but why bother? The boy was not his responsibility.

Jonathan, however, *was* his responsibility and the thought sobered him. Finding a way to remove the character flaws that made him blind without crushing the fragile human would be a delicate surgery.

The outside speakers that broadcasted hymns from the old bell tower had come to life at exactly eight-thirty and he listened for a moment, enjoying the sound. Not exactly a heavenly choir, but nice.

The moments of an earth day were passing and more and more humans were arriving to worship. Most of them were accompanied by various spirits and he could feel the tension increasing as the crowd grew. Perhaps it would be best to join Jonathan again.

As he surveyed the auditorium one last time, a vague uneasiness niggled at him. The energy fields were changing but he could not quite grasp what that meant. Surely his skills had not grown that dull. The feeling was like an expectation permeating the air. Or, maybe *threat* was a better word than *expectation*.

Moving away from the pulpit, he walked to the edge of the platform and had one foot suspended above the first step when Doltar suddenly appeared on the very back pew.

His ancient enemy was in the form of a human male and he had dressed in the exact same apparel as JaKobe. The only difference between them was

JaKobe's Assignment

Doltar's clean-shaven chin, light blond hair and eyes a deep, attractive blue. The angel of darkness smiled warmly as he leaned forward resting elbows on the back of the pew in front of him. He cupped his chin in both hands and without words passed a message to JaKobe.

"Like the outfit?"

The sudden appearance caused JaKobe to halt ever so slightly—a detail not missed by his enemy—but he quickly regained his grace and continued down the stairs. Neither changed their expression and, if humans could have observed them, none would have guessed they were anything but old friends.

"Well, Doltar. I see you are a male this time."

JaKobe had purposely responded with English words rather than the simpler communion of thought. If pride forced his enemy to do likewise, the ploy might bring him time to think.

"As for your question," he continued, "the answer is 'yes.' I like the outfit very much. Especially the pockets." He kept his voice even as he sauntered down the aisle and demonstrated the point by stretching his fingers wide under the fabric.

"You always were a sucker for human details."

JaKobe suppressed a smile. His enemy had taken the bait. He was answering with full sentences and English words.

"And to what do I owe the pleasure of this visit?" he asked with as much sarcasm as possible while removing his hands from the pockets and clasping them behind his back. Slipping the fingers of one hand inside the bracelet, he pulled slightly releasing the clasp and felt the instrument flatten in his hand.

"My visit?" Doltar replied with mock surprise. "I'm not the 'visitor' here. You are the one who's been hiding." He paused then gave a knowing smile. "Of course, I'm sure you had your reasons."

The remark was a cut, not an answer. But then, answers were not really necessary. The fact Doltar had appeared suddenly was a challenge to battle and by expressing himself in the same clothing, he communicated that he had been watching JaKobe's movements for some time and probably knew a great deal about his assignment.

Battle was certainly tempting. The only thing he wanted more than settling an old score was being faithful to the task he had been assigned. He squeezed the bracelet back into a circle around his wrist.

He continued his leisurely pace a few steps closer while his mind whirled with options as the distance between them narrowed to less than ten feet and Doltar stood. If this warrior had a weak spot, it would be his pride.

Switching to the ancient Gallic tongue they had used at their last encounter, JaKobe smiled broadly. "Earth's a beautiful place. It's good to be back." Then losing the smile he continued, "I'm sure we will be seeing each other again. Soon."

JaKobe's Assignment

With that, he turned his back and walked away with the same unhurried strides that he'd used when approaching Rachael that morning. It was a calculated risk. Doltar would want a spirit audience to see him win a second time.

At least, he certainly hoped that was the case. If not, exposing his back to the face of an enemy was either extreme bravery or the most foolish thing he had ever done.

Elizabeth Baker

9:40 AM

Gathering to Grace

The old church steeple had been fitted with woofers, tweeters, electric lines, gizmos and timers all connected to a CD player on a back shelf in LeeAnn's office. Now, the clear notes of *Rock of Ages* drifted past the parking lot and out over the yards of nearby homes. It was the same hymn that echoed through the woods when the first circuit-riding preacher passed this way.

It had taken months to get the proper level of sound and comply with all the city ordinances but after five years of operation there had been no complaints. Everyone seemed to agree the soft electronic sounds were an addition to the community not an infringement of rights or noise pollution.

For those who did not attend church, the music was a pleasant benediction that felt good yet cost nothing and came with no religious obligation. For those who attended Grace, the music and bells were a pleasant way to start their Sunday as well as a convenient way of telling time. The music played fifteen minutes before each service and bells rang exactly at church time then music continued for another five minutes to greet latecomers.

Most of the humans came in cars and although it was still early dozens of them were scattered through the halls and in various rooms. Old and young, wicked and righteous, kind and selfish. Together, they created a slightly different mix of natures than one might find at a ball game or discount store. But not much.

*****

It was 9:40 when Diane whipped her compact car into the parking lot, circled the building and stopped by a back door. Although the music had been going for ten minutes, her mind was too full of worries and schedules and plans to notice its pleasant sound.

She glanced at her watch. Five minutes before Sunday school. So, why was she rushing? She pondered the question but knew there was really only one answer: Habit. Slowing down just didn't feel natural.

Ever since Steve left four years ago, it had been her job to push against the clock, push against the budget, push against the lawyers and push against her own despair. There was no time. There was no money. Push, push, push!

She breathed deeply trying to release a little of the tension. Stretching her arms forward and gripping the top of the steering wheel she arched her back like a cat then tucked her short brown hair behind each ear and rolled down the window letting in the music and cool morning air. Better.

This morning there was no need to push. After all, she did not have the boys. She could do as she liked. Eleven-year-old Dwayne and his nine-year-old brother, Casey, were with their father for the weekend. She was free!

The music from the speakers filled the car with soft, far away tones. Air rushed into her lungs and out again in a spontaneous sigh she was not aware of holding. Who was she trying to fool? She might have a little more time with the boys gone, but it was never really better without her children.

How she missed her boys! She wondered what they thought of their daddy's new girlfriend. Hopefully, this one would be better than the last. Her mind instinctively traced the words of the melody filling the car, *Rock of ages cleft for me, Let me hide myself in thee."*[8] She needed a rock of some kind. That was for sure.

Maybe it wouldn't always be this way. Maybe one day she could slow down and offer the boys more stability. The good Lord knew she was trying.

The divorce had been bitter and long but when the judge pounded the final gavel, it sounded like there would be enough money to

JaKobe's Assignment

start a new life. Steve made a very good income working as a chemist at the Kodak lab in Longview. She had been granted three years spousal support in addition to their small home in Thyme and child support for both boys. But, something went wrong between how secure it looked on paper and the demands of real life.

She tried to prepare herself for independence by going back to school, taking her maiden name "Kirkland," and letting "Mullins" drop by the wayside. She had it all planned. With two years college on her transcript, the step from full-time Mom to registered nurse would be a short one.

Wrong.

College life and single parenting seemed to be natural enemies. Between Casey's frequent hospitalizations for asthma and Dwayne's school problems her time was squeezed to a minimum. She barely managed one or two classes a semester. Despite her best efforts spousal support came to an end last year and her dreams of building a new career faded.

When the last check came, she was ashamed and angry. Ashamed because she had not managed to become self-supporting, and angry because the things blocking her way were at last beginning to clear. Casey's health had improved and the emotional struggles which once added to Dwayne's poor school performance seemed better. It was ironic. When there was money, there had been no time. And, now that the time crunch was better, most of the money had dried up.

Elizabeth Baker

That was when she found Grace Community. She had come across a newspaper ad for a part time janitor and although she had never before considered such a low position, she swallowed her pride and sent a letter to the pastor.

Pastor Phelps hired her at their first meeting and his quick acceptance gave a much needed boost to her confidence. Although she soon realized not many people wanted the difficult, minimum wage, part-time job she quickly adjusted. Before many weeks passed found it to be a strong win-win the situation.

For Diane, the pay was enough so that when added to child support and education grants it met her needs. And, for the church, Diane became not only a dependable employee but a valuable member of the congregation as well.

After her Presbyterian childhood, adapting to the ways of Grace felt a little strange but the doctrine was much the same and best of all she found a haven for her boys. Dwayne immediately responded to his male Sunday school teacher and Casey found a real talent as part of the children's choir. The people were friendly—at least for the most part—and every Sunday Pastor Phelps had something to say that was worth listening to.

But, the thing that surprised Diane most about this new phase of life was how much she liked her work as janitor. She was paid a flat rate for the job and because she moved quickly, it averaged significantly more than the minimum wage she had been expecting. The flexible hours let her work around her new college schedule and because she worked mostly at night no boss was watching over her shoulder. She often took the boys with her. They did their homework in the church kitchen as she cleaned toilets and vacuumed. Any way you measured it the job at Grace Community had been a very good thing.

The timer on the player in LeeAnn's office signaled and a series of clear bells rang in the autumn air. It was nine forty-five. Time to worship. Welcome one and all to the celebration!

Diane rescued her worn Bible from the floorboard where it had fallen and dashed inside.

*****

In the front parking lot, Murphy Woodburn heard the bells just as the church van bounced past the familiar dip between the street and the paved parking. He hated being late. He was never late. Others were depending on him. Being late was simply unacceptable.

"Are we gonna be late, Mr. Woody?" a small voice asked from the third seat.

"No, we ain't," he replied with only a partial turn of his head. "At least not if you get with it and don't dawdle on the way in."

"It's all Carolina's fault," said one of the older girls from the very back seat.

"I couldn't help it!" five-year-old Carolina protested. "I had to go potty. I didn't know Mr. Woody was comin' so soon!"

Woody looked in the rearview mirror at his charges. Three were brown, two were black and two were white. All ranged from five to twelve and he loved them every one. "Now, hush up!" he said in an unusually gruff voice. "Carolina's all right. You kids quit picking on her. Nobody's gonna be late. At least, not much."

He pulled the van close beside a set of glass double doors and shifted the engine into park. But before opening the door, he turned and faced the youngsters.

"You all be good, now. And, remember, I'll be waiting right over there when church is over." He pointed to the space reserved for the church van. "You all done good this mornin', speci'ly since Momma Jo couldn't come."

Church policy stated two adults had to be in the van when children were being transported, but his wife woke up with another migraine, so he decided to take the van on his own. If the pastor asked out right, he would never lie, but until then he was not beyond bending the rules just a bit and keeping silent. His kids were worth the risk.

"You be good now," he said for a second time, "Mr. Woody 'll have somethin' good for you when you get back." He patted the chest pocket of his overalls with one hand and opened the van door with the other.

Everyone knew that Mr. Woody's overalls always contained something good, either hard candy or stickers or on special occasions small chocolate bars. The older children pretended it didn't matter. They were too mature to be persuaded by such small treats. But, secretly, they looked forward to the stickers and bubblegum as much as any of the small ones.

Mr. Woody watched them file out one by one then kept watching until the last one entered the church door. They were his heart.

Jolene and Murphy "Woody" Woodburn had moved to Thyme two years ago after retiring from the automotive assembly lines in Chicago. They had no children and both sets of parents were dead. So, once they had no jobs to hold them, there was no reason to face the harsh winters of the North.

They spread a map of the United States on the dining table and considered the possibilities. They had a good feel for various parts of the country having spent the last ten vacations touring. The mountains, the coast, retirement communities and even backpacking had all been tried, but they most often found themselves in the pine filled woods of East Texas camping by some small lake.

After long weeks of consideration, they settled on Thyme. It was centrally located between their favorite lakes and with such a quirky name the town was bound be a place that did not take itself too seriously.

When the move was complete, they found the little town suited them well. Their easygoing manners, country dress, frequently dropped consonants and elongated vowels fooled many into thinking they were natives of the area rather than Yankees.

There was only one problem: boredom. Woody found it strange to sleep every night after a lifetime of rotating shifts and Jolene missed her lunches out with friends. Then Grace Community introduced them to children's ministry and life came into focus again.

Every Saturday the old blue van with Grace Community Church proudly printed on the side bounced and rattled its way down country roads, through obscure side streets and around the few apartment buildings close by. Sometimes he knocked on doors. Sometimes he just looked for groups of children playing and drove up beside them.

Woody always had his pockets full of candy and he carried cards announcing who he was and his purpose for being in the neighborhood. But he was amazed that his presence and involvement with the children caused no more suspicion than it did.

The truth was, parents who kept careful watch on their children soon grew accustomed to his presence and parents who didn't care found him easy to ignore. An overweight, balding, white guy wasn't much of a physical threat, and his faded overalls and aging van didn't look like something a drug dealer would find attractive.

In the past eighteen months several dozen children had ridden his van to church. Most came only once or twice to satisfy curiosity. After that,

JaKobe's Assignment

the time away from the streets wasn't worth a piece of candy. However, a few grew to love Mr. Woody and looked forward to seeing him each week.

"Woody" Woodburn closed the van door and turned the wheel toward his assigned parking space. He shook his head and smiled at the very idea of allowing little Carolina to make him late because she had to go potty! If the guys on the assembly line could see their foreman turning to mush at the request of a five-year-old, they'd wonder if he'd gained retirement or lost his mind.

****

Inside the building, Era Lou Bridges hurried along the dreary back hall as fast as her eighty-two year old legs would carry her. The bells had only now announced it was time to begin, but she knew the T.E.L class would have been gathered for at least fifteen minutes.

She passed the bathrooms, the storage closet, secretary's office, and the cave where Pastor Phelps lived. Then she moved on to a small, hidden room at the end of the hall. Not many classes would have wanted to meet in this out of the way place, but it was perfect for the women of T.E.L. There were no stairs to climb, it had easy access to the restrooms and there were no squealing, running children to dodge in the hall. Best of all, the room had been home to the class for almost thirty years.

Era Lou remembered the uproar seven years ago when the church threatened to turn the space into a bride's room.

Bride's room! She silently scoffed at the memory. Of all things! Didn't any woman old enough to get married know enough to change her clothes at home?

But, the brouhaha had produced a few good things. First, it reminded the church old people still existed—a fact that too easily slipped out of public awareness—and second, it educated the uninitiated as to what T.E.L. was about. She wondered if this new Phelps man had any idea. Probably not.

Maybe one day she would test him. No, that wouldn't be nice. Still, it *was* tempting.

Anyone should know that T.E.L. obviously stood for Timothy, Eunice and Lois. The son, mother and grandmother commended by Paul for passing the faith on through the generations. Time was when every church worth its salt had a T.E.L. class. What else were they going to put on the door? "Old ladies with blue hair meet here"?

The door to the class stood ajar. Perfect. One could push on it rather than turning the knob with an arthritic wrist. The door swung open and she entered a cheerful room where a chorus of friendly voices welcomed her. Sunshine streamed through curtained windows and a border of flowered wallpaper was neatly pasted close to the ceiling. It felt like coming home.

JaKobe's Assignment

Norma—the teacher and youngest of the group—stood behind a small lectern resting one hand on an open Bible and holding a small pot of African violets in the other.

"Era Lou! How good that you could make it out this week! I trust you're feeling better." She held the pot of violets higher and added, "Look at the present Connie brought each of us!"

Era Lou selected one of the folding chairs fitted with a flat, chintz pillow and lowered her bones slowly into it. Five other women smiled their welcome and Connie proudly motioned to the cardboard box on the floor beside her.

"Oh, how pretty," Era Lou purred softly. "Connie you always were such a caution! I'll take that purple, ruffled one in the corner. I never knew anyone with a greener thumb."

The teacher called the women to order, anxious to get through the prayer requests and on to the lesson for the week. "Has anyone heard from Margaret?" she asked.

Alma Sparks, a bright-eyed woman in her late 70's spoke. "I couldn't believe it when you said she was in the hospital. She was fine just two days past when I phoned."

Connie looked slightly puzzled. "I thought they admitted her in right after her doctor's appointment on Friday morning."

"Yes, but we talked Thursday afternoon and that's two days past," explained Alma.

"But, this is Sunday," Connie used her fingers to count off the days, "Sunday, Saturday, Friday, Thursday. You talked to her four days ago."

"But a *past day* means that it is over and finished." Alma clarified. "You can't count Thursday because that was the day I called and you can't count today because Sunday isn't past yet."

"Oh, Lawdy," said Era Lou. "We're all so old we can't even count anymore!"

The class broke into uproarious laughter.

"Well, anyway," Norma brought them back to the subject. "Does anyone know what is wrong with Margaret or how she is now?"

"I talked with her Saturday," said Ima. "But, it was short. That nurse came in and interrupted everything. Seems Margaret had some kind of reaction to her blood pressure medicine. I think they'll let her go Monday after all the tests get in."

"Well, we need to keep her on the list." Norma turned to the blackboard behind her. "You never know about the future." She took a piece of chalk and wrote *Margaret Mc Clawson* in neat, rounded letters.

Margaret was not the only name on the board. Almost thirty individuals and families were listed. Combined, they were a microcosm of Thyme. Births, deaths, illnesses, job loss, relatives traveling, marriages, grandchildren away at college, and financial concerns. Chalk dust was thick on the bottom ledge of the board and the carpet below was permanently stained as layer

JaKobe's Assignment

after layer of names had been added and erased while the needs of the town ebbed and flowed with the rhythm of life.

Praying down the list often took half the time allotted for Sunday school, but today's list was especially long. Norma glanced at her watch and then at her carefully prepared lesson. She would have to choose.

She looked around the room at the gathered saints. "Sisters," she said softly. "Let's pray."

*****

Back up the dark hall, a corridor of white tile intersected then raced away with classrooms on either side and a kitchen at the very end. In one of these classrooms, Melody paced bouncing five-month-old Jessica. Where was Ellie? She was bound to know it was her Sunday in the nursery. LeeAnn faithfully sent reminder cards.

Anger increased as the minutes ticked by. Ellie's failure to show left an empty space and there was an unwritten law in all churches that the pastor's wife filled any spaces left by undependable volunteers. Resentment swelled inside her and she fought it down like bile.

Oh, well, perhaps being alone with the babies was what she needed. She had no right to resent Ellie. Or, Jonathan. She simply must get control of her emotions.

"Let him that is perfect cast the first stone," she quoted the words of Jesus aloud to the baby but even when she smiled it didn't do a thing for the surging, internal tide.

Maybe she should be checked out for PMS.

*****

Three doors down from the nursery, Garrison Black was grabbing the back of Jimmy's shirt and pulling him away from the door. "Oh, no you don't, young man!" he playfully jested. Jimmy laughed and returned to his seat.

"All I was gonna do was call for pizza," Jimmy pleaded with a mock whine. "You said you didn't have breakfast."

"Not quite. I said you and Brian should quit complaining because you weren't the only ones who didn't have breakfast this morning."

"Well, I was just gonna fix our problem! I figured you'd pay."

"Funny boy," his teacher stated flatly. "If you and Brian don't settle down and finish that acrostic I'll . . . I'll . . .Well...." He looked at the energetic, bright eyed group of ten to twelve year old boys. Oh, for the good ol' days in the military when he simply shouted an order and others rushed to obey.

"I'll tell you what," he continued. "You boys do a good job on that acrostic and show me what you learned. You can even help each other finish. If the whole class makes 100%, I'll take everyone out to the ranch next Saturday and you can help me burn a brush pile. I bet I could even talk Emily into rustling up a hotdog or two."

"All right!" they squealed in unison.

*****

Up the stairs, two doors down and to the right, the teenagers were giving Ward and Beverly a hard time. They had sung three snappy songs, made the announcements, and offered prayer. Now, it was time to get down to the serious stuff. The girls would follow Beverly to another room for their lesson and the boys would remain with Ward.

That was when the rebellion broke out.

"Why can't we stay together?" The new girl, Teresa, was leading the argument. Even though she had only attended the group for two weeks, she obviously felt her opinion of how things should be run was as valid as anyone's—including that of her teachers. "It's more fun when boys and girls stay together in one class!" She poked out a bottom lip in a sexy pout and slowly blinked heavily made up eyes.

"Yeah! That's a great idea!" said a surprisingly deep male voice from across the room. "We could all just stay in here and you could teach one week," he indicated Beverly, "and Mr. Newsom could teach the next!"

Ward moved closer to his wife. "Okay, okay!" he calmed the group with a wave of his hand. "You've had your say. We might stay together someday, but for now we're going to do things the way they have always been done. Girls, go with Mrs. Newsom and guys, you stay here with me"

Groans and protest were echoed around the room and a wicked spirit grinned with satisfaction. Teresa was an easy target. The spirit slipped away for a little bragging session with others who were waiting. He would be back before the dismissal bell.

JaKobe's Assignment

9:52 AM

Halls of Grace

The bells ceased to chime shortly after 9:45 and at 9:50 the music stopped. There was no sound but the wind and the occasional passing of a car along Pecan Street as Ben Phelps slipped silently around the corner.

Palms backward, arms pressed against the building, he looked left then right and slipped through the back door. Wearing khaki pants and a starched cotton dress shirt with button down collar, he looked every inch a pastor's son right down to his redish-brown, cut-neatly-above-the-ears, hair.

Ben was tall for his age, slightly overweight and pleasantly rounded in all physical attributes. His thick eyebrows were light, his nose somewhat pug and his hazel eyes set wide apart and bright. All in all he was a handsome young man whose white-toothed grin put others at ease. His manners were polite while his grades seldom dropped below an A-.

He paused in the dark, empty hall and listened. Having been in church almost every Sunday since he was born, the boy possessed a sixth sense about church sounds.

Behind him, the old ladies class was giggling and he knew Era Lou must be feeling better. He could detect her high pitched laughter above the others. No sounds came from the church kitchen. That meant the ushers had finished their coffee and probably stepped outside to visit Clint while he smoked.

Ben felt like a detective or a character out of the old *Hardy Boys Mysteries* he still read, but refused to admit he even owned. A small piece of his mind shamed him for playing super-sleuth, but there was also a strange satisfaction about reverting to kid status--if only for a moment.

The adult world was rushing at him with no hope of escape. At times he felt life was asking him to step off a cliff with nothing but fog below. There was no way to tell how far he might fall before finding solid ground.

The clicking of a woman's heels was coming toward him. Tina Bentley was going from class to class picking up attendance cards. He listened again judging the distance. Was he trapped? Not yet! The sudden shuffling of chairs upstairs told him he had timed his arrival perfectly. The youth department was separating into classes.

JaKobe's Assignment

He darted to the foot of the stairs then whispered up them two at a time and slipped inside the classroom while the girls were filing out. Stephanie rolled her eyes as her brother passed, but he knew she could be depended on not to tell. He took his place with the other boys, winking at Greg as he slipped into a vacant chair.

A moment later, Tina appeared at the door, her hands full of attendance cards and a pencil behind her ear. "You're not ready?" She spoke to Ward with an accusing tone.

"Oh, yeah," he mumbled and searched among papers for the errant card. He found it in his Bible marking today's lesson. "Sure thing," he said, handing it over with a smile.

Tina glanced at it. "The card says you have seven students and one teacher."

"O-kay...," Ward drawled with a puzzled look.

"There are eight students in this room."

He turned toward the boys and eight innocent faces looked back. Dog-gone that Ben. He was late again.

Tina removed the pencil, erased the seven and replaced it with an eight, then whirled and started back down the hall. The clucking sound she made was exactly like a hen brooding over a batch of slow hatching eggs as she when back down the hall stopping by the *Teenage Girl's* class, the class for *Young Married* and the nondescript *"Women's" Class* where unattached females settled until they aged enough to pass into *Senior Adult* status.

She went back downstairs and disappeared into her cubbyhole office where she placed the cards in a neat stack. Tina loved it when things were in order. Or, at least, when they were in *her* order. And, since she was the only one who used this six by six space, her order was easily maintained.

The pencil cup was always on the right, permanent records occupied the center of the desk, and today's attendance cards were always on the left.

In many ways Tina and Melody were very much alike. Their standards were high and every task was performed with precision. The difference between them was motive. Melody drove herself to meet standards she believed others expected and punished herself for constantly falling short. On the other hand, Tina believed her orderly ways were due to her excellence as a person and she was easily insulted when others failed to recognize that fact.

Yet, when viewed from the unseen world of spirits, both women were exactly the same in the only way that mattered. Each had a face streaked by shadows.

Tina counted her cards. Two were missing. She had been by both of those rooms earlier and the teachers told her they would send the records later. Well, now was "later" and they had not sent a student with the card.

Heels clicked against the tile with a staccato rhythm as they marched to a door with a sign

JaKobe's Assignment

reading, *Boys 10-12*. She entered without knocking. "Mr. Black, you are late again. Is there some reason?"

Garrison Black looked up from the circle of boys who seemed to be competing in some type game. "Oh, no problem, Mrs. Bentley. I just forgot." Nodding his head toward the far corner he said, "It's over on the table."

She crossed the room like an ice cube floating across hot soup, picked up the record and left without a word.

Only one class to go: The five through seven year olds at the end of the next hall.

Tina could hear the noise the moment she turned the corner. Evidently Barbara was having trouble keeping order this morning. She opened the door and found eight children engaged in almost as many separate activities. Barbara looked up with a frazzled daze and spoke before Tina could say a word.

"I'm sorry about the record," she apologized. "The teacher's manual suggested we try multiple centers rather than forcing all the children to do the same thing at the same time. It sounded good in print, but this is chaos!"

"Haven't you even started?"

"Sorry. Could you give me a hand? Carolina can't find a blue Crayon for the Sea of Galilee and if I move from this PlayDoh table we will never get it out of the carpet!"

"I'm really quite busy with my own work," Tina objected.

"Miss Barbara," Carolina followed the Southern custom of calling all adult women "Miss" no matter what their marital status. "Sharon's got a blue, but she won't share."

Tina blew out a frustrated breath. It was easy to see her records would never get finished if she didn't find that blue Crayon.

She moved to the coloring table and bent over two little girls intent on pictures of Jesus and the disciples fishing from a boat. "Carolina, I declare, here is your blue. You dropped it on the floor."

Determined to keep the girls occupied until she could locate the class record and exit, Tina bent over Carolina, placed the color in a tiny hand, and began to trace blue waves. "See, it's a very pretty blue."

That was when she made the awful discovery.

Carolina's dark brown hair was parted in the middle and as Tina stood over her she couldn't miss the small bug casually strolling down the part then slipping away among the forest of brown roots. She stared then the corners of her mouth slowly turned down in disgust.

"Miss Bar-ba-ra," she drew the name out with long, slow deliberation. "May I see you in the hall?" Her shocked look and turned-up nose let Barbara know she had better do as requested even if PlayDoh ended up ground in the carpet forever.

Carolina watched the two women exit, intuitively sensing that something important was going on. She felt uncomfortable and turned back to her picture. Her boat wasn't as good as

JaKobe's Assignment

Sharon's. Maybe she should have left the sails white rather than purple.

Voices were coming from the hall. "I don't care. I want to check each one of those children. We will have to inform the parents."

Miss Barbara came back into the room. She smiled at Carolina but something about the grin did not look right.

She took her seat at the PlayDoh table and said. "Steven, would you go into the hall. Miss Tina wants you."

"Did I do somethin' wrong?"

"No, Honey. It's all right. Just go."

"Is Steven in trouble?" asked his PlayDoh partner, Carlos.

Steven reluctantly went out the door only to come back moments later with a sheepish grin. Carolina saw him whisper something to Carlos then vigorously rub his short, stubby haircut.

Miss Barbara nodded toward the home center. "Brenda, would you step out and let Miss Tina see you?" Brenda reluctantly put down the doll she was dressing and quietly left the room.

When she came back she was grinning like Steven but her blond hair—which was neatly swept back in a ponytail when she left—now hung in wisps around her face and the ribbon was crooked. She shut the door with a loud bang pressing both hands against it.

"She was itching in my hair!" she announced to the class.

"It's all right, Brenda. Just go back to the home center."

"Tennesha, it's your turn."

One by one the children left. Most returned giggling but as Carolina watched the anxious feelings inside her increased. Maybe if Miss Tina found what she was looking for, she gave out candy like Mr. Woody. She tried to turn her attention to her picture of Jesus but it was hard to concentrate when something mysterious was going on.

At last, Miss Barbara said, "Carolina." The routine was now well established and she knew what to do. She laid her color on top of the picture, rose stiffly, and trying to look as though she handled serious matters of high tension every day, left the room.

Once in the hall she faced a tailored, navy skirt. She looked up past the skirt, past the stylish jacket and on up to the pale face surrounded by black and gray hair floating high on top of it all. "I just need to look in your hair, Carolina. This won't take but a moment."

Carolina yielded herself and moved a little closer to the skirt. Long, red fingernails began parting her hair flipping it first one way then another. It hurt. She wanted to say, "Ouch," but she had not heard any of the other children complain. She pulled her shoulders up and ducked her head down.

"Hold still," the voice looming above her instructed. "My, what a mess," she muttered. "Ugh!"

Whatever Miss Tina was looking for, it must not be good. Carolina doubted there would be a candy reward but she didn't expect to hear, "We're going to have to send you home. You can't come back to church until this mess is cleared up."

The tall figure opened the door and put her head into the room. "May I see you in the hall, again?"

Before Miss Barbara was fully out the door she continued, "It's even worse than I suspected. We have to send her home immediately."

"Carolina, would you step back into the room for a minute?" Barbara put a protective hand on her back and gently urged her toward the door. Looking back over her shoulder she could tell Miss Tina did not want her to go but Miss Barbara was the one touching her, so she let herself be guided back inside.

She sat at the table and picked up a black crayon. "What did she do to you?" asked Sharon. Carolina had stayed in the hall longer than anyone else and it was obvious that the adults were up to something.

"Nothing," Carolina avoided the subject and started coloring the robe of Jesus. The black didn't seem right somehow. She stopped coloring and sat. Turning the color over in her small fingers she listened intently to the angry voices drifting through the door.

"It won't hurt to let her stay 'till the end of class."

"They wouldn't allow that in a public school. She'll infect the others."

"I don't have the authority to send a child home."

"I insist! I'll get Mr. Woodburn right now. This is what we get for bringing in riff-raff from all over town!"

High heels click-clacked away and Miss Barbara came back into the room. She smiled sadly at Carolina then moved aimless from center to center as though trying to make things normal again.

Carolina's stomach hurt. She watched the other children play and waited even though she wasn't sure what she was waiting for.

It seemed a long time before a soft knock was heard and Mr. Woody came in. He squatted down by Carolina's small chair and put his big face level with her eyes. "Looks like we need to take you home a little early, Carolina."

"Did I do somethin' wrong?"

"No, honey, we just need to go. That's all." He took her hand and led her down the hall, but he walked unusually fast and Carolina had to take three steps to his one.

"Was I good enough to get a piece of candy?" she asked.

Murphy Woodburn slammed his big hand into the glass door forcing it open with a bang. "I'll give you two."

JaKobe's Assignment

*****

Inside the building Tina was holding her hands out in front like a surgeon as she used her shoulder to push open the door to the women's restroom. How distasteful life could become when one was simply trying to set things right!

She went to the sink and began to scrub. The label said, *Dial Antiseptic Hand Soap*, but she didn't believe it. Diane was always refilling those bottles and there was no telling what bargain brand she substituted for the real thing.

Scrubbing didn't help. She could still feel lice crawling on her skin. Diane should be told about this. Maybe she had some antiseptic spray.

A moment later she rapped lightly at the door marked *Women's Class*. "Yes?" came a surprised voice from the other side.

Tina opened the door no more than necessary and fixated her smile as her head peeped inside. "I am so sorry to disturb. I know your lesson is important. But, could I possibly see Diane for just a moment?"

Diane placed her Bible on her chair and stepped into the hall feeling like a ten-year-old being summoned to the principles' office.

Once outside, Tina talked rapidly. Never waiting for answers to her questions, she punctuated her fast monologue with snippets of laughter. For the life of her Diane couldn't quite follow. The problem seemed to be something about germs and Tina having no other choice.

"The only disinfectant spray we have is what I use on the restroom fixtures each week, but it's effective and there is an unopened can in the main closet." She led the way down stairs and flipped on the light as she entered the janitor's closet.

Tina had followed as long as they were in the hall, but she stopped abruptly at the door of the room size closet. Diane wondered if she was afraid that entering the closet of a lowly janitor might contaminate her further, yet when she returned with the spray, Tina held out both hands as meek as a lamb. There was even a whine in her voice as she said, "This won't hurt my skin, will it?"

"Of course not!" Diane batted her eyes innocently. "I use it all the time. And, just look at my lovely hands!"

She was joking, but Tina didn't seem to get the point and once satisfied the germs were gone she unfortunately began to relax. She looked over both hands front and back then let out the breath she had been holding and returned to her normal, arrogant self.

"You really must be more careful when you clean that area," she began with authority. "I suggest you vacuum the classroom at least twice between now and next week and everything should be gone over with disinfectant."

"Whoa, wait a minute." Diane protested. Her large brown eyes grew hard and defensive in her small face. "I take my directions from Pastor

Phelps. You have anything to say, pass it through him." She was surprised at the strength in her voice. Inside, she was quivering.

"Yes, dear, but Pastor Phelps takes his directions from the Elder Board and I assume you know who the senior member of that governing body is. My husband is a very busy man and he often leaves me to manage details such as this."

As Tina continued giving orders, Diane said no more but the internal quivering changed to seething. She doubted that Tina would dare approach any other member of the church in such a condescending manner, but a janitor was fair game.

At last the hateful woman drew a breath. "Well, I really must check on supplies for my niece's shower this afternoon. You did restock the kitchen, did you not?"

"Yes, Ma'am," she said, and immediately wanted to slap her own mouth. Tina had no right to be addressed as *ma'am*. The word just fell out — an automatic response to those awful child-like feelings the woman conjured up like long-dead ghosts.

She put the spray back on the shelf, flicked out the light and stood in the darkness. Her heart hammered and every muscle was taunt.

Leaning against a wall she crossed arms over her chest, threw back her head and drew in air like a runner just past the finish line. "Lord, I'm sorry I can't stand Tina, but she is such a . . . well, you know."

For a moment she could think of nothing else to say, but the silence slowly filtered into her emotions and before long, the prayer continued.

"If I could ever grow past all these insecurities I think people like her wouldn't bother me so much. Someday, I hope to respond like I should. I want to be like you and react the way you would react in these circumstances."

She thought a moment before saying the last amen. How would Jesus respond to Tina? In truth, she had no idea.

JaKobe's Assignment

10:50 AM

The Sanctuary

As Sunday school ended, JaKobe met Jonathan coming out of his office and walked beside him back toward the auditorium. The halls were crowded with children and adults. Often, the angel had to pass through the humans or allow his body to drift through walls. Human bodies of dirt were constantly bumping into one another. But this was not a problem for one whose body was composed of the weightless elements[9] within light.

He instinctively moved halfway into a wall as Diane crowded toward them, her hands full of sheet music.

"Good morning, Diane," said the pastor. "Are you singing for us today?"

"Yes. It's an old hymn. Actually, it has two sets of lyrics, an older version and a different version that's in our hymnal. I didn't particularly like either alone, so I combined the two," she said. Then with a quick grin she added, "Hope those who composed, *So Send I You*[10] don't find out. They might not like the hybrid I've created."

When she first began to speak, Jonathan grinned and waited politely. Diane's habit of providing more information than requested was sometimes irritating, yet it could also be charming when one had time to listen. But, at the mention of the hymn title his eyes jumped with new spark and his jaw hung slightly agape.

"You really chose, *So Send I You*?" he crowed with delight. "That's amazing! It's an exact quote from the text of my sermon today! The Holy Spirit must have led you to that specific hymn."

Diane opened her mouth to make a joke, but quickly decided the subject was not a laughing matter.

"Well, I do pray about what I'm going to sing, but to tell the truth, I couldn't decide what song to use. I called LeeAnn and asked about your topic."

The pastor's shoulders fell and the spark faded from his grey-blue eyes. "Well, as long as you prayed. That's the most important thing," he said. "I'm sure you will do fine." After a few polite words, he continued down the hall greeting first one human then another but his step was not as light as before.

JaKobe filed the incident for future reference. Evidently, in his desire to see God moving in real life, Jonathan had chosen to discount anything that could be explained in earthly terms. That error in thinking would certainly have to be corrected.

JaKobe's Assignment

Human reasoning was very strange. Why did they regard the forty years of manna in the wilderness to be a provision from God's hand, yet believe the harvest that provided food yesterday was their own doing? Both were equally *spiritual* and in their own way each was a *miracle*.

They turned at the door leading into the auditorium and Jonathan almost tripped over four-year-old Hope Pierce as she raced around the corner, all thirty-five pounds of her in excited motion.

"Uh-oh!" he apologized. "I'm sorry, Little Lady."

"I forgot!" The child grabbed his pant leg to steady herself and looked up with wide, anxious eyes.

"Forgot what?"

"My wibbon!"

The tiny blond girl hurried on past weaving in and out of adult legs as she traced her way back to the nursery.

As he watched the child run off, a tiny crack of sunshine penetrated his threatening somber mood. That ribbon must be important if it forced Hope to speak four words in a row.

Hope pushed her head between the nursery doorway and a woman's skirt. Her prized ribbon—two inches wide and bright yellow—lay in tangled abandon beside the story table.

Stubby fingers reverently reached out and drew it close. It was a gift from her mother whom she seldom saw and when she wore it she could feel her close. The child stroked it a moment then suddenly remembered she had no idea how to get it back around her pony tail where it belonged.

She raced out of the nursery and back down the hall where her grandmother was standing by the water fountain talking with animated hand motions.

"I'm so glad your class is praying for her," Henrietta Pierce was saying to Norma. "Lucy is really a good girl. She is just having a bit of a hard time right now. It's those friends of hers, don't you know?"

No, I don't know. Norma thought. *How any mother could take off following first one man then another leaving a beautiful child like Hope to be raised by a half-senile grandmother is beyond my comprehension.*

Hope skidded to a stop and held up her ribbon, but neither adult noticed. She patted her grandmother's leg. "What do you want, Hope?" Without waiting for an answer she added, "Have you got to go potty?"

Hope shook her head.

"Well, run along and play. Church doesn't start for another ten minutes."

Disappointed, the little girl turned away. What about her ribbon? The ponytail did not look right without it.

As JaKobe and Jonathan entered the auditorium, the angel noted Doltar was nowhere in sight. Many other spirit beings milled about but his ancient enemy had slipped away.

JaKobe's Assignment

JaKobe could have expanded his vision and looked through the walls in order to search a larger area, but held back. In their last fight, one of the tactics Doltar used to dilute his energy was to distract him with non-essentials.

It didn't matter where this emissary from hell was at the moment. The fact that he was not in this room was enough. Let him waste his power popping in and out of the room. JaKobe would keep his attention within the four walls and be prepared.

Melody had arrived from the nursery and settled on the piano bench. Her powerful playing echoed through the auditorium serving as a partial mask for the clamor of voices and laughter. Her husband moved from pew to pew greeting folks as they found seats and settled in.

For his own taste, JaKobe thought the commotion and noise rather irreverent, but he dared not lose his mental edge by considering the matter. This assignment was not about him or his preferences. He moved to the front of the room, walked up the platform steps and carefully selected his position.

He would stand to the right of the choir, six feet from the back wall, keeping Jonathan directly in front of him.

Standing with both hands clasped behind his back and feet spread slightly more than shoulder width apart the angel looked like a soldier at parade rest. But, his eyes missed nothing as they watched every detail of the room and his instincts remained on high alert.

Melody ended the hymn, then drawing even more volume from the small grand, she was joined by the organ as Allen Tippet entered through a small door, followed closely by the choir.

Embarrassed but smiling, Jonathan abruptly broke off his conversation and raced to his chair on the stage.

The choir was composed of fifteen women, seven men and three individuals who could only be described as children trying to look taller. The girls and women wore deep red robes with gold collars, while the men's apparel ranged from suits to overalls. Allen had tried to convince the men that robes were appropriate attire but getting the two older farmers into a "dress" proved impossible so he reluctantly settled for a half robed choir.

Accompanied by crisp notes from the piano and a melodic rumble from the organ, the choir was surprisingly good as strong voices blended in a familiar hymn.

A mighty fortress is our God! A bulwark never failing! Our helper He, amid the flood of mortal ills prevailing. For still our ancient foe, doth seek to work us woe—His craft and power are great, and armed with cruel hate—on earth is not his equal.

Allen turned to the audience and gave the page number while Melody played a brief interlude, then with a wave of his arms the whole congregation sang lustily.

JaKobe's Assignment

Did we in our own strength confide, our striving would be losing, Were not the right man on our side, The man of God's own choosing. Dost ask who that may be? Christ Jesus it is He—Lord Sabaoth His name, From age to age the same. And He must win the battle.[11]

JaKobe could feel himself filling with strength. Jesus! Yes, Christ Jesus. Lord Saboath! What a name! He had failed before and might fail again, but these were skirmishes, not the war. One day it would be over and things which were currently true by promise would be practical realities. Heaven and earth would be one unit; one Kingdom under God.[12]

Although he was feeling the music, JaKobe had not let down his guard. When the energy field to his back increased in intensity, he whirled to face Doltar before the opposing angel could fully appear.

Neither made a move to attack, but the eyes of every spirit in the room turned toward the two and the level of tension went up sharply.

When humans attacked one another they created damage by inserting something into the body of an opponent—a sword, bullet, knife, or piece of shrapnel, were all equally effective—and the battle continued only until the death of one or both antagonists.

But angels were different. They fought with fields of energy and concentrated more on taking something from the enemy than putting something into him. The goal was to suck energy from an opponent thereby both weakening him and strengthening one's self.

A single, well executed hit could tip the balance of power until a weakened opponent was at the mercy of the attacker. He could be shamed, battered and abused at will. The battle continued until the attacker either bored with the process or others rescued the victim. Angels cannot die, however they can suffer pain and if wounded sufficiently be sidelined as useless to the cause. JaKobe knew that feeling. It would not happen again.

The face he turned toward Doltar was absolutely expressionless and the dark spirit held up both hands palm forward as though signaling peace. JaKobe knew better. But he would not be the first to attack. He watched closely as his ancient enemy circled the room.

Allan was leading another hymn. The words to this new melody flashed on a screen that had been lowered in front of the baptistery. *What a might God we serve.*[13] shouted the congregation in union. JaKobe was troubled when Doltar showed no signs of discomfort.

Praise should have been painful for his type. A few of his loitering cohorts sulked away when the music started and those remaining looked decidedly pained. Had this warrior found some way to block the impact of praise?

His enemy seemed unconcerned as he moved about making no accommodation for material realities. Doltar unnecessarily passed through

JaKobe's Assignment

objects and people, sometimes walking above the floor and sometimes on it. He was casual to the point of disrespect and it soon became apparent that he had not come for angelic war but was looking for some human target to harass.

When he passed by the Bentley's sitting side by side on the third row, the eyes turned steel blue and JaKobe was sure he detected the smile subtly changing to a smirk of disdain before he passed on.

When the joyful chorus and clapping stopped, Pastor Phelps rose to lead the congregation in an opening prayer. JaKobe was pleased to note that whatever power Doltar used to shield himself from the music, did nothing to protect him from prayer as the angel stopped his roving motion and drew a shield of energy around him. But, as soon as the prayer ended he began to move again, his smile almost as broad as before.

There were more songs, then Allen motioned for the choir to sit and announced Diane Kirkland would provide the morning solo.

She left her place in the soprano section moving to the front, microphone in hand. She was relaxed and well rehearsed—indeed, very well rehearsed—and would be singing from memory.

Doltar moved forward. He had found his target.

Phennia saw Doltar's intent and groaned. For the past twelve years she had been charged with the care of Diane and she knew there could not have been a worse time for him to come against her.

Diane's high opposition level and the fact that her life had been going smoothly for the past six months left a large gap between her current experience and the amount of opposition hell could use against her. Doltar would have plenty of room to work. She hated it, but unless he stepped over the line, there would be nothing Phennia could do.

The messenger from hell moved in and stood very close to his victim's right side while Phennia backed up and glared at him.

Melody finished the piano introduction then Diane took a deep breath and began to sing. *"So send I you—to hearts made hard by hatred; to eyes made blind, because they will not see; to labor long, to love where men revile you. So send I you—to taste of Calvary."*

In the previous two weeks she had gone over and over both melody and lyrics. Memorizing, repeating, singing for pleasure until the song became an automated response. It was a familiar phenomenon with many performers. They sang on automation as they almost became part of the audience.

Diane listened to herself and was aware of body movements as though she were observing rather than performing. It was even possible to think of other things while the music rolled on of its own accord. In the past, she had more than once considered what to have for lunch or thought about various reactions within the audience while never missing a note or desired voice inflection. In this stage, she was not unlike a factory worker repeating a routine action with skill and ease but little thought, or a driver on a long, straight stretch of highway who is scarcely aware of the passing towns.

Doltar felt the relaxed tenor in Diane's voice and guessed she was more or less singing while on automatic pilot. From his perspective this was good. Very good. He had no direct control over the machinery of this particular human brain, but that did not mean he was powerless. Far from it. And, the lower her attention level, the better.

Humans were influenced by a myriad of things from the outside world and were so accustomed to the process they seldom resisted or even noticed his action. Emotions, memories, thoughts streams and more could easily be pulled to the surface of consciousness by external forces. The sound of a marching band could encourage feelings of patriotism. The smell of carnations might bring to mind the memory of a funeral. A cloudy day with drizzling rain encouraged a melancholy mood.

Humans did not fear external influences. Why should they? What they did not realize was Doltar and all others like him were also external realities.

If a thought or memory were already stored in the mind, evil angels could draw it to the surface of consciousness like aroma rising from a flower. They could also hover to create certain moods.

The process worked best when one knew the victim well. Specific memories could be triggered then used to torment. Insecurities and doubts could be exacerbated. Habitual sins were easy to capture and bring to the surface of the mind where human fears and appetites took over often overwhelming the weak-willed, silly creatures.

With patience and skill a human target would be scarcely aware of what was going on until hell had them well secured.

Doltar did not know Diane well, but this only increased the challenge. If he could draw some strong thought or feeling to the surface of her consciousness, he might distract her and she would make a mistake in the lyrics or melody of the song. If sufficiently embarrassed, the error might start a negative train of thought that could create severe problems for some time to come. It was a delicious opportunity and the increased level of difficulty would confirm his skill to other spirits in the room.

Diane began the second verse. *"So send I you— to loneliness and longing. . ."*

Doltar thought of sexual energy. That distracted most humans. He passed his hand through her head encouraging feelings, memories, and thoughts of a sexual nature. There was no change. Diane continued with the verse.

"To serve unpaid, unsought. . ."

He changed his tactics and reached for resentment. Surely there was something of that nature close enough to the surface that he could excite it into consciousness. He was on a fishing expedition, but thousands of years of practice had given him excellent skill. He passed his hand through her head again and by her reaction immediately knew he had hit his target.

Diane listened as her own voice sang, *"To serve unpaid, unsought,"* then she came to the word *"unthanked. . ."* As soon as the word sounded in her throat something inside her clicked.

The idea of ingratitude brought Tina Bentley into sharp mental focus. She had never seen Tina thankful for anything. Feelings of anger that less than an hour ago had been the subject of prayer came to the surface like a storm surge. Hints of superiority mixed with resentment. Tina didn't deserve to be sitting out there smiling. She deserved a kick in the butt.

Suddenly, Diane became aware that she had no idea what word should be sung next. Her own thoughts had distracted her. The chain of repetition was broken and she was totally lost. She remembered the word *unknown*, came after *unthanked*, but that was as far as she could reach. What was the word that began the last line?

Her expression did not change, but inside panic began to build. She had just finished singing the word, *"unknown"* as color crept up her neck and settled subtly in her cheeks. The signs were small, but they were enough to please Doltar.

What was the first word of the last line? Maybe she could write lyrics on the spot. She had done that a few other times when well rehearsed words suddenly failed her. She searched mental archives for ideas. Nothing.

Melody lifted her fingers for the next note, but there were still no words at the edge of Diane's consciousness.

In a fraction of a second she made a decision. She would have to repeat the last line of verse one. There was no other choice. She listened as her voice repeated, *"To labor long, to love where men revile you. So send I you — to taste of Calvary."*

In less time than it took Melody to play a quarter note, Diane's mind had shifted from relaxed performance to a memory of resentment thus breaking concentration. She became aware of the problem and felt the emotion of embarrassment as her brain signaled her body to react sending excessive blood to her cheeks and increasing her heart rate. She searched for solutions; found none, then implemented an alternative behavior. The entire process took less than four heartbeats.

Now, she felt like she had let down the Lord himself.

Sitting comfortably in the audience, Tina noticed the repetition of lyrics. How sloppy Diane had become. The woman likely believed she was so good she didn't need to rehearse properly. Perhaps Tina should mention that at prayer group. She wouldn't use any names, of course, only say she had a friend who needed to work harder if she wanted to properly serve the Lord.

JaKobe's Assignment

Diane began the third verse. This time, her concentration was totally on the song, even though her emotions surged with humiliation and failure. All week she had prayed for the Lord to bless and use the song for the benefit of others, yet any message the Lord might have desired to give was surely lost through her bungling.

She kept her face appropriately hopeful, but her heart was burning with shame as she ended the song. *"So send I you—to bear My cross with patience, And then one day with joy to lay it down. To hear My voice, 'Well done, My faithful servant—Come share My joy, My kingdom and a crown.' As the Father hath sent Me, So send I you."*

Elizabeth Baker

11:17 AM

The Pulpit

Jonathan had been sitting on the stage for seventeen minutes while the warm, secure sensations he had known since childhood washed over his soul. The music, the choir, the familiar faces of the congregation, the song leader waving his hands while no one paid attention—all melted together creating an atmosphere nothing else could match. As far back as memory reached he had always enjoyed going to church. It was the one consistent place of refuge when his father's alcoholism and mounting debt made family life unbearable.

Despite his running battle with a God who refused to show his hand, Jonathan found Sunday morning one of the most comfortable spots in his week. Church was a cocoon sealed away from the troubles of the world. In this room all else faded into the distance as music filled the air and people smiled.

JaKobe's Assignment

His early morning threat to resign was forgotten and he even pushed aside the tension between himself and Melody.

Everywhere he looked he saw people he knew and cared about. Three boys who were just entering puberty when he came five years ago were now singing bass in the choir and considering college. Allen was a personal friend. The Malone family—sitting as always in the second row to his left—had been on the edge of divorce until long hours of counseling and firm admonition drew them together again.

Within this room, he knew who he was and exactly what was expected of him. It felt good.

When Diane's solo began, he settled deeper into his comfortable chair and prepared to be entertained. Her strong voice and delivery style connected with any audience. She was not so polished common people felt they were at the opera, nor so haphazard the message of the song was lost amid twangs and mispronunciations. If any member of the choir could set the appropriate mood before his message, it was Diane. He leaned back satisfied totally unaware of the swift change that was about to unsettle his world.

Diane took her place on stage and with the clarity of crystal sang into the hand held mike, *"So send I you—to hearts made hard by hatred; to eyes made blind, because they will not see....."* The pastor was caught off guard.

Although the Bible verse in Diane's song had, indeed, been part of his text, pain and its relationship to the Christian life was not supposed to be the main point of his sermon. No longer relaxed, he leaned forward rolling his thin, well-worn Bible like a scroll. This was the flipside of Christianity that had always bothered him. The sacrificial, confusing, painful side he minimized in his preaching and tried as much as possible to avoid in his personal life.

Doubts that plagued his walk to church recycled. For twenty years he had pleaded with God to show Himself real by empowering him to do something "big," But, what if he and God were using two different dictionaries? What if his idea of something "big" didn't match that of the Almighty? What did it mean to be sent into the world as Jesus was sent?

The question burned itself into his soul. Jesus did "big" things like redeeming the world, but Jonathan was not God's First Born.

How could there possibly be any similarity between how Jesus was sent and his puny life? Then it happened. It was like a voice entering his mind without going through the pathway of his ears. *"They are the same through obedient faith that moves right through the middle of pain."*

Jonathan was a well-prepared speaker. During his years of preaching there had been a few times when he spoke spontaneously, but he could count such events on one hand. Those unusual moments had always been uncomfortable and most often not well received by the audience. He told others that was when the Holy Spirit took over and spoke through him, but in the privacy of his heart he doubted that statement. How could one ever be sure about such an abstract, brash claim?

Diane sang another verse about the end of life when Christians would be commended by God and share a new heaven and a new earth with Him forever. The audience responded with polite, expected applause and she returned to her seat in the choir.

All was silent.

Jonathan looked out over the congregation. They were waiting for him. He knew he ought to rise and go to the pulpit, but something kept him firmly rooted to the chair. His eyes dropped to the Bible in his hands while his mind turned inward.

Was this one of those rare occasions when he was to speak whatever came to his mind rather than following the notes he had so laboriously prepared? How could he be sure?

His first impulse was to argue the matter within himself. He had known preachers who used "the guidance of the Holy Spirit" as an excuse for laziness. For others, it was a statement of pride that set themselves above ordinary men and their remarks beyond the scrutiny of mere mortals. Was he like that? What if he made a fool out of himself or rambled?

He drew a breath and pushed past the arguments bouncing pro and con inside his head. At the core of his being there was something growing that was beyond argument and rationalization. He sensed a rightness about speaking from his heart rather than following his notes. An assurance.

Ten seconds of silence had passed. It was an interminably long time for a modern audience. They were accustomed to fast action and instant entertainment.

Tiny, restless noises were heard. What was wrong with the preacher? Why didn't he move?

Jonathan looked at his people for another long moment then slowly rose. He wasn't exactly sure what he would say. Part of him was terrified at the prospect of making a mistake or showing himself a fool. Shadows of childhood haunted him. Trust was dangerous!

With courage he scarcely knew he possessed, he walked forward and by the time he reached the pulpit, peace had returned.

He stood to the side of the lectern, leaning slightly against it with his weight on one elbow as the cordless mike amplified his soft words.

"Has God ever asked you to take a risk by believing something you could not prove?"

The audience detected nothing unusual in his casual style. He always preached in a conversational tone rather than the highly emotional, shouting style preferred by many Southern preachers. Only Jonathan was aware this strange introduction was totally different from the joke he had planned about four businessmen.

"Believing. That is what our text is about today. And, it's also about how believing relates to what Diane sang; being sent out into the world like Jesus was sent.

"Since she already sang about my text, perhaps we better read it. Turn with me to the twentieth chapter of John, verses nineteen through twenty-one, and twenty-four through twenty-nine."

Jonathan moved behind the pulpit, laid his open Bible on top of the lectern and clasped his hands behind his back. For the next twenty minutes he would move no more than two foot either side of that spot and never once would he raise his voice.

"Then, the same day at evening, being the first day of the week, when the doors were shut where the disciples were assembled, for fear of the Jews, Jesus came and stood in the midst and said to them, 'Peace be with you.'

Now, when He had said this, He showed them His hands and His side. Then the disciples were glad when they saw the Lord.

Then Jesus said to them again, 'Peace to you! As the Father has sent Me, I also send you.'

"But Thomas, called Didymus, one of the twelve, was not with them when Jesus came. The other disciples therefore said to him, 'We have seen the Lord.' But he said to them, 'Unless

I see in His hands the print of the nails, and put my finger into the print of the nails, and put my hand into His side, I will not believe.'

"And after eight days His disciples were again inside, and Thomas with them. Jesus came, the doors being shut, and stood in the midst and said. "Peace to you!'

"Then He said to Thomas 'Reach your finger here, and look at My hands; and reach your hand here, and put it into My side. Do not be unbelieving, but believing.

"And Thomas answered and said to Him, 'My Lord and my God!' Jesus said to him, 'Thomas because you have seen Me, you have believed. Blessed are those who have not seen and yet have believed.'"

He paused, took his hands from behind his back and looked directly at the audience. "Jesus remained on earth for almost two months after his crucifixion and resurrection. During that time, he surprised people by showing up at the most unexpected times and places. He had this habit of popping into a room without using the doors and vanishing on cue. This incident is one of those times.

"The disciples had seen the Man they trusted with their lives brutally killed and buried with finality. They were frightened, alone and living in the shadows with the doors locked.

"Suddenly, Jesus was standing in the room telling them to be at peace. When they saw him, the sadness and fear were instantly gone. Our text informs us, 'Then the disciples were glad when they saw the Lord.'

"Seeing Jesus made all the difference.

"In verse twenty, Jesus shows them his scars. Proof of his torture, agony and death. Then, he says something very strange. He tells them that he is sending them out into the world in the same way that he had been sent into the world by the Father.

"I think if I had been in that room, I would have had a few questions about that kind of commission. I suspect as I looked at those scars, I would have wondered what kind of 'sending' Jesus had in mind. If sending involved scars, I would probably have offered him a few alternative suggestions.

"How about sending me to comfort and a long life? How about sending me to financial security?

"Peter was there. He saw the scars. I am surprised he didn't say, 'Jesus, how about sending me back to my boat and giving me a good crop of fish? I'm not ready for scars.'

"Matthew could have said, 'How about sending me to Rome where I can make some real money? I'll give you a ten percent cut.'" He had not intended the statements to be funny, but the audience laughed and when he thought about it the absurdity broadened his own lips.

"But, those were not the reactions of his disciples. Evidently they were silent. The idea of being sent into the world as Jesus was sent didn't seem to overwhelm them. They accepted it.

"How could they do that?" he asked with all sincerity. He paused, looked down as though considering then glanced up and began again as though a new thought just occurred to him. It had.

"I think the reason may have been because they were so focused on something else that they hardly considered the scars at all. They saw Jesus. He was alive. Alive! And they believed because Jesus was alive, they, too, would live forever. Jesus was living proof that being sent into the world involved power, victory and peace, . . . as well as scars.

"Seeing Jesus standing right there in the middle of the room made it easy to believe. They went from fear to laughter because they saw Jesus and believed. They looked at his scars and knew that pain and scars were not the end. And believing that, made them glad.

"Yet not all of the disciples enjoyed such living proof. Thomas was not there. Believing was not so easy for Thomas.

"The scriptures tell us the other disciples shared with him what had happened, but Thomas didn't believe a word. He needed proof. He needed something real. Something beyond doubt. Something he could touch.

JaKobe's Assignment

"We are not specifically told about the emotional reaction of Thomas, but when Jesus suddenly stood before him I think he, too, exchanged unhappy feelings for gladness. He seems pretty somber as he cries, *'My Lord and my God!'* but, I don't think we stretch the text too far if we include an embarrassed giggle shortly following that statement. Thomas saw the Lord. He had his proof. And, somehow the possibility of scars didn't seem so bad.

"Once he got his proof, Thomas spent the rest of his life risking all for the sake of doing what the Lord Jesus told him. His belief took him all the way to India telling the good news. Eventually, he was cut to pieces in that land and died a martyr.

"Ouch. Talk about scars.

"But, on the balance of things, I don't think Thomas—or any of the rest of them—lost.

"When you read their stories in history you find they won personal peace, solid relationships, purpose in living, authority, spiritual power, a life of meaning and adventure. They risked all on what they believed and—even though it involved scars—they won.

"I'll ask the question again. Have you ever found it necessary to risk on what you say you believe?"

Jonathan moved away from behind the pulpit and stood to one side. He paused and again seemed to be considering a new idea. The movement wasn't a manipulation or a calculated effort to maintain audience attention; the idea really was new to him and he shared it with the audience as casually as he might have shared with a friend over coffee.

"We can give a mental ascent to something we think is true and call it 'belief.' We can debate theoretical concepts and call our opinions 'faith.' But, when we experience the genuine article—when we believe, *really believe*—we will be willing to risk.

"I'm convinced that a willingness to risk is the difference between counterfeit faith and the real deal.

"A little more than ten years ago, Melody and I took the kids to an amusement park. Traci wasn't born yet and Stephanie was so little she couldn't go on many of the rides. But Melody and Ben were ready to tackle anything that looked like a thrill.

"Now, some of you may be tempted to laugh but—I kid you not—Melody has nerves to steel when it comes to that kind of thing and Ben was too young to realize some of those rides were killers in disguise.

"We stood beside the tallest wooden roller coaster in the United States. They called the thing, *The Rattler*. It was an appropriate name. I saw some folks get off whose teeth were still making noise thirty minutes later. The entire, giant contraption was a puzzle of tracks and crossed timbers. Strings of small cars filled with screaming people dive-bombed in every direction. If I had been them, I would have screamed, too. Those tiny wheels were ready to leave the tracks at any second.

"Melody's eyes lit up with excitement and Ben stretched as tall as he could to reach the minimum height required to ride. For myself, I had a perfect excuse to stay on the ground. Somebody had to stay with Stephanie. With grace and dignity, I offered to make the sacrifice.

"The two of them allowed the attendant to strap them into seats and then lock them in place with a steel bar. Amazing. They even smiled about the fact.

"Ten minutes later they tumbled out of those same seats, red-faced and laughing their heads off. Ben wanted to go again! This time Melody thought I should have the honors, but I declined by saying something stupid like, 'I'll ride later.'"

Gentle laughter rippled through the congregation. "Melody knew I was lying.

"She teased me unmercifully. 'Jonathan, you're a scaredy-cat!' I denied the accusation with a vengeance but she wouldn't leave it alone. 'Don't you believe it's safe? Don't you believe it's fun?'

"I replied, 'Of course I believe it is safe. If I didn't, I wouldn't let my family ride. I'll have fun when I ride it. Later.'

"As Melody can tell you, my 'later' never came. No matter how much I said I believed in the safety and fun of that monster, there was no way that I, personally, would let them strap *my* body in that tiny car waiting to go eighty miles an hour straight down on wheels that were not attached to the tracks!"

"I told others that I believed, and with my head I guess I did. After all, I let my family ride. But until I was willing to risk my own body to the control of something I couldn't totally explain; my claim of belief was hollow. They knew it. I knew it, too.

"To believe something does not mean that you have no doubts. It doesn't mean that you understand. It doesn't mean that your palms don't sweat, or even that you don't worry. To believe—really believe—is to willingly risk ourselves to the thing in question.

"Sometimes those risky actions backing up our words are dramatic and the scars involve physical pain or even death. Thomas certainly found it that way. So did most of Jesus' disciples.

"At other times, the risks are small. Very small. So small, in fact, that we never use the word 'risk' to describe them.

"But, to me that's the only word that fits. I may not be risking blood but I am risking my safety. The safety of being right. The safety of being a rational human who knows what's what.

"I had one of those tiny, risky situations when I met Diane in the hall this morning. When she told me she would be singing the exact text I had planned for today's sermon, I was delighted. I believed the Holy Spirit had led her to choose the perfect song.

"Then, she confessed she had phoned the office and got my text from LeeAnn!"

Again, the congregation laughed and he paused before continuing.

"I was sorely disappointed. I wanted God to show up and *do* something! But, when her song had a perfectly understandable and human explanation, I factored God out of the equation.

"If there was no logical explanation for why her song matched my sermon, it was easy to believe God was involved. The mystical aspect provided support for my belief.

"But, when a reasonable explanation reared its ugly head, giving God credit was less sure. Perhaps I was wrong. Maybe the Almighty was involved, but then again, maybe not. Who could know for sure? I didn't want to risk on assumption, I wanted proof!

"I believe—and preach—that God is a loving father and in control of everything that happens to me. Large or small, He is in all the details. But, do I *really* believe that?

"Sometimes, I wonder if I do. How can I when I must see proof before I risk trusting?

"In fact, I have often wished that God would take away all risks from my life and make it easy for me to believe."

He saw a few skeptical faces in the crowd and felt like he was confessing rather than preaching,

"I have thought a good bit about the subject and come to the conclusion there are two ways God could make believing easier for me. I suggest

He follow the first method when I face big, philosophical questions and use the second method when I experience life in the daily world.

"The fact that these two ways are inherently contradictory shouldn't bother God.

"When I face something big and ask questions that begin with, '*why*,' it would be much easier to believe if God would explain everything in terms I could understand and not move until I had a thorough grasp of all the details. My complete understanding of these situations would remove all risk because I would know His loving purpose behind every trial and understand the end results of every difficult circumstance. In fact, if God would take me up on this idea, I wouldn't really have to believe at all. I would simply *know*.

"However, I need God to take a different route if He wants to make believing easy for me in the day-to-day experience of life. For daily stuff, believing would be easier if events were full of mystery and miracles. I want two fish to feed five thousand and disease to instantly vanish. I want visions of angels to appear. No logical explanations. No ambiguity. For daily life, believing would be easier if every turn in the road produced holy goose bumps. I want divine intervention when Diane chooses a solo, not phone calls to the office.

"I guess what I am saying is that I want the mysteries of life to have logical, easy answers and my everyday experiences to be mysterious."

The audience laughed nervously and a few squirmed in their seats.

"The Almighty has yet to take me up on that deal."

More laughter.

"God never takes away the risk and He doesn't make believing easy for me.

"It won't be easy for you, either." He paused allowing the words to sink in before continuing.

"But, God will make it possible.

"It's a risk to assume He's in control when I can't explain what's happening and the scars are making me bleed. But, those risks might be easier if I was willing to look at the everyday events and say, 'That's God at work.'

"In each of these situations, the Lord requires me to walk by faith. He expects me to lean. He expects me to trust. He expects me to risk.

"As I said, risking is difficult for me. But through the years I have found rare occasions when I took that leap and when I did, something marvelous happened. Something alive and full of strength and energy. It takes a huge amount of courage for me to believe, but the results have always been worth it.

"Jesus talked about scars, but in the same breath he said, 'blessed,' –in other words 'happy,' –are those who haven't seen yet they believe anyway.

"Never forget that part of the story. There is a blessedness—a happiness—that is available to those who believe.

"Risk? Yes. Scars? Yes. But, don't forget the happiness.

"Also, don't forget the statement of Jesus repeated three times in this short text. 'Peace.' Jesus used that word every time He greeted His disciples. It was the word He used immediately after showing them the scars and before He told them they were being sent out. *Peace*.

"How can there be peace when facing the possibility of scars? Just look at Jesus with eyes of faith and believe. Risk on Him. He will not fail you."

Jonathan stood silent for a long, uncomfortable moment. "He will not fail you," he repeated more to himself than to the audience.

He had said what he had to say and there was nothing else. He had given his people—the Lord's sheep—what he felt sure was right. The message was over.

He glanced at the clock. Eleven forty-seven. The sermon had been short. There were still thirteen minutes before dismissal and he had no idea what to say next. Nursery workers would rejoice if he dismissed early, but doing so was unthinkable. In a convoluted way, dismissing early would mean he had failed.

He could feel the tension rise and heat creep up his neck. With nothing else to grab, he fell back on the comfort of tradition: the invitation. That part of the service could be extended as long as necessary. Besides, the invitation was a litmus test showing whether or not his words had connected with the people.

"Allen, do you have something we can sing?" Jonathan made the same request every Sunday, and every Sunday Allan was prepared. He rose from his chair and motioned for the choir and congregation to stand.

"Let's all turn to 482, *Jesus Is Calling.*" Allen would repeat the verses as long as Jonathan kept the invitation open. The system was well rehearsed. People could come forward to kneel and pray privately, or they could pray with Jonathan, or offer themselves as candidates for baptism, or offer themselves for church membership. This was the moment when the real work of church was done and Allan took his responsibility seriously.

Jonathan moved from behind the pulpit to stand on level ground with the congregation. He sometimes spoke over the singing reminding the people what this special time was about. The process seemed complex, intimidating and a bit confusing to those from other denominations. But, for those of the Baptist tradition, it was the way church was done. There were no other options.

He was always tense during invitations but the feelings were especially strong this Sunday. One part of him believed that the Holy Spirit had drawn him to lay aside his prepared message, but another part desperately wanted assurance it had been the right thing to do. A large number of people praying at the altar would be just the kind of proof he needed. Especially if they cried.

He waited. Nothing.

"Allen, let's have the choir do that last verse again," he said. Then told the assembled people, "Jesus is waiting on you! If you can hear Him calling, will you respond?"

Nothing.

He remembered all those biographies telling of thousands who responded to Whitfield, Finny, Moody and Billy Graham. He didn't really expect thousands to respond to him, but still, a few sinners repenting or a couple of saints rededicating would have been comforting.

When it became obvious no one was going to move, Jonathan glanced at Allan and signaled the close of the invitation. The choir lingered on the last note then fell silent.

The mood of the room changed perceptively. Some gathered their belongings. Others shifted position, put away their hymnal and relaxed. Everyone knew that for all practical purposes, church had ended.

JaKobe's Assignment

11: 52 AM

The Flock Scatters

The pastor reached back up to the pulpit and retrieved his copy of the bulletin. Even though a lot of effort went into printing the page, people could not be depended on to read it, so he always went over the weeks' activities verbally before the congregation scattered to their homes.

He reminded the ladies there would be a shower this afternoon at two and, for those interested, a piano recital at four-thirty. The evening service would begin at seven, and anyone wishing to explore the possibility of starting home Bible study groups should contact the office. He glanced down the list to see what else might need to be emphasized and noticed the children and youth section. A Father-and-Son Banquet was scheduled to take place the weekend before Thanksgiving. After that announcement was duly made, he reminded everyone the offering boxes were located at the front of the church and asked Elder Bentley to dismiss in prayer.

"Our most gracious Lord and omnipotent Heavenly Father," Elder Bentley began while Jonathan quickly walked down the middle aisle to take his place by the front doors. Around the room, heads were reverently bowed but few paid attention to the prayer. Church was over. It was time to get on with real life.

In the choir, Diane's eyes were screwed tightly shut, but she was neither listening to prayer nor praying. Her sealed eyelids were a dam holding back tears as Jonathan's last announcement echoed over and over in her mind, *Father-and-Son Banquet.*

At times she felt church was the cruelest of all social institutions. Did anyone stop to consider the boys who had no father? Or, boys like her own whose father could care less about church? Steve's visits with his sons were scheduled by his own convenience rather than a church calendar.

How many times had she made excuses for him when he broke his promises or lightly dismissed important events? What excuse would she use this time? She may have appeared from the outside to be praying, but inside her heart had just cracked in two. Again.

The moment Elder Bentley was to asked pray, Emily Black hurriedly gathered her purse and put it over her arm ready to bolt the instant "amen" sounded. The action was not disrespectful or filled with anxiety, just natural. Emily lived her entire life looking around corners and preparing for the next event on the agenda. Going home from church was no exception. Garrison mentioned a bonfire and hotdog roast for the boys in his Sunday school class. She should probably stop by the store on the way home. No sense waiting until the last minute. Did she have enough mustard?

Barbara Tippet reverently bowed her head but it was difficult to listen. Her thoughts were with Carolina. How did her mother react when she came home early? Lice were such a messy problem. When her own daughter was in kindergarten they infected every girl in the class. Each treatment took two hours of shampooing, combing and picking and she had to treat the problem four times before the child's scalp was completely clear. Was there anyone who would do that for Carolina?

Billy Malone was one of the few in the congregation actually praying. Standing directly behind the elder, he listened intently to the beautiful, meaningful words. They sank deep into his soul and tears filled his eyes. With his arm around Stacy's waist and his son standing beside him, he was awestruck by what he had nearly thrown away. Thank God for Jonathan's counseling and Stacy's willingness to struggle through the hard times. Thank God for family and home and a loving church. He fought the tears, but one escaped and ran down his left cheek in spite of his efforts.

Across the aisle, LeeAnn, moved restlessly. Anxiously waiting for the prayer to be over, she put her weight on first one foot then the other while resisting the urge to run. However, it was not obligations or appointments that drove her. It was guilt.

Deep inside she knew her week had been one long gripe session. She complained to Melody about her husband, Glen. She complained to Diane about her college bound son. She complained to Jonathan about Tina. But, most of all, she complained to herself. Inside, she had discussed, rehearsed, dissected and ruminated on every slight and shortcoming in life. The sermon had cut her to the quick. Scars? She was not even willing to endure a scratch without resentment and complaint!

On the back pew, Stephanie Phelps sat where the teens were packed hip to hip and she snuggled tightly against Matthew Collins. She had thought of nothing but Matt for two weeks and when he squeezed in beside her as the service began the thrill went all the way to her toes. He was absolutely the coolest hunk she had ever known and his eyes could melt rocks.

She tried to act nonchalant but the electricity between them took her breath away. During the final hymn their hands touched beneath the songbook and she thought she would die. Matt must have been aware of the touch because when the song was over he made no effort to put the book back in the rack. Their hands still lay cradled in one another. Hopefully, Elder Bentley would offer a very long prayer.

Ben sat in the sound booth watching as Ward adjusted first one dial and then another. It had been tempting to sit with the other teens, but the lure of all those knobs and switches was just too great.

The instant Jonathan finished with the announcements, Ward cut his microphone then silently pointed to number six, the omni-directional wonder that swung on a thin wire above the alto section of the choir. It could pick up the human voice from twenty feet away and Elder Bentley's stood slightly over that distance. Ward twisted the knob to full volume and the Elder's smooth, baritone was clearly heard in all parts of the sanctuary.

"Cool," Ben whispered. Ward gave a satisfied nod, but kept his hand on the control. The instant the prayer ended, he would have to adjust the volume back to normal or the alto section of the choir would blast out the windows.

"Amen,' said Elder Bentley. The knob flew back to volume level two. Melody struck the first cord and Allen motioned to the choir as it joined the instruments for the recessional hymn. The congregation began to move with a noisy clatter. The choir would sing two verses then file out the side door as Melody and the organist went through the song two more times.

By the time the instruments fell silent, the crowd had evaporated into stragglers and a few cliques of friends. Alma walked by the offering box, dropped in her check for the week then went to locate Connie. Perhaps they could go to visit Margaret. Maybe she could even talk her into driving. Gas was so expensive these days.

Henrietta and Gladys stood three rows from the front discussing the latest episode of *All My Children.* Gladys had missed the soap on Friday and could not believe the two main characters were finally having sex. Henrietta clicked her tongue and lamented about how explicit the scenes had been. TV was really going too far these days.

Norma stretched her neck trying to find Tommy. He had ridden the bus to church and sat beside her during the service. Now, he had disappeared. Perhaps he was already on the bus with Mr. Woody and headed for home.

The pastor spent a few minutes vigorously shaking hands with his people, then as quickly as the line formed, it came to an end and he stood looking over the remaining stragglers. No hurry. It would be a while before lunch was on the table.

Hope was hanging on to the end of the back pew swunging one leg in a wide ark tracing curved lines on the carpet and waiting for her long-winded grandmother. All the other children had gone.

"What ya doin' Hope?" he teased. She left drawing arcs and ran to him. She hugged his knees then leaned back, looking high above to his belt, tie and face. She said nothing, just looked up and smiled.

He had been meaning to again ask Henrietta about Hope's lack of speech. He knew she could talk as well as most four-year-olds, but she so seldom did it concerned him and Henrietta could not be depended on to follow through with getting help.

He bent down on one knee, holding the other at a forty-five degree angle then drew the little girl up until she was seated on a platform of flesh and bone.

"Did you have a good time in Sunday school today?" She nodded, and then held up her yellow ribbon.

"You still hanging on to that ribbon? It must be pretty important." She nodded again and he shaped the next question to encourage a verbal response. "Where did you get such a pretty ribbon?"

She was silent at first but finally said one word. "Mama."

"I can see why it is important," he said, but was saddened by the thought of the irresponsible, drug addicted, Lucy as Hope again raised the ribbon. "If you want me to do something with the ribbon, you need to ask."

The child seemed to think about that then held up her ponytail. "Do you want me to tie the ribbon in your hair?" She nodded, but still did not speak. "You will have to ask."

"Tie it, pl e-e-z-z-e."

"Wonderful!" he encouraged. "That's my big girl."

By this time the last of the remaining adults had drifted from the auditorium and Henrietta stood nearby waiting to receive her granddaughter. He helped her down and took the ribbon in both hands. "Now, turn around," he said. Tying an expertly crafted bow, he fluffed out the loops. "There, a perfect bow for a perfect little girl."

Hope was again forced to look up past a vast expanse to his face which seemed slightly distorted from her angle near the ground. She said nothing, but inside a warm and secure feeling began to grow. She would add this brief encounter to a dozen or so other impressions from childhood and for the rest of her life, churches and pastors would represent security, help and safety. She reached out and hugged both his knees for a second time. They felt solid and secure.

When the room was at last empty, Jonathan made one more pass through the building. His footsteps echoed in the empty halls as he snapped out nursery lights and those in his own office. No need to waste the Lord's money.

He locked the back doors then returned to the auditorium, picking up a stray bulletin from the fourth pew and a gum wrapper half way down the outside aisle. All was silent.

Jonathan stood a moment surveying the empty sanctuary. His shoulders sagged and a ragged sigh escaped unbidden. Did any of the

JaKobe's Assignment

preceding activity really matter? No one responded to the invitation. Doubts began to build. Perhaps he had made a mistake and should have kept to his outline.

Slowly, he shook his head then closed the interior doors, crossed the foyer and locked the large oak doors to the outside world.

JaKobe watched him leave and wondered at his downcast appearance. In the last few hours the angel had watched as the pastor's face shone with heaven-sent glory and knew the human was connecting one-on-one with the Creator of the Universe. He observed the well ordered processes of Grace Community and knew its success was due in large part to Jonathan's skill as a leader. He felt the surge of power course through the room as over a hundred worshiping souls sang praises to Jesus and hell itself recoiled at the sound.

As Jonathan had preached, the Evaluator registered higher levels of obedience and humility in the man's character. He had observed the tender care of children as Jonathan reached out to the young and even watched as this servant-leader was responsible for such low tasks as picking up a stray piece of paper and turning out the lights.

Jonathan may not have had the advantage of seeing the spirit world, but how could the man remain so sad when heaven was breaking out all around him?

The angel passed through locked doors, walked down the steps and caught up with the pastor just as he turned the last corner toward home.

12:20 PM

Sunday Dinner

Era Lou moved from the steaming pot on the range to the lettuce leaves scattered on the cabinet while Bobby sat firmly planted in the same dinette chair that had been assigned to him fifteen years earlier. He sulked and glared at her.

"You may as well not look at me that way. I am not going to change my mind," she said.

She went on with the work, but she could feel Bobby's dark brown eyes following her every move. She felt guilty. She tried avoiding his obvious stares by singing. No luck. The guilt remained.

They had been fighting this battle for a week and he was just going to have to get used to the restrictions. She was doing the right thing. It wasn't that she wanted to be mean or was punishing him. But, no matter how logical the arguments or necessary her actions, every time Bobby turned those soulful eyes on her, guilt crept from her toes to the crown of her gray hair. She couldn't help it.

Finally, she gave up and decided to address the problem directly. "You know what the doctor said," she reminded him for the hundredth time. "If we are both going to live out our full days, we simply must have separate diets. I can't help it if the kind of food I need and the kind you must have are completely different. Is it my fault that you just happen to like my diet best?"

Bobby turned his head and looked in the opposite direction. He always did that when he was angry. He was punishing her and she knew it.

"All right, be stubborn. But I'm not going to give in. I have lived with you for fifteen years and if I have to, I can out-stubborn you any day of the week."

She turned around and went back to work. She knew his ways. He might turn away from her, but eventually his curiosity would get the best of him. He would cut his eyes trying to sneak a peek and see if his action had adequately humbled her. It was always the same.

Era Lou kept her face directed at the food while using peripheral vision to keep an eye on Bobby. She would catch him. Sooner or later.

Sure enough, less than three minutes passed before Bobby cut his eyes to see if she were watching. As best he could tell, she was unaffected by his snub and if she were not being wounded by his purposeful ignoring, the action wasn't worth

JaKobe's Assignment

the crick in his neck. He relaxed and turned his face toward her.

"Ah-ha! I caught you!" she crowed triumphantly. Bobby quickly looked at the ceiling. "That is enough of that," she stated flatly and moved toward the table with a bowl in each hand. She sat both on her own side of the table.

"Don't you dare touch a thing!" she ordered. "I gotta get me some bread and I forgot the spoon."

Bobby looked longingly at the food. Stretching his neck in that direction, he inhaled deeply. The bean soup smelled wonderful as steam rose from the top in graceful swirls. The salad was crisp, but its texture was not what attracted him. Almost anything was wonderful if enough Ranch Dressing were lathered on top. Even the tomatoes.

"Don't even think about it," Era Lou warned as though she had eyes in the back of her head. Bobby sat firmly planted. Fifteen years of obeying that woman was a habit he found impossible to break.

Era Lou returned to the table and settled into her assigned seat. "I'm sorry," she said with genuine compassion. She reached out and stroked the brown head now streaked with gray letting her hand slide to his cheek and cradled his face.

"Your food is on the other side of the room and you can eat at any time," she reminded him. He didn't move.

She sighed and bowed her head to bless her meager meal with prayer. When she looked up,

Bobby was still staring at her. Eating was impossible with those liquid brown eyes following every bite.

With lightening speed her compassion changed to anger.

"All right, if you insist on ruining my meal as well as yours, you can just get out of here!" She reached the back door with surprising quickness and jerked it open. "You heard me. Get yourself out in the yard while I eat in peace!"

Slowly, Bobby pulled his old bones off the chair and started across the floor. Moving hurt. But once he got the joints and muscles in motion, it wasn't so bad. He stopped at the door and looked one more time to see if by some miracle Era Lou had changed her mind.

"Go on. Out with you." This time she stomped her foot. There was no reprieve from the sentence, so he ambled out onto the back porch and turned to face the door. Ear Lou shut it, grateful it was made of wood, not glass. At least she wouldn't have to look at him while she ate.

But, her savory bean soup was tasteless and her throat constricted when she tried to swallow the salad. "Lord, getting old is the pits," she said aloud. The words were more statement of fact than complaint. Through the years she had developed the habit of talking to Jesus just as though He were in the room with her. She looked at the door. "It's hard on both of us."

After a few more unrewarding bites she went to the door. "Come on back, Bobby," she said. "We will make this work somehow."

He ambled into the room on stiff, arthritic legs.

"Tell you what," Era Lou said, pulling her chair across the room to the corner where Bobby's untouched bowl sat on the floor. "If you can't eat what I do at the table, we will just both sit in this corner with our own food on our own plates, 'cause I'm sure not gonna eat that mess the vet gave you."

Bobby wagged his tail as fast as his stiff spine would allow. He smelled of the dry, brown chunks in his bowl and again looked up at her.

"Well, okay. I guess a little bean juice never hurt woman or beast," she dipped her spoon toward the edge of her bowl drawing up some of the liquid then dribbled the contents over the chunks in the plastic bowl.

"Only, don't you dare tell Doc Adams it was me that gave you gas."

*****

The polished Buick Regal belonging to the Bentley family pulled to a stop in front of El Chico's. Tina was the first to step into the pleasant fall air while her husband cleaned his sun glasses and stowed them neatly in their case above the visor.

"It looks like the Lord has blessed us with a really fine day," she remarked to no one in particular. "And a parking place right by the front door," she added with satisfaction. It was good to know that the Almighty was doing His job properly. Best of all, thanks to Pastor Phelps' short sermon, there were few cars in the parking lot. They had beaten both the Methodist and the Assembly of God crowd.

But then, they were always ahead of the AG folks. Those people never seem to know when it was time to dismiss. Beating the Methodist, however, was a rare treat.

The town of Thyme had its limitations, but good restaurants was not one of them. A very respectful array had sprouted just south of I-30 giving the local people ample opportunity to engage in their favorite sport. Mexican, Chinese, Bar-B-Q and Southern cuisine were available for the price of admission. Tiny Mom & Pop offerings competed with well known chains, but none of them could match the popularity of the Tamale Palace which served its famous delicacy on a strip of butcher paper passed to customers through a wood framed window.

The Tamale Palace was closed on Sunday. So were Harold's Fried Chicken and the Bar-B-Q joint that Philip Yancy started up a couple of years back. Still, the chains offered good food and if a patron beat the other churches to a good seat, it was a pleasant way to top off a preaching service.

Inside, Kathy turned from the prep counter, both her hands full of pitchers of sweet tea as Billy passed and nodded toward the front window.

JaKobe's Assignment

"See them?" he indicated the middle-aged couple approaching the front door. "That's Jack and Tina Bentley, only never call them by their first names. If you can stand the wife, they're regulars and pretty good tippers. Carla'll probably seat 'em by the window in section 5. I got those tables today, but you can have the Bentleys if you like. I'll let Carla know you're coverin'."

Kathy smiled her appreciation. Two weeks on the job and she had already earned more than she cleared in a month at Wal-Mart. It was a good job even if the work was hard, the hours erratic and smiling at customers got pretty old after a while. Thank God for Billy. If it hadn't been for him, she probably would not have shown up today.

After closing last night, some of the crew decided to go out for beers and they invited Kathy along even though she was still under the legal drinking age. No problem. Someone with a card was always willing to share. It was well after four when she finally got in bed and she had to be at work by ten. Between the alarm, her aching head and her mom grilling her about where she had been, it had been a horrible day so far—except for Billy. Why couldn't all men be like him?

Elder Bentley and his wife settled into their familiar places, accepted menus from Carla and immediately began studying them. "Same drinks as usual?" she asked with a welcoming smile.

Jack looked up. "That's fine with me. What about you, Dear?" Tina gave her head a slight wiggle and Carla took the limited motion for a yes. "Great! Your server will be with you right away."

With the hostess gone, the Bentley's got down to the serious task of food choice. The Enchiladas looked good, but the cheese would be fattening. If they limited their selection to splitting a grilled chicken salad, they would have room to share that new offering from the dessert menu: Hot apple pie, sizzling in a skillet and topped with cinnamon ice cream.

Kathy arrived with the drinks and Tina stirred three packages of Sweet n' Low into her tea. "It's Mr. and Mrs. Bentley, right?'" she asked as she took out her order pad.

Jack looked up a little surprised but flattered. "Aren't you new here? How did you know our names?"

"Oh, you're Billy's favorite customers. He always knows the regulars by name." Her head was hurting worse, but she hoped the smile looked genuine. "I'm Kathy," she pointed to her name tag. "Billy's a little busy right now, but he said I could wait on you if I did a good job and made you welcome. What can I get for you folks today?"

Tina looked up and drew in a breath. Kathy took the cue and clicked her pen. "It's 'may,' Dear, not 'can'."

The waitress looked a little perplexed; her pen paused in midair. Tina took the expression as an invitation to teach. "One should always say, 'may I help you' never 'can I.' Proper English is

JaKobe's Assignment

important if you want to get ahead in any business."

Kathy's smile became even broader. "Oh, yes, Ma'am. I forgot. *May* I take your order?" This lady was unbelievable. They better be good tippers or Billy was going to get it. She was tempted to punched Mrs. Bentley's arrogant face, but that would only get her fired and she would end up back at Wal-Mart.

"I'll have the Number four," Jack said. "The enchiladas here are very good." He hoped the compliment helped ease his wife's critical remark.

"Too much cholesterol," Tina advised. "I'll have the Tortilla soup and maybe later a little dessert with coffee."

When Kathy had completed the orders and retreated out of hearing range, Jack said, "I certainly hope you didn't offend our new waitress."

"What? Do you mean that little remark I made about using correct English?" His wife's expression registered genuine surprise. "How could anyone possibly take offense at such a small thing? I'm sure I did the young girl a favor. Besides, she smiled at me the whole time. I think she appreciated my help."

"Maybe." Jack took a long drink from the tall glass of iced tea. "But still…"

He didn't finish the sentence. He never did.

****

The elevator doors opened with three dings of a bell and a stainless steel food cart rattled into the lobby by the nurse's station.

"Lunch time already?" A woman with a stethoscope around her neck and scrubs decorated with Charlie Brown cartoons stopped writing and peered over the counter. "Anything good today?"

"That depends on what room you occupy," Manuel grinned. "The lucky ones get chicken and dressing. The not-so-lucky get cream soup and salt-free crackers. The really unlucky ones get Jell-O and clear broth."

"Then I guess I'm completely cursed," said the nurse. "Three more hours to go on a double shift and all I've had so far is black coffee and a Baby Ruth from the vending machine."

"It's your own fault," he teased. "Maybe I can sneak you a leftover tray. Anyone dismissed today?"

"No. Margaret Mc Clawson will probably leave first thing in the morning, but no one today."

"Mc Clawson, Mc Clawson," Manuel muttered to himself as he looked over the trays on the cart. "Says here, she is still on a soft diet."

"Dr. Grimes changed that order this morning. Guess the kitchen didn't get the word in time."

"Gee, I hate to feed her soup when she could be dining on chicken and dressing."

"It doesn't matter. A couple of her friends stopped by after church. They're with her now

JaKobe's Assignment

and if I am not mistaken that room smells strangely like hamburgers from Hershel's."

****

Across town, rich smells of barbeque floated on the cool air where it mixed with the lyrical tones of Spanish and energetic Mexican music as a dozen adults and two dozen children milled about the backyard of the Saldivar home.

Everyone was laughing and catching up on the week's events while waiting for generous helpings of pork cooked to perfection and falling off the bones.

Carolina chased her cousin Alfredo playfully throwing a ball his direction in a make-shift variation of tag. Alfredo caught the ball rather than being tagged by it and immediately went on the offensive while three more cousins joined the game.

She had been overwhelmed with the tension when Mr. Woody brought her home and near tears as he turned away. Despite his constant assurances that nothing was wrong the feelings inside her stomach said that something was very wrong and when he left her stomach proved more right than his parting hug. He had not even had time to get back in the van before her mother began yelling and cursing and pulling at her hair.

But now, Carolina's world was good again. The cousins had arrived for their regular Sunday cookout and her father soon awoke from his nightshift at the plant. The smell of good food filled the air, the cousins laughed and her customary light disposition returned. Church was a wonderful and curious place. Even better than school. But, this was home. Her language, her family and best of all, her Pa-pe. Nothing could alarm her for long when curled in his comfortable lap.

"Come, Carolina!" Her mother was shouting on the other side of the yard. Reluctantly, she left the game and obeyed.

Elaine Upton Saldivar stood by her sister-in-law, Julia. Her skin and light brown hair showed Caucasian heritage, but her Spanish was flawless as she loudly expressed her anger. Even the curse words were used correctly as she pulled Carolina's hair first one direction than another, digging deeply with her long nails.

She wore skin-tight jeans and a low-cut knit top that revealed the curve of ample breast. The smell of liquor hung around her and her words were slightly slurred even though it was early afternoon.

Elaine cursed the church and the town and the prejudice of little-minded people and her boss at the tire factory while Julia only nodded and assured her the school nurse would give her some medicine to use.

Silently, Julia made a note to talk again with her brother about controlling his wife's drinking. He should never have married this woman in the first place.

JaKobe's Assignment

Michael Saldivar sat in an inexpensive lawn chair relaxing with the other men. It was times like this that made his hard work the rest of the week worthwhile. Family, friends, plenty of food, a cold beer. They were all part of the good life he enjoyed.

He looked across the yard where his beautiful wife stood talking to Julia and braiding Carolina's hair. If only Elaine could be content, life would be perfect. It was permissible to drink. It was even acceptable for men to be drunk most weekends. But a woman…? That was a shameful thing.

He watched a moment and noticed the sad look on his daughter's face. As soon as Elaine finished the braid he called to her and Carolina immediately brightened as she came running to her father's arms.

Michael pulled her close, complimented the braid and asked her about church. He knew about the lice, but thought it important to let Carolina tell the story. He assured her that lice were not unusual and medicine would soon fix the bugs and make them go away.

Then he asked, "Have you ever known another girl named Carolina?" She grinned. The question was an invitation to hear a story about herself. A story that both mama and Pa-pe told, but Pa-pe always told it best.

"No, Pa-pe, I don't know any other girls named Carolina."

"That is because until you got the name, Carolina was not a little girl. It was a place. The most beautiful place in the world."

The child snuggled closer with her back against his broad chest and her small hand lying on his muscled arm. She was glad both their skins were the same lovely brown color as her Aunt Julia. She could feel the vibrations of his deep voice and the tenderness with which he spoke. It made her feel warm inside.

"When I met your mama, I had not been in the States long. I was hired by a farmer to harvest peaches in a place called South Carolina and your mama was just a school-girl who worked selling fresh fruit to customers who drove up in big autos. She was so very pretty, but then, the whole world of Carolina is pretty. Very pretty. The air, the green trees, the little river that ran through the orchard where we worked each day, the sunsets, and the mild, warm nights—I think if God has a heaven it must look like Carolina.

"And I made up my mind right then that if I ever had a little girl, I would give her the same name as the beautiful land. And the priest married me and your mama. And we had that little girl. And I named her after the beautiful land. And you have grown to be even more beautiful than the peach trees in bloom."

He tickled Carolina and she laughed with bright waves of little girl giggles. He sat her on the ground.

"Run and play, my little daughter. And, never forget you have the best of all names."

Carolina ran to join her cousins but her father did not smile. He longed for a good life for his precious daughter. A husband, house and many children. He would pray and light a candle. Maybe that would help. Who could know for sure?

Michael Saldivar might have felt better if he could have seen the large guardian that followed his child across the yard. The angel had stood by her since before birth and his assignment of protection had been given in eternity past.

His job was to keep the way clear of overpowering wicked spiritual influence until such a time as the Spirit of God would be born in the fragile body of clay giving light to the face and hope to the heart. The angel would not force and he could not shield her from all pain. But, he would keep the playing field level and draw her heart toward what was clean, beautiful and everlasting. Ever vigilant, Remala would not fail.

*****

Five miles outside Thyme, Garrison and Emily Black were working in their large kitchen. Garrison reached into the last bag and pulled out a can.

"You bought sauerkraut?" he asked with an incredulous wrinkle of his nose.

"There may be some of the boys who like hotdogs that way. And, if no one else wants it, I'll eat the whole can myself," his wife replied.

"Well, I guess it's okay. But, you probably don't want to put it with the other stuff by the campfire."

"Why not?"

"I don't know. It just seems so... un-Texan-like."

"Tell that to the German communities around Fredericksburg." His wife as she took the sauerkraut from his hand and placed it on the pantry shelf.

"Well, for this group, I think mustard and chili would be more appropriate."

"I've got those, too."

The groceries were put away and Emily was folding the last paper bag. Garrison went to the refrigerator and stood looking inside.

"What about us and Sunday dinner? Fried chicken and cream gravy? Roast beef with fresh green beans?"

"Sure, if you want to cook any of that stuff," Emily grinned. Retirement had its benefits. At least she and Garrison now shared kitchen duty.

She still couldn't get used to seeing Major Black at the sink in overalls rather than standing straight in his Air Force uniform. Thyme was such a different life.

But, running a small ranch in East Texas seemed to fit them both just fine. They had slipped into this new way of life as though born in the piney woods.

"You never used to expect me to cook."

"You never used to wear bib overalls."

He made room at the open refrigerator and they slipped their arms around each other, both faces bathed in the refrigerator's blue light.

"What about a sandwich?" Garrison said at length. "Dutch treat. You make yours and I'll make mine."

"Add an afternoon nap to the offer and I'm with you."

"We never used to take naps on Sunday afternoon," he said.

"We never used to be so old," Emily responded with a squeeze to his waist and a bump to his hip.

*****

The key slipped smoothly into the lock on the front door of the small house on Apple Street. Diane stepped into the silence and threw her purse on the floor then stood in the middle of the room. For ten years she had prayed kneeling by the blue sofa. She had nursed her babies in that rocker. Many times she had decorated this space for Christmas.

Yet, as she stood in the awful silence, the space was strange and empty. She looked at the walls as though lost in a foreign land.

When the boys were home, every hour was packed with activity and noise. She was constantly late, running errands, racing to school, hurrying to the job and chauffeuring the boys from one location to another. Now, there was nothing.

Maybe that was why she had been reluctant to leave the church. There was no place to go and nothing to do that mattered.

When Elder Bentley announced the final "Amen," she had pulled herself together and choked back the tears as she followed the other women into the choir room to hang her robe in the closet.

She chatted lightly with neighbors and friends: The weather was unusually mild for this time of year. Yes, the boys would be back next Sunday. The youth department was sponsoring a chicken spaghetti dinner next month? No, she didn't think she could chair the event, but put her name down as one of the cooks. The empty banter went on and on while inside her heart felt like a stone.

She stood looking at the four strange walls and listening to the sounds of empty space. The judge had awarded her the house, but without family, it could never be a home. She drifted to the kitchen opening first one cabinet door then another. She tried the refrigerator. Nothing seemed worth eating.

She went to the bedroom and stretched on her back across the bed.

JaKobe's Assignment

The room had changed a good bit since the time she shared it with Steve, yet she could still feel his presence. Or, was it that she felt a longing for his presence? Or, maybe, what she felt was the longing for a husband—any nameless husband—who would share her burdens and make these walls a home.

It had been a long time since she felt the need to be caressed and kissed, but she felt it now. It permeated her being with an uncomfortable intensity. She rolled over and grabbed her Bible then rolled back and held it above her face as she began to read. It was as tasteless and empty as the kitchen.

Laying it aside she reached for a magazine and thumbed through the pages while tears welled in the corners of her eyes and dripped into her hairline.

An advertisement for diamonds showed a couple locked in an embrace. An article about cruising had pictures of handsome men and women with tan bodies lounging by the ship's pool. The monthly advice column featured a letter from a divorced father whose ex-wife refused to let him see his son.

She threw the magazine aside, curled into a fetal position and cried herself to sleep.

Phennia watched as the level of opposition filled to the maximum. The moment it was reached, she quickly moved to block a particularly obnoxious demon who had followed Diane home. She was angry and moved with lightening speed toward the imp who vanished through the ceiling laughing wickedly all the way knowing that the warrior would probably not leave the side of her charge only to chase a minor emissary of hell.

The angel was glad to see him go, but mightily wished she had sucked his power dry and silenced his wicked laughter before he left. That stupid grin had irritated her ever since he appeared cowering and fawning round the feet of Doltar.

Even though his master and been unsuccessful distracting Diane with sexual thoughts during the morning song, the imp had watched the pattern of attack and worked for hours trying to draw the right combination of sexuality to Diane's consciousness. Phennia had been forced to stand by and watch until the demon finally crossed the line.

She turned back to Diane who was still moving and softly crying in her sleep. The angel did not know much about human sexual desire, but it grieved her deeply to see Diane cry. She longed to wake her and show her the imp was gone and peace would now be restored, but that would serve no purpose other than her own satisfaction. Diane was safely asleep and she needed physical rest.

Phennia stood beside the bed and stretched both arms out over the sleeping form. For all practical purposes the protective stance was unnecessary, but it made her feel better. One day she would share the memory of this time with

JaKobe's Assignment

Diane and tell her how she drew personal comfort simply from offering the spiritual shelter of her upraised arms.

****

The oven door in the Phelps kitchen opened with a creak emitting the aroma of roast beef and new potatoes. Melody frowned. She simply must remember to do something about that hinge.

"Mom," Stephanie's voice called from the dining room. "Do you want the good china or our everyday stuff?"

Melody wished she had a third choice. Technically, Luke was company. But, he was only a teenager and the good china would have to be washed by hand. It would be hard enough to get to the baby shower on time without that added chore. She sighed.

"Go ahead and get out the china," she said. "But, use the blue cloth rather than the white one." At least that one did not have to be ironed.

"Cool! We haven't used the good stuff in ages."

As Melody transferred the meat and vegetables to serving dishes, she put the pots and cooking utensils in the dishwasher stacking them expertly around the dishes left from breakfast and her early morning cookie baking chore.

With one fluid motion, she opened the refrigerator, removed a salad with her left hand, closed the refrigerator with her foot, and retrieved a box of dish washing soap from the lower cabinet with her right hand. The art of the motion pleased her. All she needed was a little more efficiency. A little more effort and everything would work out fine

The back door opened and Jonathan stomped his way into the room. *Why didn't he use the front door?* Resentment sizzled through her brain. It would be understandable if he had driven home and parked around back, but she had taken the car and he walked from the church. *Surely the front side walk was closer to the front door. He didn't have to walk around the house picking up grass clippings to string all over the floor.*

"Hi, Hon. What's for dinner?" He talked continuously while draining the last of the morning coffee into a fresh mug and putting it in the microwave. "Thought Henrietta and Gladys would never finish gabbin'. Everything under control for your busy afternoon?" He looked around the room then took the lid from the empty cookie jar. "Got a spare cookie to hold a hungry man 'till dinner?"

Melody wanted to scream. Three questions, a statement, another dirty cup, shreds of dead brown grass all over her clean kitchen floor, and the man had not even been through the door two minutes. She jerked her lips into the tight line of a mock grin, and then threw a cookie his general direction. Without a word she turned her back and began tossing the chilled salad.

"You mad or somethin'?"

Silence.

"Okay. Don't answer. I'll be in the living room with the TV. At least it talks."

He ambled through the dining room where Stephanie was putting the finishing touches on the table setting.

"Hi, Dad."

"Hi, yourself, Steph. Where's Traci? How come she's not helping?"

"She went home with the Newsoms. They'll bring her back when Mrs. Newsom helps with the shower this afternoon. I think they were going to his mom's for lunch."

He grunted his approval then nodded in the direction of the carefully set table. "H-m-m, good china. We keep treating Luke like this and I'll expect him to show up at church sometime."

Stephanie giggled. Everyone knew Luke had little interest in spiritual things. But, he was considered a good kid and her parents trusted her brother to choose his friends wisely.

"They're in Ben's room," she tossed her head that direction. "Ya know,—not to change the subject—but it doesn't always have to be me and Traci who set the table. Ben could help. Nothing in the rule book of life says a guy can't touch dishes."

"You want me to call him?"

"Naw. Guess not. Truth is I kinda enjoy this stuff."

Jonathan hugged his daughter and loosened his tie. No sense maintaining formality in the privacy of his own home. He thought about changing into sweats, but Melody wouldn't like him eating her fancy Sunday dinner dressed like a slob; besides, he needed to go by the hospital later in the afternoon.

At times the worst thing about being a preacher was the dress code.

Jonathan turned on the television and was about to make himself comfortable in the recliner when he noticed the game wouldn't start for another ten minutes. He really should say something to Ben about sleeping late. There was time. He never could stand that pre-game commentator, anyway.

The boys were seated side by side on Ben's bed with their backs against the wall. "Hey, Ben," he said poking his head through the bedroom door. "Afternoon, Luke."

Luke used long, pale fingers to throw blond bangs back from his clear brown eyes. "Hello, Mr. Phelps," he said flipping shut his cell phone and hiding the small screen the boys had been intently watching.

Luke was tall for his age and delicately boned with wiry muscles and facial features that were as angular as Ben's were rounded. He sat with one leg folded under him and the other leg bent at a forty-five degree angle, his knee making a convenient place to rest his arm. The cell phone hung loosely in his hand. "Thanks for letting me come over this afternoon. It's a great way to relax before the recital."

"Always glad to have you, Luke," he answered then turned his attention to his son. "Ben, what's this I hear about you not getting out of bed this morning?" Jonathan's tone was more conversational than accusing.

When Ben spoke, his voice had an unusual high pitched, strained tone but Jonathan took no notice. "I got there before class," he squeaked, then cleared his throat and began again in a more natural tone. "Just ask Mr. Newsome."

"Yeah, well, you shouldn't upset your mother that way." His father took a long drink from the cup in his hand. "You boys want to watch the game?"

The boys traded glances and Luke answered. "If you don't mind, I think we'll pass. I was just showing Ben some cool features on my new phone."

"Well, don't get too carried away with all that techno-mumbo-jumbo. Dinner should be ready soon."

As Jonathan walked away, a slight uneasiness clung to the outer edges of his consciousness. Perhaps he should have said more, but he didn't want to embarrass Ben in front of his friend. They should plan another father-son time. Soon.

His mind drifted over his schedule for the next couple of weeks. Nothing jumped out as empty time. He had Friday mornings, but Ben would be in school. His thoughts circled a few times then drifted to the next subject. Exactly where had he put down that cookie?

He had barely gotten comfortable in the recliner when Melody called dinner was ready and everyone shuffled into position; Luke remembering to hold out the chair for his hostess. Small talk soon settled into a quiet reverence.

The china glistened. Bright green peas complimented fresh salad and hot rolls. In the center of the table the platter of roasted beef and new potatoes was decorated with sprigs of parsley. Large glasses of iced tea had been sweetened with Splenda and the smooth-as-silk gravy was prepared with very little fat—just the way Jonathan's health required. Like Melody, the presentation of Sunday dinner was perfect.

Jonathan loved moments like these. Good food. Family. Guest to enjoy the bounty. He was truly grateful for Melody's skills in the kitchen and the comfortable security of home. "Let's pray," he said.

A full five seconds of silence passed as Jonathan let the feeling of gratitude soak deeply into his heart and, hopefully, the hearts of those gathered with him.

Then, he drew a deep breath and prayed with a strong voice. "Lord, You have given us so much. Each other. Safety. Home. May we rest in Your provision, trusting that tomorrow is in Your hands as well as today. Thank You for putting Sunday in the week. Thank You for including rest and worship in Your plans for us. Bless this food and thank You for the one that prepared it for us to enjoy. Amen"

JaKobe's Assignment

Everyone at the table—even Luke—responded with "Amen." He had shared enough meals with the Phelps family to know the routine and found the custom both quaint and somehow comforting. In rare moments he envied the faith of Ben's family. Part of him wished that he, too, believed. It would be nice if the ship of life really did have Someone at the helm.

But, every time he drew close to letting himself embrace that philosophy, he pulled back. Believing in Someone bigger than himself would logically require him to relinquish control. He wasn't ready for that. At least, not now.

The food and physical nearness created a relaxed atmosphere and conversation flowed with an easy banter. Luke shared a joke about a fat man and his dog. They all laughed and Stephanie added to the fun because the punch line caught her with a mouthful of peas.

"Oh, well," said Melody, "that's why God invented napkins!"

When the last giggles faded, Luke told them a person could laugh all day if they went to the right sites on the Internet. That sparked a spirited debate about the benefits and pitfalls of the electronic information age. The talk was respectful, challenging and fun.

Through the entire meal, Jonathan cast surreptitious glances at Melody checking out her mood. She seemed relaxed. Whatever had caused her storm must be passing.

174

As dinner drew to a close, Stephanie pushed back her chair. "May I be excused? It's getting late and I told Bethany I would rehearse cheers with her."

Melody frowned. "Steph, you know I have the shower and rehearsal this afternoon. I could use a little help around here."

"Make Ben do dishes. Just 'cause I'm a girl you expect me to do everything."

"Hey!" Ben spoke up. "I've got company."

"Okay, you two. Settle down." Jonathan took the position of peacemaker. "We've had a great dinner and there is no need to spoil it. I can help with the dishes."

"You?" Melody raised her eyebrows as she lowered her chin.

"Yes, me. We used to do dishes together before the kids came along. I still remember how."

The truth was Jonathan was having his own second thoughts about volunteering for kitchen duty, but suspected it best not to say anything. Sundays were the most exhausting day of the week. He still had to make that hospital visit in addition to preaching the evening service and he really needed a nap.

On the other hand, he was still smarting from her outburst that morning. There was no need to make matters worse by letting her get in a fight with the kids.

"Thanks Dad," Stephanie almost tripped over her chair in an effort to leave the room before her parents could change their mind. "I'll call Brenda's mom and see you at church tonight. I won't be late."

Ben and Luke vanished into the bedroom leaving Melody and Jonathan sitting at the table alone. After a few moments of silence, Jonathan decided to risk the question. "You all right, Melody?"

"Of course." She stood abruptly and started clearing dishes. I'm just a little tired. That's all."

Jonathan hoped that was the whole truth, however, the next ten minutes made him wonder.

First, his wife complained about him throwing out the left over roast. It looked like garbage to him, but she saw the foundation for Monday's soup being ground in the disposal. Then he made the mistake of putting the soiled tablecloth in the laundry without first shaking off the crumbs. The final insult was when he insisted that the good china be placed in the dishwasher rather than a sink full of soapy water.

As soon as possible he used her disapproval as an excuse to abandon the chore. "Finish things up your own way," he sighed and left the room. "I need a nap, anyway."

As he passed the recliner he was tempted to drop and watch the rest of the game, but that wouldn't fit with the excuse he gave Melody for skipping kitchen duty. Not bothering to turn off the TV, he reluctantly passed on to the master bedroom.

He wanted to sleep. He tried to sleep. But questions picked and prodded his consciousness into full alert mode. What was wrong with his wife? She usually made his life so easy. Maybe leaving Thyme would be good for her, too. Maybe he should help more around the house but—dog gone it—his job sometimes took fifty hours a week. Maybe things would settle down in time.

JaKobe had followed Jonathan into the bedroom and watched him toss for a while. He couldn't read his mind but the significance of the man's restless turning was obvious—at least the angel believed it was.

Guilt quickly took away the peace of any human. And, since guilt was something the man would have to manage on his own, the angel left him to his repetitive tossing and drifted back into the living room where the TV was still running.

Nothing significant was going to happen to his human for at least the next hour. He might as well see if sporting events had changed much in seven hundred years.

1:42 PM

Thyme Regional Hospital

Jonathan rolled over on his side and opened one eye. How could it already be almost two? Melody had probably left for the shower. He might as well get up. If he went to sleep now, he'd might not be able to make the hospital visit and still be back in time for the recital.

Groaning, he pushed himself into a sitting position and vigorously rubbed his face with both hands. Sometimes the mundane duties of daily life were such a grind. Now, where had he put his shoes?

JaKobe was just figuring out the finer points of the Cowboy's defense when Jonathan walked through the room and clicked off the set. No matter. It was obvious the Steelers were going to win.

He followed Jonathan through the kitchen door and watched as he got into his traveling machine. Here was another thing JaKobe knew about academically, but was now experiencing for the first time. He nodded approval. The contraption wasn't a heavenly chariot, but it was definitely an improvement over the horse.

The car picked its way through residential streets as JaKobe followed with long, loping strides, but as it entered Interstate 30 and picked up speed he rose above it and floated. Of course, he could have molded his form to the empty seat beside Jonathan but he liked this outside view. There was so much activity, energy, and busyness. Large trucks carrying goods created rumbling sounds. Small cars of all descriptions wove in and out as they followed lines on a pavement and the spiritual activity around him rivaled the organized chaos of the highway.

To his left, he noticed a darkness gathering over Thyme's Junior College and wondered what prompted such activity on a day when no humans occupied those buildings. Ahead of him and almost to the horizon, a shaft of light had opened up. Several hundred angels busily ascended or descended on the beam. Some, no doubt, were headed home after an assignment; others coming down to join the battle raging on earth.

He noted all of those traveling the beam were either warriors or on information reconnaissance because even at this distance he could see none escorted a human soul.

There were angels riding in cars and others following vehicles. A skirmish between two fairly

JaKobe's Assignment

well matched spirit beings was taking place outside a convenience store.

Jonathan pulled off the highway and soon rolled to a stop in the hospital parking space reserved for clergy.

While JaKobe waited, a brief glow filled the car, and then the man picked up his Bible and stepped out. The angel nodded approval. This human had a consistent habit of prayer. More than likely he could sustain a fairly high opposition level without eternal damage. To JaKobe, the eternal perspective was all that mattered.

He followed his charge across the parking lot and through a set of sliding glass doors that silently moved out of the way without being touched by human hands. These silent, obedient doors were a marvel. He considered the physics involved and the mathematical equations necessary to make such doors work and wanted to stop long enough to examine one and see if his calculations were correct but resisted the urge.

They crossed the polished marble floor of the lobby then turned right walking toward a bank of elevators.

JaKobe felt slightly discontented. There was so much he didn't fully know. His steps slowed.

Of course, he would never forsake his assignment, but there was no requirement to stay by Jonathan's side every moment. He could still feel echoes from his trip across town. So much activity! So many stories! So much to learn!

Experiencing earth first hand rather than sitting at his station processing information was more enthralling than he had imagined.

He wondered where Rachael had gone. There had been no message from her since she nodded to him earlier that morning and drifted off among the trees. And, he couldn't forget that ominous dark cloud gathering over the college.

Jonathan was five yards ahead of him now and the angel's steps slowed even more. Doing reconnaissance in the town might be as profitable as staying by the human's side. Both courses of action were permissible. Both would allow him to better understand Jonathan's world and his needs.

The elevator arrived. More silent, obedient doors. His human entered a tiny room and pushed a button commanding that the machine take him to the third floor where eighty-three year old Margaret Mc Clawson was just beginning to stir from her afternoon nap.

JaKobe stood rooted where he was and watched the doors close. Before leaving heaven he had memorized the files of all Jonathan's acquaintances and knew Margaret to be a seasoned saint with a sharp intellect and biting wit. She was well equipped to advise and lead a young pastor.

Stuffing his hands in his pockets he made a smooth u-turn. He could safely let Margaret do angel-work for a while.

*****

JaKobe's Assignment

In the elevator, lighted buttons blinked one after another as a tiny bell announced the passing of each floor. On the third ring, the doors slid open and he stepped to the blue carpet of the hospital's geriatric unit.

Most of the pastors he knew disliked making hospital visits. The expenditure of time seldom seemed worth the effort. Patients were either unconscious or throwing up. If you knew the family well, the visit was emotionally taxing and if the family was one of those who had not been to church for the past four Easters, the situation was awkward.

It was easy to pass hospital responsibilities to a deacon or, better yet, a committee of women. At his former church the fifteen pastors of Crenshaw had averaged less than one hospital visit a year.

But, Jonathan was different. He found a deep satisfaction in hospital visitation. The long waiting time with families gave him an opportunity to hear their stories and know them more intimately. Patients were often frightened and they seemed to draw genuine comfort from his prayers. To him, visiting a hospital was ministry at its best.

"May I help you?" A male nurse with a surprising shock of black hair peered over the edge of the counter.

"Oh," Jonathan slapped his pockets then pulled a name badge from inside his coat. "Clergy," he explained, pinning the badge to his lapel. "I'm Margaret Mc Clawson's pastor. Thought I would visit her a while."

The nurse went back to his records and ignored him while the pastor was left to find his way alone. He was glad he had remembered to ask Era Lou the number of the room. Since the government's new privacy laws came into effect the friendly lady with blue hair and a striped pinafore who used to set at the information desk was gone. Come to think of it, so was the desk.

He looked for room 304, reading signs posted on the wall at the end of each hallway.

Margaret sat with the head of her bed raised and extra pillows plumped at her back. The sheet was smoothly drawn to her waist and neatly folded over in a precise line. Her pink fleece robe was decorated with tiny rosebuds and tied at the throat with a matching ribbon that looked freshly pressed. Jonathan thought her the perfect picture of graceful aging.

A touch of pastel makeup had been added to her cheeks and lips and every gray hair was smoothed into place. Her eyes were a dozen shades of blue with sapphire accents. They took in everything around her with an active interest while her placid, wrinkled face suggested an ability to hold the world at a distance while giving it honest evaluation.

"Well, if it isn't Preacher Phelps! My, but you are a sight for sore eyes! I was just laying here thinking about you."

"Now, Miss Margaret, you're gonna make me blush!" said Jonathan. "A young girl like you shouldn't be thinking 'bout a married man."

As soon as the words jumped off his tongue he wanted to grab them back. Had he gone too far? He had frequently been the focus of Margaret's quick wit, but he also knew it was easy to offend without meaning to.

The smile that lit her face put him at ease. "'Young lady?' My sweet Harold! I don't think so. These old bones feel every one of their eighty-three years."

She offered a frail hand, which he took then bent to kiss her cheek.

"At least, you're looking young and perky today," he said.

"I'll only grant you the "perky" part," she replied. "I feel fine. I wouldn't be here at all except Doc Grimes had me at a disadvantage."

"What kind of disadvantage was that?"

"I was unconscious."

Jonathan coughed trying to mask the laugh that suddenly bubbled in his throat. "Unconscious?"

"Young man, it appears no one has filled you in on the details of this case."

"No, ma'am. Not yet, anyway."

He had learned early in his ministry that people—especially women—might not want their pastor to know the exact nature of their illness, so he never asked probing questions. Physical details were most often relayed to him second hand through Melody.

"Well, pull up a chair and I'll tell you about it." He reached for the blue padded chair close by. "No, not that one. It's too bulky. Get the little gray one by the sink," she directed. "Sit it right here close by the bed and face me."

When all was arranged according to her directions, she breathed contentedly. "I don't mean to be bossy," she explained. "The truth is my eyes and hearing are not what they once were. It helps so much when I can see your face straight on and don't have to look up.

"Now, where was I? Oh, yes. Telling you about how Doc Grimes took advantage of me."

Jonathan repressed another smile.

"I was innocent. This hospital stuff was not my idea. I came to his office on Friday because I needed my blood pressure medicine refilled. –Did you know the pharmacy will only refill a bottle six times? After that, they insist on a new prescription. And, of course, the doctor can't just pick up the phone and call, my, no. They've got to have you come all the way out to their office so they can see you eye-to-eye and collect another hundred dollars for doin' you the favor.

"Well, anyway, my appointment was at three but they said he was in some kind of emergency and running late. I sat in that waiting room two and a half hours! Then I said to myself, 'Margaret, enough is enough. You might as well go home because there is no way Doc is going to see you today.'

"I guess by that time I was a little mad. And, perhaps I got up a little fast. But, the next thing I know, I'm on the floor and all these people are standing round looking at me like I was some kind of circus sideshow.

"Even Doc Grimes came out from wherever he'd been hidin' and stood there worrying over me like a hen clucking over her only chick.

"I wasn't hurt. I felt fine — only embarrassed — and I tried to get up and go home. But, when I lifted my head things went sort of black. That's when Doc Grimes took advantage of the situation and instead of getting a little water to help me come round he called the ambulance and had me carted off!

"I woke up stuck in this place and they have been prodding and poking at me ever since."

"Miss Margaret, you should be grateful for what Doc Grimes did. He was just trying to take good care of you."

"I don't know so much about that. The minute I woke up I told them I was just fine. And, sure enough, not a thing showed up on all those tests. Nothing."

She barely paused for a breath then changed the subject completely. "Oh, that's enough about me and my trials and tribulations. How was church this morning?"

"It was good. I brought you a bulletin." He flipped through the pages of his Bible and retrieved the colorful program.

Without taking her eyes from the paper, Margaret patted the bedside table until she found her glasses, adjusted them on her nose and continued to scan the document. "Looks like a busy afternoon." Jonathan grunted his agreement. "And, Diane sang! I could listen to that girl all day. What did she select?"

"She combined two versions of an old hymn, *'So Send I You.'* It was lovely, but then everything Diane sings is lovely."

"Just a moment," Margaret said. She sat straighter in the bed. "May I see that Bible you've got there?"

He handed Margaret his prized Bible and she flipped through the pages with a practiced ease. "Hum-m-m," she mused, "It's just as I thought." She closed the book and returned it to the owner.

"Diane's song quoted from the same reference you used as a sermon text."

"Yes, ma'am. Isn't that amazing? I am sure it was the hand of the Lord."

As soon as his words set the air vibrating, Jonathan regretted them. He was popping off meaningless Christian platitudes and he suspected Margaret knew it.

"Do you really believe what you just said?" She cocked her head and looked deeply into his soul.

Half of him wanted to take the barriers down and be honest with this old saint. If anyone could understand his struggles of faith, it would be Margaret. That half wanted to tell her how he longed to see God do something—anything—and how disappointed he had become at the years of heavenly silence.

But, the other half of him was too frightened to take the risk of such exposure. That half wanted to play it safe and stay hidden behind the charade of bumper sticker theology and unexplored doubts. There was a certain safety when one shut down the mind and refused to think deeper than slogans.

He had paused only a fraction of a second and the doubts were betrayed by nothing more than a shade briefly passing over his eyes, but Margaret had seen that fleeting look before and had no trouble reading its meaning.

"I see," she said softly and Jonathan was strangely relieved.

In that brief moment pastor and congregant connected with a pathos and honesty that was rare. Without discussing the matter, they understood his struggle to believe and embarrassment when the struggle was lost.

"Tell me, Pastor, do you know much about my life?" It was a strange twist in the conversation, but he knew Margaret never took abrupt vocal turns without a reason. Jonathan slowly shook his head then leaned back in the chair. Wherever

Margaret was going with this train of thought, he was more than willing to follow her lead.

"A moment ago, you called me *Miss Margaret* but did you know my name is really *Mrs. Lyde*?"

Amazed, Jonathan moved his head from side to side. He had seen this woman sitting in his congregation every Sunday for the past five years. He had been in her home. He knew her friends. He had even been part of the civic committee when the new middle school gym was named in honor of her forty years as a public school teacher. Yet, he had never heard of a husband, child, sister or even cousin. For all he knew, Margaret Mc Clawson was a spinster teacher, alone in the world.

"I am not surprised. Most people—even those my age—don't think of me as ever having married. But, I did. I even had a child." Jonathan relaxed his position and waited.

"Calling a married woman 'Miss' is an old Southern tradition that goes back before the Civil War. Everyone said it; especially the children. Out of respect they said, 'Ma'am' but out of love they said 'Miss' then added the woman's first name.

"I've had the privilege of being loved by many, many children and they all called me 'Miss Margaret.' Eventually, even the town folk and friends took up the name. My 'Mrs.' got lost over time. Perhaps that's because my marriage was so long ago and lasted only a few years."

"I'm sorry," said Jonathan genuinely touched. "What happened?"

JaKobe's Assignment

"Life." Margaret leaned her head back against the pillows and looked at the ceiling. "And, death."

They were silent as the past came creeping slowly forward and Margaret's eyes took on a faraway mist. Sixty-four years was a long way to look back.

"You probably know nothing much about the year 1943. I know it well. I lived it.

"I was eighteen that year. The war effort was in full swing. Rationing. German bombs falling on England. Speeches by Roosevelt and Churchill coming over the wireless. That was the year I met Harold."

Jonathan interjected. "I have often heard you say, 'My sweet Harold' when something seems amazing, but I thought it was only a quaint expression."

"I guess it has become that through the years," continued Margaret. "But, there really was a Harold and he was, indeed, 'my sweet.' I still find memories of him surprisingly strong.

"Pastor, my parents tried to raise me right but their good advice didn't always take. By the time I met Harold I had picked up several curse words. Harold found them very offensive."

She noticed a slight elevation in Jonathan's eyebrows. "Oh, don't look so shocked, Preacher. I was born a sinner—just like you—and the words made me feel powerful and grown up.

"But, Harold said such words were not fit for a lady. So, I had to find other ways of expressing my feelings. Somehow, 'My Sweet Harold' became a catchall phrase for whatever strong emotion I was feeling at the moment. It was not too original, but it worked and it always made him smile.

"I had graduated high school in the late spring of that year and I met Harold in the summer. He had come to Thyme on leave with an army buddy of his. I guess you could say it was love at first sight. We were afraid the war would separate us, so we married in the fall, just three days before Thanksgiving.

"I suppose today such a quick courtship would be looked down on, but lots of brides were hurrying to wed during the war. Our marriage may have been quick but it was a decision neither one of us ever regretted.

"Harold was an accountant working for a large army base in Virginia, so that is where I went after the wedding. But, not for long.

"It was about a year after our marriage and right at the end of the war when Harold was transferred to a base in Southern California. We were apart for only a short while because as soon as we could afford it I followed him out West.

"We had been married two years when my darling Peggy Jane was born. What a beautiful, perfect gift from God! California was booming, the war was over and we were so happy.

"California was good, but it always embarrassed Harold that he served during wartime and never once got shot at. I praised the Lord and thought it a blessing.

"However, the good times did not last. They never do. When Peggy was three she got sick and I was overwhelmed with panic. I pleaded with God as I never have before or since, yet all my panic and prayers did nothing to change reality.

"When they said she would die I thought I would surely die, too.

"I really didn't think I could bury my baby and still go on breathing. The idea was beyond comprehension. Harold was my rock those last three months we had her on earth. The pain. . . . The hospitals. . . . Hearing her cry. . . "

The room was engulfed with a heavy silence and Jonathan felt a tear drift down his cheek, but he did not reach for the tissues. Neither did Margaret. The moment seemed too sacred for movement.

A full two minutes passed then Margaret blinked away the tears and breathed deeply. "They said it was leukemia. It was the first time I had ever heard that word.

"I guess you have never seen a picture of my Peggy or Harold. I only keep two in frames and both are in my bedroom. Somehow memories of them are so tender and private the pictures just didn't seem to fit when displayed in the more public rooms of the house."

For several long moments Margaret seemed lost in time. Her eyes were directed downward to her hands folded loosely together on the sheet. Jonathan thought his elderly friend might have drifted off to sleep. But the moment of reverence passed and she raised her eyes with a weak smile.

"What happened to your husband," Jonathan asked.

"Oh, Peggy Jane wasn't alone in heaven for long. He went to be with her and Jesus a little less than two years later. It was 1950, to be exact.

"Would you believe an industrial accident?" she asked. Jonathan shook his head.

"It's true. My soft-spoken, accountant husband who went to war and never got shot at, who went to work each day in a business suit, was killed by a falling pipe.

"Harold had gone to work just as usual that day. He kissed me goodbye and I spent the morning ironing his good dress shirts. It was nearly eleven when the boss of his company knocked on the door. He said there had been an accident and offered to take me to the hospital. Harold and I only had one car and he had taken it to the office.

"When we arrived the doctor told me the body—I remember how I was struck by that phrase: *The body*. In a single morning, the man who was the center of my world had gone from being my husband to being *the body*.

"Anyway, the body had already been removed to the morgue.

"They said he had gone to pick up financial records at the construction site of a new 20 story building. A worker on the seventeenth floor dropped an eighteen-inch pipe. Harold was wearing a hardhat, but when he heard the worker cry out, he looked up and the pipe hit him in the throat.

"I buried him beside Peggy Jane. He didn't have other family and neither did I.

"The world was so strange after that. I knew I needed work, but I only had limited skills. Eventually, I decided to sell everything we had gathered in California and move back to the town in which I was born.

"I decided I would go back to school and spend my life educating the children of Thyme, and after I arrived it just sort of seemed natural to go back to using my maiden name. Not many people knew who 'Mrs. Lyde' was but everyone recognized 'Margaret Mc Clawson.'"

"You did a wonderful thing for hundreds of children as well as the town," he commented.

"Maybe," replied Margaret. She seemed to be rationally evaluating her service with neither excessive pride nor false humility. "At the time, I didn't have a whole lot of choices. I just trust the Lord has used what I was able offered Him.

"That brings me to the point I was trying to make." She adjusted her glasses and her blue eyes searched the naked portions of his soul. "Trust is a strange thing. It is neither stupid nor presumptive. Faith is trust in action. It has solid foundations, but it doesn't depend on those foundations to exist.

"You said that the Lord's hand was in Diane's selection of that particular song, but you and I both know that saying such a thing scares you.

"While you may hope that the Lord would be in control of such a detail, you cannot prove whether He is or He is not. You are being forced to use your faith to trust what you cannot prove and that is stretching your soul far beyond its comfort zone."

She paused giving room for her next statement to have full impact. "Pastor, if such a simple thing as the mystery of Diane's song challenges your faith, how much more struggle will you have when illness, death and circumstances that defy explanation barge into your life uninvited?"

Jonathan was stunned and silent. He remembered King David when Nathan the prophet pointed an accusing finger and said, "Thou art the man!" He felt trapped and exposed and strangely relieved all at the same time. He wanted to run, yet he also wanted to stay until he understood more. And, in the middle of the emotional confusion Margaret's piercing blue eyes never left his face. It was unnerving.

"I just wish I could go back to the days when faith was simple and all these questions didn't plague me," he finally said.

"Jonathan!" Margaret's voice was as stern as a fifth grade teacher who just caught her student cheating on a test.

"That's a wicked thing to say. Wicked! God is forever calling you forward! It may be painful, but the way forward always leads to life and spiritual growth. The way backward leads to loss and even death. Never tell the Lord you want to go backward!"

Anger flashed in him. Who was this woman to think she could instruct him? He was her pastor, not her student.

Margaret caught the spark in his eyes and felt a need to repent. "I'm sorry for being so blunt." She dropped her eyes and added, " Forgive me."

His anger had been sudden and real, but it just as quickly dissipated into a weary shadow. The whiplash of emotions was wearing his nerves thin.

"That's all right," he mumbled then continued with a sigh. "It's just that lately I have been so . . . I don't know . . . so disquieted; like I can't quite find solid ground for my feet. It's like I need something from God, but I can't tell Him what it is. I've always wanted to do something big for God, but the years have passed and . . ." He couldn't bring himself to finish the sentence. It wasn't necessary.

Compassion glowed in Margaret's eyes. She could sympathize because too often in past years she had experienced these same struggles. It wasn't easy to take a leap of faith.

"Ever read Kierkegaard?" she asked as though everyone surely had a copy of the nineteenth century philosopher handy on the desk.

"Who?"

"Never mind," she said. Then paused and finally asked, "How about, *The Confessions of Saint Augustine?*"

Again, his expression told her the answer before words came out of his mouth. "Oh, well."

She paused briefly then drew a quick breath as a new thought surprised her mind. "What about A. W. Tozer? Got any of his works on those shelves in your office?"

"Yeah, a couple. What did you have in mind?"

"Knowledge of the Holy?"

"I've read that one." He wasn't about to tell her how long ago.

"Pastor, I don't mean to even hint that any book by any author is comparable with the Bible, but we can learn from what others have written. Even when we don't agree with the author, books can challenge our thinking and expand our view. Many, many men and women have asked the same questions and struggle with the same issues that are plaguing you. Reading their words reminds us that we are not alone.

"As we move through this life, God calls us to walk by faith. You may see a dozen circumstances in one day that you could cite as proof that God is defending and guiding and blessing you. The next day you may be hit with a different dozen that could be cited as proof that you have been abandoned and the God of creation has gone on a vacation to Bermuda."

The pastor smiled at the mental pictures she was painting in his mind.

"We live daily struggling within a cocoon of circumstances and from inside that cocoon it is so hard to believe a larger, different world exists outside our cage. A real world where humans are not the measure of all things and our opinion of *big* or *small* may not matter much.

"You said you had read, *Knowledge of the Holy*. Do you remember Tozer's quote from the section on the Trinity? *'To seek proof is to admit doubt and to obtain proof is to render faith superfluous'*? [14]

"Seeking proof kills faith, but faith, repeatedly exercised as trust, will cause a heart-deep assurance to one day bloom. That deep, abiding assurance will be all the proof you need.

"Oh, well. I am prattling on like an old lady. But then, I am an old lady, so I suppose a bit of prattling is to be expected."

They both laughed out loud.

"Miss Margaret, I think I could learn a lot from you," he said with genuine admiration.

Again, she looked at him with those piercing blue eyes. "Perhaps."

It was all she said and for the second time, Jonathan felt that her statement was neither a point of brag nor an expression of humility. She was simply giving her best, unbiased judgment.

"However," Margaret continued. "It is also true I have learned a lot from you. And, if I have anything to offer in return, it might be the perspective of years." She smiled slyly, "That is, age and the many hours I've spent combing library shelves. I'm afraid I'm a bit like Erasmus,

'When I have a little money, I buy books and if any is left, I buy food and clothing.'"

"Who?"

"Jonathan! Don't tell me you don't know Erasmus!"

He pursed his lips in mock indignation. "Of course, I know him! He's the butcher at the market where Melody buys meat."

After a hardy laugh, they drifted back into serious conversation and before Jonathan noticed the time, more than an hour had passed. He could see color slowly drain from her cheeks as weariness set in but her eyes remained as intense as ever.

"I guess I had better be getting on home and let you rest," he offered.

"Oh, don't go. I'm fine," Margaret protested.

"Do you really believe what you just said?" He cocked his head in a mock imitation of the words she had used to challenge him only an hour before.

The old saint capitulated. "Well, maybe I could use a little nap. But, I'll be going home tomorrow. Perhaps you could visit later in the week? I've got a copy of *The Problem of Pain* by Lewis that I think would interest you."

"I'd be very interested, Miss Margaret."

"Then, it's a deal," she said giving him a surprisingly strong slap on the palm. "I'll even make you some limeade and hot biscuits."

"Deal."

JaKobe's Assignment

*****

A warrior in the corner of the room watched as Jonathan left. He had been fascinated by the conversation between his human and her pastor.

Faith. He puzzled over the word. In his world, obedience was necessary, but faith—the kind that humans experienced—was not. Logic, emotion, personality and even affection were familiar to him. But other things remained tantalizingly outside his grasp. Like shadows hinting at what was real.

A slight hint of envy shaded his consciousness. Or, was it longing? The human experience of faith and the birth of the Spirit that created a direct connection with God were certainly to be admired and if he could have a part in making that miracle happen, he was honored by the task.

The battle weary angel shrugged then walked to the window. Humans. What a fascinating species. He paced restlessly for a few moments then returned to the window and searched the sky. He checked his sword and paced again. It would not be much longer, now.

Elizabeth Baker

1:55 PM

The Baby Shower

It had taken less than twenty-five minutes to transform the general-purpose room known affectionately as *Fellowship Hall* into a warm, inviting space for women to celebrate birth. Five of the six tables had been collapsed and stationed unobtrusively against the back wall while a white cloth was thrown over the sixth. A rocking chair—borrowed from the nursery—was waiting for Miranda while folding chairs, placed horseshoe fashion, waited for the guest. A small table, complete with feathered pen, stood by the door and a portable crib—also borrowed from the nursery—waited to be filled with gaily-wrapped gifts.

Melody surveyed the room with a critical eye. The battered stork which served as a centerpiece had seen better days, but the overall results were not too bad. Sitting a decorated sheet cake to the side of the stork, she removed the molded plastic shield from the cardboard base then held it aloft, traces of pink icing sticking to manicured finger tips.

"Beverly, did you find the Ginger Ale?" she called back to the kitchen then followed her own voice into the small adjoining room where three women bustled about reaching over one another in order to perform various tasks.

"Do you think this will be enough?" Bev asked holding two large, green bottles aloft. "I think they used three at my shower."

"Yes, we did. But, we don't expect as many guest this time," Melody rinsed her nails under cold, running water. It never occurred to her to lick them. "I just hope enough people show up so we don't embarrass ourselves."

"If you ask me," Gladys began as she dumped a can of mixed nuts into a silver dish, "Tina ought to be grateful if anyone is here. After all, we don't know this girl. I think the entire idea is scandalous! In my day, women in her niece's position had enough manners to be ashamed."

The critical attitude and sharp tongue for which Gladys was well known made the others wince. One would think that after years of sitting on a church pew her prickly personality might have softened. But, if the grey-headed woman's nature had mellowed through the years, the original model must have been something to behold!

Melody glanced at LeeAnn who was spooning strawberry sherbet into the punch bowl. The church secretary rolled her eyes then shrugged and looked away. If anything were going to be said, it would be up to Melody to open her mouth.

"Gladys, I don't know about proper manners or how things should be done, but I do know Miranda doesn't claim to be a Christian and she is not part of any church. Perhaps showing a little love toward her is the first step in leading her to God."

"Well, at least Tina should have known better."

Melody was getting irritated. "If you feel that way, why did you volunteer to be a hostess?"

Gladys tossed the empty nut can into the trash. "I've helped with every shower for the past seven years and I'm not about to let this one break my record."

The empty can had barely rattled its way to the bottom of the trash bin when Traci, and Crystal tumbled breathless into the room. The girls had been walking in the neighborhood while they cared for six-month-old Rosaline.

"Mrs. Smith said we could pick these as long as we were careful and didn't pull up any of the plants by the roots." Traci said holding out five white mums for her mom's inspection.

Melody received the blossoms. "Would you like to donate them for the shower? If we cut the stems short and put them in a bowl, I think they would be perfect for the registration table."

Tracy raced to the cabinet where the good bowls were kept while her friend, Crystal, Beverly

Newsome's middle child, shifted her baby sister to a more comfortable position. The nine-year-old stood with her hip cocked sideways creating a saddle for the baby who clung to her with confident hands and flashed a beguiling, four-tooth grin.

Beverly gave a light, amused laugh then settled the chunky form on her own hip. Surely the child would learn to walk before all caretakers were twisted in the permanent shape of an S.

Five miles from the church, Tina gripped the wheel of her Buick with the same determined forcefulness that she used for life in general. Her jaw was as tight as her fingers, but she modulated her voice into a sweet, non-offensive tone designed to persuade anyone of reason to see the wisdom of her way.

"My dear, niece," she began for the third time. "It was necessary that everyone know the truth about your circumstance. There is no reason for you to be upset."

"But, you didn't have to say anything at all! These church people are your friends, not mine. I'll bet not one of them is under fifty. They would have assumed Brad and I were married if you had just kept your mouth closed. As it is, I'll have to sit through this entire 'party' wondering what they think of me. Most probably believe I'll be damned to hell for this. You have put me in a very awkward position."

"Young lady, your mother would be crushed to think that her only daughter would be so ungrateful! Jack and I have loved you and guided your every step since Victoria died. We paid for your college, bought you a car and have been more than accepting of the lifestyle you've chosen. How could you be so ungrateful when I arrange for you to enter polite society and receive gifts?"

Miranda was silent. She shifted her swollen belly to a more comfortable position. There was no denying that Aunt Tina and Uncle Jack had given her things. Yet, hadn't her mother's will required that? She wished she could remember exactly what the lawyers said. But, she had been only nineteen when the heart attack happened and at the time it seemed enough to know that the Bentley's were to be in full control of all funds until she turned twenty-five.

Almost four years had passed since the fateful day she came home from school and found her mother dead on the floor. Four hard, confusing years. Now, she wanted very much to know the details of her mother's estate but asking direct questions took courage. It was courage that Miranda didn't have.

The Bentley's had been kind, but every "gift" seemed to come with a hook attached. As soon as she finished out the semester at Texas Women's University they insisted she transfer to the nearby Jr. College and it was there her occasional sex and dabbling in recreational drugs changed into a lifestyle. Soon, it was hard to get to class on time and her grades were falling. She hid the trouble as long as possible, but last year the web of lies finally came unraveled.

Tina had responded by cutting off all funds and threatening to take back the car that was still registered in the Bentley name. She said she was going to, "show tough love and straighten out Victoria's daughter."

Uncle Jack said she needed to learn the value of a hard-earned dollar. So now she was clerking in his lumberyard three days a week while she and Brad were forced to move to an apartment in Sandy Flats to shorten her commute.

Miranda laid her head back and stared at the softly padded ceiling of the car's interior. It was smooth and orderly as it stretched from one point to another and molded perfectly around each curve. Why couldn't life be more like that? No bumps, rips or sharp turns; just orderly progression and smooth days.

She found out about the baby in early spring and within days everything in her world was different. The idea of returning to school faded as the prospects of parenthood grew larger and for the first time Miranda began to consider the future with more than her own immediate pleasure in view.

Every time she lit up a joint, she thought about the baby and within days her marijuana habit was a thing of the past. She considered Brad and saw him as more than a good sex partner. What kind of father would the underemployed, part-time student be? She looked at their cramped, disheveled apartment and wondered if it would ever be a home.

If she could hold on until the trust fund was under her control, maybe her future wouldn't look so dark. She would be twenty-five in two more years. Until then, she would just have to play whatever game Aunt Tina organized. But, smiling through the next two hours was not going to be easy.

Tina and Miranda arrived on the stroke of 2 PM. The room was almost empty. Only one guest, three hostesses, two little girls and a baby greeted the guest of honor.

"I am sure the others will be here soon," assured Melody as she tried her best to make them feel welcome. Tina was invited to become involved with last minute preparations as Beverly led Miranda to the rocking chair then sat beside her with Rosaline on her lap.

At first, Miranda felt stiff and unnatural. She had only been inside a church for weddings and funerals. She didn't know what to expect from this group of religious strangers but the charm of baby Rosaline and Beverly's easy style encouraged her to lean further into the comfort of the rocker and rest.

"Tina says you are working in your Uncle's lumber yard." Beverly opened the subject and then paused briefly to see if Miranda would respond.

"Yes. They thought I needed a little practical business experience before finishing college." The statement might not have been the whole truth, but at least it wasn't a complete lie.

"My husband, Ward, is a plumber and he often buys supplies in Elder Bentley's place. Perhaps you have run into him."

As the conversation continued, Miranda decided she liked this unpretentious woman. They talked of children and school and family and work. Beverly moved with ease as one subject faded into another and she made it easy for Miranda to feel an important part of everything that was said.

It wasn't long before Miranda was tempted to mention something about Brad, just to see if Beverly knew of the circumstances surrounding her pregnancy. But, before she could decide exactly what to say, others began to arrive. By 2:15, eighteen adults and several children were standing around in small groups.

"Miranda!" It was Tina's voice. "You've got to see the cake before they cut it!"

She would much rather set in the rocker talking with Beverly, but she obediently stood and walked to the decorated table. Maybe the shower would not be so bad. No one pointed a finger at her or whispered while throwing side glances her way. She even felt a certain excited curiosity growing as she watched the crib filling with gifts.

They only gave because she was Tina's niece, still, it was a nice thing for all these ladies to do. She had no idea her aunt was so well liked!

While Tina and Miranda posed for pictures, Melody drifted closer to Bev. "Could I ask a really big favor?" she whispered.

Her friend rose from the chair snuggling baby Rosaline against her shoulder. "Let me guess," she said as a good-natured grin spread across her face. "You need someone to supervise cleanup."

"Well, more or less," she confessed, relieved that her friend could anticipate her need without her asking.

"More or less?" Bev cocked her head. "With a schedule like you have this afternoon, you will not only need cleanup help but an extra dose of vitamins and a pair of roller skates!"

The laugh they shared was soft and private.

"Thanks, Bev. I don't know what I would do without you," she said and felt her shoulders sag with relief. "Jonathan told me I was trying to pack too much into one Sunday."

"Oh, I am glad to help. Gladys and LeeAnn will be here and we should be done in no time. Besides, . . ." She paused while her eyes fluttered downward. "I'm going to owe you big time around Christmas."

Melody felt the floor move beneath her feet. The Newsome family was such an integral part of church function, that whatever Beverly was trying to get up courage to say could not be good news. Her friend raised her eyes and stumbled into an explanation.

"You know how much I've wanted to go back to Ohio to see my Mom and Dad."

"Yeah, so..."

"Well, that last job Ward finished paid really well. It looks like we we'll not only be able to make the trip, but spend several days there.

"It will be wonderful to be home for Christmas, but that means I've got to" –she pulled in a breath raced through the remaining words as though saying it quickly might somehow soften the blow—"cancel out on helping with the Christmas program."

It took a moment for the full import of what Beverly was saying to sink in but when it did Melody began naming all the holes she would have to fill with the Newsome family gone for the holidays.

"So, you can't be there to direct the children's choir."

"Sorry."

"And, Ward can't do our sets."

"I guess not."

"And, I'll need to replace Donny in the roll of Joseph, and Crystal won't be doing the angel bit."

"Nope."

"I don't suppose you could ship Rosaline back by UPS to do the baby Jesus gig?"

"I told you I was going to owe you big time."

While the activity of the shower continued to swirl around her, Melody felt that strange, separated feeling come again.

She didn't know the first time the sensation overcame her. It just had happened gradually as year after year she worked to present the proper façade to an approving public. In her teens, she learned to play the role of a perfect daughter. She smiled on cue and constantly performed for an audience—even during those times when she knew the theater was empty.

Later, she learned to play the role of a preacher's wife. She had also learned to play the role of perfect mother and the perfect Christian. She had played so many roles and performed them so well that finally, the roles became bigger and Melody—the real Melody—began to shrink.

Then, about a year ago something new began to happen. There were times when the real woman became so small and the plastic actor so large, that Melody found herself stepping off the stage and leaving the well-rehearsed shell to say the dull, repetitive lines all alone. It was a strange sensation and after it passed, the experience frightened her. Yet, drifting away was also enticing. She was so weary. The façade was so heavy. At times, stepping off the stage was the only way to manage the tension.

Like now.

The mask came on and the actor took over. Inside, Melody felt almost as though she were standing somewhere else in the room watching the scene rather than being a part of the action.

"It will work out all right," the actor said with a light air. "You have a good time with your folks. We can manage. I'll just make a few calls. After all, Christmas is over two months away."

From somewhere else the real Melody recalculated. The program was set for December 5th cutting twenty days from her optimistic schedule.

Across the room, Miranda balanced her cup on the side of her plate and picked up a napkin. This experience might not turn out to be so bad. Who knew? Maybe one day she and Brad might have a life that included attending church. Most good families did that. Didn't they?

Her hopeful mood was suddenly broken when three latecomers breezed through the door. Henrietta Pierce had arrived with little Hope and this time they were accompanied by Lucy, Hope's mother. Everyone seemed to know the woman with the little girl clinging to her legs, but one look told Miranda that this lady fit with the group like a lion fit with lambs.

Everything about her was subtly wrong. Her eyes were too bright and her jeans too tight. Her voice sounded somehow fake and her once lovely brown hair had a dull, dry cast to it. Her makeup was perfect, but at the same time seductive, and the way she moved confirmed her sexual style.

Yet, Lucy's appearance was only a small part of what startled Miranda. The biggest shock was the sweet smell of marijuana that hung around her like an invisible cloud. The odor was faint and covered by a hint of patchouli perfume but she knew that scent well and smelling it stirred a longing in her that was hard to deny.

Suddenly, what Miranda wanted more than anything else in the world was a joint and a cold can of beer.

Miranda had been clean and sober for almost four months, but the cravings had not gone away. Certain situations or people or scents brought back the longing as strongly as ever. Last week she had searched the Net reading blogs of former users. Some of them said it was five years before they stopped wanting a joint. She was hoping that wasn't true, but now, she wondered.

The moment she locked eyes with Lucy, they recognized themselves as kindred spirits. It was a fact Lucy acknowledged by holding her gaze a moment too long and giving a slight nod.

Then, suddenly she was off chatting merrily and greeting one and all. She flitted from group to group often hugging people or standing with her arm around their shoulder while the little girl called Hope trailed behind her.

Only minutes earlier as Miranda sat quietly talking to Beverly she felt a warm glow of acceptance, but after she saw Lucy nothing was quite the same. Now, she knew the truth. She didn't belong to this group anymore than Lucy.

"Melody!" Lucy purred and moved toward the pastors' wife. Hips leading the way, shoulders thrown back and both hands extended, she looked like a bad imitation of a movie star on opening night.

"As pretty as ever I see, and still keeping the good citizens of Thyme in line."

Melody offered her hand which Lucy took in both of hers, then the younger woman moved in closer for an embrace. "I am so glad to see you again!" she almost squealed.

"Hello, Lucy" Melody pulled away from the embrace. "Will your stay be a short one?"

Instantly, she wished she had chosen other words. The last thing she wanted was to make this troubled, wayward girl feel unwelcome.

"Only a couple of weeks. I simply must get back to Dallas. I'm finishing cosmetology school, you know, and they won't hold my place if I am late. Maybe you have heard of it. Jason's School of Beauty over on Harry Hinds Boulevard? It's quite famous, you know."

The only thing Melody knew was that Lucy had started various college programs and trade schools half a dozen times in her young life. At least three times she had announced she was getting her beauticians license. But, there was no profit in going over old history, so Melody's eyes softened and her voice was genuine when she said, "I wish you every success."

"Thank you! I'm so excited!" Lucy pulled her shoulders up and arched her eyebrows making her look like a little girl waiting for Christmas. It was enough to make the pastor's wife believe that maybe this time things would be different. One could hope.

"And, how are you and Pastor Phelps these days?"

"Oh, about the same. The children have a Christmas program the fifth of December. Hope has a part. Perhaps you could come back and see her perform."

"Of course! I never miss anything in my little girl's life," she lied then changed the subject. "I guess you stay busy with all the church activities and your piano lessons, too."

"Oh, yes! We are having a recital this afternoon. After church this morning I barely had time to finish lunch, run a brush through my hair and dash on some makeup before heading out the door for the baby shower."

As she spoke, Melody flipped the edge of her hair on the word 'brush' and swiped her index finger lightly across her eyelid illustrating the speed with which she was forced to apply her makeup.

"Oh, no, no, no!" Lucy took the offending hand in one of her own then placed the other over her heart as though overcome with tragedy. "One should never do that!"

"Do what?"

"The muscles of the index finger are far too strong to use on the delicate tissue of the eye area."

Melody gazed at her open mouthed, but Lucy took her amazement as admiration.

"One should always apply eye makeup only with the ring finger." She spread Melody's fingers and pointed to the proper digit. "The muscles here are among the weakest in the hand; perfect for

JaKobe's Assignment

spreading eye shadow without damage to the skin." Letting go of her hand she smiled with the benevolent glow of a benefactor. "Proper makeup technique is one of the first things we learn at Jason's."

"I'll remember that," Melody stammered and studied Lucy with an incredulous gaze. The girl stirred such strong, conflicted feelings. Pity was there. And, outrage. She hated Ludy's arrogance and had just been personally insulted. But, she was sad for little Hope and longed for the day when things might truly be different for the tragic family. In the end, all the feelings converged in a flood and froze somewhere in her throat allowing none to achieve dominance.

"Glad to be of help," said Lucy then she raced across the room to embrace Beverly and coo over baby Rosaline.

By two-forty most had been served. Miranda was back in the rocker with Tina on one side and Beverly on the other. Melody stepped to the center of the room and cleared her throat calling for attention. It was time for the next stage of the affair to begin and she dare not let things fall behind schedule.

"Well, ladies," she said in a clear, strong voice, "I want to thank you all for coming. New life is always a welcome and blessed event and we are glad to honor Miranda with this little party.

"There is a card that will be circulating while Miranda opens the gifts. We ask each of you to sign—even if you have already signed the register—and add a special prayer or blessing for baby, . . ." She paused and looked directly at Miranda. "Have you decided what to name her yet?"

"It's not firm but it will probably be Nicole."

"A blessing for baby Nicole.

"As we begin, Norma, will you lead us in prayer?"

In her role as pastor's wife, Melody often led in prayer. She was a good speaker, polished and fresh. Praying in public had never bothered her.

Until lately.

For the past several months there had not only been those strange, disconnected times of drifting away, but something deep inside her was restless, on edge and agitated. All the activity and schedules and projects were empty. Even the spiritual rituals of prayer, Bible study and church had an unreal element to them. At the moment, she didn't want to pray before this group of women. Maybe she couldn't.

Norma's lyrical voice thanked the Lord for the church, for family, for Miranda's new baby, for another day. She asked God's blessing on all who had come and expressed appreciation for the hostesses who had sponsored the event then said "Amen" with a finality that signaled the start of the next thing on the agenda.

Beverly handed Miranda the first present. It was large pink striped bag stuffed with white tissue and Beverly poised her pen over a tablet ready to record the gift and name of giver for later

JaKobe's Assignment

convenience when writing thank-you notes. The rocker began to slowly drift back and forth and in spite of her earlier discomfort Miranda felt her shield slowly dissolving. Lucy was still in the room, but she wasn't talking at the moment and the only thing Miranda could smell was baby powder.

As socially required, the mother-to-be read it completely before diving deeper into the sack, but when her hand touched the present a smile spread across her face, lighting up her eyes and brightening her cheeks. It was a basket containing power, baby oil, tearless shampoo and a small, soft brush.

One by one the packages kept coming. Each item drew an assortment of coos and comments from those assembled. Then each gift was passed hand-to-hand down the line for the guest to inspect more closely. When the gift came to the open space in the horseshoe of chairs, two little girls made a game of ferrying the packages from one side of the room to the other.

This was fun.

About half the gifts had been opened when Miranda was handed a box wrapped in pink paper and tied with real, three inch wide, pink gingham ribbon.

"Oh, look," someone said and a hush fell over the room. She cast a curious glance at Beverly.

"Is this something special?"

"Yes and no," Beverly teased.

A voice from the crowd said, "I thought Margaret was in the hospital."

"Oh, but you know Margaret," said another. "She dropped her gift by the church on Monday."

Beverly whispered an explanation. "The present is from Margaret Mc Clawson. She always wraps her gifts this way. It's her trademark. Pink if the baby is a girl or blue if a boy."

When the paper and ribbon came off and the box was opened, a tiny dress with embroidery on the yoke, ruffled hem, and matching ruffled panties was held up for all to admire.

"Isn't that darling!"

"One of her best!"

"Where does she get those patterns?"

"Her little girl outfits always look so dainty!"

"Margaret is quite the seamstress," Beverly spoke low so only Miranda could hear. "Dozens of babies have been brought home in outfits she created."

It was Norma's turn to examine the little dress. "Do you remember when everything in the nursery had to be yellow or white because we didn't know what kind of baby we were having until the child got here?" The comment drew quizzical looks from the younger women and Norma laughed. The room had suddenly been divided into those over fifty and those younger.

"You young ladies don't realize how much times have changed!" she continued. "When my Judy was born in World War Two, Herman was overseas with the army. I was living with my parents. My daddy would not let me put my feet on the floor for the first two weeks. He even carried me to the bathroom!"

A chorus of "No way" and "You must be joking," encouraged other older women to join the conversation.

"I was never allowed to look directly at a fire. My aunt said that it might create a red birthmark on the baby's face."

"It was a bad sign to have a child born on Wednesday."

"Remember confinement?" One of the oldest in the group asked. "In my day, once a woman began to show, she was expected to withdraw from society and not reenter until the child was a couple of months old. We were not allowed to go to town or even to church."

"I remember when it was very poor manners—even shocking—for anyone to say the word 'pregnant.' A woman was always 'with child' or 'p.g.' but never 'pregnant'. Only animals were talked about in those terms."

"Remember the ring test?" Era Lou asked. Several of the younger women shook their heads and looked at each other. "The only way we had of knowing if the baby was a boy or girl was with a ring. The expectant mother tied the ring on the end of a string and then lay down on a bed. A female relative held the string above her tummy. If the ring began to swing up and down the baby was a boy, but if it moved side to side the baby was a girl."

"Did that work?"

"Well, it predicted each one of my six kids correctly."

"That doesn't count," said another voice. "All you ever had were boys so the job wasn't too hard!"

Laughter spread around the room.

Norma joined back in the conversation. "Yet, we had an advantage in those years that you younger gal's don't," she smiled. "You have to stay pregnant much longer."

A flood of voices challenged her. "It's true! I swear it!"

"Norma, you know better than to swear," Era Lou scolded.

"Miranda, how far along were you when you found out you were expecting?"

"I guess about three or four weeks."

"Okay. Era Lou, how far along were you before you knew for sure another baby was on the way?"

"That all depends. When my last, Ronny Joe, was born the doctor thought I was going through the change. We wasn't sure he was coming until a little more than two months before he got here!"

"See! That proves my point," Norma stated triumphantly. "Miranda has to stay pregnant for eight months and you got by with two."

Era Lou caught the point and laughed with the rest of the women, but felt compelled to continue the argument anyway.

"You know that doesn't count. I carried my child just as long as Miranda will hers. My only problem was that old Doc Spencer didn't know how to kill the rabbit."

"What are you talking about?" a young voice asked.

"Child, child," said Era Lou shaking her head, "Way back in the dark ages, the only way we knew for sure that we were expecting was with a test that the doctor did with a rabbit. I am not sure how it all worked, but it involved me giving the doctor a small bottle of pee—which was very embarrassing—and if a child was on the way, the rabbit died."

"Oh, gross!"

"Not as gross as finding out you had to make room for baby number six in less than three months!"

Norma's voice joined the group again. "There's a sermon in there somewhere."

The statement was a familiar thing for Norma to say, but Era Lou groaned.

"Norma, you always see a sermon in everything. What are you thinking-up now?"

Her tone was mildly exasperated and tinged with a little jealousy. Norma seemed to have a talent Era Lou did not possess. The sermons she saw illustrated through every day events were always clear after Norma explained them, but Era Lou could never spot them first. It gave her the uncomfortable feeling of being slightly dense.

"Don't you see?" said Norma. "The rabbit had to die for a woman to know her body contained new life. Jesus had to die not only for us to know we had new life but to be the source of that life." The laugher changed to serious expressions and several around the room nodded their understanding of the strange thing Norma was explaining.

Miranda followed the conversation with a light spirit, but now she was completely lost. It was great fun to hear how females of a different generation experienced childbirth but, when the subject shifted from babies to religion, she was adrift in a sea without shoreline. Babies were within her experience. Jesus was not.

"Oh, I get it!" The voice came from a child of no more than ten. "Jesus died to make us alive and when the rabbit died it let the mother know the baby was alive."

"Close enough," Norma smiled.

Miranda smiled, too, pretending she understood it all perfectly but inside she felt uncomfortably like a charlatan who had crashed a party uninvited. Even the children in this group seemed to know more about this religious stuff than she.

The rest of the packages were opened while Beverly kept a list of each gift and the donor then, carefully looking in the empty crib, she said, "I think that was the last one."

"No, there's one more," announced Tina. "I saved the best for last." She fished deep inside her

JaKobe's Assignment

oversized handbag and pulled out an envelope handing it to her niece. "Your uncle Jack and I wanted to do something special."

When Miranda opened the large envelope, two items fell into her lap. The first was a stack of money still wrapped with the strip of paper from the bank and the second was a card with a photograph inside.

"The money is given in the name of my dear, departed sister, Victoria Elliott, and the picture is of the gift your uncle and I want you to have."

She spread her hands wide and faced the audience rather than her niece. "As you will all see, the bassinette is too large for a car. It will be delivered by one of Elder Bentley's company pickups next week."

The picture appeared to be some kind of small bed or covered basket. It was about three feet long and a little over one foot wide, mounted on a frame that held it off the floor, but the thing that caught everyone's attention was its elaborate covering. Yard after yard of satin and lace drifted from the tiny bed in all directions. There was even a canopy above the bed mounted to a frame and more yards of illusion net hung from it in graceful folds.

A hush fell over the room.

Miranda sat holding the picture and the money in her lap. Thoughts of her mother brought tears to her eyes, but at the same time, she wondered about how much money was actually left in the trust fund.

Worst of all, if the bassinette was anything like its picture, finding a place to put it in their small apartment was going to be a real problem. It would easily take up a space six foot long, four foot wide and five feet high and, unless she missed her guess, all that lace was probably dry-clean-only.

Tina was delighted by the drama her gift caused. "Well, pass the picture around, dear" she encouraged. "You can deposit that thousand dollars through the ATM as we go home tonight."

With two short sentences, she had managed to stage a grand end to her niece's shower with herself as the star. She had also satisfied everyone's curiosity about how much money was bound in the thick wrapper. She also demonstrated the future she envisioned for the baby. The new princess had just been given her first throne.

JaKobe's Assignment

2:30 PM

The Streets of Thyme

The yellow Chevy Cobalt belonging to Steve Mullins whipped around an eighteen-wheeler and took possession of the inside lane. His eleven-year-old son felt the car sway and briefly lost sight of the tiny images on the three-inch screen of his Game Boy.

"Da-a-ad! You're making me mess up!" Dwayne complained from the back seat, but his dad ignored him and continued his conversation with his new girlfriend.

No matter, thought the boy, *I don't need him anyway.*

His score for Super Mario was better than ever and the weekend had not been as bad as he feared it might. Even his little brother, Casey, had not been too much of an ass.

Letting the word "ass" be part of his private thoughts gave him a feeling of power. He knew his mom would not approve, but there were a lot of things in his mind that his mom knew nothing about. Or anyone else.

He was sitting in the back seat by the driver-side window with Amanda Fisher sandwiched close beside him, but he knew how to seal himself off and be alone no matter what swirled around him. He simply closed his mind and she didn't exist. That, too, had a powerful aura. He felt like a man with his own secrets and his own mind. Nothing could violate that private space.

Amanda yawned as she watched glimpses of scenery pass in between the heads of her mom and the new boyfriend in the front seat. The girl was pouting but she worked hard at not letting it show on her face.

It wasn't fair for her to be stuck in the middle between the Mullen boys. At thirteen, she was older than either of them and should have been given first choice of where to sit. The place she was now perched wasn't even a real seat. The manufacturer had put in a third set of safety belts, but it was obvious they never intended for someone to actually sit there. Her legs were spread apart with one foot on each side of the hump in the floorboard and the raised, convertible armrest felt like a lump between her shoulder blades. At least the boys should have been made to share.

She wanted to ask how many more miles before they reached Thyme, but her mom had promised a new pair of jeans if she would be "good" this weekend and not upset anyone in the

Mullins family. It had been a long, boring weekend. She had earned those jeans and they better be Tommy Hilfiger.

In the seat on the passenger side, nine-year-old Casey was feeling uncomfortable for entirely different reasons. He was watching the space between the front seats as his father's hand moved to rest on Julie's knee. He wasn't sure why the sight made him feel strange, but it did. He turned his head and tried to concentrate on the passing scenery. It was no use.

Girls. They messed up everything. His dad had promised to take him alone on the paddleboat but when they started down to the dock Julie came, too. Bitterness and self-pity began to rise. Hot tears pushed behind his eyes but he was determined not to let them out. His Dad was always ga-ga over some new girlfriend leaving his son out in the cold. Casey felt as useless as the lifejackets that his dad tossed on the dock before they left.

Amanda leaned forward. "Mom, will we be stopping to eat before Steve takes us back to our apartment?"

Her mom shot a glance at Steve and cleared her throat. "Amanda, I wanted to talk to you about our apartment . . ." she began, but did not finish the thought. Steve felt her reluctance and filled the gap with a voice that was authoritative and clear.

"Kids, listen up," he began. Everyone turned toward him except Dwayne who studied his game and under his breath encouraged Mario to the next level.

"Julie and I have been talking about what a great time we all had being together this weekend. We're just like one, big family. It seems silly for people who are just like family to pay rent on separate apartments.

"You kids know that sometimes I sleep over at Julie's place and sometimes she is with me when you boys wake up in the morning. We're more than good friends and we have even been talking about getting married someday. So, while we are figuring out what we want to do, we thought we might as well rent a house together and save the money. Wouldn't it be great to be with each other all the time?"

At first there was only stoic silence from the backseat then Amanda did a few quick mental calculations. She was tired of the cramped apartment and since Steve had no daughters, if they got a house that meant a room of her own. The boys would only be present every other weekend and perhaps if her mom were married again, she would quit going out so much. "I think that would be great!"

Casey stared at her then tried to catch his father's eyes in the review mirror. "Aw, Dad. . ." he began.

"Now, Casey, you have always known that I might get serious about someone someday. I want your mom to be happy and I am sure she wants the same for me. Nothing would have to change.

Diane would still be your mom and Julie would be like a big sister. Don't you want me to have a chance to be happy?"

The statement was a terrible burden to place on the shoulders of a small boy. He squirmed and looked down; his dad added a bribe to the deal. "If we got a house with a backyard we could put up a trampoline and all have fun learning to do flips."

Everything was happening too fast. Casey was intimidated but did not know how to express his feelings, so he swallowed and followed Amanda's lead. "I guess it would be okay."

"That's my big boy. What about you Dwayne?"

"All live in one house? Sure." Super Mario was on level sixteen.

Julie leaned her cheek against the headrest and looked tenderly at Steve. It was so wonderful to have a man she could depend on.

Her soft, sun-kissed blond hair was falling in graceful waves as it flowed over her shoulders. "You handled that so well!" she complimented. "I never knew there could be a man like you. I think I must be the luckiest woman in the world."

Steve felt ten feet tall and invincible as he looked in her eyes. No condemnation. No demands. No arguments. Just pure admiration. In her eyes he found validation for everything he wanted to do and everything he longed to be. He winked at her and while driving with his left hand, pinched her breast with his right making her draw back and giggle.

The sign by the highway announced Wilson County and Steve eased off the accelerator slowing the car to seventy-five. Thyme would be just over the next hill. "You kids in the mood for McDonald's?"

Even Dwayne cheered. It had been a long time since breakfast.

They coasted to a stop in the parking lot and stretched muscles cramped by long hours of driving.

As they entered the restaurant Steve reached for Julie's hand. She smiled and glanced up at him through long lashes. Julie made him feel like a king and he was determined to keep that feeling no matter what it cost. Nothing could stop him. This was the kind of simple, satisfying life he wanted. Cool autumn weather, tables on the playground in the open air, Big Macs all around, obedient kids and the smile of a woman who adored him. Any tense moments the group experienced when he announced the possibility of moving in together melted into laughter.

Dwayne put his Game Boy aside long enough to inhale the food then feeling exhilarated by the fresh air, rose from the table and reached overhead for the bar that served as a brace between the overhead tunnel and a slide for small children. Pulling with his biceps and forearms he raised his feet off the ground and tipped his chin above the bar with a smooth motion.

"I can do that," said Amanda. "Watch."

Dwayne watched. She reached her arms overhead drawing up the red knit top to expose perfect skin and a slender waist. Half inch of panty rose above the top of her low-cut jeans and he wondered if they were like the thongs he had seen advertised in the newspaper. She pulled up smoothly and tipped her delicate chin above the bar dropping back to the ground with a smug grin.

"Bet ya can't do as many as I can," he said. He took her place and pulled up three times then sat down again to watch. The competitor in him was interested in the number of repetitions this girl might pull, but a deeper instinct was interested in another display of long legs, low-cut jeans and bare midriff.

*****

Although completely unnoticed by the humans, benevolent spirit beings were also watching this childish competition. Two guardian angels and a warrior had followed Diane's children onto the playground.

A guardian had been assigned to each of the boys since before birth. As their name implied they were purely defensive spirits and their only job was to guard the human will thus making sure it remained fully functioning and free.

Under normal circumstances their protection would have been enough. But, Diane was well known in the spirit world and powerful in prayer. This, along with her high opposition level, made her—and everything she loved—an open target of the enemy, so the extra precaution of a warrior seemed warranted and several weeks ago one had been dispatched to join the group.

Vinyon was a warrior angel of the first rank and if human eyes could have seen him, they might have guessed him a page out of history. Ancient history.

Although the angel's clothing was, in truth, a living extension of his being, what appeared to be garments told much about him and the role he had played in Kingdom work.

His light brown tunic seemed to be woven of heavy threads and it hung loosely to just below his hips. His legs were wrapped in a more finely woven fabric of dark brown. His boots were soft tan suede, almost moccasin in construction, and laced up to his knees with thin strips of leather. The wide belt at his waist appeared to be heavy, ornately carved leather. Jet black hair streamed shoulder length while piercing eyes, high cheekbones, broad forehead and prominent nose gave him the aura of an American Indian.

Vinyon had been a warrior for over fifteen hundred years and he wore the same form he had chosen when first assigned to earth.

This wasn't a statement of pride or even preference of style on his part. He had simply found the form useful and never seen the need to

JaKobe's Assignment

change. It served him well and he cared little for anything beyond that.

His orders were simple: act as a support for the guardians and watch for opportunities to serve Diane's children. It seemed far too small a task for one of the first rank but, like any good soldier, he didn't question only obeyed.

Vinyon had willingly joined this group and watched and learned but, so far, found very little use for his sword. The minor demons who presented themselves were dispatched by the guardians and it had been an uneventful tour of duty.

As to be expected, when Dwayne and Amanda started their competition, the spirits moved to a higher level of caution. Not that there was any cause for alarm; sexual attraction was natural for humans—even very young ones. Yet, the spirits also knew that many natural attractions could go wrong in a hurry if proper controls were not applied.

Many permissible—even blessed— appetites such as food, security, power, and even a desire for comfort were potential opportunities for the enemy. So, as Dwayne's eyes locked on Amanda's exposed navel and slowly sinking jeans, spiritual tensions rose.

The guardians moved to place the children at their backs while scanning the immediate area before them for signs of danger. Vinyon floated upward taking a position just above the playground slide where he watched both distant and near activity with keen, dark eyes; his feet wide apart and his sword drawn.

It was the guardians who saw them first: Five demon spirits rising through the pavement just outside the playground fence. They were small beings, but lightning-quick and ready for battle. The guardians began their defense.

Moving their hands with large, circular motions, small burst of energy were released from their fingers and palms until they formed glistening streaks green and blue. Faster and faster the streaks whirled and blended until becoming solid shields of energy. Any spirit coming in direct contact with the shields would instantly be stripped of power and few would risk getting close.

Vinyon, too, spotted the enemy and dropped to the ground taking his place between these new invaders and the guardians. He was ready for war, but would not be lightly drawn into battle until the enemy made a move.

The demons separated from one another forming a semicircle while they studied Vinyon with yellow eyes. They looked more like the gargoyles fit to adorn medieval castles than creatures of the earth and howled and hissed as they moved.

Three of the beings had leathery, bat-like wings with feet like those of wolves. Two others had claw-like feet similar to an eagle's talon yet their bodies were covered with fur rather than feathers and they had hands, but no wings. All were uniformly dark ranging from true black to purple and varying shades of black-green. They all possessed wide mouths with fangs and bulging, unblinking eyes.

The spirits continued their apparently aimless motion yet did not attack. They feared the shields of the guardians but Vinyon was torment waiting to happen. Warriors had been known to chase spirits to the very gates of hell inflicting pain and loss all along the way.

It was all they could do to hold their ground as he watched them with steady, piercing eyes so they gnashed their teeth and howled louder encouraging each other. They, too, had orders and they dared not turn back.

The warrior's whole body seemed alert. With his feet wide apart and knees slightly bent, he looked as though he could spring in any direction with equal ease, yet he stood as motionless and unmoving as a rock. Even his eyes did not move but rather took in all five creatures at once and the glow of his sword pulsated like something alive.

As the standoff continued Vinyon became suspicious. There was a strong smell of fear emanating from the five spirits. He suspected they must have been unusually hungry or abnormally frightened. But, before he could consider the question further, the semicircle widened and the two on the left pulled together as though grouping for a possible joint attack.

Suddenly, the central being rushed low at Vinyon while the one on the right flank jumped and flapped his stubby wings in an effort to land on the warrior from above. He countered both with swift, decisive strokes making glancing contact with their membranes and drawing away energy that flowed from their wounds like ink dissipating in water.

The two drew back letting the stronger ones form the first rank, but still, the group did not withdraw. The three in front made quick, false starts keeping Vinyon alert trying to predict their next move.

With the warrior focused on the five enemies before him and the guardians busy holding defense shields before the boys, no one noticed the two wisps of smoke slowly materializing on the other side of the slide.

Unseen and unchallenged, the smoke became dark shadows then thin strips of color appeared. Finally, two more beings from hell took form. Angels from the dark side.

They shuddered and shook themselves as they adjusted to earth, then appraised one another with a smiled. The two spirits looked exactly like the sons of Diane Kirkland.

*****

In the small house on Apple Street Diane rubbed her eyes. Her heart was still heavy and lonely but the intense grief and sexual need had been washed away by sleep. How long had she been out?

JaKobe's Assignment

She pulled around the clock on the bedside table and looked at its face. Strange. She never took naps, but the clock said she had been asleep almost two hours. Maybe she was coming down with something. She lay back and listened to the silent house. Even clocks didn't tick anymore. Steve would keep the boys tonight and take them to school Monday.

Silence.

With a suddenness that surprised her she threw both legs off the bed, sat up and opened her voice. Marching to the bathroom military style, the volume of the melody increased as though she were trying to fill all the empty, silent spaces with joyous, colored notes.

"When God created living things He knew He'd need a way to share our fears, our questions and our dreams." The Gather hymn[15] flooded her small space. "Oh, there were words, but words won't do when joy swells up inside. There simply had to be a better way!"

Diane finished her physical obligations, flushed the toilet and cranked up the volume until the windows reverberated with the sound. "Then He said, 'Sing!' From a laughing heart. Just sing! When the night is darkest. Sing! Let your joy explode and let music fill the air!"

She stomped to the refrigerator and opened the door. Nothing in there worthy of note. She slammed it shut and continued a concert designed for her own heart alone. "Then He said, 'Sing!'"

She tossed her Bible, a package of crackers, three stale cookies and a warm can of Dr. Pepper into a backpack. Throwing it over her shoulder she continued the melody. *"Just sing! When the night is darkest. Sing! Let your joy explode and let music fill the air."*

Very little within Diane felt like singing, but she instinctively knew that she needed space and air and a new attitude. Singing accomplished all those goals. There were country roads outside brimming with brisk fall weather. She would get out of this silent house and enjoy it. Out there, alone in the car, no one would care how loud she sang or how long she cried. Everything else could wait. Right now, she needed the Lord!

*****

Across town, another kind of spiritual activity was unfolding. Having left a wise woman to work with Jonathan, JaKobe was looking for Rachael. He traced her energy through several streets and finally caught up with her on a Farm-to-Market road just north of town. She and Centrace were following the pickup belonging to Garrison Black and from a distance it sounded like they were arguing.

"Will you please give Rachael a new assignment?" said Centrace as JaKobe approached the two. "Angels wondering around earth without specific duties become a real nuisance to those of us who have work to do."

JaKobe's Assignment

"Give her an assignment? You know perfectly well that I don't make assignments while robed in this garb," said JaKobe indicating his human appearance.

"Well, excuse me!" said Rachael with mock offence. "But I still say your tactic is wrong and you would have better results using an emotional appeal."

"Children, children," JaKobe repeated the phrase he had heard exasperated parents use then floated down, squeezed between the two angels and put an arm around each angelic shoulder. "How can we settle this matter peaceably?" He knew their banter was good natured, but it seemed to have a serious undertone.

"The problem," explained Centrace as he moved away from JaKobe's uncomfortable closeness, "is that I have a human male who has spent years in the military. He thinks like a soldier. Yet, Rachael wants me to work through silly emotions rather than logic to accomplish my mission. I know my human and I don't think he would respond to an emotional appeal."

"All humans respond to emotion," said Rachael defensively as she, too, moved away from JaKobe. Mimicking humans was all right within limits but JaKobe sometimes took the game too far.

"What's the assignment?" he asked.

Centrace sounded more than a little exasperated. "It's Diane again. She is not my responsibility and I don't think I should even be involved with this, but you know the compassion of the Final Authority." He spread his hands helplessly palms upward.

"So, why did you get involved?"

"It's that *Father and Son Banquet* over at Grace Community. Diane knows her former husband cannot be depended on to take the boys. More than once he has broken their hearts by canceling out on a big event at the last moment. She is deeply grieved and has been petitioning heaven for a solution.

"So, the obvious solution is to have a man who is faithful take the boys. My human is their Sunday school teacher and he has been selected for the task."

"That still doesn't explain why you are involved." said JaKobe. "Wouldn't it be simpler to get Diane's angel to encourage her to ask the man?"

"I already thought about a direct approach and discussed it with Phennia. But she believes asking for the favor would embarrass Diane and since that human's opposition scale is already at the limit, I could not insist. Phennia even had the cheek to suggest that getting my human to take the initiative would be good for his character! Imagine that! My human's character is none of her concern."

"I heard about that banquet this morning," said JaKobe. "I have a temporary assignment with the pastor of that church."

"Well, next time the banquet idea comes up, remind your pastor-friend that his choice of words is certainly creating problems for the rest of us." Centrace grunted with disgust. *"Father and Son Banquet.* The very idea! Doesn't he know the pain that creates for fatherless boys?"

"Maybe next time they'll call it, *Men-and-Boy's-Eating-Time."* JaKobe smiled.

"Maybe," said Centrace without mirth, "but meanwhile, I have to find a way to complete this assignment."

In the truck below them, Garrison fiddled with the radio trying to bring in the public broadcasting station in Louisiana. *Prairie Home Companion* kept cutting out while the host described a problem in Lake Woebegone. It was frustrating.

For ten years listening to the program had been a Sunday afternoon tradition. He hated it when cloud cover cheated him out of a clear signal. Oh, well, he would not have had time to hear the end of the story anyway. The Pick and Pay was just ahead.

Garrison could not believe he had interrupted a perfectly fine nap for another trip to the store! They had already stopped by the supermarket on the way home from church, yet here he was headed for the Pick and Pay convenience store.

Why was it impossible to get everything at one stop? During his military years he would never have put up with such disorganization!

He shrugged and sighed. Perhaps there were just some fundamentals of civilian life to which he would have to adjust. After all, in a way, it was his fault. If he had remembered that there was no coffee for breakfast during the first stop, he wouldn't be in the truck now.

He had lain there on his back with Emily sleeping soundly beside him and glared at the ceiling. Why had neither one of them thought about the coffee? The more he considered the problem, the more complex it became. They could pick up some on the way back to evening services; that would save gas and the coffee would be there for breakfast. But, they also needed some filters.

Filters at Pick and Pay would cost too much, and, besides, the store was small. They probably didn't have the right size. Their only good selection was the well stocked ice cream freezer. Only place in town that consistently carried Butter Pecan with Chocolate Chunks.

The more he thought of the ice cream the more discontent he became. That sandwich for lunch hadn't lasted very long. The coffee could sit in the car, but if they got ice cream on the way to evening service it would melt. They could stop to get the ice cream after church, but if they did, he wouldn't be able to snack on it this afternoon.

The discontented human lay on his left side and then his right. It was foolish to go to the store for one item, but he really wanted that ice cream.

If he got the filters along with the coffee and included the ice cream, that would be three items.

JaKobe's Assignment

He could also fill up the truck with gas while he was there. That made four things. Was that enough to justify a trip?

Exasperated, he threw back the light blanket and put both feet on the floor with a thump. The lure of a big, cold bowl of Butter Pecan with Chocolate Chunks was just too much. Having yielded to temptation and justified his action, Garrison was soon on the road.

As he approached the outskirts of Thyme, he dropped his speed from 75 to 60 then slowed again as the convenience store came in sight.

"Okay," said JaKobe as the truck pulled to a stop, "How are you going to handle this Centrace?"

The angel sighed. "You win, Rachael. I'll try the emotional route. Only, this better work."

Rachael focused her vision looking through the walls of the store. Inside, an unknown man and young boy were standing in line ready to pay for gas. She smiled. This would be easy.

As Garrison entered the store and made his way to the back for ice cream, Centrace closed his eyes for a quick review of his records. Surely, somewhere in all that data there was something he could use as an emotional trigger.

His eyes opened a slit and noticed Rachael. She was standing behind a man and boy. She gestured toward them with both arms wide. "Why not use these?"

Why not, indeed? It did seem providential. Garrison's mother had been widowed when he was twelve, so he had memories of personally being a fatherless boy, but the angel needed something to encourage those memories and make an emotional connection with Diane's sons.

Nodding, Centrace smiled then reached over and drew the attention of the child to the red candy on the bottom shelf.

Six-year-old Tommy surveyed the tempting array. "Dad, can I have a Twister?" he asked as a stranger walked up behind him with a half-gallon of ice cream in his hands.

"Not this time."

Garrison smiled down at the boy. Red "licorice" had always been his favorite, too. Memories of being small returned to him. He knew how it felt to stand by an unavailable rack of candy.

The little boy steadied himself with both hands on the rack and gently thumped the base of the display with the toe of his sneaker. "I could share it with my sister," he offered smiling up at his dad who responded with a small laugh. Garrison smiled, too.

"So, you want to bargain with me, is that it?" the dad asked.

The boy seemed a little confused by the concept of bargaining but wouldn't give up. "Can I have it, Dad? I'll share."

"All right." The father looked at the man behind him in line. "Kids," he grunted. "They sure get disappointed when they can't have something." Then he changed the subject. "This is

JaKobe's Assignment

a really long line. Hope your ice cream doesn't melt."

"Yeah, me too." Garrison responded as he watched the small boy take a box from the shelf.

"Can I open it now?" asked the boy.

"No."

"Please?"

"We haven't paid for it."

"Please?"

His dad let out a long breath. "I guess we can pay for an open box as easily as a sealed one." He ruffled his son's hair with his fingers. "Save some for your sister."

Garrison smiled as the aroma of cherry drifted upward and with the fragrance came the past. One thought pulled another into consciousness:

Why did we call those sticky, red ropes "licorice"? > They aren't even black. > That kid sure seemed attached to his dad. > My dad bought me cherry licorice. > (feelings of loneliness.) > Boys really need their dads. > The banquet will be good for fathers and sons. > Probably all ages will be there. > Mike'll bring his boy. > Dwayne and Casey weren't in Sunday school this morning. > Wonder who'll take them? > Not Steve, that's for sure.

The line moved, Garrison paid his bill and returned to the truck.

The trio of angels took up their positions floating in the air some ten feet behind the truck. Garrison looked both ways and turned onto the highway.

"What do you think?" asked Rachael. "Did it work?"

"Too soon to tell," said Centrace. "I picked up an increased level in compassion as he looked at the kid and the scent of the candy should have encouraged memories of himself with his dad. But, I don't know if he made the connection between those memories and the loneliness of Diane's boys."

"Probably not," said JaKobe.

Rachael watched as Garrison fished his cell phone from his pocket and began pushing buttons. "I'll bet my halo he did," she said.

"Well, if he is going to do anything, it will have to be soon" said Centrace, "because once he gets home he'll be one mad human."

"Why?"

"He forgot the coffee."

*****

Balancing the back pack over one shoulder, Diane scooped her purse from the living room floor where she had left it. *"Just sing! When the night is darkest. Sing! Let your joy explode and let music fill the air."*

Despite the loud, joyous sound of her voice, a tear trickled down her cheek. There had been so many disappointments; so much pain. She didn't think her heart could stand the weight of another trial.

JaKobe's Assignment

"You can sing when there's nothing else to do. Sing! When something deep inside of you tells you that life is still a wonder, just throw back your head and sing!" Diane continued the concert as the front door slammed shut behind her.

In the now silent house, a telephone began to ring.

*****

As they stood side by side the two dark angels were one of hell's strangest oddities: rivals who moved in concert with one another in a way that looked very much like cooperation.

For as long as hell had memory these two challengers had competed. On a few occasions they inflicted more wounds on each other than on the enemy when their fierce competition drove them to a fever pitch. Yet now, they stood quietly passing congratulatory smiles between themselves as they prepared for the next stage of battle.

Together they had conceived the current strategy and were pleased to see it working so well. As far as they were concerned, the five demons now teasing the warrior were bottom feeders in hell's food chain. They were expendable vermin with whom they agreed to share the spoils of victory out of necessity rather than generosity. In fact, the warrior, the guardians, the five demons and the other humans were all expendable. Their only concern was the two boys and even they were only means to an end.

The situation that had given birth to this strange partnership was the open attention heaven had given one earthly woman: Diane Kirkland. She was constantly surrounded with activity from the Light and it was rumored that she would one day wield strong influence in the heavenly realm.

When the warrior was dispatched to protect her children, hell took notice and the stakes of the game were raised. Anywhere the favor of God appeared to shine, the attention of hell was drawn with corresponding fervor. Diane was no exception.

Yet, it wasn't really even Diane that drew hell's notice. Their real target was the object of her worship: The Alpha and Omega; the Beginning and the End, the total and ultimate Final Authority.

To damage Diane would be to insult the Power that she depended on. To break her heart would be the same as breaking the heart of Jesus. To strengthen and accentuate her poor character traits would be to destroy the work of the Holy Spirit. To create pain and distress in her life would open her to the temptation of disbelieving God, thus changing her future role in the Kingdom.

Thwarting God's purpose in her life would be a victory for hell. And, the best way to achieve all of those goals was through her children.

Diane's children were her weakest point. She could release her own life to the will of God. She could let go of her dreams. She could watch her marriage crumble and be rejected as her husband walked off with another woman. But, the prospect of surrendering her children totally to the will of a God whom she could not see was a step she had only imperfectly taken and even then with much trembling and disbelief along the way.

To hell, the children were a means to an end. They were a tool for fighting God and destroying His work on earth. The children would be a path leading them to the ultimate satisfaction: rebellion that inflicted pain on the God of the Universe.

That was a thing for which they constantly thirsted and the possibility of enjoying the satisfaction of God's pain had drawn Arilus and Benkat together.

The team of spirits had studied their targets well and their plans were clear. They could not overpower the children and take possession of their wills directly because of the guardians, but that did not mean they were helpless.

Just as the human body might have a helmet protecting the head, while an arm or vein in the leg was exposed to attack, so with the soul. The will of the children might be sheltered and free for the time being but with care and planning other elements could be targeted and exploited.

In the physical world, if any part of a body was sufficiently wounded, that site could be made to fester until the human became concerned with little else. Over time, such wounds could poison and destroy the whole organism. In a similar fashion, if a demon could use shame or hopelessness or addiction or selfishness to sufficiently wound, the entire organism—body and soul—would eventually be vulnerable to decay.

Before they left hell, each dark angel had carefully studied the boy's behavior and marked character traits that appeared to be the most vulnerable. Dwayne had learned to manage the pain he had experienced thus far by growing hard and independent. He pulled himself aloof and moved in a fantasy world of invincibility scoffing at other humans from behind his shield of pride. Casey had chosen the path of self-pity and was quickly learning to manipulate and punish others when they slighted him.

Setting up a base of operation inside these ripe fields would be easy. If everything went according to plan, they could dispose of the warrior, circumvent the guardians and enter the children at the designated character points.

Once inside, they would be somewhat sheltered from the guardian's reach, and then slowly, over time, as they pushed and tempted working that one weak trait, corruption would spread and eventually even the will of the children could be eroded until only fragments of human likeness remained and the spirits held full sway.

The five imps they had bribed still held Vinyon's attention with constantly shifting motions. Arilus glanced anxiously at Benkat. Although breathless and bloodless, they could feel the excitement build. With unhurried precision

JaKobe's Assignment

they crouched to the ground. Vinyon parried first left then right with his five antagonists as the dark angels inched closer.

Lower, still lower to the ground, they pushed themselves. They wanted to be above the pavement for instant reaction but if Vinyon glimpsed them as the slithered behind him, he would ignore the demons before him and escape would be impossible. The timing was critical. An experienced warrior would soon suspect the demons were only a diversionary tactic.

Together, fingertip to finger tip, they made contact between them while stretching their opposite arm wide and forming a semicircle. Vinyon's feet danced before them and the demons moved left pressuring him backward and to the right.

The moment of victory came as Vinyon thrust directly forward impaling a demon clean in the center. He also stepped backward grounding himself and giving more power to the thrust and his foot made solid contact with Benkat's arm.

The arc of power was like an explosion as righteousness and unrighteousness collided. Like a vacuum, the darkness sucked up life while giving back nothing.

Vinyon felt the jolt like searing heat and knew he had seen his last battle. Power flowed from him in an instant. Weak, disoriented, and helpless he tumbled toward the ground.

But, at that critical moment, three other events took place. Events that would forever change the life of two human children.

For the first event, Arilus and Benkat were knocked stiffly erect as more power than they had ever imagined surged through them. What phenomenal success! They turned toward the children with curled lips and exposed teeth. The rest should be easy.

All they needed now was to concentrate on a specific character weakness, draw it to the surface and grab hold.

Second, the guardians saw Vinyon fall and knew their power was no match for whoever had caused such catastrophe. With high-pitched screams they called for help even as they drew into tight knots around the will of each child.

And, third, Vinyon saw a bird.

*****

Amanda was determined to pull one more repetition than Dwayne. Her muscles began to shake with the strain, but on the count of four her chin came even with the bar. She dropped to the ground, put her hands on her hips, and gave him a flirtatious flutter of her eye lashes. "I told you I could win."

Julie and Steve who had been watching the competition, were startled by the open flirting. Julie laughed nervously and Steve choked on his

JaKobe's Assignment

cola. "Are you sure my son is safe with your daughter?" he teased.

Then, they both laughed as the tension eased. Casey looked up from his fries and ketchup. "What's so funny?" Their laughter increased as they watched his naïve, innocent eyes.

That was when the blackbird fell.

The bird had been sitting on top of the slide considering the half-eaten hamburger that a former patron had thrown beside the trashcan. The tempting morsel lay in plain sight and no other living thing paid it any attention. No enemies. No competition from other birds. The only problem was the humans.

The bird cocked his head considering whether he could get the burger and fly before they attacked him. But as he sat there feeling his desire for food struggle against his desire for safety, the bird was suddenly and unexplainably seized by another instinct.

This last instinct was far stronger and more compelling than either food or safety. It was a sudden, undeniable urge to protect one's young and it consumed the bird as it fluttered to the ground with pitiful cries landing less than three feet from where Dwayne stood.

Dwayne jumped and Amanda squealed.

"Dad! Look! A hurt bird!"

"She's not hurt. That's a mother bird and she's pretending she has a broken wing in order to draw us away from her nest."

"No, she's not. She's really hurt!" Dwayne reached for the bird as it fluttered in circles then moved toward the table where the family sat.

"I can catch her!" Casey joined the race. "Watch out, Julie. She's under the table!"

Julie squealed and pulled up her feet.

"She's not hurt!" shouted Steve, "She's just pretending!"

"Dad! She's coming your way!"

Unable to resist being caught up in the fun, Steve at last joined the chase and as the bird fluttered past him, the family dissolved in laughter.

The man was as determined to show his powers to Julie as Dwayne had been to win over Amanda. He chased the bird through the tangled web of supports for the ball pool. "I've got her trapped!" he announced as he straddled the end of the slide and blocked the bird underneath with his hands.

The black bird, seeing the solid slide above, the ball net behind and large tennis shoes to the left and right, panicked. The little creature was driven to the only available exit: Straight forward. Like a shot, it darted between Steve's hands and burst into the sunlight.

"I got it!" he foolishly declared. Grabbing for the blur of black feathers, he tripped headlong, landing on his shoulder and rolling to a stop by the trashcan.

*****

As Vinyon collapsed, the five demons rushed forward to suck way any remnants of energy still within the fallen warrior. Like vultures, they bit and tore away pieces glutting themselves with the life of another.

Arilus and Benkat ignored them. They didn't need them. Knowing they had only a fraction of time before reinforcements responded to the guardians call, each turned toward their target.

They readied themselves and lunged at the laughing, running children but were shocked beyond measure as they slipped clean through their targets and landed rolling across the pavement on the other side. Both clutched and grasped and screamed as they felt the small humans slip past. Latching on to the children was like trying to hold on to the surface of a sheet of glass that had been covered with oil!

Something had gone wrong. Very wrong. All their work and planning and efforts netted them nothing but one disabled warrior. Fury consumed them and as heavenly reinforcements arrived they turned on one another with accusations and curses then vanished from sight.

Responding to the call of the guardians, heavenly host came from every direction. Warriors and personal angels and others who were simply unassigned rushed to the aid of their fallen comrade and as quickly as they arrived, the battle was over.

Outnumbered and overwhelmed the hell's emissaries had fled. Only the battered, emaciated form of Vinyon languishing on the ground gave evidence of what had transpired.

Maltus was the first to Vinyon's side. It hurt to see his old friend so destroyed and in pain. He reached cradling his head with his hand. A small amount of warm, life-energy flowed from his touch and Vinyon turned his face toward it.

"Hi, Maltus," he moaned. "Glad you could make it."

"Yeah, I didn't have anything else to do, so I thought I would stop by this afternoon."

Others gathered around. One by one they touched Vinyon sharing small bundles of energy. They could not heal him—that would take time and the Final Authority—but they could show their concern.

It would be many earth years before Vinyon saw another battle but when he could finally lift his head unaided Maltus asked, "What happened, here?"

"Oh, I was careless. I thought the five in front of me were the entire force of the enemy."

"Five of them?" Maltus interrupted arching his eyebrows.

"They were little ones.

"Anyway," Vinyon continued, "I was concentrating so intently on the five in front that I didn't see the two stronger enemy who had materialized to my back. I suspect they combined forces. I only took one hit."

"Know what they were after?"

"Yes. The two boys belong to Diane Kirkland. She has such a high opposition level that I was sent to work with the guardians."

"Seems like the enemy is always after the young and the weak."

"Are you surprised by that?"

"No." Maltus said then paused, considering Vinyon's condition and the laughing human family. It was a lot of damage for one blow. "You must have been disabled in an instant. Why didn't their attack succeed?"

"As I was falling, I knew I had almost no power left and the other demons would be on me in a flash. I could either call for help or use the last fragments of my energy another way."

"It was the guardians who called," said Maltus. "I recognized their tone."

"I suspected they would. But with power so limited, the only defense for the children I could think of was a diversion tactic."

"Diversion?"

"Yes. I needed to fill up the children's minds and draw them totally away from any thoughts or feelings related to their weak character traits. That is when I called to the bird.

"It was obvious that hell had been planning this attack for some time. I hoped that with all their planning and debate, they might have forgotten some basic element of warfare."

"Had they?"

"Yes. They forgot the most fundamental reality of all."

Maltus offered Vinyon his arm which he gratefully took even though he was not sure he could stand.

"Before any spirit can have an impact on a human," he paused and groaned as he tried to rise on shaking legs then fell back to a seated position. "You have to possess their attention.

JaKobe's Assignment

3:15 PM

Benjamin's Bedroom

It had been almost two hours since lunch but Ben was still full. Those last three hot rolls with crisp, brown tops and pull-apart centers had been just too tempting. He possessed his father's aptitude for enjoying the comforts of life and though still a teen, these pleasures were beginning to show around his waistline.

Ben flopped across his bed, feet dangling on the floor and face toward the ceiling. "Oh, man. I ate too much!" he said rubbing his tummy.

"Well, ol' buddy," answered Luke, "you've got no one to blame but yourself."

"Sure I do. I can blame Mom."

"Yeah, right."

Luke sat on the end of the bed with his back to the wall and reached for his phone. "Now, let's see. Where were we before your Dad so rudely interrupted?"

He flipped open the cell and punched buttons. "M-m-m. Now, that is what I call a delicious dish!"

Keeping the screen toward himself he murmured, "Who'd want roast beef when you can wrap your appetite around legs like those!"

Ben kept his eyes fixed on the ceiling. If he didn't move maybe Luke would leave him alone and not notice that his cheeks were turning pink.

"You've got to see this one, Ben. I mean this is one hot chick!" He leaned forward holding the phone in front of Ben's eyes. "Taking on something like this will never make you fat! You'll be too busy exercising!"

"Aw, quit it Luke," he lamely protested. Ben was accustomed to being teased by the older boy. He pulled the corner of a pillow over his face.

Luke pushed the pillow away but his friend's eyes were closed. "Just take a look." he tempted. "You'll be glad you did."

Ben could feel the warmth of Luke's hand above his face, the tempting picture just inches from his nose. He let out a sigh of resignation and opened one eye. A picture of a Lean Cuisine chicken dinner filled his vision.

Luke let out peals of laughter while Ben picked up the pillow bopping him beside the head. The other boy ducked and poked him in the ribs.

"Hey, you two! What's so funny?" It was Stephanie.

JaKobe's Assignment

"Nothin' you'd understand," said her brother, working Luke into a headlock.

"Well, maybe I understand more than you think," she said lifting her chin. "You guys want to practice a little catch in the backyard? Or, are you just gonna punch each other all day?"

"I thought you were going to practice cheers with Bethany?" said her brother letting go of Luke's head.

"I am. But her mom couldn't pick me up until three thirty, so I've been laying low in my room. You want to toss a ball around or no?"

"Come on," said Luke. "Let's make your sis happy. Besides, you need to work off a little of that gut."

Although Luke had the build of an athlete, it was Ben who picked up the well-worn baseball glove. Once outside, the teens separated far enough to practice a little three-corner catch while still talking. Ben threw to Stephanie who immediately ricocheted the ball to Luke.

"That's some pitch you've got. Practice with your brother?" He tossed it back to Ben.

"When I can pull him away from the table," she answered.

"Come on, Steph, quit teasing," Ben defended. "You know I taught you everything you know."

The ball made another round and for a second time Stephanie threw fast and hard to Luke. The ball hit his bare hands with a smack.

"Take it easy," Ben warned. "Luke's got to have those hands in a couple of hours. Mom will kill you graveyard dead if you bruise her prize pupil."

"Sorry, Luke. I forgot about the recital," Stephanie apologized. "Want to borrow a glove? We got a couple of extra."

Luke grinned. The truth was, playing without a glove added a bit of spice to the game. Something in him liked tempting fate. Probably nothing would happen to his hands. It was only a game of catch. Yet, the slight element of risk was tantalizing.

"I'm fine," he said.

"Are you sure? I can get a glove. I think one's in the house."

"If you are that worried about my hands, just don't throw so hard."

The ball made a couple more rounds, Stephanie lobbing easy catches to Luke. They reversed directions, and then started throwing in random patterns.

"What were you boys looking at when I came in the room?"

"Aw, nuthin'" said Ben.

"Well, I think it's something pretty special," said Luke. Then to Stephanie, "I got a new cell phone. It has all kinds of cool features. I'll have to show them to you."

"Can you take pictures with it?"

"Not only that, I can download from the Internet, set dozens of ring tones, text-message friends, use the calendar to send reminders and even watch video clips or TV."

"This I've got to see!" said Stephanie catching the ball and holding it. She moved a step toward Luke.

"Stephanie, don't be a nerd. Throw me the ball," called her brother.

Something surged inside Ben calling him to protect this younger, female sibling. He knew Luke would probably behave himself and not alarm his sister with those nude pictures, but he couldn't be sure. One could never quite be sure of Luke.

"I'm not a nerd," she stated flatly and shot him a low, inside fireball to prove her point.

"It's okay, Steph," Luke said. "We can look at my phone another time. After all, sharing is the 'Christian' thing to do." He caught Ben's eye and winked.

The ball made three more rounds while Ben argued with himself. Everyone knew the older boy made no pretense of being a Christian and hearing him use the word so lightly make Ben mad.

But on the other hand, he really liked Luke and felt responsible for his spiritual welfare. He even liked all the God-stuff that surrounded him: Attending a Christian school, going to church several times every week, Dad praying at meals. But, he knew what really mattered was getting people saved and he felt guilty about not doing enough to make that happen for Luke.

Saved. That was the goal. It was a kind of fix-all. Sinners were miserable even though they tried to look happy on the outside. Christians were joyful both inside and out because they knew Jesus. Christians were supposed to work hard for Jesus by getting others to say the sinner's prayer so they could be happy, too. It was simple.

Ben watched Luke chatting lightly with Stephanie as the ball made another round. Yeah, it's simple. But, it sure is hard.

How long had he known Luke? Two years? Holy smoke! Luke would finish high school in a few months, go away to some big music college and Ben would never see him again. They would probably both get married and have a couple of kids and then the next thing you know, Luke would get killed in a car wreck. They would both stand at the Judgment Day and Luke would point a shaking, bony finger in Ben's face saying, "You never told me about Jesus and now I am going to hell and it is all your fault!" He shuddered at the thought.

"Here's one for you, Buddy-Roe," said Luke drawing him away from the unpleasant thoughts and lobbing a high, slow ball his direction. He stepped backward, stretching high and caught the ball on the tip of his glove.

A horn beeped and Stephanie waved to Bethany and her mom. "Gotta go, guys." She ran toward the car, turning a cartwheel on the way bouncing feet over head with surprising grace.

"Show off," said Ben under his breath.

Without Stephanie, the game soon dwindled. "Let's go back to your room and rest a while," suggested Luke glancing at his watch. It was

JaKobe's Assignment

three-forty. Both parents were gone so it would be pleasantly quiet inside the house and his hands were beginning to sting from the repeated impact of the softball. He knew he would soon need to start the process of stretching and focused exercises before the recital.

Luke never let others know how much he longed for a career as a "real" pianist but the truth was it guided every thought and action. Dreams of one day touring on the concert stage were as real as his breath and just as vital. At eighteen he was too old to be thought of as a prodigy, still, he was good. Very good. Recent contest and comments from judges were indicating just how good. And, if all went right, a scholarship or professional music contract was a real possibility.

Who knew what might happen after that? Standing before an audience in Vienna or London would prove his talent to the world, but most of all it would prove his personal worth to himself.

As the boys entered the silent house, they shuffled big feet against the rough mat at the door—both remembering how upset Ben's mom got about grass clippings on the floor— then slipped inside without conversation while their thoughts whirled in two very different worlds.

Ben was guilty and struggling. He simply had to tell Luke about the difference Jesus could make in his life. It was now or never.

Partly, he was motivated by a desire to see good things for his friend, but the recent thought of Judgment Day loomed large and the idea of being responsible for Luke's eternal damnation was too much. "Lord, help me get this right," he prayed with an emotion that bordered on desperation.

Luke's thoughts were far away. Italy to be exact. He flipped open his phone and noticing his friend's discomfort said, "Don't worry, Ben. I'm just checking my email." He punched a few buttons then sighed. "My uncle said he would text me before the performance. Guess he hasn't had time."

"You used to live with your uncle Raffa---, what was his name?"

"Raffaello Machiavelli"

"Yeah, that one!" Ben laughed. They had reached his room and he was putting away his glove. He never noticed Luke's discomfort as he turned his back and examined the assorted items scattered on the desk.

"What a mouthful!" Ben continued, then paused and added seriously, "Funny, you don't look Italian."

Luke turned to face his friend. "Well, you don't look dumb, either." He studied Ben with cold, level eyes as the air in the once friendly room became stale.

Ben reached into the closet and hung his glove on a peg while his throat tightened with emotion. This certainly was not going the way he had hoped.

Luke broke the silence. "I'm sorry." He wanted to say more, but something inside him froze. The story was too big to be told in one afternoon. It was too complex to be understood by someone as sheltered and naive as Ben. It was too tender to be exposed to the light and too emotionally charged to be left in the dark.

He turned back to the desk and picked up a picture album he had seen lying there.

"Hey, I showed you my pictures, how about you showing me some of yours?'

Ben glanced at the black and gold photo album in Luke's hand and breathed a prayer of thankfulness. Surely this was a God-thing. The pictures were of his mission trip and would be the perfect tool for talking to Luke about getting saved.

The boys settled on the edge of the bed facing each other, each with one foot on the floor and the other folded under a thigh. The book lay open between them.

"I forgot I hadn't showed you these," Ben started. "You remember last spring when I went to Padre Island with the youth group?"

Luke thought a moment. "Oh, yeah. I was jealous because you were romping on a beach during spring break and I had to stay home for that stupid piano competition."

"Stupid? You walked away with $1,000 in scholarship money!"

"Well, you got a vacation!"

"Only part of one. We spent most of our time handing out tracts to the college kids who had come down for spring break."

"Tracts?"

"Yeah, you know. Little folded pieces of paper that tell folks about Jesus."

"You mean propaganda."

"No, tracts."

"Whatever."

Ben turned the first page of the album. He hoped that by giving Luke a pictorial journey through the two-week trip, he might introduce him to Jesus along the way.

"Here we are all packed and ready to go. This was taken just before the bus left the church parking lot. That's our teacher, Ward Newsome, leading us in prayer and asking God to bless and keep us safe."

Luke listened patiently and commented occasionally giving the illusion that he was interested. It wasn't particularly fun but he knew he had hurt Ben's feelings with that crack about being dumb. Listening to him tell about the trip was the least he could do to make amends.

However, they were not far into the album when Ben's real intention became evident. He was using the pictures as a means to ask personal questions about Luke's relationship with God.

In the past, Ben had talked about religion in general terms and invited him to church, but this was shaping up as an all out assault. Luke didn't know whether to be insulted or amused. Ben was the closest thing he ever had to a brother, but at times the kid could be as clueless as a stump and

JaKobe's Assignment

his stumbling efforts to "witness" were almost humorous.

Luke thought about taking him for a ride by giving each well-rehearsed question some off-the-wall answer that would set Ben's sensitivities reeling. Or, it might be fun to play spiritually dumb and answer each question with another, more complex question that Ben could not possibly answer. Both ideas were tempting.

Luke knew he was smarter than Ben. He was also older and far more versed in real world issues. He was a deep thinker and had probably considered spiritual matters from more angles than Ben had even dreamed. He read a lot from the Net, surveying Christian sites as well as Eastern religions and the view of evolutionists such as Carl Sagan. It would definitely be fun twisting Ben into a mental pretzel, but he could never convince himself that it would be nice.

They had been through the album page by page when Ben brought out a copy of the little paper that the youth group had handed out to vacationers on the beach. Luke grunted in all the proper places but made no significant comment. At last Ben cleared his throat and asked the "big" question that they both knew would come.

"Luke, would you like to pray with me and receive Jesus as your savior?"

Having put aside the temptation to frustrate or confuse, Luke opted to simply be honest and try to move this naive kid a notch closer to reality.

"Ben, I love you like a brother, but I don't think it would be very profitable for me to go through your formula prayer just to make you happy."

"No, I guess not." His disappointment was obvious.

"Let me ask you a couple of questions instead." Ben looked at him with wide innocent eyes. "Why do you want me to become a Christian?"

"I want you to have peace and go to heaven," Ben replied.

"Okay, peace. Let's start with that one. What makes you think I am not peaceful? Ben you have known me for a little over two years. Do I look unhappy or anxious? Think about it. Can you honestly say you know that I am not peaceful?"

"Well, I've seen you pretty upset. . ." his voice trailed off.

"All right. I grant that on rare occasions I have expressed strong emotion. Is that so bad?" He flipped the picture album back a couple of pages. "Look at those young bucks on the beach? Does that one dunking the girl in the red bikini look distressed? How about this old guy asleep under the umbrella? Think maybe he is full of anxiety?

"Ben, I've got more peace than most people I know. When I play a lyrical melody by Tchaikovsky my soul soars to the stars on a wave of peace."

"But, don't you want to go to heaven? I mean, this earth is not all there is, you know. If you don't accept Jesus, you will end up in hell."

"Okay, let's talk about that one. What about heaven? Or, even hell for that matter. You've grown up in a home with a preacher father who taught you about those places before you could walk. I don't have any objection to that. If that is what he believes and how he wants to raise you, that's cool. But, I have never seen any evidence that those places are real.

"I think you believe in them just because others told you and you have never questioned or thought about it for yourself."

Luke had finished his argument, but felt badly for Ben. He had no desire to destroy the faith of his friend. He saw his down cast eyes and tried to soften the blow just given.

"I don't know, Ben. Maybe those places are out there somewhere. It's a very big universe. Maybe there is life on other planets. Maybe even intelligent life. Maybe there are all kind of places and possibilities." He paused and let out a long breath. "I surely don't claim to know everything. But my problem is, you seem to think that you do."

Ben picked up the album and gently closed it. He wanted to hug it to his chest and cry, but resisted the urge. He was embarrassed and frustrated and felt like a first class fool. Yet, showing these feelings in front of Luke would be worse than what he had just been through.

It wasn't that Luke had told him anything new. He occasionally wondered about these things, but quickly turned away from such doubt. Questions were uncomfortable; his world was safe only when it was neatly divided into "us" and "them." It was like an Old West drama where Christians were the good guys in the white hats, everyone else were victims who needed to be rescued and Satan was the bad guy in the black hat.

Yet, deep inside, Ben knew the reality of his faith was more than his need for simple answers. There was something inside him that was awake and alive. He couldn't explain it. He couldn't even say for sure if this something had always been there or exactly when it had arrived. He remembered the first time he had been burdened by his sense of personal sin and separation from God and he vaguely remembered being baptized when he was five, but there was something else. Something deep in his soul and he knew that something was real.

Gently and quietly, like a sunrise coming over the horizon, a certainty dawned in Ben's mind and his feelings of foolishness melted into the background. It wasn't that he heard a reassuring voice, but that he felt a reality and knew he was supposed to ask his friend a specific question.

"Luke, you doubt religion, hell and heaven. But, do you believe God is real?"

Luke was tempted to argue the definition of God. Was Ben asking if he believed there was a power behind the universe? Did he mean a cosmic intelligence? Was it the Force? But such arguments, which were so fitting for the classroom, seemed to have no place in this intimate setting between friends.

Luke knew exactly what Ben was asking. Did he believe in a personal God? This was not a question about some abstract power or theoretical spiritual construct. It was about a God who could think and feel and connect with people. Did he believe in a Being who was in some small way like a human, yet without limitation, eternal, all-powerful and all-knowing? Did Luke believe in that kind of God?

He had promised himself that he would be honest with his friend. The question repeated itself ringing through the hollow spaces in his heart. Did he believe in that kind of God? He sat silent for a moment, thinking about the answer.

No doubt there were powers, laws and dynamics that ruled space, matter and time. But, were these powers and laws self-existent or did they come into being because Someone willed an order into the universe? Someone called, God?

"I don't know, Ben," he said at last. "There are times when I would like to believe Someone is behind all I see. But, at other times, . . ." He didn't finish the sentence only let his voice trail off into silence.

For the second time Ben felt an unaccountable knowledge inside his heart. He knew exactly what Luke intended to say. He knew it so thoroughly that he finished the sentence for him. "But at other times, the idea of such an all-knowing, real and personal Being scares you spitless."

Luke looked at Ben and tossed his head throwing the long, blond bangs out of his eyes. He grinned.

"Well, I don't know that 'scared' is the right word." It was the first time that afternoon he had lied to his friend.

JaKobe's Assignment

Year of Our Lord, 1807

Boston, USA

It was Sunday in the fall of 1807 when a different Ben—Elijah Benjamin Stonemeyer, to be exact—thought he heard the voice of the Lord. What he heard and how he slowly grew to believe it, would change the fate of his descendants for generations to come.

Melody's great-great-great grandfather was sitting in church with thirty other souls on that bright Lord's Day while—according to Quaker tradition—the Society of Friends waited in silence. They had been sitting for almost half an hour. Not a sound; not a disturbing movement broke the spell. Quietly, peacefully they waited.

Every Lord's Day it was the same. With the women on one side of the aisle and men on the other, they waited in silence until someone in the group felt the Spirit of God encouraging them to speak. Often the one feeling the Spirit would begin to tremble or "quake," thus giving the group their informal name. At other times, no one spoke and after a period of silent waiting, all went home refreshed. On this particular Sunday the silence had continued for so long, it seemed as though this might be one of those silent occasions.

Elijah waited along with everyone else but his internal world was not passive. Behind his eyes, he was alive with ordered activity as he pursued a thought that had captured him somewhere around corn-planting time. The thought was not a constant companion, but it had returned regularly all summer and fall and seemed to grow as the corn reached higher in the fields.

The thought first came late one night while reading from his Bible. Exodus was not the usual fare for a Quaker—his branch of Christianity centered almost exclusively on the New Testament—yet this particular passage captured and fascinated him; a curious statement that refused to let him go.

Making every effort to turn the pages as soundlessly as possible, he thumbed open his Bible to the twentieth chapter of Exodus and read the words again.

Thou shalt not bow down thyself to them, nor serve them: for I the LORD thy God am a jealous God, visiting the iniquity of the fathers upon the children unto the third and fourth generation of them that hate me; And shewing mercy unto thousands of them that love me, and keep my commandments.[16]

JaKobe's Assignment

The words intrigued him. God clearly stated something bad would happen to the third or even fourth generation of a man who rejected God, but also some kind of extra "mercy" would be shown to the future generations of those who loved God.

Elijah had studied the New Testament enough to know—although no one could keep the commands perfectly—wanting to keep them was one evidence of loving God. Examining his own life, he knew his failings all too well, yet he also knew that as much as possible for a man of clay, he did love God. What did all that mean for the children and grand children of Emma and Elijah Stonemeyer?

He looked at the verse again. Strange. The Bible didn't indicate how many generations would receive that special consideration of mercy, but it seemed logical to Elijah that if God would reap vengeance to the fourth generation on those that turned against Him, He ought to go at least that far with the children of those who loved Him.

He tried hard to visualize what future generations might be like. He and Emma had five children. How many descendants would they make after four generations? Would they be wealthy? How many would be government leaders or store owners who lived in town? Craftsmen? Would they stay Quaker? Education had always been important to the Stonemeyers, but surely, most descendents would be farmers.

He thought of the needs and possible struggles his future generations were likely to encounter long after his body had turned to dust in an unremembered grave. As he considered these things, Elijah watched the golden light stream through a glass window high on the church wall.

Even though future generations might never know him, according to the scripture he could touch them. His actions, his faith, mattered to generations yet unborn. He could reach through the years and believe a gracious God would offer a special measure of mercy to them simply because an ancestor loved God and believed.

He thought of the Exodus promise and a quiet assurance grew in his heart. The seed that had been struggling to grow all summer was ripening to harvest. Like dawn moving across the landscape, realities that had always been there emerged into clear focus. Truth dawned on Elijah Benjamin Stonemeyer. He could claim this promise if he chose to. He could believe God's words. As he slightly tilted his brow in reverence, his heart reached out to his Maker with silent words of gratitude.

Emma lifted her head and cast a covert glance at her husband sitting with the other men. The sunlight spilled over his hatless head and she thought she saw a faint glistening of tears on his weather-worn cheeks. Elijah would not speak out loud in this meeting. He seldom did. But one thing she knew for certain. Her husband had heard the voice of the Lord.

JaKobe's Assignment

*****

It was true that Elijah Benjamin Stonemeyer had heard the Lord. But, it was also true the Lord had heard him.

At that very moment the command went out and half way around the world the angel Jubilee was told to drop what she was doing and to go to Boston, Massachusetts where for—not three or four—but six generations she would follow the descendents of one man who believed the Almighty knew how to extend mercy.

Elizabeth Baker

3:50 PM

Gathering Home

Melody Stonemeyer Phelps slipped out the side door of the church and began the short walk home. The shower wasn't technically over, but Tina and Miranda were packing away their booty and Bev assured her it was all right to leave a few minutes early. She quickened her pace and turned south on Pecan with long, determined strides.

The quick steps were only partly due to her heavy schedule. A larger reason for haste was simply to avoid thinking and the sense of futility that hung around her like a fog.

The unexpected exit of the Newsom family from the Christmas program was more than just another problem; it was a stark example of everything her life had become. It was a weary cycle of problems, followed by huge effort, followed by success, followed by more problems. Around and around the cycle went with no end in sight and no way to get off the treadmill.

JaKobe's Assignment

There had been a time—oh how far away, young and naive it seemed—when the cycle had been exciting. Back then, she assumed that each trip around was moving her closer to the goal. Now, she knew there was no goal.

She considered that bleak reality as her heels beat a faster staccato against the sidewalk.

Of course, there was heaven somewhere in the sky, by and by. She had been taught about that place since a child and found it easy to believe God was out there—somewhere—existing in another dimension beyond time and matter. The beauty of the world; the steady cycle of seasons; all spoke of order and creative thought. There was no way that chance could account for an awesome reality ranging from invisible bacteria too the vast distance between stars. Nothing smaller than God could be the source of all that.

In some ways Melody's faith was much stronger than that of her pastor-husband. Jonathan seldom shared his deepest thoughts with his wife, but she watched him closely and listened with ears that often heard things not said with words. She knew of his discontent and she understood its source: The man who stood in the pulpit encouraging others to believe, struggled to believe for himself. He kept looking for the Almighty to show up and prove His existence.

But, Melody did not share Jonathan's doubt. God didn't need to prove Himself. For her, God was all around and shouting from every corner of creation.

What do you want, Melody? An internal voice quietly but persistently pushed at her. It was a good question. What *did* she want? She had smiled and volunteered and been good and willingly solved one problem after another all her life, but something was missing. All that effort to be good had somehow left her stuck. She didn't want to perform any longer, but every time she tried to stop, guilt drove her back to the old patterns.

What do you want, Melody? The internal words echoed again and she considered the question. There was a longing in her heart for something different but she couldn't put the desire into words.

Freedom? The word welled up from deep in her spirit and burst on her mind. It was almost as though a sound had entered her mind without using the door of her ears. But before she could question the experience, the joy of at last having a name for her struggle over took her.

Yes! That was it! She longed for a deep internal freedom. The very word seemed to heal the sharp, jagged edges of her soul. Freedom. It was what she had always been seeking.

But, how could there ever be true freedom? She had a job. She had a family. She had obligations and responsibilities and commitments and schedules. How could freedom and the rat race of modern life coexist?

People talked about the carefree days of childhood, but was even that a reality? Was anyone ever free? Even a child?

JaKobe's Assignment

Images of days gone by drifted through her consciousness. Scraped knees. Tears. At age eight she cried for weeks over the death of her beloved dog. Frequent bouts with infections had caused physical pain and often restricted activity. There was the hurt when her family moved away from friends. The fear of a new school. The rules her parents laid down. The rules of her school. The rules that she learned in church telling her what God expected. Had she experienced freedom as a child?

She considered the question.

Yes! The surprising answer within her own soul almost shouted. Childhood was freedom! Those years had not been free from responsibility or rules or expectations or limitations or even pain. But, inside, she was indeed free.

As a child, she could relax. She could play. Children could live without masks, work without dread, dream without fear, play without shame and enjoy all of life because they trusted that someone strong loved them without reservation or condition and stood taller, bigger and beyond any temporary pain that invaded her world.

Childhood was "free" because it was safe.

Isn't God safe? The internal voice came again causing her pause.

Years of church attendance had indoctrinated her to believe that God was Someone big. After all, He created the universe. Did not He stand taller, bigger and beyond any temporary pain her world might hold?

As she rounded the last corner and cut across the yard, a sadness rolled over her like an ocean wave. Yes, God was "out there" but inside her soul there was no freedom. Not a thread. Not a hair. She was bound to the treadmill of performing for an unidentified audience who could never be satisfied. Yet, adding God to the equation didn't seem to help.

It wasn't that she did not believe in God. It was rather that in the secret places of her heart, she didn't think God believed in her.

*****

But, God did believe in Melody and the presence of an angel standing in her kitchen confirmed that this was so.

Jubilee arrived in the early afternoon and had been waiting around the Phelps home for several hours. Because she was assigned to a family, not an individual, she took no character readings and seldom stayed focused on one individual for an extended amount of time. But that did not mean she was idle.

Elijah and Emma had been quite prolific. Their five children had multiplied and the angel currently had a hundred and seventy-two individuals under her care.

For six generations Jubilee had been kept very busy as she encouraged prayer, gave reports to higher authorities, dispersed spiritual shields, coordinated the efforts of personal angels,

JaKobe's Assignment

supervised births and deaths and when extra help was needed fought as a warrior. It had been a fascinating assignment watching how the choices of one generation impacted the next, and how the new generation guided and shaped the raw material they had been given.

Two hundred earth years had passed since the day she was so abruptly pulled off assignment in India and during that time she had grown to know and love this family quite well. Indeed, she would be saddened to see the assignment end.

And, coming to an end would certainly happen soon. Although most of Elijah's decedents were Christians, no one in generation six had stepped forward to pick up the challenge of faith by claiming the promise for generations yet unborn. They were all too concerned with the whirlwind of their days and never thought about their possible impact on the centuries. Humans were strange that way.

*****

Melody pushed open the back door to her home and at the same time pushed the troubling thoughts from her mind. What she needed to do was get busy. Very busy.

The door shut with a bang and she entered her large, country kitchen with floor to ceiling closets covering a large part of the nearest wall. Coats, homework, shoes, sports equipment and more were all assigned specific places behind these cream colored doors and every member of the family had a private cubbyhole of their own.

Melody opened hers, hung a light colored purse on a peg and, kicking off her shoes, left them in the middle of the floor. Those pinching, restrictive pumps reminded her of everything she did not want her life to be.

Grabbing the door to the dishwasher, she jerked it open letting out a cloud of steam from the delayed wash cycle. She would add putting away the dishes to her list of things to do before returning to the church for the recital. That ought to keep her busy enough.

Jubilee watched the angry, jerking motions and wondered how it was that this great-great-great granddaughter could look so much like Emma yet have so little of her gentle spirit?

Every time Jubilee looked at Melody, she saw Emma's eyes and Elijah's strong chin but, the darkness on her face concerned the angel deeply. This woman was already past the age when most humans received spiritual Life. It would be a challenge, but Jubilee was determined not to lose another of the Stonemeyer offspring to the enemy.

Ben heard the back door slam and jumped up off his bed headed for the kitchen. "Dad's back!" he informed Luke who followed at a more relaxed pace.

As he swung around the corner, Ben saw his mom in her stocking feet rapidly moving items from the dishwasher to the open cabinets. Surprised, he paused before speaking. His mom never slammed doors and she certainly never walked around the kitchen without her shoes. It was a though she were attacking the dishes rather than putting them away and her face looked unnaturally tense.

"Mom, you're the one whose home?" he asked and paused only a heartbeat before adding, "Say, can I have some of those cookies with milk?"

Two questions and both of them dumb. That boy was so much like his father he hurt.

"No, I'm not home. I'm still at the church," Melody said with more sarcasm than humor. "And, no, you can't have any more cookies. They're for the recital tonight."

"Hi, Mrs. Phelps," Luke said pleasantly. "Did the shower go well?"

"Thanks for asking, Luke," she answered. His mom's face seemed to relax a bit and Ben frowned at his friend. How come Luke could always think of the right thing to say while Ben was continually putting his foot in his mouth?

"The shower went fine." Polishing the flatware with a cloth, she tossed each fork into the proper drawer slot with a clang. "Are you all prepared for the recital?"

"As prepared as I ever will be; thanks to a great teacher."

"That's a laugh." Melody knew it was empty flattery, but it pleased her all the same. "With the power and precision you possess, your teacher was left in the dust a long way back. About the only service I perform is listening with a critical ear and helping you enter all those contest!"

"Well, I still think of you as my teacher and I'll try to make you proud tonight."

Melody slammed the dishwasher door. "I assume you have all your music in order. Have you rehearsed this afternoon?"

"I wanted to but Ben forced me to play catch with him and Stephanie."

"Me?" Ben protested.

"Catch? I trust you wore a glove. Stephanie has a mean fast ball."

"Oh, yes ma'am!" Luke lied and winked at Ben. "But, I do need to run through some scales and exercises before the program. Do you think I could use one of the pianos at the church without disturbing anyone?"

Melody started to offer her own instrument sitting in the living room, but she knew Luke's penchant for privacy and decided against it. "There's a piano in the church basement that is good enough for finger exercises and the church is never locked on Sunday. Do you know your way downstairs?"

"Yeah, I remember the way from our last recital," he said heading toward the door. "Thanks, Mrs. Phelps."

Melody tossed the damp towel on the cabinet leaving it in a heap. She opened the junk drawer and rummaged through its contents. Evidently not locating what she wanted, she left the drawer open and moved to the closet where she began to

JaKobe's Assignment

dig. Changing her mind, she slammed the door and moved to the kitchen desk, picked up a pen and chewed on it for a moment. Then, she returned to the closet, opened the door and pulled out a large tote full of piano music which she dumped unceremoniously on the kitchen bar. She tossed a couple of old music books over by the sink.

Ben watched his mom openmouthed. What had happened to his always neat, never-do-anything-half-way mother? Something was obviously wrong but he couldn't figure out what. He tried to open a conversation. "Did anything special happen at the shower?"

"No." Melody answered in a flat tone and continued shifting the sheets of music from one place to another.

Silence.

"Are you sure everything is okay? Can I do somethin'?"

More questions. Everything *had* been okay, until Ben opened his mouth. She was becoming irritated. How could she prepare for the recital if Ben kept interrupting her?

"Everything is fine," she said crossly. "I'm just busy. Why don't you get out of my way and give me room to breathe? I need to change shoes."

She flowed from the room like a rushing river on its way to the sea, sweeping up her discarded pumps along the way.

Alone in the kitchen, Ben tapped the bar lightly with his fingers. Mom wants me to get out of her way so she can change shoes? It didn't make sense and the empty silence around him seemed strangely threatening.

Maybe he should just do as he was asked. He would stay out of his mother's way, sit on the front steps and wait. Dad should be home soon. Maybe he could explain what was going on.

But, if Ben could have seen the spiritual world around him, he would have known there was good reason for his feelings of threat. Evil beings, like gray smoke, were gathering in various places about the room.

Jubilee saw them clearly and she puzzled over their presence. The shadows increased in volume as they moved and swirled about but did not materialize. They only remained shadows, more of hell than of earth, and because of this it was difficult even to determine their number much less their battle tactic.

She hesitated, caught between three possibilities. She could call for help; wait for more development or draw her own sword and challenge them to battle. What was needed? What was best?

Melody flowed back into the room. She was still barefoot, but now she carried a paper in her hand and mumbled to herself as she read.

Unfortunately, with her attention on the paper, it was not on the path. As she passed a heavy barstool she slammed her still bare toes against it with a force that made them snap and brought the stool down with a clatter.

JaKobe's Assignment

The stabbing pain brought tears to her eyes as she crumpled the paper in her hand while reaching out to the cabinet for support. Curse words flooded her mind, wedged their way between clinched teeth and slipped into the air. Her ears heard the words and a small portion of consciousness wondered where she had learned such foul language. The rest of her didn't care.

Pain. For a full minute her whole world was consumed with it. Then, hopping on her one good leg, she found an upright stool and sat to examine her injured foot.

The third and fourth toes were already beginning to swell and turn blue. Great. She would stand before the audience tonight in her smart, cream-colored dress and fuzzy, pink house slippers.

Anger rose up and tightened her throat. *What a stupid life I'm trying to lead. Why didn't I have sense enough to schedule events further apart?*

After a few more moments of tears, Melody pounded her fist on the bar. Time was passing. The recital would be here soon. It did no good to sit and cry.

Spreading the crumpled list of chores on the counter she tried to prioritize: One: Find music for Paul. Two: Get credit card back from Jonathan. Three: Call Linda. Four: Remind Stephanie about Monday's orthodontist appointment. Five: Pack tote bag.

Number three was not as important as the others, but it was quick and if the call to Linda was successful, she might feel better. As the pain subsided to a level that allowed her to breathe, she checked her watch. It was 4:05. The recital was scheduled to begin in twenty-five minutes. Perhaps Linda had not left yet.

She dared not attempt walking but by stretching her arm and shoulder full length across the bar she could just catch the phone's receiver cord with her fingertips. Pulling the object toward her, she punched in the numbers from memory and on the third ring, Linda Amesworth, mother of her newest piano student answered.

After Melody assured her that there was no problem with the fast approaching recital, she cleared her throat and got to the point.

"I was just calling to see if Melissa might be interested in performing a small part in our church's Christmas play this year. . . . Yes, I know she is already involved with school and piano, but the angel only has one line and she would look so cute with the halo and wings. . . Aw-huh, . . . Of course. . . . I understand . . . No, it won't be any trouble at all. I'll just make a few calls. . . . Sure. I'll see you in a little while."

She slammed down the receiver then crossed her arms on the bar, leaned forward and dropped her head face down.

By now, the room was filled with shadows and as Jubilee watched they gathered around the head and chest of the depressed woman. Although Melody could not see them, she sensed their presence in both her body and spirit. Her chest tightened and her sad mood deepened. The spirits added to her burden in much the same way that physical discomfort adds to the burden of an already foul mood and encouraged her to drift even deeper into the gathering depression.

The angel put her hand to her sword. Melody was a child of Elijah Stonemeyer and that gave Jubilee rights and responsibilities. This woman had no Life within to comfort her, no personal angel to defend her and keep the enemy in control. Enough was enough.

But, the moment she made the decision to defend, the spirits released their victim and dissipated, drifting about to all corners of the room.

Melody raised her head drawing a deep breath and stretched her arms stiffly before her, fingers outspread over the cool surface of the bar. She slapped one hand down hard and uttered a mild oath.

"There's work to be done! If you can't do item three, work on item five."

Balancing on one foot she limped to the other end of the bar and pulled the tote bag closer. Rummaging through its contents she haphazardly tossed items around, ignoring where they landed.

A stack of programs for this afternoon's recital were pulled from a side pocket and laid to the right. A handful of old music sheets were tossed to the left where half of them immediately spilled onto the floor. *Stupid sheet music. Never was good for anything.*

Her grade book was pulled from the bottom of the tote. She would need that. The back page had a list of awards that each student should be given at the end of the performance. Where was Paul's music? *Maybe I still have a copy of Book Two.*

Limping over to the closet, she yanked a stack of beginner books from the top shelf then limped back to the overcrowded counter. Making room, she tossed the crumpled dishtowel in the sink while the neatly wrapped platter of cookies landed with a thud in front of the canisters and on top of two previously discarded books. She never noticed the precarious angle of the off balance stack.

Jubilee noticed. But the main reason she did so was that every shadow spirit in the room suddenly converged at that point. Her brow wrinkled as she considered the puzzle. Why would dark spirits be interested in an unstable platter of human sweets?

The shadows began to blend with one another and whirl, creating a synergy of power while Jubilee stood transfixed. These spirits were evidently intent on toppling the platter. But, why?

Humans often attributed misplaced objects or odd sounds to spirit activity but that was almost never the truth. While it was not impossible for pure spirit to influence matter, it took such a huge amount of energy to achieve such small results that spirits and matter seldom ever directly impacted one another.

JaKobe's Assignment

On rare occasions when spirits partook enough solid substance to be seen by humans, they touched and moved matter at will, but such a thing might occur once a century. What were these spirits after?

She studied the platter of cookies sitting half-on / half-off the book's edge. It would take ten grams of weight to tip that platter to the floor. Such a touch would be a feather's weight to the human hand, but for spirits reaching from one world of reality into another, it was analogous to tons! This was not a normal battlefield.

For a second time Jubilee decided she had been passive long enough. She drew her sword while channeling power into the blade and leaned forward.

Then came the most shocking realization of all.

As soon as Jubilee made the decision to fight, she was frozen in place by what felt and looked like being encased in a thin, but solid wall of liquid fire. A fire she recognized. This apparition was not from darkness, but from the Light. This was holiness. For the first time in memory, the Giver of Light was preventing Jubilee from fighting the darkness.

"Here it is," Melody grumbled to herself. "*Beginner Book Two*, page 51, 'Counting Stars'." At least Paul would have no excuse. Maybe something was at last going right in her horrible, pitiful, frustrating, pain-filled day!

At that precise moment, Melody's attention was drawn sharply to the right. As though in slow motion she watched as her grandmother's crystal platter slip from the unsteady stack of music books and began its plunge to the floor.

She lunged as the crack of glass shattering against ceramic tile sent shockwaves around the room. Shards of glass and cookie fragments scattered in a wide pattern.

She landed on the floor among broken crystal and crumbs, cutting the heal of her hand. Crying and cursing she picked up a book that had fallen on top of the mess and slammed it against the nearest cabinet door.

Across the room Jonathan gazed in horror at his wife. He had entered just in time to see her helplessly lunge for the falling platter and for a fraction of a second stood frozen as the scene unfolded. Then, breaking out of the slow motion mold that trapped him, he cried, "Melody!" and raced across the room.

She was on the floor pounding her fist against the tile, ignoring the broken glass. "I can't! I can't! I just can't do it anymore!" She shouted as tears began to flow. He reached to hold her but she sat back covering her face with bleeding hands.

"Melody!" he shouted again. She didn't seem to hear. Lifting her upright by her forearms and standing her before him he repeated, "Melody! What is it? What's going on?"

Pulling her hands from her face he saw small streaks of blood. But it was not the blood that caught his attention. It was her tear-filled eyes.

"Oh, Melody," he said with the tenderness of a lover, then still holding her hands moved to the sink and turned on the cold tap. Running water spilled over manicured nails as she sobbed and soon drew a ragged breath relaxing against him with her head on his shoulder.

He turned off the tap, dried her hands and gently turned them palms upward surveying the damage. His eyes drifted from her hands to her face. The cuts on her hands were minor and would quickly heal, but in the eyes there was something he had not seen for years. It was something tender and open and childlike.

For a brief moment, the all-efficient stranger she had become changed back to the tender young bride he once knew. She bit her quivering bottom lip and looked up through wet lashes.

Jonathan gathered his wife of twenty years into his arms and stood for a moment, silent and motionless. Then, breaking the spell, Melody sniffed and pulled back.

"The recital," she said with finality. "I have to get this cleaned up. They're depending on me." She turned and limped toward the broom closet.

"Did you cut your foot, too?" he asked.

"No, I stumped my toe like a stupid ninny when I kicked over a bar stool."

She kept limping toward the closet, opened the door and removed a broom and dustpan before Jonathan could react.

"Sit down. I'll get that."

"It's all right, I can do it."

"Melody, sit down!" He surprised both of them with his forcefulness as he took the cleaning tools from her hands and nodded toward a still standing barstool. She obeyed.

The tension between them began to rise again as Jonathan swept up crumbs and broken glass.

"I've got to go." Melody looked at her watch. "It's 4:25. They are already wondering where I am. The program needs to start in less than five minutes."

"Melody, I think we have something going on here that is more important than a piano recital."

"Like what?"

"Like you and me, and why we are arguing, and why you fell apart over a broken plate of cookies and…" He knew there was more, he just couldn't think of it at the moment.

"I need to go. They are depending on me."

"The world will not stop spinning if you don't show up. I'll call LeeAnn and tell her there has been an accident and you can't make it."

"Great. That ought to start tongues wagging. I can see the headlines now, 'Pastor's wife loses mind over cookie crash.'"

She pouted in silence for a moment then the absurdity of it soaked in and she began a cynical chuckle. Jonathan, too, caught the ridiculousness of the moment and laughed softly as the tension eased.

The brief laughter was replaced by silence then Melody sighed.

"Jonathan, I have worked hard for this. So have the children. I want to go."

He hesitated then capitulated. "All right. But we have a lot to talk about. Soon."

"I agree."

"You still have spots of blood on your face. Go wash and slip into some kind of shoes. I'll call LeeAnn and tell her we are on our way."

"There won't be enough cookies for the reception."

"Easy fix. I'll drop you by the church and pick up a package at the store. They'll be on a platter and ready for guests before the last note sounds."

Melody limped toward the bedroom while Jonathan searched his pocket for a cell phone. She paused and turned back toward him before he could finish speed dial.

"Jonathan." He looked up hoping to see tenderness again and waited expectantly. "Make sure the cookies are not the cheap kind."

Ben had waited patiently in the yard but his dad had not said how long he should stay and the tension was growing unbearable. Surely, whatever problem his mom had must have been solved by now. The air was brisk and a slight wind was kicking up from the West. Perhaps it would be warmer on the porch.

He got up from the curb, brushed his pants and walked up the steps. Under the shelter of the wide porch, he paused briefly to listen at the front door. If anything was going on inside, there was certainly no sound of it. Settling on the porch swing, he twisted to see if he could catch a glimpse of internal activity through the curtained window. Nothing.

Ben drew a deep breath and blew it out between pursed lips. He needed to talk to his dad and if they delayed much longer everyone would race off to church again. No telling when there would be another opportunity.

It wasn't only the weird way his mom was acting that had him upset. His world had been spiraling downward ever since his talk with Luke this afternoon. His friend hadn't said much, but what he did say sure made sense. The kind of sense that left Ben without answers. Many people really did seem to get along without Christianity just fine. And, there were lots of religions in the world. His Christian school provided a protective environment and when he was there or in church things seemed so clear. But, there was a wide world out there and it was providing answers, too. Answers Ben had never considered.

But now, that outside world was invading his with surprising persistence and making sense of both worlds was becoming more difficult. If he could only talk to Dad!

He turned to the windows again. This time the blurred images inside were moving.

"Hey, Dad," he asked as he opened the door. "Is Mom all right?"

Instead of answering, his father held up his hand indicating his son should keep quiet and continued talking into his cell. "That's right. Just tell them we will be there in a few minutes. No. There is no need for that. Everything's fine."

He clicked the phone shut and turned his attention toward Ben.

"Nothing's wrong. Your mom just cut her hand. She is changing shoes."

"She still hasn't got on any shoes?" Ben looked confused.

Melody came to the door smiling weakly and carrying her large music tote bag. "Ben, you have grass stains on your khaki pants," she sighed.

"And you have on fuzzy house slippers."

Jonathan's voice was succinct and commanding. "Your mom hurt her foot, too. Don't be disrespectful. Get your clothes changed and don't disturb the recital when you enter late."

"But, Dad!"

"Never mind. Just do as you were told."

Jonathan reached for his wife's large bag and held her elbow as she limped out the front door toward the waiting car.

"But, Dad . . ." the boy said softly as the front door closed firmly shut.

Alone in the silent house, he turned slowly looking at the empty room then ambled back to his own private space to do as he was told.

Yet, the room was not as lonely as Ben assumed. JaKobe stood by the door exchanging sad glances with two other spirit beings. Rimnon, Ben's personal angel, hung his head while Jubilee thought of the future and three united hearts reached out to the Final Authority seeking hope.

JaKobe's Assignment

4:15 PM

County Road 3052

Diane had been traveling almost two hours. Part of the time she twisted her hands on the steering wheel while crying gut-wrenching sobs. Part of the time she talked out loud to a God she couldn't see. But, mostly she just drove letting the car eat up mile after mile of black pavement as her heart wrung itself dry of the emotions choking her. By the time she reached Jefferson a settled state of numbness was all that was left.

    The afternoon was growing late and she had not eaten anything since breakfast, so she pulled into a Dairy Queen, ordered a large cup of ice and paid the attendant with a sigh. The ice cost less than a dollar, but that was probably as far as the budget would stretch. Sitting in the parking lot, she dug into the backpack, popped the top on her warm Dr. Pepper, opened the crackers, and then pulled back onto the highway.

As the blacktop rolled beneath her again she noted the position of the sun; a couple of hours of light were still left in the day. If she remembered correctly, there was a seldom used road that ambled across the lower half of Wilson County before reaching Thyme from the west side.

The scenery would be beautiful and with luck she might come across a pecan tree loaded with nuts shedding them freely for anyone who would stop and pick them up.

Carefully watching for crossroads, she was soon rewarded by a small green sign announcing that County Road 3052 would reach Thyme in another 23 miles. She turned the wheel, slipped a Selah CD into the player and settled deeply in the comfortable seat.

The road was narrow and empty as it contorted around curves, dipped into bottom land and stretched over low, rolling hills. While the music fed her spirit, the picturesque scenery fed her soul and the tensions of the day began to ease. She loved this land and she understood the stubborn people it produced.

This forgotten corner of the big state had originally been populated by a few scattered tribes of peaceful Indians. When the first white men came little changed. The land was large and generous and for a time the two races shared the tranquil forest undisturbed by governments.

For a while, France claimed the land and then Mexico said the trees and lakes were hers, but each of these would-be authorities faced a local

JaKobe's Assignment

population who refused to believe the land belonged to anyone other than those who trapped, built, and cultivated it. The only government that came close to winning their allegiance was the one claiming Texas was a country all its own.

Although the republic only lasted nine years, the fierce independence and often wild nature of the people remained unchanged until after the Civil War. It was then the sparse population suddenly mushroomed as disillusioned families fled their beloved, destroyed South and brought with them a more civilized way of life.

Small, family-owned dairy and cotton farms sprang up in a patchwork of fifty to three hundred acre plots. Tiny towns replaced the scattered trading posts, Indians, and trappers.

Those remaining formed a new generation that mixed prejudice attitudes with generous hearts; big, boastful dreams with small bank accounts; and a high moral code with much rule bending on the side.

Then, sometime in the late '40s, another development forced a second wave of major change. The arrival of huge tractors and electrically powered irrigation systems combined to move farming profits to flatlands in the western part of the state. Small acreage farms on hilly land were left to die.

But they didn't die.

Even though most farms could no longer support families, they brought in limited income. Residents clung to their land, culture, and guns with the same stubborn resistance that their pioneer forefathers possessed. Some adapted by raising chickens. Others turned to fruit production. But many held on by becoming two-income families. Husbands worked to feed the cattle and pay interest on the farm mortgage, while their wives worked to provide groceries and pay bills.

Diane smiled. It was amazing how creative and determined humans could be when it came to holding on to something they loved. Even when what they held was more illusion than practical benefit, still the human heart found a way to hang on.

As her blood sugar responded to the soft drink and her stomach settled to munch on the crackers, her mood softened. Maybe she, too, clung to dreams that were more illusion than reality. Steve had left four years and six girl friends ago, but something deep inside still waited for him to come home. Something seemed to be stuck, frozen in time. How could the years get by so quickly?

She stretched her neck and looked at her face in the rearview mirror. Unsatisfied, she slowed the car to a crawl, pulled down the visor, flipped up the lighted mirror behind it and studied the reflection.

Tears and a nap had not helped the eye makeup. Pulling a tissue from the door pocket, she wet it with saliva and rubbed away black circles.

JaKobe's Assignment

The mirror reflected a pleasant, pixie face with a short tousle of chestnut hair and large, brown eyes. Fluffing the hair on top of her head and tucking short fragments behind her ears, she turned her face first left then right.

She suspected she had less wrinkles than other women in their mid-thirties. Or maybe that was just wishful thinking. She sucked a wad of crackers from between her teeth and raised her chin. All in all the view was not bad.

The words of a scripture echoed in her mind, *Man looks on the outward appearance, but the LORD looks on the heart.* [17]

Yeah, well, maybe that was true. But, that sure wasn't where Steve had kept his eyes!

Memories came back and the same questions that haunted her four years ago resurfaced. Had she overreacted when she found the emails and websites he had been visiting?

She had uncovered the first emails shortly before Casey was born when she accidentally opened his mail instead of hers.

Steve said it was a prank sent by a male from friend from work. He said was getting even by playing along. She wanted to believe that. She *did* believe that. At least, she believed it for a while.

Within months of the first discovery, Steve changed. He was critical, distant and often stayed up at night. He dropped out of church and alternated between sexualizing everything and withdrawing from her. She told herself it was the new baby or maybe he was having trouble accepting the weight she had gained while pregnant. But, at last, she did the thing that she swore she would never do. She started snooping.

A computer savvy friend taught her how to open emails after others thought they had been trashed and to pull up lists of websites that had been visited then simply erased.

What she found was both appalling and frightening. She felt as though someone had kicked her in the stomach and she might never draw another free breath. Yet, she kept silent.

Her first reaction was to blame herself. Surely, if she had been pretty enough, exciting enough, Steve would never have needed electronic satisfaction.

She booked an appointment with a counselor under the pretence of seeking help with a communication problem, but as she and Dr. Standish talked in the privacy of his office, she broke down and told him what she had discovered. By the end of the second session she realized the gravity of what she was dealing with and risks the future might hold.

Dr. Standish assured her that the problem was not her fault but those words were not what she wanted to hear. The solution would have been so much easier if the fault were 100% her own! If she possessed all of the blame, then she also possessed all control! She could force the situation to change simply by changing herself.

It was much harder to listen as Dr. Standish repeatedly encouraged her to recognize Steve was an adult who made his own decisions. Diane had never been so frightened in her life and she terminated counseling without Steve ever knowing she had sought outside help.

The situation rocked on for almost two years. It might have gone longer, but then she found the check stub. There was no denying the depth of the problem and no turning back.

She could remember the day as clearly as if it were happening in the present. She was standing in the utility room sorting laundry when she saw a white paper sticking out of the back pocket of Steve's jeans. Unfolding it, she noticed it was the receipt for his paycheck that was automatically deposited. Thinking nothing of it she laid the paper aside, but then something drew her back for a closer examination.

Diane had always written checks and paid bills from an account Steve funded, but other financial matters were in Steve's capable hands. It was a mutual agreement. She hated financial details and when she was honest with herself she enjoyed the privilege of leaving her husband with the full burden of planning the future and balancing the books.

But, as she examined the stub, she realized that the year-to-date totals were significantly above the amounts Steve budgeted for family expenses and savings. She tried to ignore the implications, but couldn't lay aside the haunting fear in her gut. So, with a regretful sigh, she found herself snooping once again.

She knew Steve thought of her as mentally rather dull and regarded her former success tracking his Internet history as a fluke. He had no idea the extent of her computer capabilities, so he was comfortable storing most of his passwords for automatic recall and it never occurred to him that because she knew his social security number she had immediate access to a great deal of his private life.

Diane had no trouble viewing checks from old bank statements and tracking purchases made by credit card. Within hours the shocking reality could was in her face. Within the past two years, seventeen thousand dollars was missing.

Well, it really wasn't "missing." She knew exactly where the money was. It had been given to places that peddled phone sex, chat lines and pornographic pictures. A significant amount had even found its way to a casino in Shreveport.

Steve had evidently received a raise eight months earlier and negotiated for the increase to be paid in bonuses rather than hourly. Adding these to his already significant semi-annual bonuses, made keeping her in the dark easy.

When she confronted him, his response was to move out and blame the separation on her. He said he could no longer live with a wife who invaded his privacy.

She was stunned. It all happened so fast! The divorce was long and ugly.

Perhaps the lowest point was that first Christmas without Steve. Casey had only recently been released from yet another hospital stay brought on by his ever present asthma and her depressed seven-year-old, Dwayne, never smiled.

She tried to pretend like nothing had happened and spent Christmas Day with her folks, but something inside her had died with the marriage. She doubted it would ever come alive again. That night, for the first time in her life, she deliberately drugged herself to sleep.

Yet, time truly did have a way of healing. Another Christmas came and went. Then, two more. Less sickness for the boys. A new job and back to school for their mom. Life in the piney woods rolled on just as it had for two hundred years. Sometimes, she could even smile.

It was while thinking of all this that Diane rounded a sharp curve and with delight saw what seemed to her a most beautiful sight designed by God and given to her, personally.

Five old pecan trees stood sentinel on both sides of the road bathing the area in dappled shade. They were showering leaves, hulls and nuts all over the ground and she applied the breaks so hard she nearly gave herself whiplash.

"Eureka!" she squealed tumbling out of the car to stand beneath the trees. "Thank You, Lord!" A sudden wind that stirred the limbs and a fresh shower of brown leaves fell around her. It was almost as though the Almighty had answered.

Diane stood very still for a moment breathing in the fresh, early evening air, amazed at the transformation the last few hours worked in her soul. In one afternoon she had walked through anger, bitterness, disappointment, sexual need, sorrow, confusion and had at last come to this moment of gratitude where she could feel the nearness of God.

Life wasn't always easy, but it certainly was an adventure!

With a smile on her lips and a light in her eyes, Diane returned to the car moving it as far to the shoulder as the one lane road would allow. She retrieved a couple of old Wal-Mart sacks from the trunk and surveyed the bounty around her. Ready-to-eat pecans were nine dollars a pound in the store and she would get hers free for only a little work. Well, maybe a lot of work.

The nuts were of good quality and larger than she expected from native trees. They had evidently been falling for a couple of weeks and many had rolled into the ditches that lined the road. Others were nestled under banks of leaves. Soon, the first bag was comfortably full and she started on a second.

As the rhythm of bending and stooping continued, she felt so good she started to sing. This time the words and music were not a defense but the bubbling over of a joyful heart.

"You shall go out with joy and be led forth in peace. The mountains and the hills will break forth before you. They'll be shouts of joy, and all the trees of the field will clap, will clap their hands.[18]"

The cows beyond the fence lifted their heads with curiosity and Diane found herself singing to the dumb beast.

Deciding the noisy human meant them no harm the cows went back to grazing, but joy was welling up inside and she lifted her hands toward the sky shuffling her feet in an impromptu version of mid-Eastern dancing.

"And all the trees of the field shall clap their hands (clap, clap). *The trees of the field shall clap their hands* (clap, clap). *The trees of the field shall clap their hands* (clap, clap) *while you go out with joy."*

Shrill laughter from behind a hedge interrupted the concert.

Her first instinct was to run, then she realized by the tone the laughter must be coming from children. Placing her hands on her hips she faced the bush.

"It's not nice to spy on people. You better get home before I tell your parents."

"It weren't me!" said a hidden voice with a decided Mexican accent. "He started it."

"Huh-uh. Did not." A small white body naked from the waist up jumped out from behind the brush. "Manny was the one who laughed first. All I did was giggle."

The scamp before her could not have been more than ten years of age. He was blond with a wiry, muscular body, canvas shoes and ragged jeans. Diane was so shocked by his lack of clothing that she forgot to be insulted. Her motherly instincts trumped the wounded ego of the singer.

"Young man, where is your shirt? You will catch your death of cold running around like that in this weather!"

"I ain't cold. Me and Manny never get cold. Ain't that right, Manny?"

By this time a second young boy was peering cautiously through the branches. His coal black hair was thick and windswept while his dark, wide eyes sparkled within the frame of a handsome brown face. He was fully dressed and perhaps a year older than the white boy. Diane crooked her finger encouraging him to step fully into the open and he cautiously obeyed. A shy smile edged its way to his face but he said nothing.

"And, your names would be . . .?"

"I'm Caleb," said the thin boy, "And, his name is Immanuel, but I call him Manny for short."

"Well, Caleb and Manny, my name is Diane. You two live around here?"

"Not far. Manny's got a four-wheeler just over that ridge. We was walkin' the pasture lookin' fer snakes."

"Snakes? There are no snakes this time of year. They've been hibernating for weeks."

"Shows how much you know." Caleb crossed his arms and shifted his weight. "I told you, I ain't cold. I got me a shirt back on the four-wheeler. And as fer snakes, you can sometimes find 'em under brush piles or rocks. If you do, they is easy to catch 'cause they've cooled down a bit. We was hopin' to find us a couple but we heard you singing and the cows all lookin' this way, so we snuck up to see what was goin' on."

"Aw-ha! So, that's why you laughed. You didn't like my singing!"

Manny exchanged a glance with Caleb who seemed to read his mind and speak for both of them.

"I guess you sing pretty good. But, you dance funny and the song don't make no sense. Trees ain't got no hands and they sure can't clap."

"The words are symbolic," she said without thinking. Then realizing the word symbolic was likely beyond their vocabulary, she added, "The words are out of the Bible."

"Then the Bible don't make no sense."

The Mexican boy seemed slightly alarmed by his friend's assertion.

"You should not say that, Caleb. The Bible is a holy book."

"You're right, Manny. Most of the words of the song were from the book of Isaiah and they just mean that when people love God, they sometimes get so happy that it *seems* as though the trees around them are clapping with joy."

"I love God," Caleb said defiantly. "And I don't hear no trees clappin'"

Diane was torn between a desire to set the boy's theology straight and the temptation to ignore the whole matter because explaining it would do no good. She chose the latter and changed the subject.

"Aren't your parents getting worried about you two? The sun will be down soon. Isn't it about supper time?"

"They never worry about me when I'm with Manny," Caleb said.

"And mine never worry about me when I'm with Caleb."

"Besides," Caleb continued, "we know how to find plenty of food if we're hungry."

"Like nuts?" Diane asked.

"Sure. And other stuff."

"Well, why don't you help me finish filling up this sack and I'll give each of you a cookie."

The bargain was quickly struck and Diane watched as the boys darted here and there picking up nuts, scattering the leaves as they went. She really didn't need their help, but she missed her own boys and these two youngsters delighted her with their wit and energy.

In less than fifteen minutes both plastic sacks were filled to overflowing and she safely tucked them away in the trunk of the car.

"Okay, now for your reward." Once more Diane rummaged through her backpack, locating the Ziplock at the very bottom. Three, slightly stale, oatmeal cookies were soon being passed around.

Immanuel received his with a polite, but doubtful look. Caleb was more vocal.

"I don't like oatmeal. And, this one ain't even got raisins."

"Sorry. You didn't ask what kind of cookies when we made the deal."

Caleb took a large bite out of one side and swallowed with an exaggerated, dry motion.

"I can get better stuff than this outa the pasture."

"Are you trying to tell me you think my cooking is as bad as my dancing?"

"Maybe. But, I can still get better stuff in a tree."

"Is that true, Manny?" Diane looked at the Mexican boy who had yet to take a bite. He grinned then replied with a slow nod.

"Se, Signora. Caleb gets good food from the land and trees."

"No way," said Diane. "Maybe I would believe that was true any other time of year, but not now. There are wild plums and berries in the spring, grapes and native pears in the summer and a host of other things. But the only wild food being produced this time of year is nuts."

"Naw. They is persimmons, too," said Caleb authoritatively.

"Not for several weeks," she corrected. "It isn't cold enough yet."

Caleb sighed and shook his head. "First you was wrong about snakes and now you think you know everything there is to know about persimmons."

Diane was taken back at the brashness of this bare-chested urchin. She wondered if he talked to all adults with such impudence or if that privilege was reserved for lonely old women he found by the roadside.

"Show me," she challenged.

"Sure. I got me a tree not far from here." The boy seemed to revel in his role as guide and provider. "You take yer car and go 'round the next two curves, then crawl through the fence on that side." He pointed to the left. "Me and Manny 'll take the four-wheeler and meet ya."

"Are you sure the property owners won't mind?"

"Never have afore."

Diane was up for this little bit of adventure and chuckled to herself as she settled behind the wheel. This was fun. Nothing like following a sassy little kid through the underbrush to get your blood flowing.

It wasn't hard to find the place Caleb mentioned and she hadn't wiggled her way through a barbed wire fence in years. She could hear the four-wheeler roaring just across the meadow and followed the sound.

Manny was driving with Caleb straddled behind him and, sure enough, the long forgotten flannel shirt was tied to the back, waving in the wind like a flag.

"Your parents let you boys ride around without helmets?" she asked as the expensive bike pulled to a stop.

"Don't need no helmets," Caleb said and Manny nodded in agreement.

"Well, if you were my boys, you sure would wear them. No sense getting killed if it can be avoided."

Each boy looked at the other with an expression of pity and shook their head. A woman this dumb probably came from the city.

"This here is a persimmon tree." Caleb announced.

"I know a persimmon tree when I see one." Diane defended herself in a flat tone. "But, I still say that until we get a good freeze, that fruit will pucker your mouth worse than a lemon. At least a lemon tastes good, but the tannin acid in those things will make them as bitter as gall."

The phrase, *tannin acid*, impressed the boys, but they didn't say so.

"I know how to get some good ones. You watch me."

Caleb was already clinging to a low branch with both hands and working his feet up the trunk. Within moments he was clinging to an impossibly thin upper branch like a spider monkey. He selected one of the highest, thinnest twigs and began shaking it. Several rust colored balls a little over an inch in diameter tumbled to the ground.

"Well, ain't you gonna catch 'em? They're no good if they splat."

Diane laughed. "What do you expect? The fruit is small and catching it as it falls is nearly impossible!" She looked around for a solution.

"Tell you what. How about if Manny and I use your shirt like a big basket? That should help."

"You got good ideas, fer a girl."

Manny unwrapped the plaid flannel shirt from the back bar of the four wheeler and soon a makeshift landing area was stretched almost three feet square. "Okay, Caleb. Let 'em fall!"

The boy carefully picked among the thin upper branches until he found one to his liking. With a firm hand he grasped the base and gave the twig a shake. Five globes fell and bounced on the smooth surface of the tautly held shirt.

Diane squealed with delight and scooped the fruit into her hands. Their wrinkled, orange-red rinds were the texture of thin plastic and the fruit beneath was as soft as mush. She split one rind with her fingernail, sucked out the fruit and spit the seed.

"Caleb, that's delicious! Send down a few more!"

The boy beamed and the brief game of catch continued. The tree was full of fruit, but only a very few globes in the topmost branches were eatable. Within minutes Caleb gave up the search for ripe fruit and dropped to the ground.

Diane wondered if he would smugly announce that she had been wrong about the persimmons. But, he surprised her by looking up with hopeful expectation and asking, "Did I do good? Do you like 'em?"

"Yes! Those very top branches must have been exposed to enough cold so that the acid in these

JaKobe's Assignment

particular fruits has turned to sugar weeks ahead of fruit on the lower branches.

"Look," Diane held out her hand. "I saved some for you and Manny. And, they really are much better than my stale cookies."

Each boy took some fruits, pierced the rind and sucked out the sweet, bright orange pulp. "Are you a teacher?" Manny asked thoughtfully.

"What makes you think that?"

"You use big words and you knew about the Bible. You even know about persimmons."

"No, Manny, I'm not a teacher. I'm just a mommy with two little boys about the age of you and Caleb."

"What's their names?"

"Dwayne and Casey."

"Could you bring 'em to play sometime?"

Diane remembered how hard it was to juggle school schedules, visits with Steve and church activities, not to mention her own class schedule and her janitor job.

"Well, not any time soon," she said. "They have a lot to do and I go to school, too."

"No way," said Caleb. "Y'er too old. They don't let grownups go to school."

"Yes, they do. I go to college and I hope to be a nurse in a couple of years."

"Really?"

"Cross my heart."

"Will you give shots and everything?"

"Probably so."

"I don't like school. Ner shots neither."

"Well, I can't say I'm fond of those two things myself. But, if I want to be a nurse, I guess I'll have to put up with plenty of both."

Caleb looked at the remaining fruit in Diane's hand. "There ain't but two left. Why don't you take 'em to your little boys? Maybe then they could come back when the rest 're ripe and help us pick?"

She smiled and dropped the two small fruit into her shirt pocket thinking how wonderful it would be to let her boys romp the pastures for a long, lazy afternoon with Caleb and Immanuel.

So many of the good things in life seemed to get squeezed out by the necessary and urgent. She hated to say no, but the reality was …

While she contemplated how best to phrase her answer, Manny's eyes grew wide. "Caleb," he said in a soft voice. "We better go now."

Caleb frowned. Manny ought to know who was the leader of this team and it sure wasn't the Mexican boy even if he did own a four-wheeler.

Then, he noticed Manny's eyes. They were looking right past him to a rise in the meadow. He turned and so did Diane wondering what had the boys so fascinated.

It was a bull.

"Uh-oh," Caleb said. "Big Red is back."

"I take it you two know that monster."

"He done chased us a couple-a times, but the farmer moved him in the spring."

"Well, I guess he's come home for the winter," said Diane. She was not terribly frightened, just respectful. Very respectful.

She watched as the beast lowered his head and pawed at the dirt. He was standing less than a hundred feet away.

"Boys, you two get back on the four-wheeler. Move slowly and don't start the motor until I tell you. We don't want to give Mr. Bull any reason for concern. The noise might cause him to leave, but it could just as easily make him charge. Just move slowly and get on the ATV."

As the boys began backing away from the tree, Diane considered her own situation. The ATV could easily outrun the bull, but it would not hold three people. The strong branches on the persimmon tree were too low to offer safety and the higher ones were too thin to hold her weight. The only option was to put the barbed wire fence between herself and that mass of steaks on the hoof.

"What about you? Caleb asked.

"I'll be fine. I'm going to walk backward toward the fence. Big Red is probably just as frightened by us as we are by him."

All three humans moved with a casualness they did not feel. The boys reached the ATV and straddled it. Manny put his hand on the key and waited while Diane continued to walk slowly backward.

When she was ten yards from the fence she shouted, "Okay, boys, get home to supper!" and headed for the fence at a dead run.

The bull froze briefly, surprised by the sudden movement and noise. He gave a lazy, half-lunge to the right and then to the left as though undecided as to which target posed the most threat. Then almost instantly, he lost interest in the fight and watched the invading humans leave without further protest.

Diane reached the fence, pulled the two center wires apart with her hands and ducked her body through the hole tearing the sleeve of her shirt in the process. By the time she was safely on the other side, the sound of the four-wheeler was fading. Caleb and Manny would cross the pasture and probably negotiate a gate or two before the ATV reached the road. She would not see the boys again.

She got in her car, took a moment to compose herself, and started the motor, then remembered the two persimmons. Fishing them out of her pocket, she gently placed them in the passenger seat for the ride home.

Dwayne and Casey would be back on Monday after school. She would serve them milk and cookies and ask about their weekend. Then, she would tell them about the two boys she met. She would show them the persimmons and tell them how God used the buffeting of cold and exposure to change the acid in the fruit to sugar.

Casey would probably think the story "cool" and maybe be adventuresome enough to sample the fruit. Dwayne, . . . well, he would likely ignore everything she said.

But, she would tell him anyway.

The car ate up mile after mile of black, twisting ribbon. Thyme couldn't be much further. The late afternoon was shifting toward sunset and soon the roads became familiar as the outskirts of Thyme came in sight.

What now? The words were gentle, yet persistent on her mind.

Indeed, she thought, what now? She really did not want to return to the house on Apple Street, but there was no place else to go. The idea of going to church seemed confining—almost suffocating. What now?

She drove with one hand, pulled her backpack from the floorboard and rummaged through its content. Her Bible. An old paperback song book. Some gum. Three dollars and change. Two pencils. It was enough.

She'd buy a hamburger, fix some tea in her own kitchen, take the Bible and songbook to the back yard and watch God bring out the stars. It would be cold, but so what? If a little discomfort could turn acid to sugar, maybe it could do the same for her disquieted heart.

*****

Phennia was leaning forward from the car's backseat watching Diane shuffle through the contents of the backpack. The woman seemed interested in the Bible and the money. Phennia wondered if she had plans for each. Probably. Her human often spent time considering both those objects with great interest.

When she left the house hours earlier Phennia had decided to check on the boys and drift around town for a while. She thought it would be safe enough since Diane's opposition level had been reached and the angel doubted any evil being would start trouble.

She hadn't counted on the bull.

When Diane's fear level spiked, it took angel speed to intervene. Fortunately, animals were much easier to manipulate than humans.

She settled back and considered the situation. What was next for Diane? Her mood was much improved, but she seemed somehow ... empty.

It was something like the way humans became when they were ill or very weary. Only this was different. She pulled out an Evaluator, aimed it at the back of Diane's head and took a reading.

Nothing too unusual. Hope was low, but not alarmingly so. Maybe there were some things about humans that angels would never understand.

She settled back then smiled. Diane might think life was an adventure from her perspective, but if the woman wanted a real sight, she should see it from Phennia's view!

JaKobe's Assignment

4:40 PM

The Recital

Soon after Ben went to change clothes, JaKobe nodded to his fellow angels and vanished from the Phelp's living room. A moment later he was standing at the front of Grace Community sanctuary, his Evaluator resting loosely in his left hand while he waited.

LeeAnn had just finished announcing that Melody had been in a slight accident, but she and Jonathan were on their way and a murmur rose from the crowd as friends shared questions and concern.

JaKobe could have eves dropped on any of the human conversations swirling around him, but instead he chose to listen for a noise from the street. He believed his man would be at his best about the time he stepped through the doors.

It had been a good day for Jonathan. He obediently yielded to the Holy Spirit for his morning sermon and the way he took over in the recent family crisis was commendable despite the failure with his son. The visit with Margaret had stripped some of his defenses and the stress of the last hour would make the pastor keenly aware of his own inner world. It should be an excellent time for a reading.

Knowing when to take a significant reading was important. Humans were such emotional creatures readings could easily shift according to momentary events. A full understanding of one of Adam's children was never easy yet a full understanding was exactly the goal JaKobe sought.

Recommending a change in the level of opposition would impact Jonathan and everyone he loved for years to come. The right level, rightly responded to, would strengthen, bring reward and mean new advancement for the Kingdom. The wrong level would provide opportunity for the enemy. Too low, and the enemy fed on weak character traits encouraging humans to remain soft. Too high, and there was risk of overwhelming or discouraging the frail creatures of dust.

He stood alert as the sound of rusting metal hinges indicated the outside doors were opening then extending his arm to eye level took aim.

As the interior doors swung open, all eyes turned to see Melody enter leaning heavily on Jonathan's arm. She smiled then glanced at her husband who reassured her with his eyes.

JaKobe's Assignment

Purposely withdrawing his arm, Jonathan let her walk alone using the ends of the pews for occasional support. She moved a few steps then glanced back. He offered a nod and smile. JaKobe gave the command and lights of the Evaluator began to glow.

"Thank you for waiting," Melody said as she moved up the center aisle. "Did you ever have one of those days when nothing goes as you planned?" The audience laughed politely.

At that moment Melody remembered she left her tote behind, but Jonathan lifted it, indicating where the it would be, and dropped the bag on the end of a back pew. He pointed to the door and mouthed the word *cookies*. She returned his silent message with a nod and continued speaking to the audience.

"I know everyone is wondering what happened, but it is really nothing. One of our kitchen stools and I had an argument. I lost."

Again, the audience laughed—a little louder this time—as they began to relax.

"But, you didn't come this afternoon to hear about my fights with the furniture. You came to hear your children and to enjoy an hour of music.

"I promise we will get out on time, so without further delay—Jamie, could you bring me that blue bag on the end of the pew? That's it. Thanks—we will have our first budding prodigy, Paul Baker, who will play. . ." she paused, took the bag from Jamie and pulled *Beginner Book Two* from a side pocket.

"Paul is going to play, 'Counting Stars,' she announced then reaching to the piano, spread open the music to the proper page.

From the left side, third row back, a five-year-old boy in a suit stepped forward and took a bow. His thick, brown hair, dark eyes and light olive skin gave him a slightly exotic look while his suit and well proportioned body made him seem more like a tiny man than a child. He mounted the steps to the stage and took his position beside a waist high piano bench.

"I will play for you, 'Counting Stars.'" Using both hands and a knee, he climbed on the bench. "I hope you like it."

He breathed deeply and announced, "And-a-one, and-a-two," The audience chuckled while his parents beamed. The tiny virtuoso sounded like a miniature Lawrence Welk.

Then, to everyone's surprise, Paul continued to count out loud all during the song. Melody remembered telling him he could do that if that made him feel more comfortable but even she had not expected him to be so loud. *A-one-and-a-two, and a-one.* It seemed the stars were not the only thing being counted. Mild laughter rippled through the gathering.

Paul wiggled off the bench and bowed again to the audience. "Thank you," he said, graciously accepting their applause.

Melody had taken a seat on the front pew. Now, by using the arm and backrest for support she stood and turned to the audience. "We will

JaKobe's Assignment

next hear from Kara Lynn McKinsey. She will be playing, 'Winter Roses.'" Another child, nervous and dressed in Sunday best, took the stage.

Melody looked at her watch and calculated the minutes each performer would take. There was no way to follow the planned schedule and still keep her promise to end the program on time.

Normally, the situation would have set off alarm bells inside her over-stressed mind, but not tonight. It was as though the emotional catharsis of the last hour had released something tight and festering. Inside, she felt better than she had all day and as she considered the situation with calm objectivity, a solution bubbled to the surface of her mind. She would award the ribbons during the refreshments. That would add almost fifteen minutes to the schedule.

By five forty-seven, the program had moved from the newest student to the most experienced teen. Parents had bitten their nails and snapped pictures while their children performed and then hugged and patted their offspring as they returned to their seats.

Now, it was time for the best student of all and Melody rose for the final announcement. It was time for Luke to shine.

But, when she stood to announce him, Melody was surprised as he interrupted. "Folks, if you will be patient for just a moment, we have something special for our teacher."

He reached behind the pulpit and drew out a dozen roses placing them in her arms. The audience applauded. "Now, Mrs. Phelps, if you'll be seated I have another surprise for you."

Not knowing what else to do, Melody sat back down on the front pew while Luke removed the roses from her arms and replaced them with a bound music score. The front cover indicated it had come from London. *Symphony No 3 by Charles Ives (1874-1954).*

He whispered, "You may not be able to critique this on such short notice, but I highlighted the appropriate passages in case you might like to try and follow." He grinned wickedly and added, "If you can keep up, that is."

Melody vaguely remembered hearing this work years ago, but to the best of her recollection there was no concerto movement. When she opened the score, the music, as expected, was for full orchestra, not piano solo.

Luke stepped to the piano, seated himself and placed his fingers on the keys. He relaxed his shoulders and concentrated on his breathing as a tiny moment of expectant silence. Then, with a sudden burst of energy the room erupted as Luke's fingers flew over black and white keys.

Melody was shocked. He was not strictly following the score, but improvising. She knew Luke composed occasionally and that he was skilled enough to do a little musical translation work, but this was amazing.

He had tabbed the beginning of the Andante Maestoso and she quickly turned trying to keep up with his rapid progress.

The original composer had interspaced his symphony with bits and pieces of popular gospel music from the turn of the century.[19] Some cords were unmelodic and rhythms almost jazz-like as fragments of hymns wove their way in an out in tiny, repetitive themes. Luke had expanded the gospel themes without losing the character of Ives' work.

The dissident cords gave way to, *"O for a thousand tongues to sing / My great Redeemer's praise / The glories of my God and King/ The triumphs of His grace!"* Then, just as suddenly, the music flipped back into Ive's unique style. The sharp, unexpected notes jerked then melted seamlessly back into the hymn and she found herself humming, *"Oh what peace we often forfeit / Oh what needless pain we bear / All because we do not carry / Everything to God in prayer."*

Melody thought she would jump from the pew! She had known Luke was good. Very good. But, this was far beyond anything she expected. How long had he worked on memorizing those transitions?

The tempo picked up to an even more rapid pace. He was moving into an Allegro and she fumbled with the tabs searching to find the spot to which he was so effortlessly racing. This time she heard pieces of "There is a Fountain Filled with Blood" and "Down at the Cross." She wanted to hum the quick stucco, *"Redeeming love has been my theme and shall be 'till I die…and shall be 'till I die"*

A gentle Largo movement was next and the hymns were more clearly heard as they gently drifted their way in snatches through complex cords. *"Just as I am, without one plea / but that thy blood was shed for me / O Lamb of God, I come"* "What a friend we have in Jesus / All our sins and grief's to bear"

Then for the last time, he cycled to the beginning theme and she quietly repeated, *"His blood can make the foulest clean / His blood availed for me,"* finishing with a sound that moved from tender expression to explosive passion, he suddenly dropped to a whisper for the final notes.

Forgetting her injury Melody jumped up, winced, and began to applaud wildly. The complexity and talent of what she had just heard took her breath away! For a moment she was in a concert hall begging a famous pianist to follow with an encore. Then, she turned to face the audience and reality came back with a rush.

The crowd of parents, children, and amateur music lovers were clapping politely but showing little enthusiasm. They had enjoyed Kara Lynn's "Winter Roses" far more.

It was time for cookies and punch and the children were anxious to receive ribbons for their semester of work. The loud popping of her own hands and shouted *bravo* were completely out of sync with the rest of the room. She stopped making a fool of herself and the room grew quiet.

Melody announced the end of the recital, invited the guests to refreshments in fellowship hall, reminded them that ribbons would be awarded during the reception then thanked everyone for coming to support the children. The crowd of some fifty people broke up and milled about pushing their way into the halls.

Luke slowly stood from the piano bench and drifted down from the stage with a lazy, loose gate.

"You were amazing," she said when he at last stopped before her.

"Yeah? Well, I practiced a lot," he tossed back the blond bangs from his face. "Can I help you with something?"

She smiled her appreciation handing him the heavy tote bag. He shrugged the strap over one shoulder then offered a steady arm to lean on. "Shall we go, ma'am?"

They traveled only a few steps when Melody stopped and looked up into his face. "Luke," she called his name and then paused until she had his full attention. "Don't be too disappointed."

Indicating the crowd of retreating backs she tilted her head. "They just don't understand the beauty and enormous complexity of what you just did."

"Aw, Mrs. Phelps, it's all right. I was just trying out something new to please you."

She searched his eyes. "No, Luke. You have the fire of a true artist. There is something sad about giving a performance like that and having only one person in the audience who understands."

He responded with the same crooked grin she had frequently seen in the last few years and, as always, she wondered what lay behind that half-smile.

They were almost to the auditorium exit door when they met Jonathan fighting upstream against the crowd. "There you are!" he greeted. "I was coming to see if you needed help, but I see you are in good hands."

"Yes. Excellent, talented hands," she smiled encouragement at Luke. "Were you able to hear that unbelievable performance?"

"I caught it over the speakers while LeeAnn and I finished up with food detail." He reached for Melody's hand and relieved the teen of the blue tote bag.

"I had never heard anything quite like it, Luke. I recognized some of the hymns, but the rest of the composition...well, I don't have Melody's training or ear, but I know quality and technique when I hear it. Who was the composer?"

"An American," he answered. "I improvised some, but the original work was Charles Ives. He didn't receive much recognition during his life, but later they began to realize his genius. Some call him one of the greatest composers of the 20th century and often he is said to be uniquely American."

"I wonder what that means?" Jonathan huffed. "Seems to me that being 'unique' is a pretty vague and probably useless quality."

Melody thought she felt Luke stiffen slightly at Jonathan's remark, but they had reached the reception area and other matters needed her attention. She hugged each pupil, congratulated parents and someone handed her a glass filled with water for the roses.

Jonathan insisted she take a chair and even retrieved a stepstool from the kitchen for use as a foot prop. With her tote bag sitting on the floor and a list of student names in her lap, she began announcing rewards, feeling just a bit like Santa Claus. The ribbons and a few trophies were soon in the hands of smiling students and even the most stoic teen seemed pleased with the small recognition.

At six fifty-two Melody glanced at the wall clock. Surprised, she looked around the room. She had been so busily engaged in congratulations and small talk, she hardly noticed as Jonathan and a few other volunteers cleared away the leftovers and took out the trash. The room was almost empty as Luke approached her with his easy style.

"Well, Teach, another semester is gone." He looked around the room. I think the ladies have most everything packed away and your husband has gone to the auditorium. Need help making the trip back there?"

"Oh, I'm sure I could make it, but a little help would be greatly appreciated."

He picked up the tote and extended his arm. "Glad to accommodate."

They walked in silence for a moment then Melody said, "You know the Van Cliburn International will be held in Fort Worth this August."

"I know."

"You might have a chance to be part of the competition."

"Do you think I am ready?"

"After tonight? I think you are ready for about anything the piano world might throw at you!"

He grinned, but said nothing.

They were well down the hall when Melody paused and turned toward him. "I hope what Jonathan said about being *unique* didn't hurt your feelings."

She knew by the shadow passing over his eyes that for some reason the remark had stung, but Luke only shrugged. She waited until he felt obligated to say more.

"I wasn't offended."

She lowered her chin and looked skeptical.

"Well, at least not much." He paused, and then added, "I always took pride in the fact that I was a bit *unique*."

They continued on. She wanted to know more about her mysterious prize pupil and tonight their joint understanding of the music gave them a connection just strong enough to risk the question she had wanted to ask for two years.

"Ben mentioned that you have an Italian uncle. Have you ever been there?"

JaKobe's Assignment

He laughed without humor and Melody paused by the door making no attempt to enter the auditorium. The service was beginning as Beverly sounded the first notes of the evening prelude, yet Luke instinctively knew his teacher was not concerned with the time and would wait if he chose to talk. It was an unspoken and tempting invitation.

"Look, Mrs. Phelps, not even Ben knows this, but I was raised in Italy from the time I was five until I was eleven. My dad's name was Luigi Machiavelli and my mom was Alice Smith. They met in college when he was an exchange student in this country.

"I had no idea."

"Most people don't.

"Mom and Dad divorced when I was three and he died when I was four. For a while I lived with grandparents somewhere in Iowa. Then, grandpa had a stroke so I was shipped back to California with Mom. She couldn't handle a budding career and a kid, too, so I was sent to Italy to live with Uncle Raffaelo, his wife and their two girls."

"So you speak Italian?"

"Si, parlo l'italiano," Luke grinned. "But divorces keep me moving around the map. When Raffaelo and Ramona split, she took the girls and he was stuck with me. That didn't work out too well for Uncle. He had a job and wanted to start a new life. I guess he tried. I was almost eleven when he finally gave up and sent me back to America."

Melody knew that Jonathan would be wondering what had become of her, but something inside told her this conversation was important. Luke had been her student and Ben's best friend for almost two years but this was the first time he had been willing to share anything beyond surface information. She had never even met his mother but twice.

"By that time, Mom had gone back to her maiden name and moved to a place called, Texas." His teacher smiled knowingly. To a young, Italian boy, Texas must have seemed as foreign as the moon.

"Things were better financially by then, but having a little Luigi Machiavelli running around the house reminded her too much of things she would rather forget. So, since I looked like her side of the family and spoke fluent English …" he waved his hand like a magician. "Behold, Luke Smith was suddenly "born" at age eleven and Luigi Machiavelli Junior vanished forever.

"What do you think? Does having two names and two cultures and God only knows how many "parents" who took part in my raising, make me unique?"

Melody heard the pain and resentment in his voice, but said nothing. She studied his eyes until he looked away then studied his shoes. He seemed both reluctant and hopeful when he continued.

"The one consistent thing in my life has been the sound of a piano. Dad started teaching me when I was three. I've had good teachers in two countries, but I've usually gone beyond them within a few months.

"When I turned fifteen, I called the college and asked the head of the department about local teachers. The professor said that you didn't have as many degrees as some, but as far as encouraging students to reach their full potential, you were the best."

Melody cocked her head and her eyes widened in amazement.

"Oh, so you didn't know your reputation reached that far?

"Anyway," Luke continued his story. "As I said, I was only fifteen and you lived twenty-five miles away. I didn't have a driver's license but Mom didn't care, so after she signed me up for lessons, I would drive to Thyme, park around the corner and tell you my Mom dropped me off."

"Why, you scamp!"

"What can I say? It worked."

They were laughing too loudly when Allen announced the second hymn.

"Think you can make it the rest of the way by yourself?" Luke loosened the tote from his shoulder.

"I could tell you, no, but that wouldn't be the truth." Melody reached out taking hold of familiar blue bag. "But you've come this far, why don't you stay for the service? Jonathan's not a bad preacher. You might just find you enjoy the experience."

"Aw, Mrs. Phelps, I can't go in a church. The roof would cave in."

"Fat chance. Why not try adding God to that unique history? It could be your adventures are only beginning."

His only answer was that mysterious, crooked half-smile.

JaKobe's Assignment

6:45 PM

Twilight on the Hills of Thyme

JoKobe left the church shortly after Jonathan returned with the cookies. His readings were complete and he wanted to reflect and pray before coming to a final decision. In his travels that afternoon, he had noticed a particularly lovely hill not far from Grace Community and decided to catch the sunset from its summit. Instead of concentrating on earth, he would turn his mind heavenward for a while and refresh.

The angel was moving up the hill with long, purposeful strides when a breeze stirred the grass on the far side of the meadow. It rushed his direction making the grasses move as though dancing with joy and for the first time in his earthly sojourn JaKobe missed being able to interact with matter.

As a creature composed of light, he experienced the same sensations humans enjoyed, yet he lacked one critical element: the ability to freely exchange with matter.

As the wind raced past it blew through, not around him and the smells of sun-warmed earth and damp evening air were things he chose to understand, not the natural interaction between chemicals and bodily sensors.

With feet that could have walked above or through the ground, he chose to press against the surface of the soil and topped the hill just as the sun dipped behind the trees some fifty yards beyond him. The blue horizon turned to pink and lavender while branches became black etchings scratched against the softness. *Beauty. Handiwork of the Final Authority. Nature. Knowledge of God freely given to all who had eyes to see. Glory.*

How wonderful to be in this place and behold the wonders unfolding around him. He was so glad he had made it in time to watch the colors form.

Time. How strange to be concerned with that illusion. For seven hundred years on the other side he had enjoyed the realities of before and after without the constraint of time as earth experienced it. Here, he was constantly aware of hours and schedules and clocks.

He bent to examine the shape of a pebble just as Rachael came over the ridge. Angels often greeted one another with bits of memorized scripture and as she approached her friend, words flowed from her smile.

"*To Him be glory; world without end!*"[20] she shouted. The words were heartfelt, yet she quoted

JaKobe's Assignment

facts as a child might quote truths they had learned but never personally experience.

"Welcome, Rachael! Welcome indeed!" JaKobe's face brightened at the presence of a fellow soldier. Worship was always enhanced by the presence of others and multiplied when shared. He was delighted she had sought and found him in this place.

They walked together in silence for a moment then he asked, "Do you ever wish you could pick them up?" She looked at him with puzzled expression. "You know, the pebbles. Or the flowers, for that matter. Do you ever want to pick them up?"

She didn't have time to respond before his face cracked open with a wide grin and he looked up. Gentle laughter rippled as Maltus and Rimnon joined the group.

"The earth is the Lord's and all its fullness," Maltus began and was immediately joined by Rimnon, *"The world and those who dwell therein."*[21]

Rachael laughed out loud. "More friends! Welcome!" Then she turned more sober and asked, "Do you miss moving rocks, Rimnon?"

"Rocks?" It took a moment for him to realize she was serious. "No, not really. I can touch and move real objects on the other side anytime. I have plenty to do on this side managing the powers I've already been given without adding a physical element."

"So you think it's unnecessary to respond to physical realities?" asked JaKobe.

Rimnon's face grew serious as he considered the question. "I've never found response necessary..."

He had only began when an object that looked like a pinecone raced toward him narrowly missing his head. He ducked just as the missile dissipated behind him in a rainbow of sparkles and three angels dissolved in laughter.

"JaKobe! Behave yourself!" he shouted with mock anger.

"You said you didn't need to respond to matter," he teased. "I was just taking you at your word."

"That wasn't matter," argued Rimnon. "You made that 'pinecone' out of pure energy."

"Yes, but you didn't know that when you ducked!" They all laughed.

"Well, he won't fall for that trick next time," Rachael put in with a chuckle. "I'll bet my hallo on that."

The laughter slowly settled and JaKobe seated himself on a nearby stone. "Rachael, that is the second time today I have heard you say that silly phrase. You know angels don't bet on outcomes like foolish humans."

He reached her direction, palm extended upward in an almost pleading motion. "Besides, you don't even own a hallo."

"Of course I do," she stated flatly. With a mock pout she crossed her arms stubbornly over her chest as she had seen humans do. "I just left it in the closet back home."

Angel laughter again pealed loudly over the meadow. It increased and soon left the moorings of the joke far behind. They laughed for the pure pleasure of laughter. They laughed with, at, and for each other. Joy flooded them all. Joy because humor was a quality they had been given by a gracious Creator. Joy because they could see and participate in both the worlds of spirit and matter. Joy because of friendship. Joy because color and light existed on this third planet from a star.

"We heard laughter and came to join you!" It was the voice of BaLanna as he, Zobath and two others cleared the tops of nearby trees and approached the group at lightning speed. "It sounds like a celebration."

"All of that and more," replied Maltus. "We celebrate the pink and gold sunset on this planet of blue and green. We celebrate our comradeship and the adventure of battle. We laugh at the joy of watching son's of God come into their own inheritance and most of all we celebrate the Creator and sustainer of it all!"

BaLanna quoted scripture. *"I will be glad and rejoice in You, I will sing praise to Your name, O Most High!"*[22] He said it a second time as JaKobe, Rachael and Maltus joined in. They repeated a third time more loudly as every angel on the hill joined in.

"Your name, O Most High!" shouted a new group flying directly out of the sitting sun and landing a few yards away. These new comers did not actually join the group, but dropped to the

surface over by the trees. The new angels set up a discussion among themselves and occasionally laughter was heard, as a fresh reason to rejoice became the topic of the moment.

JaKobe began to speak addressing only those nearby who chose to listen. "The glory of our heaven is beyond compare, yet here, in this simple, tree lined meadow there is a different kind of glory: A rhythm. A created balance. Earth holds a special kind of glory like nothing else in the universe."

"We understand," replied three voices, unrehearsed yet in perfect unity.

There was silence for a moment. Three more angels joined the group. One moved away. Seven arrived across the meadow.

"Do you ever wonder why He made this place?" asked Rachael taking the lead.

"It is the beginning of man's home," offered BaLanna, then added, "Although surely not his final one."

"Why create a temporary way station?" she asked rhetorically. "If it is not man's final home, then what is the purpose of earth?"

"A battlefield." Maltus was thinking of his still suffering friend, Vinyon.

"A schoolroom," said two voices in unison.

"A place to prepare creatures in His image" said another.

No one argued any particular answer as wrong or right. None competed for space to explain their particular viewpoint. All listened and

JaKobe's Assignment

considered, rehearsing the wonder within themselves.

The voice of a newcomer who appeared to be a battle weary negro took the lead. *"The heavens declare the glory of God, the skies proclaim the work of His hands. Day after day they pour fourth speech, night after night they display knowledge. There is no speech or language where their voice is not heard."*[23]

"Glory shown in the skies," said another single voice.

"Glory shown in the trees and fields," said another.

"Glory shown in the waters, rivers and seas," said a third.

"How much poorer we would all be if God had not condescended to show us something of Himself through creation!" replied Rachael. "Because of earth—because of man—we see so much more of Him. If the Almighty had not chosen to show us Himself through these material things, some of His attributes would forever have been locked in the boundless abyss of His divine nature, unknown to any but Himself alone. God brought all creatures into being that they might know Him."

"That they might know Him," repeated several voices in unison.

"To know the unknowable and behold the unapproachable Light of Life," JaKobe offered. "What honor God has given His creatures!"

By this point over a hundred heavenly beings were scattered around the fifty-acre meadow.

They had been drawn to this place by the sound of praise to be refreshed together. Five at one time arrived from Tel Aviv where an unusual moment of Sabbath rest in government function provided opportunity to be with others of their kind. Some arriving angels were waiting for new assignments and others, like JaKobe, were catching a brief reprieve while their human charge remained close in the vicinity.

BaLanna floated upward a few feet and began to speak. "Our God is the only self-existent One."

He stated a fact they all knew yet each angel attending to his voice recognized something unique and wonderful about that single statement. Without plan or compulsion they gathered around as BaLanna led them in antiphonal response to his simple statement.

"The Almighty has no creator."

"Nothing existed before the I Am."

"He owes His being to Himself alone."

They spoke one at a time while perhaps fifty feet away a group of ten began to respond in unity. One word was all they offered. One word repeated again and again. It was like the undertone of a base drum supporting and driving all other notes. "Holy, Holy, Holy!"

"Transcendent! The Divine stands separate from creation." As BaLanna spoke again, the sound of "Holy, Holy" went on consistently, resolutely.

"Timeless, spaceless, single, lonely. / Lone in grandeur, lone in glory!"

"God is other; nothing is His peer." A vibrant and clear voice sounded.

"Above and beyond all else." Higher pitched and soft.

BaLanna shouted one word: "Omnipotent!"

"Nothing and no one can stay His hand," came the response.

"His power will never be overcome."

"His desires will be accomplished."

"Holy, Holy, Holy!" The foundation voices rolled on.

Calling out a new attribute BaLanna cried, "God is the source and definition of all that is good."

"All have received of His bounty." A single angel voice.

"Leading His creation to know what is good." Two voices joined.

"Opening His hand with mercy abundant." Five spoke

The colors of sunset had gently faded and now light was refracted by earth's atmosphere.

Without shadow, a deepening blue light enveloped everything and mist began to rise from the creek. Twilight had come.

"Holy, Holy, Holy!" The beat drove on relentlessly as one group then another took up the call. "Holy, Holy, Holy!" Unheard by human ear, the hilltop rang with praise. "Holy, Holy, Holy!" every voice in the meadow took up the theme.

JaKobe longed to stay. How wonderful! How like heaven! If he could only stay on the hilltop with others of his kind filling his being with the satisfying joy of worship! But, duty was calling. It was time to leave.

He turned toward the town and saw darkness, not of earth but of spirit. Consuming fury boiled like dark clouds ripped by a storm. Surrounding the angels of light it pulsated with hatred. Any angel leaving the meadow would have to fight their way through the blackness before returning to their stations.

It was as expected. No matter how brightly the glory of earth shown, the reality of sin and sorrow could not be ignored. The created order and beauty of this planet had been marred and twisted.

JaKobe drew his sword, but before plunging into the darkness he turned back and raised the sword in salute to fellow soldiers. Shouting above the praises, he quoted a scripture they all knew well, *"Bless the LORD, you His angels,/ Who excel in strength, who do His word, / Heeding the voice of His word. / Bless the LORD, all you His host; / You ministers of His, who do His pleasure. / Bless the LORD, all His works / In all places of His dominion: / Bless the LORD O my soul."*[24]

Then refreshed and with renewed vigor he plunged into the fight. Destiny was calling.

7:55 PM

Three Battlefields

Twilight had passed and darkness was settling in by the time Diane picked up a burger and reached the house on Apple Street. The white frame structure with its wide front porch and green shutters stood back among the trees in a manner that was neither welcoming nor foreboding. The non-descript residence attracted little attention but it was home and she was grateful to be there.

There was a detached garage in back but instead she parked by the curb and rolled down the windows. The catharsis of the afternoon had cleansed and quieted her. A night bird sang a few cheerful notes and then moved on to a neighboring tree. She inhaled deeply of the brisk, cool air.

Life was hard, but God was good. The Almighty had interspersed painful times with spaces of hope and rest, and through it all she intuitively felt something was being built. There was purpose to life. There was a plan. By God's design life on earth was a step-by-step progress toward ... what?

She paused, considering the question. If life had a goal, what word expressed it? The streetlights cast sharp shadows and the night bird again took up a tune.

Kingdom, she decided at length. Life was moving step by step toward what the Bible called the Kingdom of God.

The finished Kingdom would be when the rule of God covered the earth like the waters covered the sea. Yet, here and now, in some mysterious way the small events of her life were also part of that vast, eternal sweep. It was a Kingdom begun in eternity past and sweeping on to some infinite point in eternity future.

The thought was big. Too big. She tried to hold it; to wrap her mind around all it implied, but found she could not. Understanding it all was like comprehending the distance between stars. There was a certain academic sense in which the subject could be conceived, but efforts to capture it emotionally and personally hold it, fell apart like scorched threads of old fabric.

Phennia waited patiently. The expression and brightness of Diane's face gave evidence that something good was going on inside her, but the angel could only guess at what it might be.

Suddenly, Diane roused herself as though stirring from sleep. Jerking her backpack from the floorboard she shrugged it over one shoulder, grabbed the sack of fast food, picked up the two persimmons and opened the door.

Phennia followed as her human walked down the drive, entered the back yard, dropped her pack on an old glider and opened the rear of the home. Diane would not leave her pack without plans to return, so the angel settled herself on the edge of a large planter and waited.

As the door shut behind her, Diane felt her mood plummet. One moment she was sitting in the car feeling the goodness of God and contemplating His rule on earth, the next she was standing in her kitchen waiting for the water to boil while a heavy weariness settled over her. When she left the car, she made up her mind to sit on the deck and pray but now everything in her resisted that notion.

As the rebellious mood settled, she wanted nothing more than to indulge herself someway. Or sink into a pity-party. Or—even better—argue with somebody. She wanted anything and everything, but she did not want to pray. Maybe she should get back in the car and drive. Maybe she should forget the budget and go out for a steak.

The kettle began to whistle and she poured bubbling water into a mug drowning the tiny paper bag of tea leaves. Waves of caramel color drifted through the water as she unwrapped the burger and took a tasteless bite. She ate with large bites while standing with her back against the range. The food didn't help. Something inside was still restless.

She struggled into a hoodie and poured another cup of water over a fresh tea bag. Perhaps the cold would chase whatever was bothering her. With luck the chill might even clear her head.

She flipped up the hood ducking deeply inside and held the warm mug to her face inhaling the steam as the screen door banged shut behind her and cold air hit her face.

Phennia looked up as Diane settled into the glider and chided herself for not paying closer attention to duty. Over the past few hours the opposition level had cleared just enough to allow an oppressive spirit to attack.

Worse, because Diane was willingly focused on the negative emotions it provoked there was little the angel could do now to remedy the situation. The human had freely embraced these negative feelings and now the battle of resistance belonged to her alone.

Diane could not see the shadow which was as near as her skin, but she could feel it. Heaviness and a hovering anger soaked into her like the damp night air. On one level she was repelled by the feelings and wanted to shake free, but at the same time, there was an attraction in the darkness. It held a sensation of power and a stubborn hardness that answered to something bubbling up from the hidden places in her soul. She took a long swallow of the tea barely noticing its pungent taste.

JaKobe's Assignment

She had come here to pray, but she neither felt like praying nor could she think of a subject fit for that holy activity.

Thoughts of Steve and his new paramour drifted in and out but mostly her mind was occupied with feelings rather than thoughts. Dark feelings.

The lonely woman sat down the tea cup with a loud clink and arched her back stretching her hands high above her head. This would never do. She could either sit here, and sulk or she could fight. The choice was hers.

Diane decided to fight.

Rummaging through her backpack, she pulled out a large print Bible and a tattered songbook. The only light was a faint glow coming through the kitchen window but it combined with the street light and was enough.

She tossed open the pages to the psalms and began to read. Nothing seemed right. She went to John and perused the upper room discourse in chapters 13-17. The long reading helped, but still fragments of darkness lingered.

She flipped back to the Gospel of Luke and began reading scattered passages she had underlined through the years. Then, her eyes locked on the thirty-second verse of chapter twelve: *"Do not fear, little flock, for it is your Father's good pleasure to give you the kingdom."*[25]

Kingdom. There was that word again. If Jesus Christ was King of Kings—and He definitely was—then He must possess a Kingdom. He told

Pilot before the crucifixion that His Kingdom was not built of the things so highly prized by the world. His Kingdom was different.

But, it was also real.

One by one the souls of mankind came under His command. Through obedience to God, Christians put sinew and flesh on the prayer Jesus offered to His Father, when He said, *"Thy kingdom come!"*[26]

Phennia watched as the shadows began to fade and Diane's face glowed more brightly. Peace permeated the atmosphere and a holiness surrounded this child of Adam who, though made of dust, was destined for the sky.

The angel wanted to worship with the woman, but knew such an act was not advisable. Not because she was made of light and the human of dust, but because her sword would be needed. Soon. She could sense it. She loosed the clasp on her bracelet and stretched the silver circle into a solid strip.

Sometimes when Diane prayed, she used a list. At other times, her prayers might take the form of an internal dialogue or a song thrown on the air. But, always as she prayed she trusted— and most often could feel—that Someone beyond her was out there and listening. It was a warm, comforting experience.

On this occasion, it could not accurately be said that her mind was drifting, although the process certainly resembled that aimless act. It was more like she was quietly, gently moving from

JaKobe's Assignment

subject to subject. Her consideration of the Kingdom, had brought the world to mind. The planet contained so many people; so many needs. A news report seen last week rolled back into conscience.

The reporter had called it, "The Sock War," but to Diane it seemed more like conflicting hopes built on capitalism. A company in Alabama that manufactured knitted socks was competing with a firm in Belize. The reporter interviewed both sides and Diane remembered a young Belize girl who spoke through an interpreter.

The girl was only seventeen with small bones, dark hair and large intelligent eyes. Her family lived in the hills about six miles from the new factory. She had just finished the technical training offered by the company and would soon be allowed to work on the knitting machines. Her whole family depended on her income. They were looking forward to having enough to eat without worry and perhaps even buy a radio.

The girl had no idea the new company in the valley would probably close due to American labor contracts and international negotiations which at that moment were taking place in a country she had never seen.

Diane remembered the hopeful tone in the girl's voice and a surprisingly deep emotion gripped her heart. She found herself praying for the family to have enough provisions for the coming year. She prayed their farm products would bring a fair price. She asked that the family somehow be given a radio to bring them comfort, joy and solid Bible teaching.

But, most of all she prayed that spiritual life be given to the nameless, dark-haired girl. The reporter had stated poverty forced many of the young people from the hills into crowded cities where they were cheated, lied to, and often drifted into prostitution.

Phennia opened her sword and scanned the area trying to anticipate the enemy's most likely approach. But still she was caught off guard when an evil energy of astonishing force broke on her from the south.

The force was violent and like a wall of hurricane wind. It moved silently from the darkness and she had only a fraction of a second before the impact. Rolling from her seat on the planter, she kept close to the ground and called for reinforcements with a loud, undulating, screeching wail as violence passed and she braced for the second assault.

Grabbing each end of her sword she twisted the device into a short staff. If the enemy was this close and powerful, hand-to-hand combat would likely follow and the defensive qualities of a staff were greatly preferred; at least by this angel. Diane must have broken through and now it would be the job of others to keep the way clear until the communication was complete.

Diane sat motionless, wrapped in the tender secure feeling of prayer. It was as though time didn't matter and she was walking in a garden

JaKobe's Assignment

rather than huddled in the cold. If asked to explain it, she would have had no words, but the experience was as real as her hoodie and the mug of tea that sat cooling beside her.

There had been a moment while praying for Belize when tears rimmed her eyes. Then, they faded and she thought of friends and family: her boys>Pastor Phelps>his children>his wife.

Melody seemed like the world's one perfect woman. Yet, as she considered her, something seemed amiss. She didn't know what to pray but distinctly knew she should plead with God for Melody. Was the pastor's wife sick? For a moment the strength of the spiritual connection faded as she thumbed through a mental index of possible problems then she pushed them all aside.

"Lord, just be with Melody. Touch her." The words sounded lame and far too generic to be effective, but somehow they were the only ones she could form.

The wall of energy returned and shattered around Phennia like thousands of fragments of hot glass. Each shard grew and took form. There were warriors, demons and spirit beings of every description. Phennia had never seen such an array.

An angel in bright colored clothing brought a glistening sword down in a blow aimed directly at her head. She placed her hands about two feet apart on the staff, dropped back on one knee, raised the staff and took the blow with a force that rammed her arms into her shoulders.

She was grateful to have been able to exchange the sword for a staff. The power of the enemy was so great she needed the strength of both arms to deflect each hit and defending herself was the best she could hope for at the moment.

Reinforcements began to arrive but they were outnumbered by the enemy and her position was walled off from help by fierce warriors. She shielded herself from the point of a sword that jabbed at her from the right then whirled in time to deflect another coming from the left.

As the battle continued Phennia realized this was a fight she would probably lose. There was no way others could reach her isolated position and no way she could hope to overcome the sheer number of enemy pressing from every side.

She desperately wanted to exchange her staff the sword. If she must lose, there would have been satisfaction in taking a few of the enemy with her. But there was no time to make the exchange, and the angel resigned herself to her fate.

Sitting peacefully on the glider, Diane was unaware of the battle raging around her. She had already won her skirmish and was no longer the enemy's main target. Now, their focus was on the shaft of light that carried her prayers flashing toward heaven. Interfering with that light was the prize for which they thirsted.

Three powerful enemy warriors closed in around Phennia and she knew this was the end of her usefulness on earth. There was no way she could defend against them all but she chose the particularly hateful looking one on her left and charged anyway.

At first, she thought the noise was an enemy sword striking her staff, but in an instant she realized the sound behind her was a friend. JaKobe!

Somehow the mighty warrior had broken through the lines and joined her in the tight circle. Standing back to back she could hear the sizzle as his sword crossed that of an enemy.

"Change to a sword!" he called over the battle sounds.

"What a novel idea!" Phennia scoffed as she blocked a waist high slice intended to cut her in two. "Tell this warrior to back off a moment and I'll be glad to make the switch." She grunted as the force of another impact jarred her body.

JaKobe pierced the arm of his assailant diluting his power with a hissing sound, then whirled switching places with Phennia. She now faced the weakened enemy while he parried with the other two foes.

"Thanks," she exhaled in surprise.

Shocked and wounded her antagonist missed a beat while adjusting to this new turn in the battle. It was just long enough. Phennia focused her mind on her weapon, ran her finger along the side of the staff and it became a sword once more.

"Better," she breathed then jumped aside barely missing her opponent's thrust.

"That was some move!" she complimented JaKobe as the wounded angel withdrew giving them only one warrior apiece to fight. It was no wonder he held Superior rank. He deserved it.

Shifting the glider backward and forward with a gentle grace, Diane continued to move mentally from one subject to the next. She prayed about her assignment in anatomy class that was due in two weeks. Casey was going to need braces soon. Maybe Steve could be encouraged to pay for them. Feelings of peace settled over her as she remembered the falling leaves and crisp air as she picked up pecans that afternoon. She hummed part of an old Christmas carol giving the song up as an offering to God.

Then, for some strange reason, Miranda came to her mind. What did the girl look like? Hopefully, it wasn't at all like her aunt. No, that wasn't nice. She had never met the girl, but it must be terrible to be pregnant and alone. She considered the situation and prayers began to form in her mind.

*****

The church service was nearing its end. Jonathan left the pulpit and moved down the steps until he was level with the congregation. For slightly less than an hour, one-hundred-and-three people had put aside the many other things that could have occupied their time and instead gather to sing, pray and listen to what he had to say.

Back upon the stage, Allen was coaxing one more verse of *Just As I Am* from the yawning congregation while Jonathan spoke above the sound of the music.

"Can you feel the Spirit of God calling you? If so, why not come to this altar and talk to Him about it?"

Standing by the back pew in the left hand corner of the room, Luke shifted his weight from one foot to another and waited impatiently. He recognized the song from a Billy Graham crusade he'd once watched on TV. But, all his study in religion had not prepared him for this strange place.

As a child he occasionally attended church in Italy with his uncle, but this was far different than anything he had ever experienced. There had been a reverence and mystery about the Catholic services that seemed to fit with what religion ought to be. The casual noise of this place unnerved him.

The people were overly friendly and the auditorium, although nice enough, was too bare. There were no statues, pictures, or even a single cross in sight. The only useful religious thing as far as he could see was some kind of recessed area behind the choir that was painted with an outdoor scene. He had read about emersion baptism and guessed that was where the ritual was carried out.

Pastor Phelps kept referring to an "altar," but for the life of him Luke couldn't find one. It was only after the preaching was over when a couple of folks came forward and dropped to their knees by the steps that he figured out the "altar" must be the steps leading to the stage. Strange.

Yet, there was something else about the place that was far harder to identify than differences in architecture or ritual. This was something . . .well, . . .personal.

Or, maybe emotional was a better word. At any rate, whatever this unidentifiable something might be, it was certainly making him uncomfortable. He felt like a kid with his hand caught in the cookie jar. He was somewhat embarrassed, but didn't know why. He knew he was behaving in a thoroughly acceptable social manner and no one had indicated any displeasure with him, yet his skin seemed to crawl with guilt.

The sermon had been a simple one about some Jewish tradition involving temple worship. It seemed two guys went to pray. One of them was real religious and the other a bit of a scoundrel. The religious dude reminded God of all the good stuff he had done, but the scoundrel kept his eyes to the floor and just asked God to have mercy on him.

The preacher hadn't mentioned hell or pounded the pulpit or yelled or any of the things he had heard about happening in some Protestant services. So, why did he feel judged?

Ben's question rolled back into his mind with a forcefulness that surprised him. Did he believe in a personal God? Other questions quickly followed. Was it possible God really did make the universe? If so, had the Almighty lost interest after that? What if God stayed involved with the planet and even knew the individual lives of people who lived there? Did God judge people after they died?

Luke thought about it a minute then shrugged. Well, so what? Not that he believed such a God existed, but even if by some outside chance He did, Luke was as moral as the next guy. He did good stuff and had never really hurt anyone. He wasn't weak like his mom who jilted her responsibility for her son the moment she didn't have a man to support her. He wasn't selfish like uncle Raffaello who rejected a boy that needed and adored him. He wasn't useless like the drug addicts or dumb like most of his classmates.

Even if at some distant future he might stand before a God who was concerned about his morality, Luke figured he would fare better than most.

The defensive self-talk should have brought comfort but for some reason it did not. Feelings of being caught and exposed still hung around him. He fidgeted and glanced at his watch. *How many times are they going to sing that same song? Oh, no, now the church secretary is coming forward. Is this mess going to go on all night?*

Slipping quietly into an outside aisle, LeeAnn made her way to the front where Jonathan acknowledged her with his eyes. He would have been glad to take her hand and pray, but she turned toward the steps and fell to her knees. Folding her arms, she leaned her head against the second step and Jonathan turned his attention back to the audience. Surely, his faithful friend was praying again for her wayward husband and needed a moment of privacy.

However, his assumption could not have been further from the truth. LeeAnn's thoughts had nothing to do with Glen. She had also forgotten her son. And, the needs of the mission committee. And, her mother's arthritis. And even the ache in her own left hip.

It had started that morning as Jonathan talked about scars being part of the Christian calling. She left the service feeling sure a large rock had been jammed in the middle of her chest leaving no room to breathe and creating a dull ache that extended up into her throat. It was a feeling that grew worse as the day progressed.

Willingly embrace scars? Not on your life! Complaining was her gift to the world! Every time a pain of any kind came close to her vicinity, she was insulted and let everyone within hearing know of her displeasure.

It didn't even have to be a big pain. Any twinge, any discomfort, any resistance to her will, any perceived moral infraction by another—no matter how distant—could set her off. Politicians, telecasters, her family and even the weather were instant targets for her grumbling, moaning, protesting tongue.

Not that all of those things couldn't use some improving, but her constant stream of complaining was certainly a long way from accepting the buffeting of life as a natural part of the Christian experience. Even her prayers had become little more than gripe sessions aimed heavenward.

When the morning service dismissed, she had sat briefly in the church parking lot and considered her situation, then used her cell to call Glen telling him she had a busy week ahead and needed to buy groceries before coming home.

The truth was she just couldn't face sitting still in that house and being forced to think. So, she invented an excuse to stay busy.

But, shopping and filling the car with gas did little to relieve the dull ache in her chest. When she finally drug herself through the kitchen door, if she had told someone she felt like dirt it would have given her mood too high a status. She was beneath dirt and falling fast.

The first thing she saw was Glen—beer in one hand and bowl of popcorn in the other—doing a highly animated job of armchair-quarterbacking for the Cowboys. "Throw a Hail Mary pass!" He was screaming at the screen and before the first bag of groceries hit the cabinet she was screaming at him.

She complained about having to do all the work herself. She complained about his addiction to sports and what a poor example he set for their son. She even complained because he had gained weight. And, as the steady stream of complaints flowed from her lips, the rock in her chest grew proportionately.

Glen pain little attention to his wife's scalding voice. To him, it was nothing new.

But, something was new for LeeAnn. For the first time in years, she was listening to her own voice and could hear—really hear—the meaning and impact of her words. Hour by hour the stone grew larger and by the time of the evening service, she felt weary and broken and old.

As she knelt by the step she dissolved into tears while gently, almost imperceptibly, the Spirit of God moved in her heart.

The invitation had been extended longer than usual and Allen began to repeat verses that the congregation had already sung. *Just as I am and waiting not / To rid my soul of one dark blot, / To Thee whose blood can cleanse each spot, / O Lamb of God, I come! I come!* [27]

The words pierced deeply into her soul with fresh meaning. She raced forward and fell to her knees. *Yes, Lord. Cleanse me. I come.*

The rapidness of the change that swept over and through her soul filled her with amazement. Instantly, like water draining from a steep incline, the tensions left her body and peace replaced the turmoil. She sighed. LeeAnn had at last come home.

Across the room, Luke was considering how he might slip out without others noticing when Pastor Phelps signaled Allen bringing the invitation to a close. Another quick prayer and it was over. He gathered his jacket and moved toward the door.

"Thank you for coming tonight, Luke." The voice at his shoulder belonged to Melody. "It meant a lot to me."

"No problem, Mrs. Phelps. You folks worship a bit differently than I'm accustomed to, but it was nice. I enjoyed it. Thanks for inviting me."

He didn't mean a word of what he said, but that was no reason to be impolite. He pushed on toward the door. The cool evening air was waiting. He longed to take a few deep breaths of it and shake the awkward feelings. But, if that didn't work, his mom had a bottle of vino in the fridge that would surely do the trick.

*****

Coming from a late night trip to Wal-Mart, Miranda had just turned East on Pecan Street when she noticed people spilling from the open door of the church. It was all she could do to keep from staring. These people were certainly different than she expected.

In the past, she had thought of *church people* in rather generic terms and assumed they were all cookie-cutter images of her aunt and uncle. But, that had not been her experience at the shower. The women she met there were very different from one another. Old Henrietta seemed a bit daft. Beverly was charming and real. The pastor's wife seemed a bit aloof but not unkind.

A blue sedan was waiting to exit the parking lot. Miranda slowed to a stop, politely motioning the driver to proceed. She waited for a blue then a brown car and wondered what the people inside were really like. Surely, they all led good lives, married their childhood sweethearts and earned a middle class income. They would be small-town, all-American, mom-and-apple-pie type people.

Although the thought surprised her, she found herself for the first time wishing that she could be "that type" people, too.

There had been very little traffic on the streets of Thyme but once she reached Interstate 30 travelers multiplied. It was only a fifteen-minute drive to Sandy Flats. When the sign for Whispering Pines apartment complex came into view, she pulled off the highway and stopped in the familiar space reserved for Unit 2.

Struggling with three bags and keys, she opened the apartment door. A rush of warm air mixed with the scent of fried pork skins and salsa assaulted her.

"Get what you wanted?" Brad asked never taking his eyes from a Karate match on TV. He was sitting on the sofa in a muscle shirt and short sweat pants, the low table in front of him was scattered with crispy fragments of pork skins, a half empty bowl of salsa, and his ever present soft drink can.

"Yeah, more or less," she replied. "They had diapers, but I couldn't find a basic pink gown in newborn size."

She sighed deeply and added, "I got the duplicates exchanged and spent everything on the gift cards, plus some."

"Well, the kid's got to have clothes and with your aunt's money in the bank there ought to be plenty extra."

"Plenty until the Discover card comes due."

Miranda crossed to the dining table where the shower gifts were spread and sat down the bags.

"It's hot in here. Why don't you put on more clothes and turn down the thermostat? Money doesn't grow on trees, you know."

Brad ignored her, so she turned her attention to the table. "Where are we going to put all this stuff? In fact, where are we going to put a baby? That tiny bedroom barely holds the two of us and the dresser is crammed full."

"Aw, don't worry. Babies don't take up much room. Just relax and it'll work out."

"Sure," she scoffed. "That's your answer to everything. If a problem is more complicated than a new karate move your only solution is 'relax, it'll work out.' That's what you said when I told you we were pregnant."

"Well, having a kid this soon wasn't my idea."

"You think it was mine?"

Silence filled the room as though the air had become cotton.

At last Brad broke the quiet by swearing at the television. "That idiot doesn't deserve the black belt he's wearing."

Having no solution for the crowded conditions, he balanced his discomfort by assuring himself of his superiority on the karate floor. "I can execute a better palm heel strike than that slob."

"Is karate all you ever think about? Why don't you dust off that chemistry textbook and see if you can manage to pass this semester. And, while you are at it, turn down that heat!"

"Listen, I'm sick of your nagging! I work part time. I go to school. I bust a gut trying to take care of you and that kid and all you ever do is gripe."

"And I work full time!" she interrupted, shouting the words. "If it wasn't for my paycheck you would be back living with your mama." She injected the last word with as much venom as possible.

"I was doin' fine before you came along and I can do it again! But, if you think you can get along without me, you're welcome to give it a try!"

"You're weak and you're a dreamer, Brad. If you didn't have a woman to patch things up for you and stroke your ego, you would end up on the streets!"

"I don't have to listen to this!" He grabbed a jacket that had been tossed over a chair and shoved his bare feet into worn sneakers. "Maybe I'll be back, but don't bet on it," he shouted as he slammed the door.

"Don't be so sure I'll let you in!" Miranda shouted behind him.

Emptiness flooded the room. Only the television pierced the silence as the young, dark-haired, mother-to-be aimlessly shuffled the packages on the overflowing table.

She thought about turning off the television but the idea of total silence frightened her. She tried to make order of the baby clothes, but the energy of thinking was just too much. So, she sat and looked straight ahead with large, soft, unseeing eyes.

Life was not supposed to be this way.

After fifteen minutes of trance, Miranda began to cry. First, the tears trickled out as frozen emotions began a slow thaw. Then, the flood came with painful, wracking sobs.

Life wasn't supposed to be this way. It really wasn't.

8:20 PM

One Mile Above Earth

Residents of heaven crowded together at the top of the light corridor and waited. Preparations were complete. Assignments clear. All systems go.

"Has it been long since your last trip?" one asked another as he leaned over the railing and looked below.

"Not too long. Perhaps fifty earth years, but I'm sure no more than that. I like being in the thick of things."

"I know what you mean."

There was a pause as both angels inched forward moving with a thousand or so other individuals waiting to use the easy passage way connecting spiritual dimensions with those of earth. Changing into an appropriate form and preparing for battle was draining enough. No need to use energy popping in and out of earth's atmosphere if one didn't need to travel that way.

JaKobe's Assignment

The corridors might not be faster, but their convenience made up for that flaw.

"What's the assignment?"

"Recognizance. There has been some question about the home churches in Lanchow. I need to get a feel for the level of opposition in that part of China. And you?"

"Routine request. Say, do you know anything about the quality of radio reception in the mountains of Belize?"

Elizabeth Baker

Time: Eternity

Place: Heaven

It would be inaccurate to say she rushed. No one rushed in heaven. But her insistent movements were certainly the closest thing to that activity seen in this celestial place. She was like a fish darting in and out among rocks and underwater vegetation as she smoothly, persistently slipped through busy crowds making her way with steadfast determination and no wasted motion.

Three friends were coming out of a building across the street. They shouted greetings, but she only smiled, dismissing them with a wave of her hand. The project they had all been working on would have to wait. Farther down the street, two angels were moving toward each other but abruptly stopped as she swiftly passed between them. Amused, they looked at each other. Where ever this human was going, it certainly must be important!

Indeed, to her mind it was the most important thing that had happened in a long while. The message had just now come and if her plans were to be successful, she must see the King. She must see him now.

The trysting place was not far ahead and her steps slowed as she neared the familiar, ornate, iron gate snuggled deep in the garden wall. Both the bricks and the gate had the pleasing appearance of age and as she lifted the latch the gate squeaked a welcome on rusty hinges.

Once inside, the solid surface beneath her feet gave way to the comfortable crunch of pebbles and she could feel the peace of solitude as the gate closed behind her.

The open vistas, busy streets, public halls and homes of heaven were wonderful places. But here, in this private garden, Mesah felt a special kind of belonging. It was here she first became accustomed to heaven and here she met with the King.

Her movements relaxed and mind centered on Him as she slowly made her way to the meeting place, thinking of what she would ask Him and imagining His answer. Many times she had rehearsed this moment. She could list the reasons why her request should be granted and she had even considered arguments against the idea, developing counter reasoning for each.

As she followed the path, songbirds kept up a lively tune in the trees overhead and the chatter of a chipmunk was not far away.

This place was so alive! She marveled at the sounds, inhaled deeply of the sweet air, felt a branch brush her arm, and reveled in the fragrant mixture of green, growing things and new blossoms. How real and solid it all was! As real as her love for Him and His for her.

The path came to an end at a clearing of no more than thirty feet where the garden had been planted with a more formal feel. In the center, a bubbling fountain and small fish pond added movement and melody, while all around it neat beds of colorful flowers were artfully placed at strategic points and two benches invited visitors to pause.

But, the Master was nowhere to be seen.

His absence surprised her yet, in another way, it didn't. The real surprise was that He came at all. Not to mention the mystery of *how* He came.

All those strange, incomprehensible words like omnipresent and omniscient rose up in her mind. She saw Him on the throne with the seraphim crying, "Holy! Holy! Holy!" She knew His reality as terror and overwhelming light. Yet, somehow, when she called, He came to meet her here, without leaving there.

It was so fearfully strange and incomprehensible but once she accepted the reality of the experience rather than trying to comprehend it with her mind, the beauty and the tenderness of their moments together became as real and precious as life itself.

She entered the space with reverence and settled on a rock by the pond to watch the fish flashing blue and yellow in the shallow water.

JaKobe's Assignment

They had built this pond together, *she* and the Master. It had been not long after her arrival so, of course, He did most of the work. She was far too new and inexperienced to be of much help, but He graciously took time and let her feel a part of everything. Even to the point of incorporating her choice of color for the fish. The memory brought a smile.

Where was He? She stretched and looked in all directions. It was not like Him to be late.

The instant the thought entered her mind she almost laughed. Of course He was not late! How could anyone be late in a place without time? And, if anyone could be late, it certainly would not be the Lord of Glory! Perfection was never anything but, . . . well, . . . perfect!

Still, He most often arrived first when she sent a request to see Him. So, if He was not here, there must be a reason. One thing for certain, the reason would not be because He was occupied elsewhere or did not get the message. No, the reason could only be for her benefit. He must be giving her space and a moment of peace.

Why?

Her thoughts turned inward and she rose from her place by the pool to walk one of the many paths twisting among the trees.

Her request was not totally out of line, but she had to admit it would be a bit unusual. After all, she had been here long enough. She should have power to do this on her own. But, she didn't.

For the first time, she questioned the wisdom of asking the favor. He was her mentor, her Father, her Friend, her Hope and her Foundation, but He wasn't to be taken lightly or manipulated.

She had been chosen to walk with Him; chosen to know Him, yet familiarity or equality with the Holy Creator of the Universe was not part of the privilege. No matter how tender His presence or how intimate their conversation, He still was God and she was not.

Turning down a path bordered on each side by lilacs, she felt small and not at all as self-assured as she had been. To her mind, the request was still a good one but she was no longer positive that her judgment was infallible. She walked on with her head down and eyes on the path.

"Have you found your walk in the garden pleasant, Mesha?" He breathed the words tenderly and she turned to see His face. What a beautiful name He had given her and how she loved to hear it on His lips! No one else knew that secret name.

"Oh, Master," her hands dropped to her side and her eyes shone as she looked up to see Him there. He had been sitting close by all along but with her eyes fixed on the path, she had not seen Him until the moment He called her name. How strange that it would be possible to overlook Him!

"May I never cease to be amazed that you come to my garden," she whispered.

He seemed pleased with what she said and rose to stand beside her. "That's a good request," He said. "It will be a joy to honor that one."

He laughed. Mesha laughed, too, and He reached for her hand. He must have known that she had called to Him because of a special request. He was making the way easy for her by showing his willingness to hear petitions.

They walked on together in silence. She could make her request any time but for now His nearness was all she desired and to know he understood made patience an easy thing.

They meandered past the jasmine and laughed at a squirrel-like creature vainly struggling with an especially obstinate nut. Soon, the path turned back to the fountain by the pool and He asked, "Do you remember when we worked together building this?"

"Well, I am not so sure how much I contributed to the project but at the time I thought that nothing could be more fun than playing in the mud with the Lord of Glory!"

His laughter rang across the clearing and echoed in the trees. "I'm glad you enjoyed it. There was another time when my 'playing in the mud' as you call it resulted in a planet teaming with life! But, I also enjoyed building our small fountain."

He paused and she could feel that something significant was about to be said. "Tell me, do you see a difference in yourself between when we built the fountain and this moment?"

Mesha thought seriously before answering. "Ye-s-s," she said slowly drawing out the sound. "I feel a deeper connection with You now. This place has become my home. I've hundreds of friends and I love going to the music festivals with my earth Dad. There is always something new to do and another challenge is always waiting. These things don't intimidate me as much as they did once."

"So, you recognize the value of change?"

"Ye-e-s-s," she drew out the word. She suspected where He was going with this line of questioning and wondered if she could follow without being embarrassed. She had changed and grown, but perhaps not always in the way she should have. Yet, as she considered this, the Lord seemed to abruptly change the subject.

"Was there something you wanted to request of Me, Mesha?"

As always the sound of her special name warmed her heart. No one called her that but the Master. No one else had the right to. What a wonder that He could be seated on the throne as God ruling both the physical and spiritual universes and at the same instant walking here in the garden with her. Omnipresent, Ancient of Days, Jesus, Lord, Spirit, Master; above all and beyond comprehension, but just as truly by her side as Friend.

She waited a reverent moment then pushed forward. There was no delaying the matter. It was time to make her request.

"I have received a message she is coming."

"That is true."

"I want to greet her looking as she knew me on earth. Would you grant me the power to do that?"

"You cannot do that on your own?"

Of course, He knew the answer to that question. There was no detail of her life with which He was unacquainted. It was not that He lacked the information, but that He desired to hear her admit a truth they both knew.

She had not sinned as those on earth knew sin. She was not being punished. She did not cringe under His disapproval. It was rather an opportunity had been placed before her long ago and she had ignored it. Changing form at will and knowing which forms were allowed for one's station was an elemental lesson. She should have mastered it by now.

"No, Lord. I have not applied myself to learn this skill." It felt good to have the truth out in the open. If He decided not to grant her request, it would be for the good of all concerned. She could relax knowing that, but still she waited anxiously to hear His judgment.

"Is there a reason why you believe this is needed?"

Mesha cleared her throat and glanced up into His eyes. He let go of her hand and they settled side by side on one of the benches. Only totally honesty would do.

"At first, I told myself that changing back into the form she knew on earth was a fun thing. A simple expression of pleasure. A happy gift I wanted to give. Then, I realized it was far more. Getting my request granted instantly was an opportunity for me to short circuit the step by step learning process."

"So, you do not appreciate the concepts of challenge and learning?" He probed.

"I understood none of these when we built the fountain. Even after I had been here a while I did not embrace them as I should have. Now, I am seeing more clearly the wisdom of the plan. Some of that new knowledge came only as I walked in the garden today and waited for You to appear."

The Master smiled, but He did not say a word, only waited for Mesha to work out her own thoughts.

"I know now the one who's pleasure I sought first was my own, not hers. I wanted to greet her in a familiar form because of the joy it would give me. Consideration of her was secondary. And, applying myself to learn the skill was not a consideration at all."

Mesha was uncomfortable with the confession but felt no condemnation radiating from Him. "I guess I have not yet learned the challenge of true loving or the value of working to acquire new skill."

"Yes. I would think there is room for improvement." His words were not an accusation, but agreement with facts that would guide her to a higher level.

They shared a moment of silence as the fountain played its eternal music. At last, He spoke.

"But, even understanding all this, you have still asked Me to fill your request. Why?"

"Changing to the form without the effort of learning would give me great joy, but more than that, I think it would ease her way."

"How?"

"When I came here, the angel first brought me to this place. A place that would one day be my garden. You let me discover heaven bit by bit rather than in one overwhelming wave. People. Foods. Expected behavior. Sounds."

She looked up at Him, then tucked both hands under her thighs and swung her crossed feet back and forth like a child. "You even built a fountain with me and let me choose the fish."

"Do you think she needs such slow introduction?"

"No. She is well prepared and looking forward to all this place holds."

"There are over five thousand people waiting to greet her. It should be quite a party," He said.

After a pause, she continued. "It was so hard for her to let me go." Mesha's voice trailed off into silence.

"And, you believe it would help her heal if she had a moment to adjust to what is truly real before being greeted by the others?"

"That seems like truth to me."

"But, you have not prepared yourself for such a privilege."

"No."

"Mesha, one of the greatest gifts I give to those I love is the opportunity to change. To be alive is to grow and reach for the next level. My call to My people is always, 'Higher! Move higher with Me!'

"Yet, you have been slow to come higher, slow to accept adventure, contented with the satisfaction of what you have already attained."

She had no words to respond. He was right. She pulled in a deep draught of celestial air and stretched. The party would be wonderful. Things would be as they should.

He stood and Mesha did, too. They would walk to the gate together.

Half way down the path He stopped and turned to face her. Putting both hands on her shoulders, He looked deeply into her eyes and read her soul.

"You have your request." He smiled and tapped her nose with a strong finger, "Only next time, Mesha, learn a lesson from earth. Embrace each challenge when it comes and grow on schedule. You will be pleased with the results and so will I."

JaKobe's Assignment

9:15 PM

The Cordless Phone

They came through the back door with a clatter. Like camels unloading burdens, they dumped things on the kitchen counter. Traci sat down two trophies belonging to a sick piano student who didn't show up for recital; Stephanie dumped a megaphone and pom-poms she had picked up at Bethany's house and ferried home for next week's practice; Jonathan unloaded a laptop, cell phone and Melody's blue tote bag. There were also two sweaters, one jacket, five Bibles and a doggy bag filled with leftover pizza. Ben balanced two almost empty cookie platters wrapped in plastic and looked for a clear spot to set them.

"Hold it right there!" Melody's voice was stern. She came through the door last after gingerly negotiating the steps one at a time. Still clinging to the doorway for support she glared at the others.

"I have worked very hard making sure there is a place for everything in this house. And, in case none of you have noticed, that place is not the kitchen counter top."

They looked at each other a little dismayed. Mom never talked like that before. Sure, she made everyone clean their room occasionally and fussed about things being left around the house, but something in her voice was different this time. It wasn't her usual wistfulness or pleading. This was a command.

Ben looked at his dad who cocked his head and clicked softly with his tongue but offered no explanation. "What about these?" he looked back at his mom and held the cookie plates higher.

"I'll bet with a little effort, you can figure that out. Where do dirty dishes usually go?"

"The dishwasher?"

"Good! And, what do you do with the plastic wrap?"

"Trash?"

"Right again! And, the left over cookies?"

"In the jar on the counter that looks like a little fat man in an apron."

"Young man, you are batting a thousand!"

"But, don't these belong to the church?" Again, he lifted the plates.

"And, your point is. . . ?" His mother raised her eyebrows and placed one hand on her hip.

This was dangerous territory. It was time for a joke. "My point is that as a dutiful, Christian young man, I recognize the value of hard work and responsibility. Iptso facto, I will clean the plates before returning them to their proper owner, post haste."

Stephanie frowned and his parents exchanged surprised looks. "What can I say?" Jonathan shrugged to Melody. "Our kid speaks Latin."

Ben's sense of humor did much to lighten the moment and before long most items were snuggly put away. Even the leftover pizza found a home on the second shelf of the fridge.

Counters clear, the family scattered to pursue their favorite evening activities. Traci turned on the TV and inserted a movie CD while Jonathan headed for his recliner carrying his laptop and a mug of coffee. But, before he could get there, the phone rang.

"I've got it!" he announced sitting his burdens on the end table by the recliner. The ringing was muffled but insistent. He tossed pillows from the sofa and rummaged under the afghan. "Hello?" he asked on the sixth ring.

"Hi, Bethany. . . . You want Stephanie? Yeah, let me call her."

"Stephanie!" He shouted toward the back of the house. "Telephone!" Placing the cordless receiver on the arm of a seldom used chair, he rescued the remote from Traci who was frantically pushing useless buttons.

"Steph is in the bath!" It was Melody's voice from the bedroom.

He grabbed the phone again and held it with his chin as he punched buttons on the wicket remote. "She can't come right now, Bethany. Call back tomorrow. . . .Yeah, well . . . Maybe you could get her in about an hour. . . .uh-huh. . . .Good night."

Then handing the receiver to Traci he added, "Tray, would you put this in the girl's room? Bethany is going to call Steph back in a little while."

"What did Bethany want?" asked Ben entering the room from the hall as his little sister squeezed past.

"Oh, she just needs some advice on what to wear to school tomorrow."

"She called for that?"

"Seems they're taking pictures," his father responded without looking up from the remote. "Ben, do you know how to stop that wavy line from messing up the picture?"

With the rebellious remote safely in the hands of the younger generation, Jonathan settled in the recliner and picked up his laptop. At least this was technology he could understand.

He opened a file of HTML code, and then a browser to view his work thus far. "Not bad for a novice," he mentally complimented himself. It was about time Grace Community entered the twenty-first century via a web page and Jonathan hoped to surprise the Elder board next month with his progress toward that goal.

As the movie credits began to roll, Traci curled on the floor and Ben sprawled on the sofa throwing the afghan over his bare feet. Jonathan breathed a restful sigh. This was one of his favorite things in all the world. An evening with the family gathered home; a well-worn recliner molded to his back, his laptop open to creative work, and the TV blaring in the background.

The computer made him feel productive and the TV kept his family close, but not directly involved with him. The combination preserved the illusion of togetherness without the work of actually relating and the computer was proof that he wasn't wasting time. Melody hated the setup. Jonathan regarded the arrangement as life at its best.

Except on those frequent occasions when the phone refused to cooperate.

"Dad," Stephanie appeared at the door with her head wrapped in a towel. The phone was in one hand and a hair dryer in the other. "It's Elder Bentley. Says it's important."

With a sigh of resignation, Jonathan took the phone and listened for almost fifteen minutes as his head elder explained half a dozen details. Jack might have many flaws but he was also punctual, faithful and efficient. Not a bad combination for an elder.

When he at last pushed the button disconnecting the call, Jonathan tossed the receiver back on the sofa behind Ben's feet. Hopefully, it would get lost under the pillows and never be found again.

No such luck. When it rang for the third time, he ignored the irritating, muffled jangle, but that did not mean the call would go unanswered. Melody came in holding the handset from the bedside table.

"It's Kristi," she said holding out the phone.

Without making a sound, his lips pantomimed the reply *I don't want to talk to her!*

Melody put her hand over the mouthpiece. "She is your sister and she certainly didn't call to talk to me."

Reluctantly, Jonathan reached for the phone and tried to put a smile in his voice.

"Hi, Kristi. How's my big sister?" That was all it took. Kristi knew exactly how she was and looked forward to the opportunity of sharing the details. After about five minutes of monologue, Jonathan interrupted.

"Kristi, it's good to hear from you, but I was just about to go out the door when you called." As he spoke he closed the laptop and shoved sock covered feet back into polished loafers. "I have a bit more work to do at the office tonight. Could I give you a call tomorrow afternoon? Late?"

He nodded, silently accepting his sister's advice about not working too much and how pastors needed a day off just like the rest of the world. He then said goodbye three times before he could extricate himself. Looking up, he saw Melody's disapproving eyes.

"It wasn't a lie!" he defended. "Look! My shoes are on. I've got my laptop. I'm going to the office. Really!"

Jonathan retrieved his suit jacket that had been tossed on a dining chair and slipped out the back door.

Melody picked up his half empty cup and Sunday's bulletin that had slipped between the recliner's seat cushion and arm rest. It always amazed her how much work that man could create just by entering a room.

The phone rang twice more and then the house settled into a quiet routine. Stephanie finished her call to Bethany. Traci decided the movie wasn't worth watching and Ben went to his room for the night. Peace.

Melody went to the kitchen and again pulled her tote from the closet. Might as well take advantage of the quiet and organize music for the new students scheduled to start in two weeks. Paul would be moving to *Book Three,* but Carol Bonn was an adult learning to play for the first time. She would need something different for her, but simple. The separate piles began to grow as organization replaced chaos.

When the phone rang again, she jumped. Silence in the home was so rare she hardly knew how to respond to a sudden, loud disruption.

As she had done early in the day, Melody reached as far across the bar as possible and pulled the kitchen receiver from its wall base by the cord.

"Hello," she spoke softly hoping the strain of the stretch didn't sound in her voice.

There was a pause then a vaguely familiar, uncertain voice asked, "Is this the Phelps home?"

"Yes."

"Is this Mrs. Phelps, the pastor's wife?"

"Yes, may I help you?"

"Oh, I am so sorry," the caller apologized. "I really didn't mean to disturb you. I guess I dialed the wrong number... I mean it's the right number, but I thought it was the office phone. I mean... this is Miranda and I just wanted to say thank you for the shower and all the stuff.... I only planned to leave a message. I didn't intend to call your home." The obviously embarrassed voice trailed off.

"It's all right, Miranda. Pastor Phelps has gone back to the office for a little while and the kids are in bed. You are not disturbing me at all. I was just sitting here getting music sorted out for my students next semester."

"Oh, of course you are." she affirmed. "Uh,... My aunt said you were a wonderful piano teacher." Melody pulled the phone away from her ear and looked incredulously at the receiver. She couldn't imagine Tina saying she was a wonderful anything; the woman had never bothered to attend a recital. She listened as the voice at the other end of the line continued, "I think teaching someone to play an instrument is very special. It's like a gift you give them that lasts forever."

"Thank you."

An awkward silence followed, and when Miranda continued there was a slight shaking in her voice. "I just wanted to thank you. I mean, you know, for the shower and all. It was real nice."

"You're welcome," said Melody, "but I had a lot of help."

Something was wrong. She could sense it. Miranda may have accidentally dialed the number, but expressing gratitude for the shower was not the only thing this call was about. The girl was troubled.

"Will you tell the others I said, 'Thank you'? I'm not sure I know all their names. I just remember that Beverly lady. She was real nice. And she had a pretty baby."

"Sure, I'll tell them." Another awkward silence. Melody drew courage from deep inside and asked a direct question. "Miranda, are you all right?"

"Yeah. Sure. I'm fine," she sniffed as though sobs were threatening to overtake her at any moment. "I mean, . . . well, Brad and I have a few things to work out. That's all."

Melody was about to respond when a familiar voice spoke loudly. "Mom, did you wash my blue top? Stephanie entered the kitchen. "Oh, sorry. Didn't know you were on the phone."

Holding off her daughter with an upturned hand, Melody spoke into the receiver. "Miranda, could you give me your number? Something has come up on this end and I need to call you back."

"Oh, no ma'am! You don't have to do that! I didn't mean to bother you. I mean . . ."

"Miranda, I really want to call you back. Please?" She gave the number and Melody scribbled it on a sticky note then turned her attention to Stephanie.

Within ten minutes the drama of the missing blue top was settled and all was quiet again. Melody retreated to the master bedroom where she could be alone. She sat in her favorite rocker, Miranda's number in her hand and the cordless phone on her lap.

What could she tell this troubled girl? It wasn't like she was a novice at this sort of thing. As a pastor's wife she had been "counseling" others since her early twenties. She had gone to soul winning classes, memorized the Roman Road.[28] But, somehow, none of that seemed to matter anymore.

She could not put the vague feeling into words, but something inside her had shattered with that platter of cookies. Now, all memorized answers—indeed her entire robotic life!—seemed ... She searched for a word.

Second hand? The phrase formed in her mind unbidden, but the more she thought about it, the more appropriate it seemed.

That was it. *Second hand.* As good as the answers may have been—as good as all of her actions might have been—they never really belonged to her.

"Lord," she prayed. "I don't know where this is going. I don't have any plan. I just know I am tired of holding up a front. Let me listen as You would listen, and if I offer her nothing else, let me offer her my honesty."

Miranda picked up on the first ring and Melody wondered if the girl had been sitting by the phone waiting. They exchanged pleasantries then drifted into a few moments of unsatisfying small talk. Melody broke the spell when she summoned her courage and reminded them both of why she called.

"When we hung up last time, you seemed upset. You said there were some difficulties that you needed to work out. Could you tell me what is going on?"

"Nothing much. He'll come back. I know he will. He always does."

"Brad left you?"

"Well, probably not for good."

Melody waited. She had experienced being pregnant and broke, but could not imagine what it must be like to face those things with the added burden of an on-again-off-again, father-to-be.

"I guess I can't blame him," Miranda offered timidly.

"What do you mean?"

"I got so mad! And, I said I some things that weren't very nice."

"Do you often get angry?"

"I try not. Really I do! It's just that things are so hard and Brad is so irresponsible!"

They talked for another twenty minutes while Melody listened to the young mother wash back and forth like the tide. She blamed herself for the trouble; then gave excuses for her actions and explained why it wasn't really her fault. She blamed Brad; then switched and talked about how wonderful he was. She wanted to get married; but probably not now. They were saving money for a *real* wedding; but it *wouldn't be fair to the baby* if they got married just because of the pregnancy. She talked about how much she loved the baby and wanted to be a stay-at-home mom, yet she also planned to finish her education and wanted to make a career as an art broker or museum curator.

Miranda's youthful, illogical approach to life left Melody's head spinning. Yet, the thing about the conversation that amazed her most was the way the girl peppered her speech with a lot of God-talk.

She said she knew God would *make everything turn out fine,* and although He probably didn't like her and Brad living together, He *understood* and therefore it was all right because they loved each other. Several times she mentioned praying and once she said spiritual things were very important to her. But, she had never gone to church and thought that studying any religion *cheapened* the spiritual experience.

Melody had almost come to the conclusion there was nothing she could offer, when Miranda asked a question. It was the first logical thing the young woman had said.

"What does it mean when they say God loves us?" Miranda queried. "Last Sunday I saw a preacher on TV and he talked a long time but somehow I couldn't understand. If God loves us, why doesn't He just fix everything for everybody?"

"I've wondered about that a lot myself," admitted Melody. "Especially lately."

"I thought a preacher's wife would know stuff like that."

"Yeah, well it might seem that way, but having the right answers about God doesn't come automatically just because you're married to a preacher. She paused then continued with a smile.

"Come to think of it, I don't believe those answers come automatically to a preacher, either."

"That's okay. I guess spiritual stuff isn't supposed to make sense. I mean, . . . like, if we could understand it, then it wouldn't be spiritual 'cause it would be real, ya know?"

Melody rubbed her forehead again squeezing the temples between extended fingers. She wanted this girl to talk, but every time Miranda opened her mouth the contradictory flow of twisted logic made reasoning impossible. She felt like they needed an interpreter.

"Why not start with definitions?" Again, the words formed somewhere deep inside. It was almost as though the thought was not her own. She wondered briefly about the experience, but didn't have time to pursue it.

"Miranda, I believe spiritual things should make sense and are real. However, I also think before we can even consider your question we have to ask ourselves what we mean by *love* and what it would mean for God to *fix* everything."

The young woman wasn't accustomed a systematic approach and she really didn't want to go there. But, Melody's voice was a balm for her silent, lonely apartment and she longed for her to talk on and on while the pleasant sound washed over her.

"Ok," she replied as though volunteering to take part in a game. "What do *love* and *fix* really mean?

Melody wasn't sure where to start but as she began speaking, the words felt right and seemed to fall in place almost of their own accord.

"When we say things need *fixing* we are recognizing this world is broken. Wars, terrorism, global warming, poverty; all testify that something is badly wrong out there. And I suppose God could start to *fix* things by tackling these big problems first.

"But, when you honestly think about it, these *big* problems all find their root in people. If people were not broken, then the world would not be broken either. If people did not hate, kill and oppress, there would be no war. If we really cared about each other and voluntarily shared, there would be little, if any, poverty. Even global warming would be cured if all people everywhere were conscientious and careful with the resources God has provided.

"Because all of these *big* problems find their root in the *little* problems of people, it makes sense that if God is going to fix the world, He will have to start with individual hearts.

"The Christian faith teaches that is exactly what He has done.

"You said earlier you realized the words you said to Brad were unkind and hurtful. You didn't want to say them, but they came out your mouth anyway. Isn't that right?"

The answer on the other end of the line was weak, but clear and affirmed the truth of the statement.

Melody continued, "The reason that happened is because inside—in your soul and heart—your nature is to hit back and hurt others when you have been hurt."

This time the response was only silence.

"Before God starts changing the world, He has chosen to change us—one person at a time—by giving individuals new natures.

"The way God does this is by exchange.

"When Jesus came, He took on the nature of man and opened the way so we could take on a bit of the nature of God. For centuries Christians have called this event the *new birth*. In fact, that is what Jesus called it.

"When we admit we are broken and ask God to fix us, He has promised that He will. And, He starts that *fixing* by putting a new nature or heart inside us then He keeps on training us to do better deeds from that point.

"Well, I don't think I really need that much fixing" Miranda broke in. "I just want Brad to love me and this baby and be responsible!"

"I guess that brings us to the definition of the other important word in your question, *love*. You said earlier that you loved Brad, but you also said that you were so angry you didn't know if you would let him come back. You say Brad says he loves you, but he won't be responsible and refuses to take fatherhood seriously.

"These are examples of how our love is broken. Yes, our love is real and it's good, but it is also confused, inadequate and when push comes to shove it can be very selfish. We become centered more on our need to be loved than our giving love freely to another.

"Sometimes what we call *love* is nothing more than our desire to consume or control or get the feelings we want. Human love is limited. Our love comes with conditions and agendas that have nothing to do with the benefit of another."

"Love with strings attached," said Miranda thinking of her aunt.

"Yes, exactly!"

Miranda was delighted that she had said something of which Melody approved, so she continued. "It's like that saying, 'If you love something, let it go. If it comes back it is yours forever.'" She paused then confessed, "I found that on the Net."

"I like that. There is a freedom in the highest, God-kind of love."

"Yeah, but the next guy in the blog said, "If we loved something we should it let go, but if it didn't come back, then we should hunt it down and kill it!" She laughed at the joke.

Melody was appalled. "I guess that is what I meant by human love being tainted with selfishness. We want our way and refuse to give unless another gives back to us."

Miranda sobered. The truth was coming home in a way she could understand. "God is not like that?"

"His love is not selfish, if that is what you mean. It is strong enough to give us freedom. He always seeks our good, but He will let us go our own way if we insist."

"That's scary."

"Yes. But, Miranda, there is something else. God really does love us without strings and unconditionally, but it is also true that our actions matter. Our bad actions separate us from God. He is holy and we are not.

"If we could never do anything bad our whole life—not even have a bad thought—we would stay connected and near Him all the time. But, we can't do that because our natures won't let us. Our actions show what we are inside. Anytime we do even one selfish thing it shows that we have a selfish nature. God does not have that kind of nature, so we are separated from Him."

"But, I sometimes feel connected to God." Miranda defended. "I walk in the park or sing or get high and everything is cool." She had not intended to add the remark about getting high. It just slipped out. Color began to creep up her cheeks and she wondered if Melody was shocked.

The pastor's wife heard the remark but ignored it. Personally, she had never so much as drunk a glass of wine, but she understood what it was to enjoy moments of happiness and assumed some drugs provided those same feelings. Temporarily.

"I understand about being happy and content," she said. "In a way, those moments are evidence of God's unselfish love scattered freely on the world and everyone in it.

"But, that is not exactly what I mean by connection. To connect with God, we must have a nature like His. Our brokenness is not just about what we do; it's about what we are.

Melody scarcely heard the conversation after that point. Miranda talked. She talked. And, by the time they hung up, their conversation had drifted back into a discussion of everyday events and the shower.

But, Melody couldn't get past the phrase, *not what we do, but what we are*. The words held a curious, haunting quality that drew and fascinated her.

Like a moth that can't resist the light, she was mentally and emotionally drawn to the words going over them again and again long after the phone was resting in her lap.

Nothing she had shared with Miranda was new. All of the words; all of the spiritual jargon;

all of the concepts had been a part of her for as long as she had memory. Yet, somehow everything *was* new.

How often had she confessed the wrong things she had done and beat herself up internally for not doing better? How often had she resolved to try harder; struggled, prayed, resented and fought? How often had she rededicated and sought a new start so she might please an angry God?

Less than an hour ago, she had prayed asking God that she might be honest with Miranda. Was she now, at long last, being honest with herself?

How much longer would she hide from others pretending to be what she knew she was not? Would she continue to drag her "best" before God pretending it was good enough and knowing it was not? Wasn't it time to just stop? Wasn't it time to stand before Him in rags admitting how helpless and broken she really was?

Yet, everything in her resisted the idea. Something inside was insulted by the idea of helplessness. All her pride and training and talent and life history were geared toward working hard and making things happen.

It was only natural that she should take on fixing her own nature just as she took on any other project. Giving up was for cowards and weaklings and those who were lazy. Melody Stonemeyer Phelps was none of these things. She was strong and capable.

Wasn't she?

A broken platter of cookies said, *no*.

It didn't matter how hard or how long she tried; no amount of effort would make her what she longed to be. Deep inside, she was as broken as the shattered platter. Nothing inside her could ever produce the freedom for which she longed. All her efforts only produced more guilt which in turn drove her toward more efforts.

She had never seen herself in that light before. Yes, she had known theoretically that all people were helpless to save themselves, but the reality had never soaked so deeply or personally into her view of herself.

Now, seeing herself as empty and helpless and broken seemed a bit strange. Worse, these things were not only true at this moment they would always be true no matter how hard she tried to make them different.

It was a new idea that both grieved and freed her.

It grieved her, because she deeply desired to be capable and strong. She wanted to walk up to God and have Him pat her on the shoulder while she proudly displayed her handiwork of a perfect woman she had produced for Him.

Yet, helplessness also freed her. If she accepted to the depth of her soul that she had no power to change, then her efforts that direction became foolish. She could not change her own nature any more than she could pull herself out of quicksand by tugging on her shoe laces. She might as well rest. There was nothing to lose.

Melody sat for a quiet moment toying with the phone. The old ideas that she had known for so long were becoming fresh and new. It was like a strange, slow moving light that gradually reached out to illuminate one room of her soul and then the next. The feelings were warm. And relaxed. And gentle.

She took in a long, ragged breath. Freedom. For the first time, she realized that it was not about her. It never had been. It was not her effort but His great love. A love that was so unselfish, it existed to give. A powerful, free love so amazing it would willingly share a spark of its own nature with all who reached out in faith.

Melody didn't bow her head. She didn't have to. Because for the first time, she bowed her whole being to His control.

"Lord, change not only what I do, but what I am."

*****

The gentle glow from the light on the bedside table was the only thing that held back the darkness of the night. Its yellow softness spilled over the chair, the woman and the floor holding them all in a small, intimate circle. But as BaLanna entered the room and took up his new assignment, he saw something else. Life—real, Divine, new-born LIFE—fluttered then took hold making the most wondrous glow of all stream from Melody's face.

Elizabeth Baker

10:16 PM

Between Two Worlds

The only sound coming from room 304 was air being pulled into lungs and softly expelled. Soft, natural, and peaceful it was the sound of life.

The patient tossed and moaned as the nightmare assaulted her. A child was crying. She longed to rescue it but was trapped; the lower half of her body immovable and sunk in mire. More pitiful than before, the child's cries turned to wails.

Margaret Mc Clawson had tried to fall asleep shortly before nine, but the cramped room seemed purposely designed to thwart her efforts. Getting comfortable in the too hard, too small bed was nearly impossible and the blinking lights of a nearby machine didn't help. She finally requested the machine—along with its clothespin-like pincher that attached to her finger—be removed.

No luck. Hospital policy, they said.

After another hour of fruitless effort, she clandestinely located the off switch and removed the pincher without permission.

But, she had only begun to drift off when Attila The Nurse found the silent apparatus and reconnected it. She even had the audacity to scold the former school teacher who promptly scolded right back and again removed the offensive finger pincher.

The squabble was at last settled around nine-thirty when a less-than-happy Dr. Grimes was contacted by phone and suggested a don't-ask/don't-tell policy be implemented. The nurse would connect the finger pinch then walk away. What Margaret did with the devise after that was her own business. It seemed the perfect solution. Hospital policy would be adhered to in every detail, his cantankerous patient would get some much needed sleep, and he could get back to his wife and their movie.

Soon, the rhythm of breath was the only sound: blood pressure 135/85; temperature 97.6; air moving in and out sixteen times each minute. But no offensive machines announced those facts to the world.

10:16:00 PM

Approximately 60,000 miles of blood pipeline course through the body of a healthy adult, but Margaret was thin and old and small, so her miles had shortened with the years. She possessed only

56,235 miles; enough to stretch around the earth twice with a few thousand miles left over.

It was a vast system of channels and branches, bypasses and overlaps without a single dead end, all powered by a pump that to date had constricted and relaxed over three billion times. It was a dependable system with tireless accuracy and it worked to perfection while the old woman slept.

If Zorbath had wanted to exert the effort, he could have followed the pipeline, but instead he was observing the whole woman. Ignoring the thinning grey hair, wrinkled, discolored face, and hands with swollen knuckles, he saw something deeper. Much deeper. Something even deeper than the blood cells and electrical impulses and pumping heart.

The angel saw a daughter of the Most High. She was a charge he had been given years ago and looking back he felt he had performed his duty well. After a few bumps in the initial training period, serving her these many years had been a joy. To him, she was more beautiful this night than she had ever been. The prospect of her translation filled him with excitement and the battered warrior could hardly wait to escort her home. It was time for rest.

10:18:05 PM

Red blood cell number six trillion, three hundred and forty-two had been born ninety-seven days ago. Shaped much like a toy Frisbee, it was small enough so that eight thousand copies of itself could fit side by side on one-third inch of ruler. It raced along in a river of liquid fats, platelets, water, proteins, vitamins, white cells, hormones, sugars, and acids.

Aging fast, the cell would be dead in less than a month but at this moment it exploded from the heart carrying on its back the means of physical life: a single molecule of oxygen destined for Margaret's brain.

The tall, red-haired angel could feel death approaching. It was time. With silent efficiency he readied his sword then called for reinforcements. Stationing the fresh recruits above, below, before, and behind, he effectively encased Margaret in a bubble of protection. Separating the human soul from its body would draw forces from the darkness and he would take no chances with the one entrusted to his care.

As he worked, Zorbath studied the silver threads radiating out from Margaret's body. Thousands of threads. Millions of threads. All of them reaching, pulsing and stretching out like an aura.

These were touch points of caring, longing, affiliation, memory, relationship, and desire. Together, the threads formed connections binding Margaret's soul to the earth. He reached the tip of the sword and snapped one which recoiled trembling toward the body then disappeared.

10:18:07 PM

The dream returned and the cycle repeated. Color, sound, smell, emotion they were all there. A baby was crying. Her body responded appropriately by dumping adrenalin into the blood and as the red cell raced along searching for the next, smaller branch pressure against artery walls began to rise. A baby was crying. She needed to rescue it.

When the pressure reached 180/100 a weak spot in the tunnel up ahead began to puff slightly. Nothing unusual. The same spot had expanded slightly and relaxed thousands of times. Less than 1/8th of an inch long and bubbling out no more than 1/16th, the tiny bubble could hardly be considered significant.

Adrenalin surged and emotional tension increased as the red cell raced on. It was destined for a capillary branch where it would fold itself into the shape of a bullet, squeeze into the tiny canal, and release its burden of oxygen.

But, the bubble lay between the cell and its goal. This time it would not be allowed to pass.

The angel's sword dipped again snapping more silver threads that quivered and retreated toward the body. Each thread held a memory. Each was a reason why Margaret desired to see another earth sunrise.

Most often the threads were voluntarily released as one by one a weary human let go of dreams and interests. Occupations that once held hope and security became empty goals.

JaKobe's Assignment

Fascinating hobbies faded and lost purpose. Relationships that gave life meaning became too heavy to hold.

Other times, the threads were ripped away suddenly through accident and a startled human entered eternity scarcely aware of the transition.

But Margaret maintained such energy and thirst for living that she had released very few threads during her years on earth. So, Zorbath aided her separation from the world as one silver thread after another was silently snipped and fell away.

10:18:08 PM

Rising adrenalin and constricted artery walls caused the pressure to rise still further and as it moved to 210/105, the bubble of tissue stretched dangerously thin.

Seven more angels of various ranks arrived and Zorbath dispatched each to their station. His force now numbered a hundred and twenty-seven. Tension rose as he continued to snip the silver threads for dark spirits were also gathering.

The dark ones could smell approaching death and they were drawn to it with delicious anticipation hoping that the soul was unprotected and owned by hell. But when they arrived and encountered Zorbath's defenses, their anticipation turned to anger and they fought the forces of light purely to dissipate their fury at being robbed of the prize. If the dying human were out of their reach, at least the nearest warrior was not.

Zorbath judged the strength of the enemy and continued to deploy arriving troupes while staying close by Margaret's side.

Where was a guardian? He needed to choose one quickly and scanned the available candidates looking for the best prospect.

10:18:09 PM

As the red cell with its precious load of oxygen reached the junction between artery and smaller arteriole, pressure reached 230/126 and the wall gave way.

The sensation of a crying child abruptly stopped and Margaret briefly rose to a state of semi-consciousness. She sensed there was pain located somewhere in the vicinity of her head, but the sensation faded as she was folded into a formless void.

The red cell was pulled by the force of blood under pressure as it poured through the small but widening rip pushed by the pressure of a beating heart.

Fibers, tissues and nerves were displaced as delicate brain cell connections ripped apart.

10:18:18 PM

Blood continued to pour through the opening. Soon, two teaspoons of liquid displaced brain tissue.

Sensing the crisis, the body fought to stay alive. Blood pressure suddenly dropped reaching 90/50 and tachycardia sent the heart racing. Desperate to provide needed blood and oxygen to the wounded area, the heart constricted over 150 weak, fluttering beats a minute.

As the pressure dropped, the flow of blood through the rip slowed, but the disruption to brain circuitry would not be repaired. Signals that should have passed among brain structures with lightning speed were suddenly unsure, slow and occasionally scrambled.

The heart continued to flutter and agonal breathing began. Occasional, irregular gasps replaced the smooth breathing of the past and her temperature began to rise.

The red cell had stopped moving. Now, it drifted in a pool of blood and water. The load of oxygen it protected slipped away and stuck uselessly to a fragment of severed nerve.

Zorbath made eye contact with a guardian that was just arriving at the scene of battle. Without words he requested she take up resurrection duties. Also without words, the guardian agreed.

Zorbath motioned her inside the defended circle of light stationing her to the left side of the body while others spirits continued their fight with the surrounding enemies.

10:20:45 PM

Even though the flow of blood had slowed, it continued to ooze from the severed arteriole. Two teaspoons became half an ounce slowly increasing pressure on delicate brain tissue.

Suddenly, a second barrier gave way. Swelling, rupturing tissue pushed its way down toward the brain stem where the most fundamental, life sustaining, instructions went out to the body.

Although technically the blood continued to flow, the pressure of 50/20 could not have been measured by any machine and ventricular fibrillation replaced the previous faint, quick pumps of the heart. Now, irregular twitches and random jerks substituted for heartbeats while no significant amount of blood passed through the system.

As others fought to keep the way clear, Zorbath reached for Margaret's hand and held it fast.

Still physically alive, she hung between worlds. She could feel his hand, but not understand what it meant or why such warmth and encouragement came from the strong grasp. Instinctively, her own fingers tightened around his and Zorbath smiled.

If conscious to only the earthly world, Margaret would have been in agony but between the worlds she knew nothing except a vague sensation of pain and the pressure of a friendly hand.

JaKobe's Assignment

10:21:10 PM

The brain ceased to give out any signals and as the last breath exited her lungs her body lost all tension. The journey from sleep to death had been less than 4 minutes.

For Margaret Marie Mc Clawson Lyde, time had stopped.

Elizabeth Baker

10:55 PM

The Pastor's Office

JaKobe might have been less pensive if Phennia had not been wounded earlier in the evening. But he watched as the sword burned her forearm and the event sobered him. He had slapped the contact point away instantly, but the damage was done. Earth was not a dress rehearsal or a lark. It was real and the stakes were eternal.

He shifted his position, crossing his arms over his chest, leaned back against the wall and studied the pastor before him.

In many ways Jonathan was both blind and foolish, yet the angel felt a grudging admiration. At least this human wanted to be part of the war. He was honest enough to struggle with God while maintaining a respectful awe of Deity.

That was more than he could say for most humans. It was even more than could be said for many of his own kind. One third of them had made choices that put them at odds with their Creator.

What about himself? Were his choices always good ones? Perhaps it had not been best to withdraw for so long from direct human contact. His decision to stay heaven-side had not been an act of disobedience.

Yet, what might have been if he had requested to stay?

He smiled ruefully. The human writer[29] had been correct. When considering our past, one question Heaven never answers was, *What if?*

Pulling the Evaluator from his pocket, he once more studied screen after screen of charts, reports and graphs. The current opposition level of three/seven was extremely low. How much pressure would it take to open Jonathan's eyes to Kingdom realities?

He was considering the value of taking one more reading when his thoughts were interrupted by a jangle of earthly noise.

Startled, Jonathan jumped and grabbed at his pocket for the phone. "Hello," he stated abruptly.

"I'm sorry, to bother you," it was Melody's voice.

"Oh, it's you, Honey." Jonathan relaxed. Late night calls usually meant emergencies and trouble, but his wife sounded peaceful enough.

"The hospital just called. Dr. Grimes is requesting you come see Margaret."

"See Margaret?" he asked a bit confused. "I just saw her this afternoon and I thought I would stop by her home in a day or two. Can't this wait until then?"

"It was some nurse or receptionist that called, but she was very clear. Doc Grimes wants you to see Margaret tonight."

"Did she say why?"

"Not really. I tried to get more information, but she would only say it was Doctor Grimes' request for you to come immediately."

"Oh, these stupid privacy laws!" he complained. "The government has made them such an issue it's impossible to get a straight answer out of anyone! I wonder if he knows I already saw her today?"

"Shall I call the hospital and ask them to page him?"

"No, that's ok. Maybe they got late results from one of those test and she is upset or something."

He glanced at his watch. It was almost eleven. "Well, the hospital is not far and it's time I called this quits anyway. I can drop by and still be home before midnight."

"I hate you to be out so late."

"I'll be fine. You get some sleep. I'll be home soon."

"I love you, Jonathan." It was the same salutation she had used for years, but tonight there was something different in her voice. It made him uneasy.

"I love you, too. I won't be long."

JaKobe's Assignment

Within moments he had shut down the laptop, locked the office and settled behind the wheel of his trusted Chevy Coup.

In less than twelve minutes he was making his way through the emergency entrance of Thyme Memorial. He glanced again at his watch. With a little luck he could keep his promise to be home before midnight with room to spare.

Elizabeth Baker

Time: Eternity

Place: Earth

The pressure on her forearm increased. A strong hand was holding her wrist, pulling her. The vague sensation of struggle faded and was replaced by a knowledge that more than anything else, she wanted to follow that hand. She wanted it more than the inertia that only moments before lured her into nothingness. She longed to jump up and follow wherever the hand was leading.

So she did.

Gasping like a drowning victim breaking the surface of the water, Margaret drew her head, shoulders and back free from the binding shell that had been her prison for eighty-three long, hard years.

She sat up, her eyes growing bright with wonder. Angels were everywhere! Some had their backs to her as they fought a rolling darkness beyond the capsule of light that surrounded her. Others faced her and laughed as they welcomed her to join the ranks of spirit. But the angel she noticed most of all was the one who still held her hand in a firm grip and continued to pull until she stood on her feet and faced him.

"Welcome!" He said it with an almost musical lilt in his voice. "Welcome, child of the King!"

So many emotions flooded her. If she had been in her earthly shell, Margaret would have been terribly frightened. But she was not in that shell—thank God—so she stood and let the joy of the moment wash over her in waves.

What a thrill it was to be alive! She could hear, see, smell, feel and, if someone would offer her a morsel, she was quite sure she could taste, too! Yet, each of the familiar sensations was sharpened and accelerated to a whole new level. She was alive. Truly alive!

Margaret wanted to laugh. To sing! She looked back at the worn, ugly shell from which she had emerged. Wonderful! I don't have to take those stupid blood pressure pills anymore! As soon as the thought entered her mind, she laughed out loud at the ridiculousness of it all!

Zorbath laughed, too, and she turned to see him still holding her hand. Suddenly, a second, more urgent thought came; one that bordered on panic.

"Where's Jesus? Where's my Lord? Oh, tell me, Zorbath, tell me quickly!"

The instant the words formed, other questions came. How had she known the angel's name? Was it stupid to ask for something to be done quickly when there was no such thing as time? Had she actually spoken words or was she communicating via thought only? Could the angel speak English?

It was all too much. She closed her eyes and drew a breath, then immediately wondered how she could breathe if she were dead? Slow down, old girl. Slow down. She admonished herself with the same words she had once used to force unstable legs to behave.

Calming a bit and curious, she gently cracked opened her eyes.

"It's all right," Zorbath's words comforted her. "Give yourself a little space to adjust to the translation."

What does he mean by "translation" and why did he say "space" rather than "time"? The questions rattled around without answers and she again tried to limit the multiplying thoughts by closing her eyes.

"It's all right," Zorbath reassured. "You will see Jesus. He knows you have arrived and He will not delay coming to you."

With the angel still holding her hand and eyes shut, Margaret stretched her neck left then right and rolled her shoulders; a habit she had used on earth to dissipate tension. She simply must relax and take one thing at a time while she got used to being in heaven.

Wait a minute. Her eyes popped opened and looked around. There was the hospital bed. That silly corpse and even the machine with its finger-pincher were still here. She was on earth!

Zorbath laughed again. "It really is all right," he assured for the third time. Margaret glanced at the turbulent warfare taking place just outside the bubble of light in which she, Zorbath and a few others were encased.

"The warriors will keep the enemy at bay. Soon, you will see them no more."

The angel did not seem to be in a hurry, so Margaret found it a little easier to relax. He moved his arm slightly as though asking permission to release her. She loosened her fingers which until that point remained clamped to his wrist and let her arm fall to her side.

Zorbath's proud smile made her feel as though she had just accomplished something great.

Well, maybe simply standing in this strange new place without hanging desperately on an angel's arm was something of an accomplishment. She smiled.

Zorbath smiled, too, and moved back a step. That was when she noticed the sword. While she had been clinging to his left hand, his right held a glowing, three foot long blade.

The angel moved back one more step indicating with his raised, free hand that she should wait. He glanced around as though checking the position of his troops and evidently satisfied, held the hilt of the sword in both hands with the blade pointed up and arms extended straight out before him. He seemed to concentrate as the color of the blade changed from orange to blue.

Then releasing the pose, he struck horizontal and vertical slices in the air with two quick strokes creating what could only be described as a doorway in the fabric of reality.

The four pointed edges of the cut rolled back like scrolls as hospital wall, bathroom door, window and trees responded like pictures on a screen. Beyond, a narrow cobblestone street led into a different world.

"Honored, Daughter," he said with a polite bow, "Heaven awaits."

Music poured through the opening. Wondrous, complex, fascinating, joyful music. Music from every tribe, tongue, nation and century flowed in a pleasant cacophony of harmony.

Strange, she thought. I always assumed cacophony and harmony were antonyms. Now, somehow the dissidence blended without competition or clash and she instantly knew she could choose to focus on one melody or listen to the full spectrum with equal enjoyment. Amazing.

As though reading her expression, Zorbath explained. "The sound of praise is ever present, but you will find it only enhances your experience. Something like the way many different colors on earth are always present but never disturb."

Grateful for the explanation, Margaret wanted to pick the angel's brain for at least a century gleaning delightful tidbits of information. Wait a minute. Do angels have brains? She shook her head at the thought. Of course they do. Don't they?

Zorbath laughed out loud. "Would you like to step through the door?"

Had she been speaking aloud? She made a mental note. One of the first things she must learn is the difference between thinking and speaking in this strange place.

Zorbath became serious, "My Lady?" He used the archaic earth term for royalty, bowed, and turned slightly toward the opening.

Margaret began to move. Slowly, step by astounded step she moved not with caution, but with reverence and awe.

"There is a great reception waiting you, as befits a child of the King. But, before you experience that joy, a special request has been made for your presence. Follow the path and go through the gate."

She turned briefly and caught his eye.

He said, "Do not fear. I have a few things to finish here. I will see you at the celebration on the other side."

The last glimpse Margaret had of earth was Zorbath still holding open the door and beyond him the boiling clash of angels at war just outside the circle of light that had protected her.

Nothing in her wanted to go back to that place and she was comforted at the thought of meeting Zorbath once more. She suspected she owed him much and it would be a delight to reminisce.

Once inside the door, she had the distinct impression that much activity was going on, but it was shielded from her view. Like the sensation of walking a quite side street while knowing New York City was only a block away. There were buildings on each side of the narrow street and up ahead a small iron gate was fixed into a wall.

As she approached the gate, she could smell the scent of roses and over the top of the wall a huge bough tumbled looking very much like the summer blossoms she so laboriously cared for back on earth. The gate itself seemed to be fashioned of iron and she marveled at the pleasant touches of rust and aged patina. Bhings age in a place where there was no time? It was another curiosity waiting for her delighted investigation.

The gate opened with a pleasant creaking sound and as she stepped through she had to push back a bough of roses. *No thorns,* she noted. Petals scattered over the gravel path.

Zorbath had told her to go through the gate, but he hadn't said exactly what would happen after that. Maybe this was just a quiet place where she could become more oriented to the new realities around her. On the other hand, he had said someone had requested her presence.

There were earth-like sounds of birds and the sight of green, growing things and because no other option seemed logical, she followed the path as it lead deeper into this private, well tended garden. All around was the secure feeling of home

JaKobe's Assignment

and as she walked the gravel crunched under her very real, very alive feet.

The sound of water splashing drew her around an azalea blooming vibrant pink. A fountain must be ahead. She entered a small clearing where two benches had been placed by a pool. Water trickled over rocks and splashed.

Someone was sitting on one of the benches with their back toward her. A child. A little girl dressed in blue.

The child stood. There was something familiar about the way she used tiny hands to smoothed the folds of her dress. She looked up and smiled, light pouring over soft, golden curls.

Margaret felt her heart leap into her throat as it constricted with both laughter and tears. She choked and staggered as she ran forward scooping the child into her arms and feeling thin small arms encircle her neck.

Laughing and spinning she shouted for joy, "Oh, my beautiful Peggy Jane!"

11:07 PM

Thyme Memorial Hospital

The halls were empty and he was the lone occupant in the elevator on the short ride to the third floor, but once the doors slid open it was evident that hospitals never slept.

A young man in a lab coat entered the car as Jonathan stepped out and behind the central desk one nurse was pulling records from a large file while another counted pills into a small paper cup.

Doc Grimes stood with his back to Jonathan. He was bending his tall frame at the waist as he leaned on a counter for support and scratched notes in a chart.

When he heard Jonathan approach, the doctor turned and his wide-jowled face took on a scowl. Dark, hooded eyes peered at the pastor beneath heavy, white brows.

Jonathan thought nothing of the foreboding look. Doc Grimes was famous for his bad temper, poor bedside manner and permanent frown.

"Preacher Phelps." He stated the obvious. "So, you finally got here."

"Sorry. I came as soon as I got the call." Jonathan wondered why he always felt as though he were apologizing in the presence of this man. "How's Margaret?"

"That all depends on your viewpoint," the doctor replied, tossing his pen into a receptacle on the other side of the counter. "I suppose from your take on such things, she is doing better than she has in years. From my point of view, she's dead."

The words seemed to rattle in the air without meaning. "I beg your pardon?"

"Guess I didn't put that very well." It was the closest thing to an apology Doc Grimes had spoken in years. "But, it is not like you were related to her or anything like that."

"Did you say Margaret is dead?" Jonathan asked incredulously. "But, I spoke with her this afternoon."

"Talking to a preacher in the afternoon doesn't keep people from dying that night."

Jonathan's head was spinning. Margaret was dead? He took in the information but somehow it kept slipping away. Then a second thought pierced his consciousness.

"Why did you call me?" he asked.

"It's on the form," said the doctor unceremoniously.

"Beg your pardon?"

"It's on the form," he repeated. "Item twenty-six. Standard Admission Form."

He turned the record he was holding around and tapped the bottom of a page then flipped it shut before Jonathan actually saw what was written. "Emergency contact. Everyone has to name one when they are admitted. Margaret named you as emergency contact. Dying qualifies as an emergency."

Jonathan stood dumbfounded. How could Margaret be gone? Bewilderment showed in his eyes as he tried to take it all in.

Doctor Grimes glanced at him. For a preacher, the man didn't have much stamina. The middle aged man in a white shirt, suit, and loosened tie seemed rooted in place and suspended in time. Perhaps he had been too abrupt. He had heard that some preachers grew quite close to those under their care. He cleared his throat and tried to soften his style.

"Would you like to see her?"

"Huh?"

"See Margaret. Would like to see her? Maybe you need to say goodbye or something."

Jonathan had never thought of that.

"Ah, sure. I guess so. Yes." He stammered.

With Grimes leading the way, he followed to room 304. It was dark inside and the sour-faced physician flipped on the light as they entered. "Nurses have been busy, so they haven't cleaned things up yet. Death occurred at . . ." he searched through the papers in his hand, "... ah.. 10:40 PM. Give or take a little."

The doctor reached over and felt Margaret's hand then checked his watch. "Yeah, the body is quite cool. That time ought to be about right. At least, that is the time I got here and found her, so that's what I wrote on the forms."

Jonathan stood silent looking at his friend. Her sheets were still folded neatly just below her arm pits with both hands lying on top. Her mouth was open and the eyes were tiny, dark slits. Her slack jaw and ears laying flat against her head indicated more than sleep. He found himself wondering what the face must have looked like the first time Harold saw her smile.

"W-what happened?" He was stammering again.

"Hard to say. Margaret was getting on up there, but I never found much wrong other than a slight blood pressure problem. She was pretty healthy for eighty-three."

He reached and jerked open one eye between two fingers then did the same to the other eye then closed both with a sweep of the palm of his hand. "One pupil's dilated." He rubbed his chin and thought.

"Judging by that and how fast it evidently happened, I'd guess she first had a cerebral aneurysm close to the Circle of Willis, then a second event finished her off. Probably a tonsillar herniation." Seeing the perplexed expression on the pastor's face, he translated for laity. "She had a stroke."

Silence filled the room. A prolonged silence that lasted until both men became uncomfortable.

"You want to be alone?" the doctor asked.

"No, that won't be necessary." Jonathan answered too quickly.

"You want to pray or something? I can step out."

He ignored the offer. Praying with Margaret earlier that afternoon seemed natural. Praying now seemed stiff, formal, and without purpose. He coughed slightly to hide his uneasiness then asked, "What will happen next?"

"I guess that depends on you."

"Beg your pardon?"

"You know for an educated man, you sure *beg pardon* a lot!" The displeasure of the physician was clear. "You are on the papers as emergency contact and if I remember right she once told me that she had written the church in as beneficiary of her property."

"Yes, that is true."

"She had no kin?"

"Not that I know of."

"Do you know who the executor of the will might be?"

Jonathan shuffled his feet uneasily. "I think I remember signing something to that effect."

"Well, all I can tell you is that we can't hold the body long. It needs to be moved to a funeral home. Soon."

JaKobe's Assignment

The old physician almost grinned. He seemed to be enjoying the discomfort he was creating. "Preacher, you can probably fight this in court, but it seems to me like Margaret has spoken from the grave and said, 'Tag, you're it'."

As the two humans continued to discuss such things as the disposition of the body and how long one could be legally left above ground without embalmment, an unobserved sentinel silently looked on.

The guardian understood what the humans were saying. She had as much power, curiosity and personality as any other angel. But while on duty she did not interact with her surroundings as they often did. Silent, unblinking, never weary, as guardian she had only one task and a sense of duty so strong nothing else mattered. She did not care if the task lasted five earth years or five-thousand; a guardian never abandoned the post.

This guardian was named Reaobah and the moment she accepted the assignment from Zorbath she knew where she would be until the day earth was no more. She would follow and preserve at least one copy of this particular human's DNA until it was called for by the Final Authority.

At the end of time the master code in her care would be surrendered and used to collect the proper elements of earth once again. Arranging the elements in the exact order prescribed by the code it would recreate a body for Margaret to again inhabit.

The code had been given at conception. Long before Margaret had a name or drew a breath. The unique code was settled and sure. It had been duplicated as one cell became two, became four, became ten thousand, then a million.

The code was in her hair and brain and skin. It had been washed away as cells died and flushed away in excrement, but constant duplication marched on cell after cell until at last well over a hundred trillion copies of the code were duplicated.

Reaobah crossed her hands behind her back. Considering the huge amount of data available, preserving one copy would not be a difficult task. She would wait and listen for the last trumpet.

11:37 PM

The Back Steps

Jonathan pulled under the carport and turned off the motor. He was bone weary but doubted he could sleep. Sleep required the mind to downshift. His seemed stuck in overdrive.

It was always difficult to unwind after preaching twice on Sunday but today had been especially draining. First, there was the packed schedule then Melody's strange behavior. Finally, Margaret's sudden death with all the unanswered questions about her will.

It was too much. He had not enjoyed a moment's peace since early morning. Not even an afternoon nap.

Reluctantly, he opened the door and got out. One thing for certain, sitting in the carport all night would not make him feel any better.

The house was dark as he stepped through the back door and entered a silent kitchen. He flipped on the light over the stove and made coffee in semi-darkness. Decaffeinated. No sense antagonizing a reluctant Sand Man. When the perking stopped, he poured a large mug then walked outside into the damp night air and settled on the back steps.

Moonlight flooded the scene giving a surreal essence to familiar objects. Trees that once formed a leafy umbrella now stretched black branches against a clouded sky. A tire swing hung limp. Fragments of used charcoal gave up a faint acrid smell from the rusting barbeque grill. Melody's flower bed had been a riot of colorful chrysanthemums only weeks before. Now it lay as a twisting heap of spent stems against the grey fence. Even the picnic table seemed a little crooked and less square in the pale, filtered light.

The somber scene fit his mood. He held the coffee close to his face inhaling the pungent aroma and warming his fingers on the thick ceramic cup. Home. It was good to be here with the long day finally behind him.

"I thought you might need this." Melody's voice caressed him as a quilt draped around his shoulders.

"Did my rattling in the kitchen wake you? I'm sorry. I know the kids will have you up at the crack of dawn."

"It's all right. I was having a little trouble sleeping, anyway."

Jonathan adjusted the colorful patchwork around his shoulders and scooted over on the steps.

JaKobe's Assignment

"Want to share?" he asked holding open a pocket of warmth. Melody nestled beside him with the quilt covering her right arm and his warm body comforting the left.

Less than fifteen feet away JaKobe shared not only the pastor's somber mood, but his picnic table as well. Sitting backward on the bench, he faced the steps with both elbows on the table top and long legs stretched over dead grass, feet crossed at the ankles. His Evaluator dangled loosely in his left hand while the palm of his right cradled the final report waiting for transmission.

For some reason he could not completely explain, he had been reluctant to actually release the memorandum. Instead, fingers still closed over it like a protective shield.

Was this what Rachael felt when she received orders to clear the way and answer the human's oft repeated prayer? It was not unusual for angels to grow fond of their charges and Rachael had been with Jonathan since birth. Did the idea of causing him pain grieve her?

He uncrossed his ankles and sat forward, elbows on his knees. That was one of the biggest mysteries of earth yet to be solved: why was there so much pain? What good was it?

He knew the place was a fallen, fractured planet. He had been there and watched when Eden died. But, why had God not simply wiped the place clean at that instant? Why not throw it all out and start over. Why seek to redeem something so broken?

An earthly philosopher noted a human could endure any amount of pain so long as there was a goal.[29] It was only empty pain—pain without purpose—that destroyed. Perhaps there was some truth in that insight.

Would Jonathan value the goal of spiritual insight enough that it balanced the pain of a high opposition level?

Only the Final Authority could reset the opposition scale, yet the angel knew God would honor his work. Very likely the level he suggested would be something Jonathan would live with for the rest of his life. The warrior was confident of his choice, but the responsibility still lay heavy on his heart.

Melody spoke. "I see you were able to make it back before midnight, just like you promised." Her body relaxed and molded to the small shelter. "How did it go with Margaret?"

When he didn't answer right away, she pulled back to look him in the face. "Was something wrong?"

His eyes searched hers for a moment then he responded slowly, "I guess it's like Ol' Doc Grimes said, 'That depends on your perspective.'" She studied his face waiting patiently. "Margaret died around ten tonight."

"What happened?"

"Doc used a few big words but, basically, she had a stroke. There must have been a weak place in a vein somewhere inside her brain. It just gave way."

"This will really hit a lot of people hard. Margaret has been a pillar in Thyme for years." She paused a moment as the memories rolled past one by one then added. "Wasn't she a charter member of Grace Community Church?"

"No, but her parents were. She was a small child when the church was organized. She will definitely be missed."

He took a large swallow from his steaming cup. Soon, he would have to tell his wife about the job they had inherited: disposing of the body, settling the estate. It would be a lot of work. And, probably a lot of controversy. Margaret was generous and well known. Without family, dozens of individuals and organizations would feel they had a right to profit from her demise. He took another gulp of decaf then continued on a safer subject.

"Remember when Thyme named the new elementary gym in her honor? It was amazing as we went through that woman's history. She almost single handedly improved the public library when no one else seemed to care. She badgered every city council member and civic organization for miles around. I believe reading was her passion."

"She also worked with the food bank and other volunteer activities" Melody added. "I don't know how she found time to teach school for forty years."

There was another silence and Jonathan again felt the need to tell his wife of their upcoming responsibilities. Again, he avoided the unpleasant reality. "Did you know Margaret was married?"

A quick intake of breath made it obvious that he was not the only one who would be surprised at the news. "Yep," he said, "for several years. She even had a daughter."

"What happened?"

"It seems both her husband and daughter died early in the marriage."

"I had no idea."

"Neither did I."

"Strange," she mulled over the new information. "We think we know someone then find some of the most important events of their life are hidden in the shadows. Makes you wonder how much we humans ever truly know one another."

"Well, I don't think Margaret ever intended to keep her marriage a secret. It's just that it happened a long time ago and through the years the importance to others began to fade. Let's face it we have only been here five years. As far as Thyme goes, we're still considered interlopers and greenhorns."

Melody's laughter was as musical as her piano. "I think you are exaggerating that point just a little."

They lapsed into a comfortable silence and her thoughts cycled around to how her life had changed within just the past few hours. Something inside her was as clean and as fresh as a child. She wanted to share, but at the same time, this

JaKobe's Assignment

newness was so precious and so private she resisted. She would tell her husband. Later.

The night closed around, sealing off the outside world. No sounds of traffic on the sleepy residential street. No squealing children or music from a neighbors' television. Even nature was silent. The last of the crickets, katydids and frogs had settled into the quiet of winter. Several minutes passed before Melody spoke.

"I'm sorry, Jonathan."

"Sorry about what?"

"Oh, a lot of things. But, mostly about today."

Her husband listened intently. There was something in her voice he couldn't quite identify. Melody often apologized for imperfections. He half-expected one day she might apologize for breathing and taking up space on planet earth.

But, this apology was different. There was no despair. No tears. No promise to do better. No shame. There didn't even seem to be a hidden message designed to squeeze a compliment or reassurance from him. He waited, not sure what would come next.

"I know my need for perfection can be a stress on others." This was a new approach he'd never heard before. Then his wife totally surprised him by laughing out loud. "It can be a heavy stress on me, too!"

She became serious once more and continued. "I have spent a lot of today falling apart at the seams. I know it added to your burden."

He wasn't sure how to respond. He kept waiting for her to elaborate, but there was nothing. Maybe this was a new manipulation technique designed to get him to confess something. He thought about Ben and cleared his throat.

"It's okay, Hon," he said. Then thinking he ought to offer some olive branch added, "I really will try to find time to talk with Ben."

"Ben? Oh, I am sure that will work itself out. You have always been such a good father."

He squirmed. It was hard to be defensive when you hadn't been attacked. Now, he really did feel guilty about Ben.

At length she remarked, "It really is a lovely night." They cuddled closer under the quilt. He rubbed the top of her head with his chin. Beard stubble tangled itself in the threads of her hair. He pulled back and smoothed the strands down with his free hand.

Something tender and warm began to bloom between them. Something he hadn't felt in a long time. Then, suddenly, as though pinched Melody jumped and stiffened.

"Oh, Jonathan, I forgot! I was supposed to tell you about the problem Carolina had in Sunday school this morning."

"Problem? I didn't see her today. I didn't think she even came."

"She came, all right. But Tina Bentley sent her home."

"What?" He was too confused to be offended.

"It seems Tina discovered lice in the little girl's hair and after examining all the students in the room she insisted Woody take her home immediately.'

"Who gave her authority to do that?" he asked then just as quickly answered his own question. "Never mind. Tina needs no authority but her own."

"Woody called right after you left. He was very upset and said Carolina's mother was livid when he left the child."

"Great. Next thing you know we will have the whole Hispanic community angry with us and the Department of Health knocking at our door."

"Jonathan, . . ." she spoke his name with a gentle drawl he had heard a thousand times. It said, *slow down, stop exaggerating and take a calm approach to circumstances.*

He didn't want to calm down. "I mean it. Every word!" He huffed and blew between his lips. "Tina is an arrogant fool who's married to a pompous windbag! If there is any way to make trouble or stir up dissension, the Bentley's will find it!"

His words scalded Melody's new born spirit, but she said nothing.

"Lice! Next thing you know we'll be facing a lawsuit by some young hot-shot lawyer trying to collect for damages. If not that, we will be personally shampooing the girl's hair and picking nits."

He huffed again as though disgusted with life. "Welcome to doing church in twenty-first century America!"

Her husband seldom lost his temper but when he did, molehills quickly became mountains and he ruminated on the negative for hours. She offered no solution or reprimand, only waited.

It was an eloquent silence that not only calmed but encouraged him to look at himself and at last it squeezed out a confession he had been holding inside all day.

"It's just that I want to see God do something big. I get so discouraged and tired of this petty church stuff."

"What 'stuff', Jonathan?"

"You know. Church stuff! Building programs that go bust because the people won't give. Petty personality clashes. Gossip. Counseling situations where no one wants to listen. Strangers who show up at the door expecting a handout. Not enough volunteers for Sunday school classes. Resistance to new ideas. People who expect you to marry them and bury them but never walk through the church door on Sunday or give a dime. Budget committee meetings. All the yucky stuff we call doing 'church'!"

She remembered Ellie not showing up for nursery duty and how she paced and checked the clock every two minutes. It was easy to understand his frustration. Sometimes "doing church" felt like dragging a wagon through mud with no horses attached.

"Yeah,..." she breathed out gently. "But, Darling, couldn't all that be part of what your sermon was about this morning? Isn't it possible part of being scarred is dealing with the yuck of bumping against other humans beings? And who is to say? Maybe the pain of serving one person at a time *is* 'big stuff.'"

In a flash, his resentment was back. That afternoon Margaret preached at him and now it was his wife delivering a sermon!

Jonathan drew himself up a little taller on the step and responded with dry, measured tones. "I suppose there might be something to what you say. I hadn't thought of this morning's sermon in exactly those terms."

He managed to get out the calm response but his soul smarted under the cross-examination. Could daily irritations be part of the "scars" in a Christian's life? Who was to say what "big stuff" might be?

The truth was he hadn't thought of this morning's sermon at all. He preached it spontaneously then in the rush of the afternoon forgot it. It was uncomfortable having his own words returned.

"It is just that I get so sick of being involved with the petty stuff. We claim we have a big God. He ought to be doing big things!

"In fact, I suspect He *is* doing big things, while I'm stuck here in the backwash of Texas dealing with late night calls from cranky doctors and head lice! I just want to be a part of something significant before I die."

"Do you want to go back to Crenshaw?"

"No. Crenshaw was just a heavily advertised, overgrown version of Grace wrapped in a four color brochure. I want . . ." He paused, unable to articulate the rest of the sentence.

"I guess I just want to see God's doing something that matters and know that I'm part of it."

"You don't see that here?"

"In Thyme?" he asked incredulously. Melody nodded. "No." He stated the word with flat finality leaving no room for argument.

"I preach, but no one listens. I pray, but I don't see answers. I work, but the church doesn't grow."

His spurt of anger and subsequent confession had helped dissipate pent-up emotions. He took another long draught of his rapidly cooling coffee and studied the sky. The blanket of low clouds had broken into scattered clumps exposing a bright quarter moon and distant stars. He sighed.

"Nothing significant ever happens in Thyme."

Across the yard JaKobe listened to the complaints. He knew the man was blind but the comments still surprised him. For a place where nothing significant ever happened, he and the rest of the crew had certainly been busy!

He cocked one eyebrow and slowly shook his head. If that was what the pastor wanted, so be it.

JaKobe's Assignment

The angel raised his arm straight over his head, opened wide his hand, and released his final message of the day toward the sky.

Recommended resolution of current assignment: Facilitate spiritual sight through elimination of dominate character flaws. Move current opposition level from three point seven to eight point five.

Elizabeth Baker

Author's Note

My only hesitation when writing *JaKobe's Assignment* was a concern readers might elevate my personal flights of fantasy to the level of theology. This would be a grievous mistake. For, while every effort was made to not contradict any biblically revealed truth about angels, it is also true that where the Bible was silent I took much assumptive latitude filling in the blanks with whatever fit the plot and my whim at the moment.

This work originally contained an end note with many Bible references to help readers distinguish the difference between truth and my imagination. However, the note became so extensive it was distracting from the plot and I suspected contained far more information than would interest many readers.

Therefore, this research note has been uploaded to the cloud and given its own URL. The download is copyright free. See "Free Downloads" page at the end of this book.

JaKobe's Assignment

Endnotes

[1] Pronounced: Ja-KO-be
[2] Shekina: The Hebrew word used to describe the presence of God expressed in any form, particularly light.
[3] Chambers, Oswald. *My Utmost for His Highest*. Reading for October 4th.
[4] Exodus 40:34-38
[5] Isaiah 6:1-8
[6] Matthew 17:1-7
[7] Psalm 87:5 NKJV
[8] "Rock of Ages" Augustus M. Toplady and Thomas Hastings in *The Celebration Hymnal*, Word Music. Integrity Music, 1997.
[9] Although no one has any idea of the elements composing an angel's body, the author has reference to the possibility of *neutrin*; an elementary particle of light with zero electrical charge and zero mass. Part of quantum physics, this element has only recently been discovered and is not fully understood.
[10] "So Send I You," E. Margaret Clarkson & John W. Peterson. In *Soul Stirring Songs and Hymns* complied by John R. Rice, D.D. and Joy Rice Martin. Singspiration Inc., copyright 1954. Also "So Send I You," Margaret Clarkson & John W. Peterson. In *The Celebration Hyman.*, Word Music/ Integrity Music, 1997.
[11] "A Mighty Fortress is Our God," words and music by Martin Luther. Translated by Fredric H. Hedges. In *The Celebration Hymnal*. Word Music / Integrity Music, 1997.
[12] Revelation 21:3

[13] "What a Mighty God We Serve," words and music anonymous. In *The Celebration Hymnal*. Word Music / Integrity Music, 1997.

[14] Tozer, A. W., *The Knowledge of the Holy The Attributes of God: Their Meaning in the Christian Life*. Lincoln, Nebraska: Back to the Bible Broadcast, p. 25.

[15] "Then He Said, 'Sing', William J. & Gloria Gather Music Company / ASCAP, 1985.

[16] Exodus 20:5

[17] I Samuel 16:7

[18] 'The Trees of the Field" by Steffi Geiser Rubin & Stuart Dauermann, Lillenas Publishing Company, 1975.

[19] Symphony No 3, S. 3 (K 1A3), *The Camp Meeting*, by Charles Ives.

[20] Ephesians 3:21

[21] Psalm 24:1

[22] Psalm 24 9:2 NIV (pronoun capitalization altered)

[23] Psalm 19:1-3 NIV (pronoun capitalization altered)

[24] Psalm 3:20

[25] Luke 12:32

[26] Matthew 6:10

[27] "Just as I Am" Charlotte Elliott and William B Bradbury, in *The Celebration Hymnal*, Word Music / Integrity Music, 1997.

[28] A set of scriptures from the book of Romans uses as a format for leading some to experience salvation. Usually given as Romans 3:23; 6:23; 5:8; 10:13; 10:9 and 3:20.

[28] Lewis, C.S., *The Chronicles of Narnia, Book 4, Prince Caspian*. New York: HarperCollins, 1951,1979. Pp 148-159.

[29] Frankl, Viktor, *Man's Search for Meaning*, 1946.

JaKobe's Assignment

For FREE Downloads:

Find out the difference between the angels in JaKobe's Assignment and what the Bible has to say about those beings. Read the story behind the story and find why certaub scriptures led the author to use certain example.

http://tinyurl.com/cv8a88w

Discussion Questions for JaKobe's Assignment can put life in your reading group without leading to argument and provide plenty of room for individual opinion.

http://tinyurl.com/cv8a88w

Share your personal opinion about what was right with JaKobe's Assignment or how it could be improved

http://tinyurl.com/aykd4q3

Elizabeth Baker, Ph.D. is a Fellow with the Oxford Society of Scholars and she served twelve years as a church counselor. Currently living in Pittsburg, Texas, Elizabeth is semi-retired dividing her time between grandchildren, gardening, and freelance writing.

A widow since her mid-30's, Elizabeth has four fantastic grown children, three amazing children-in-laws, fifteen remarkable grandchildren, and six astounding great-grands. But, she identifies her greatest joy as helping others apply biblical principles to real-life situations.

Licensed as a Professional Counselor with the State of Texas, Elizabeth holds a Master of Arts degree in counseling from Liberty University and a Doctor of Philosophy in Religion and Society from Oxford Graduate School. She has been writing professionally for more than thirty years.

Contact Elizabeth at

www.ElizabethBakerBooks.com.
FaceBook.com/grannywritesbooks
Follow on Twitter: @granny_writes

JaKobe's Assignment

Book 2: Angel Trilogy

The Silent War

Coming Summer 2013

Made in the USA
Charleston, SC
05 December 2012